Books by Carol Lynne

Campus Cravings

Co
Side-
Sacking the (
Off-Se
Forbidden F
Broken Pottery
In Bear's Bed
Office Advances
A Biker's Vow
Hershie's Kiss
Theron's Return
Live for Today
Incoming Freshman
A Lesson Learned
Locky in Love
The Injustice of Being
Watch Me
Coming Clean
Professor Sandwich
Big Man on Campus

Cattle Valley

All Play & No Work
Cattle Valley Mistletoe
Sweet Topping
Rough Ride
Physical Therapy
Out of the Shadow
Bad Boy Cowboy

Slow-Play
Pocket Pair
Different Suits
Full House

Bodyguards in Love

Brier's Bargain
Seb's Surrender
I Love Rock n Roll
Taming BlackDog Four
Seducing the Sheik
To Bed a King

Neo's Realm

Liquid Crimson
Blood Trinity
Crimson Moon
Royal Blood

Seasons of Love

Spring
Summer
Fall
Winter

C-7 Shifters

Alrik
Seger

Buck Wild

Cowboy Pride
Cowboy Rules

Fighter

ISBN # 978-1-78651-949-8

©Copyright Carol Lynne 2017

Cover Art by Posh Gosh ©Copyright 2017

Interior text design by Claire Siemaszkiewicz

Pride Publishing

Published in 2017 by Pride Publishing, Newland House, The Point, Weaver Road, Lincoln, LN6 3QN, United Kingdom.

Printed and Bound in Great Britain by Clays Ltd, St Ives plc

1

The Brick Yard

FIGHTER

CAROL LYNNE

Dedication

For my dad, Asa Gillette. Although it's been eight years since I lost you, you will forever remain in my heart and memories. Love you, Dad.

Prologue

Lucky Gunn looked around the dark Chicago alley in search of the milk crates he usually used to climb into The Red Dragon's dull green dumpster.

"You! Boy! Get away from there!"

Lucky saw the owner waving his arms in the air. He wanted to tell him he was only after the food the restaurant threw out, but he knew the small Asian man wouldn't listen.

After a last glance at the dumpster that held so much promise, Lucky took off as fast as his short legs would go. He didn't have to run far to get away, and slowly lessened his pace once he was clear of the restaurant. Looking around, he weighed his options. The pizza place usually had crusts and half-eaten slices in its dumpster, but digging them out was harder because the workers hadn't left the milk crates sitting in the alley. With a resigned sigh, he decided to walk the three blocks home without dinner. He was luckier than some kids because at least his mom had signed him up for free lunches at school.

Lucky spotted an empty Coke can lying on the sidewalk and kicked it along as he made his way back to the apartment he shared with his mom and whatever lowlife she was using that week. Two blocks from his building, he stopped and tried to see through the big window of The Brick Yard. It was so cold outside that the glass carried a heavy amount of condensation, making it nearly impossible. He wondered if the boxing gym's heater was cranked or if the number of sweating men inside helped warm the place. *Probably both.*

Someday he was going to be a fighter. He'd promised

himself that very thing a few months earlier when they'd moved into their current apartment and he'd discovered the gym. If he could learn to fight, he'd be able to keep the drunk men away from him and his mom. Unfortunately, the sign on the door said you had to be eighteen to become a member, and he was only eight.

Ten years. Lucky shook his head. He wasn't sure he'd still be alive in ten years.

The door to the gym opened, startling Lucky. He jumped back into the shadows as a big man came out of the building with an old bag slung over his arm. The man passed Lucky without even knowing he was there. Lucky had become very good at hiding in dark places. The last apartment he'd lived in had had a small door that led to a crawl space behind the bathroom sink and shower. He wasn't sure why it had been there, but he'd used it to hide three or four times a week. It wasn't everyday his mom had men over, but when she ran out of drugs or alcohol, she'd leave the apartment for an hour or so and come back with a new man.

Unfortunately, they'd been kicked out of that apartment, and the only place to hide in the new one was the roof. He reckoned it would be a nice spot to hang out once the weather grew warmer, but it was only January and winters in Chicago were freezing.

The gym door opened again, and another man walked out. Lucky decided it wouldn't be a good night to watch the fighters. After the man had pulled his car away from the curb, Lucky picked up his can and continued home.

As he neared his building, he stuck the can into his pocket. Like he always did, he approached the rundown apartments cautiously before ducking down the alley. The last time he'd tried going in through the front entrance, he'd been harassed by a group of teenagers who liked to hang out on the steps. That night had been bad because he'd managed to score an entire loaf of bread from one of his dumpster dives. It hadn't mattered to him that there was some funny-looking green stuff on one end because it was an entire loaf. With that much food, he wouldn't have had to go out at night for another three or four days. Unfortunately, one of the teenage boys had seen what was tucked under his jacket and had demanded the food as payment to pass. The guy had called it a toll, whatever that was. When Lucky had refused to give up his score, one of the other boys had pushed him down half a flight of stairs. He'd ended up with sore ribs on his right side, a small cut on his cheek where his face had slammed into one of the steps and no bread.

Since that night, Lucky tried to sneak up the fire escape to the third-floor hallway window. From there, he still had to pass several doors, but no one on his floor hung out in the hall.

Lucky let out the breath he'd been holding since sliding open the window. He dug the key out of his pocket before pressing his ear against the door. Hearing no sign that his mom had someone in the apartment, he quietly fit the key into the lock. He winced when the old hinges let out a loud creak.

"Lucky," his mom slurred from the sofa.

Lucky closed his eyes. He could tell by her tone that she was angry and either drunk or high, so he held perfectly still, praying she'd pass out before doling out punishment. She had given him ten dollars and strict instructions to get her more vodka. He'd tried to tell her that the man at the liquor store in their new neighborhood didn't know him and wouldn't sell it to him, but she'd ordered him to walk to their old neighborhood if necessary. Their previous apartment was miles away, but he'd known there was no sense in using that as an excuse because she wouldn't have cared. Instead, he'd hoped she would have passed out by the time he got home after looking for something to eat. He could have spent the money on food, but that would have garnered him a harsher punishment.

"Where's my vodka?" she asked.

"I'm sorry, Mom. They wouldn't sell it to me." Lucky

backed toward the door. It was so cold outside that the warmth of the apartment felt like heaven, but he'd happily spend all night huddled in the hallway if it meant getting out of there before his punishment was handed down.

Lucky ducked just in time to avoid the empty bottle his mom threw toward his head. He was grateful the thick glass only broke into a few pieces when it hit the heavy metal door behind him. Being careful, he bent and started to pick up the shards, but stopped when he felt his mom's hand press down against his shoulder.

"You're a very bad boy," she slurred. "You know what happens to bad boys?"

Lucky's eyes filled with tears. "They need to be punished."

* * * *

By the age of ten, Lucky knew the neighborhood like the back of his hand, which was both a good thing and a bad thing. It meant he knew exactly where to go for the best garbage for dinner, but it also meant the restaurant owners were on to him. He'd never understood why they cared whether or not he went through their dumpsters, but some owners treated him as though he were stealing something valuable from them.

Lucky huddled in the doorway of an abandoned store across the street from The Brick Yard and watched two men box through the window. Since he was on a school break for Christmas, it had been nearly two weeks since he had eaten anything that hadn't already been on someone else's plate. He might be the only kid alive who hated holiday and summer breaks from school.

Lucky watched as the old man who ran the place handed a white paper-wrapped package to one of the younger boxers. The fighter laughed as he lifted a shiny red bathrobe out in front of him. He pulled it on and spun around with his arms out to his sides. There was a giant gold and green dragon printed on the back of the robe. Lucky doubted he'd ever seen anything more beautiful. That was, until he saw the fighter throw his arms around the gym's owner. The two men stood holding each other for several moments before breaking contact. A lump formed in Lucky's throat at the show of affection. He couldn't really remember a time when his mom or anyone had hugged him like that.

Needing to get a better look at the dragon on the robe, Lucky moved to cross the street. A blizzard five days earlier had dumped almost a foot of snow on the city. It had been pretty that first morning, but since then it had been reduced to piles of grayish brown. He tried to jump over a mound at the edge of the sidewalk and ended up jumping right into a puddle of dirty, melting slush. Worn and tattered, his secondhand canvas sneakers offered zero protection from the freezing cold water as it seeped through the holes.

With a grimace, Lucky shook each foot before continuing across the street. He cursed his clumsiness when he reached the window of The Brick Yard just as the fighter was walking toward the back of the gym. *Shit.* He pressed his cold hands against the glass and scowled.

The owner's face appeared on the other side of the window. Lucky gasped and jumped back. The last thing he needed was to get run off from the one place he wanted to be. He started to flee but heard the old man yell from behind him.

"Don't go. Come on in here and get warmed up!"

Lucky slowed to a stop before peering over his shoulder. He wasn't sure if the man was talking to him or not, because why would he?

"You look cold, kid. If you're interested, you can come inside and I'll have the guys show you a few moves."

Lucky turned around and faced the owner. "Why would you do that?" In his experience, adults weren't nice to kids, so he wasn't sure he trusted the old man.

"Like I said, you look cold." The man's gaze traveled down over the coat Lucky had found in one of the dumpsters to the ratty sneakers on his feet. He shook his head before gesturing to Lucky. "Come on."

Lucky pointed toward the sign on the window. "It says you have to be eighteen."

"No, it says you have to be eighteen to become a member. You got money for a membership?" the old man asked.

Lucky's heart sank. He shook his head as he started to turn back around.

"Maybe we'll amend that policy someday, but for now, I have to heat the gym regardless, so you might as well come in and get warm." The man held out a big hand. "My name's Tony Brick, but everyone calls me Brick."

Lucky appreciated the way Brick spoke to him, so he squared his shoulders and shook Brick's hand. "I'm Lucky Gunn."

Brick whistled. "That your real name?"

"Yeah," Lucky replied.

"That's a good fightin' name." Brick held open the door.

Although warmth cocooned Lucky the moment he stepped foot inside the gym, the smell nearly knocked him on his butt. He wrinkled his nose.

"Yeah, these assholes sweat like pigs, but that's how I know they've given me a good workout." Brick led Lucky to a metal folding chair next to the ring. "You into boxing or MMA?"

"MMA?" Lucky questioned.

"Mixed martial arts. It's a combination of boxing and wrestling with karate and judo mixed in. It's a full-combat sport and definitely brutal, but the men I train love it."

Lucky stared up at Brick, fascinated by the idea of mixed martial arts. "Can I watch?"

"Sure, kid. My best fighters won't be here until after dinner, though." Brick narrowed his eyes. "Can you stay that late or do you need to get home?"

"I can stay." Lucky felt his stomach rumble at the mention of dinner. He prayed the noise in the gym had drowned out the sounds of his growling gut.

"Your mom won't be worried?"

Lucky shook his head and said the first thing that popped into his head. "She's probably passed out by now anyway."

Brick crossed his arms over his chest and stared down at Lucky. "You need a job?"

"A job?" Lucky couldn't believe Brick had just asked him that. "Don't I have to be older or something?"

Brick lifted one hand to scratch at the gray stubble on his cheek. "Technically, yes, but all I really need is someone to wash the towels and clean up after these lazy assholes. I wouldn't be able to pay you much, but it'll give you somewhere to hang out when you're not in school."

"Thanks." Lucky got to his feet. "You want me to start now?"

"No time like the present," Brick said.

A warmth that had nothing to do with the temperature of the building filled Lucky. He wasn't sure what Brick's game was, but working at The Brick Yard meant he'd have a safe place to go to get away from his mom and her endless stream of boyfriends.

* * * *

Dray glanced at the guy who kept watching him. It was normal for him to drop by his favorite bar after a fight—even more so after a victory. Brick didn't like it when he drank, but Brick still remembered what it was like to be twenty-one, so he simply cautioned Dray to be careful and show up on time ready to train regardless of whether or not he was hungover.

"I thought I might find you here."

Dray closed his eyes as the familiar voice warmed him. He took a deep breath before looking over at Vince, who had taken the stool beside him. "Hey."

"I heard you won another fight." Vince turned his attention to the bartender. "Bring me a shot of tequila."

Dray shook his head. He'd never understood the lure of shots. They cost nearly as much as a beer and only lasted one swallow. He supposed the aim of shots was to get a person as drunk as possible, as quickly as possible. That was something else he'd never understood. He'd always hated himself the morning after drinking too much. It was too damn easy to get careless and ruin everything he'd built.

"Did you lose my phone number?" Vince asked.

"No." Dray and Vince had dated, if you could call it that. Actually, they'd spent roughly a month fucking each other's brains out. Their time together had been awesome, but once Vince had started pushing for more, Dray had had little choice but to break things off. "I told you the last night we were together that I can't be what you want me to be."

"You can't be in a relationship?" Vince asked.

"I can't be public." Dray had tried a dozen different times to explain his reasons for staying in the closet, but none of them seemed to matter to Vince. What Dray didn't understand was why it was so important. They might not be able to hold hands or kiss in public, but they'd gone out to eat several times in the month they'd dated.

"Maybe I'm okay with that," Vince said. He stopped speaking when the bartender set down his drink.

"For how long? I'm close to getting a local endorsement deal for Waverly Athletics. Do you know what that kind of money can do for my family?" Dray shook his head. "I know it's not fair, but my mom and little brother are counting on me to help make their lives better, and MMA is the only way I can make that happen. Brick told me tonight that a scout from the UFC was in the crowd. That's the second time they've sent someone to one of my fights."

"That's great," Vince said before downing his tequila. "You're good in the cage." He leaned closer. "But not as good as you are in the bedroom."

Dray lifted his mug of beer to his lips. Maybe he was crazy for believing he'd someday earn a spot in the Ultimate Fighting Championship, but the UFC had been his dream since the day he'd wandered into The Brick Yard. He tipped the glass back and finished his drink. "Why're you here, Vince?"

Vince grinned. "You want to get a table or something?"

Dray looked around the bar full of straight people. Although he had occasionally run into other gay men at the bar, it had never been the reason he frequented the place. "We can't talk here." He leaned in and spoke into Vince's ear. "You want to go back to my place?"

Vince licked his lips. "Yeah."

Dray nodded. He knew he was taking a huge risk, but he was horny and lonely. Vince wasn't flashy, and he'd been subtle so far. What would it hurt to give Vince another chance? "I'll meet you there in fifteen minutes."

Vince slid off his stool. "I didn't drive. Can I just meet you in the parking lot?"

Dray fished into his pocket for his keys. "My car's in the back lot." He set the keys between them. "I'll sit here for a minute then be out."

"Right." Vince took off, and Dray wondered if he'd made the right decision. He'd gone back and forth with himself about the importance of staying in the closet. Unfortunately, his grades hadn't been enough to get him a college scholarship, so fighting was the only shot he had of making it out of the life he'd been born into. His career was still in the early stages, but he'd already made enough money to get his own small apartment and help his mom out. Those might have seemed like little things to most people, but they meant everything to him.

Dray half hoped Vince would be nowhere in sight by the time he reached the parking lot. Trust had never come easy for him. He just prayed he wasn't making a huge mistake by trusting the wrong person with his secret.

Chapter One

Lucky knocked on his boss's door before sticking his head into the messy office. "Hey, Brick? Okay if I crash in the back room again tonight?"

Tony Brick glanced up from a dog-eared UFC magazine. "Sure, kid."

"Thanks." Lucky didn't need to explain why he needed a place to crash. His mother, Alana, loved men and meth a hell of a lot more than she loved him. It wasn't something he hated her for, although he should. Instead, he blamed his father, the bastard who had sold her the shit in the first place. Yeah, Lucky was the product of a whore and a drug dealer. Queue the tiny violin that would bleed out a tune for him.

Lucky snorted and shook the thought away. His home life sucked, but the tiny apartment he shared with his mom was a world away from the gym where he'd practically grown up. Thanks to Brick, the sixty-something ex-fighter who'd taken him on as a charity case years earlier, Lucky had managed to never take drugs while making enough money to pay the rent and keep the lights on. Not bad for a teenager, he reckoned.

He was halfway across the gym when Brick called after him.

"Lucky? You get that book report finished?"

"Not yet," Lucky said over his shoulder. "But I'm workin' on it." Truth was, reading didn't come easy and writing his thoughts on *The Great Gatsby* had proven even harder.

"Take your work to the laundry room while you wash the towels," Brick ordered. "That report's due in two days, and if you don't get a decent grade, you'll flunk that damn class of yours."

"Sure thing." Lucky groaned to himself. Laundry was his least favorite chore outside of cleaning the locker room, but he'd jump into a steaming pile of shit if Brick asked him to.

He thought about the book while he walked around the weight room, gathering the dirty towels people were too fucking lazy to drop into the bin. Jay Gatsby had started his life as a poor kid from North Dakota who'd wanted more. He'd climbed his way to wealth and power by doing anything and everything he had to. Lucky knew he was supposed to write a report on how the money Gatsby had worked so hard to obtain had shriveled his soul, and that was the problem. Lucky didn't see it that way. He knew what it was to yearn for more — to dream of a day when he didn't have to turn on the kitchen lights and wait for the roaches to scatter before fixing a sandwich that was more bread than meat. In his opinion, Gatsby's actions had been justified, and someone who didn't understand that hadn't been forced to dumpster-dive as a kid to find something for dinner.

A deep laugh caught his attention and he glanced up just in time to see Dray walk into the gym with that asshole friend of his. Dray was cool, but his buddy Vince was a piece of work. The fucker always made a point of talking down to Lucky.

"Hey," Dray said, acknowledging Lucky.

"Your face is healing nicely." Lucky winced. Why the hell did he say shit like that to Dray? It was bad enough he was obsessed with the fighter to the point of distraction, but did he need to turn into a chick every time Dray was around?

Dray touched a finger to the bandaged cut on his coal-black eyebrow. "Gettin' there. Although, I have another fight next weekend, so it won't last long."

Lucky couldn't help but stare at the tattoos covering both of Dray's arms below the stretched T-shirt sleeves. The designs were incredibly intricate and inked in nothing but black. Lucky had been fascinated to discover Dray had drawn the artwork and had asked some old dude down the street who was a UFC fanatic to ink it into his skin. The guy had been so impressed with Dray's designs that he'd been teaching him how to tattoo. Lucky had never fully understood why drawing on someone else's skin was fun, but Dray seemed to really enjoy the hours he spent at the shop.

"Are you getting a boner?" Vince asked.

Before he could think better of it, Lucky peered down at his fly. "No," he mumbled, although he'd been close before the asshole had called him on it. "I was checking out Dray's tats."

"Really?" Dray asked. "You thinking of getting one?"

Lucky nodded. He didn't have the money for anything half as nice as what Dray had. "Something simple. Irish. Maybe a four-leaf clover."

"Like a fuckin' leprechaun?" Vince laughed. "Yeah, that sounds about right."

Once again, Lucky cursed his red hair. It didn't matter that the shade was more mahogany than fire engine. It was still red, thanks to his mother, who was one hundred percent Irish.

"Lay off," Dray warned Vince before returning his attention to Lucky. "When you decide what you want, come by the shop and make an appointment. I'll give you a discount."

Lucky warmed. He wanted to ask how much a small tat would cost, but no way would he do it in front of Vince. "Thanks. I'll have to save up, but I'll let you know."

Dray grabbed a fresh towel off the stack and draped it over his shoulder. "You are eighteen, right?"

Lucky felt like a giant weight had settled on his chest as he shook his head. Although he'd taken care of himself for years, he still had nearly sixteen months before he'd turn eighteen. "Not quite."

"Oh, shit, man, sorry, but it's against the law in Illinois to tattoo anyone under the age of eighteen," Dray explained. "But find me on your eighteenth birthday, and I'll give you something you can be proud of."

Lucky wished Dray was the kind of man who would bend the rules, but he supposed no artist, who was any good, would jeopardize his career over a tattoo. Unfortunately, Dray was moving up in the UFC ranks, so Lucky doubted he'd still be tattooing by the time Lucky reached his eighteenth birthday. "Thanks. I'll do that."

Dray pointed at Lucky, a stern expression on his handsome face. "Promise me that you won't let some asswipe do it just because he's willing to ignore the law?"

"I promise."

Dray gestured to the raised ring. "If you see Brick, tell him I'm going to pull one of his fighters to spar with."

"He's in his office. You want me to get him?" Lucky knew how much Brick hated it when Dray trained without him.

Dray blew out a frustrated breath. "Sure. No sense in getting my ass chewed over it. But tell him I'm going to take it easy, so if he has something else to do, it's not a problem."

"Okay." Lucky leaned the towel bin back on its two wheels and pulled it toward Brick's office. He wished he could forget the laundry and watch Dray train instead, but he still had his report to write up, and Dray usually trained for hours. Maybe, just maybe, he'd be able to get Dray off his mind long enough to finish his homework and still have time to watch the training session.

* * * *

"Grab that tape for me," Dray said, pointing to a roll next to Vince's hip.

"That kid gives me the creeps." Vince tossed the white tape to Dray. "He's always watching you."

Dray ground his teeth together. He and Vince had been together for nearly six years and in that time, he couldn't believe the changes in Vince. In the beginning, Vince had been content to stay in and watch television or take a walk around the city, but lately, all Vince wanted to do was go out and be seen. It was like his sweet young boyfriend had transformed into a fame whore.

"Leave Lucky alone," Dray ordered. Vince didn't have a clue what it was like to grow up without enough food on the table. He came from a typical middle class family in a typical middle class suburb of Chicago. Vince talked like his childhood had been boring, but Dray, Lucky and quite a few others would trade everything they owned to have known that kind of boring.

Vince picked at a split in the vinyl that covered the weight bench. "I'll be glad when you finally dump this place and start training at a real gym. You've made it to the big time for fuck's sake. I doubt any other fighters in the UFC still train in the dumpy gyms they started out in."

"Never going to happen, so get that right out of your head," Dray said. "Brick's been like a father to me."

"Brick's held you back," Vince said. "You should be training in a gym with all the latest equipment with a swimming pool and sauna."

Dray stared at his boyfriend. There were days when he wished he'd never started up with Vince. In the beginning, Vince had still been in college so Dray hadn't minded picking up the tab when they'd gone out or ate in. However, Vince had graduated four years ago, and he'd yet to look for a serious job in his field. Even with a Masters of Business Administration degree, Vince seemed perfectly content to work three days a week at one of the local public libraries.

"Brick's made me who I am," Dray argued.

Vince sighed. "You don't get it. You could be huge if you really tried. Think of all the endorsement deals you could get your hands on. Think of all the money you'd make."

Dray studied Vince for several moments. "Aren't you always the one on my ass about coming out of the closet? How can you care so much about money and still want me to acknowledge you as my partner?"

"Because I think you're full of shit. Your fans love you. They wouldn't turn their back if you told the truth."

"Yes, they would." Dray narrowed his eyes as something finally hit him. "You don't give a shit about me or what I want. All you're after is the limelight that would come your way if the city found out about the two of us."

"It's not just the city, Dray. This thing could be huge. We would probably make the front page of every newspaper in the country." Vince slid off the weight bench to kneel in front of Dray. "Seriously, just think about it. I know it's a risk, but I believe it's a risk worth taking." He started to reach for Dray but pulled back before connecting. "I love you. You know that. It's time to tell the world how you feel about me."

Dray got to his feet. "You need to figure out which you want more, me or your face in the paper, because you can't have both. I'm not sure why I can't get this through your head, but I'm going to try one more time. If it gets out that I'm gay, I might as well kiss my career goodbye." He flexed his hands to make sure he'd applied the tape to his knuckles correctly.

"Just think about it," Vince said before Dray threw his first punch at the heavy bag.

* * * *

Lucky shot up, blinking at the sound of knuckles rapping against the table he'd fallen asleep on. "What?"

Brick chuckled. "I'm calling it a day. Dray's in the shower, so do me a favor and lock up when he leaves." He eyed the spiral notebook Lucky had used for a pillow. "How's it coming?"

Lucky shrugged. "I'll get it done." He still had more than half the report to write, but at least he'd started the damn thing.

Brick laid his hand on top of Lucky's head and mussed his hair. "I'm proud of ya, kid."

Uncomfortable with the tender gesture, Lucky swiped at Brick's hand. "I haven't been a kid in a long time, old man."

"And for that, I'm truly sorry," Brick said, slapping Lucky on the back. "Don't stay up too late."

Lucky got to his feet and stretched his arms over his head. "Can we train this weekend?" It wasn't often Brick had spare time to work with him, so he tried to train on his own, but he knew how important it was to learn from the best.

"Yeah. You been keeping up with the routine I wrote down for you?" Brick asked from the doorway.

"Every day." There were times when Lucky's days had been so busy he'd had to do the circuit training at night after the gym had closed, but he was starting to see the difference in his body when he looked in the mirror. He'd never been big and would probably never bulk up enough to compete in anything beyond the welterweight class compared to Dray's light heavyweight status, but he was proud of his muscle definition.

"Keep it up, and you'll go far. You're quick and hungry and those are two things you have in your favor."

"Thanks." Lucky acknowledged the compliment. Brick didn't give them out easily when it came to fighting, so to hear his mentor's praise meant everything.

"Get some sleep." Brick gave Lucky a surveying glance before turning to walk away.

Lucky opened the dryer and began to fold the towels. They were cold, which meant the dryer had finished its cycle while he'd been sleeping.

Towels folded, he lifted the stack and left the laundry room, secretly hoping he'd catch Dray in some sort of undress in the locker room. He'd done just that several weeks earlier. Dray had walked out of the shower while Lucky had been mopping the locker room floor. Instead of waiting for Lucky to finish the job, Dray had dropped his towel and started rifling through his gym bag before pulling on his clothes. It had been one of the best and worst moments of Lucky's life. He'd been struggling for a while with his attraction to men. The girls he went to school with were okay for a blow job behind the equipment shed, but he didn't dream of putting his hands all over them like he did with Dray. He hadn't said anything to anyone—and he'd definitely never acted on his desire—but it was always there in the back of his mind.

Hoping to catch a peek of Dray, Lucky entered the locker room and was assaulted by steam and the sounds of fucking. *Holy hell.* He quietly loaded the shelf with the clean towels before sinking onto one of the benches. It wasn't Dray's grunts that surprised him as much as the echoing moans of an equally deep voice that shocked him. *Fuck, was that Vince?* He shook his head, trying to wrap his brain around the fact that Dray was with another man.

"Fuck," Dray drew out, his voice lower than Lucky had ever heard it. "You're always so fuckin' tight."

"Yeah," Vince answered. "You love it."

Lucky pressed the heel of his hand against the growing bulge in his jeans. If he'd had doubts of his true sexual preference before, he didn't anymore—he wished he was Vince. He couldn't think of anything he'd ever wanted more than to be bent over while Dray drove inside him.

After unzipping his jeans, he felt a moment of guilt, but shoved his hand down the front of his underwear anyway. He wrapped it around his aching dick and squeezed as Dray groaned again. *Fuck.* He'd had a few sexual experiences in his life, but he'd never made noises like Vince and Dray were making. He wondered if it had something to do with his partners.

The steady slapping sound of skin on skin drove Lucky to pump faster. There, among the smells of Clorox, sweat and clean towels, he closed his eyes and listened to Dray fucking. What would it be like to have access to Dray's muscular, tattooed body? Would he sink to his knees and worship Dray's erection with his mouth or just bend over and offer himself fully?

"Tell me I'm the best," Vince begged between moans. His

voice echoed in the tiled locker room, and Lucky suddenly hated the asshole more than he ever had.

"You know you are," Dray said, sounding out of breath.

"I'm tired of being your secret," Vince continued. "At least acknowledge me to your friends."

Lucky heard a loud slap followed by a cry of pain. *Shit!* Had Dray slapped Vince's face or had it been his ass?

"You don't give a shit about my friends. All you're after is attention, and that kind of attention will end us," Dray growled.

Lucky's balls drew tight, seconds before he shot a volley of cum into his hand. "Fuck!" he ground out, trying to keep as quiet as possible. He continued to squeeze his shaft, milking his dick for every drop of seed.

The shower shut off. "Did you hear something?" Dray asked.

"What the hell, man? You can't just pull out like that. I was close," Vince complained.

With one hand still down the front of his jeans, Lucky jumped up and raced out. He didn't stop running until he reached the storage room he'd called home more nights than he cared to think about. There were only three people in the entire building, so if Dray'd heard him cry out, he'd know exactly who'd been listening.

Lucky stripped out of his soiled jeans and underwear, and reached for his jock and the only pair of workout shorts he owned. Once dressed, he hurried to the laundry room and began to transfer another load from the washer to the dryer.

"Hey," Dray said from the doorway.

Lucky glanced over his shoulder. "Hey." He returned his attention to the job. He silently prayed Dray wouldn't mention the most embarrassing situation of his life.

"I know you heard me and Vince."

Lucky cringed. He shut the dryer and switched it on. Turning to face Dray, he hoped his pallor had returned to its normal Irish pale instead of the embarrassed crimson it had been when he'd caught a glimpse of himself in the storage room mirror. "Don't worry about it. I won't say anything."

Dray held Lucky's gaze for several seconds. "I'd appreciate that. Things could get messy if word got out."

"Yeah," Lucky acknowledged. There had never been an openly gay UFC fighter, and he doubted there ever would be. It was a brutal sport, both inside the cage and out. "I get it."

* * * *

Dray rested his cheek against the cool porcelain rim of the toilet as he continued to spit into the flushing bowl. He'd barely made it back to his one-bedroom apartment before he'd lost the entire contents of his stomach. His gaze landed on the crumpled magazine a few feet away. He'd known the truth about his sexuality would eventually come out, but he hadn't expected to find naked pictures of himself staring back at him from the checkout stand of his local grocery store. Sure, his genitals and Vince's head had been covered by a black box with the word 'WOW' written across it in bright-red letters, but it was obvious by his expression what Vince was doing to him.

"So fucking stupid," he said to the empty bathroom.

He wiped his mouth with the back of his hand as he tried to come to terms with Vince's betrayal. It still didn't make sense. Free concert tickets, free meals at restaurants and VIP status at every nightclub in Chicago were just a few of the perks Vince had seemed to enjoy at Dray's side, and the asshole was *always* at his side.

Dray lifted his hip enough to reach into his back pocket for his phone. While his initial reaction to the photo spread had been to storm over to Vince's place and pound his fist into his boyfriend's face, he'd had enough control to stop himself. Beating Vince bloody would only harm his career further and most likely land him behind bars. Instead, he'd run flat-out toward the home he'd worked so damn hard to get.

After hitting Vince's name in his list of contacts, he held the small flip-phone to his ear.

Dray wasn't surprised when his call went straight to voicemail.

"I'm busy. Leave a name and number and I may or may not get back to ya."

"What the hell did you do?" Dray closed his eyes and took a deep, calming breath. "I trusted you." He stopped himself before he lost control. He knew the call was being recorded and the last thing he needed was to give Vince more ammunition to use against him.

"Call me." Dray hung up. He doubted Vince would have the balls to contact him again, but Dray had to try. Less than eight hours earlier, Vince had been in Dray's bed after celebrating in the VIP section of their favorite nightclub. The last discussion the two of them had had about Dray coming out had occurred the previous month. He'd reminded Vince, once again, that if news of his sexual orientation ever got out, his career would be over.

Dray reached for the paper and forced himself to stare at the photo. He recognized the setting as Vince's shitty apartment, but Vince lived alone, so Dray had no clue who had taken the picture. Although, after studying the image more closely, he decided Vince must have had a hidden camera tucked away somewhere on or near the big fifty-inch television Dray had given him for Christmas. There was slight bruising noticeable around Dray's left eye and the stitches closing the cut on his cheekbone that he'd suffered in his last fight nearly six months ago. Bile burned his throat when he realized Vince had spent at least half a year planning to betray him.

The forgotten phone in his hand began to ring. One look at the display and Dray groaned. He flipped it open and held it to his ear.

"Get in here," Brick said before hanging up.

Dray closed the phone. Brick's call was the wake-up he needed because being outed by Vince wasn't just about him. The Brick Yard had become home for Dray, and not only would the news ruin his career, but it could also harm the gym that had saved his life years earlier.

"Fuck!" Dray yelled and hurled his phone against the tiled wall of the shower.

He stared at the mess he'd made. The broken shards of plastic were the perfect metaphor for his current situation. After years of fighting in every match he could find, he'd finally worked his way up to the UFC. For the first time in his life, he was important enough that people listened to him. Now, because of one stupid story, everything he'd worked so hard to achieve would be taken away.

* * * *

Dray slowed his car as he drove through the crowd of reporters and UFC fans that lined the sidewalks on both sides of the street in front of The Brick Yard. A few of the fans held signs condemning Dray to hell and dubbing him the 'Fighting Faggot'. Others simply shouted their disgust at his perceived betrayal.

The Fighting Faggot? "Jesus," he muttered. He'd known the fans wouldn't like finding out the truth about his sexuality, but condemning him to hell?

Dray found a parking spot a block behind the building before entering the gym through the back door. He tried to slink in without the other fighters spotting him, but no such luck.

"Quite a crowd out there." Flint was one of Dray's sparring partners, and, usually, a fairly nice guy.

"Yeah." Dray headed for Brick's office.

"Want us to get rid of them?" Flint asked.

Dray paused with his hand on Brick's door. "Wouldn't hurt to tell them I'm not here. I doubt you'll get rid of all of them, but maybe some of the fans will give up and go the fuck home."

Flint nodded. "I'll give it a try."

"Thanks," Dray replied.

"By the way, I kinda always knew something was going on with you and Vince, but I told myself it wasn't my business. I mean, it's not like it affected your fighting or anything. You're one of the best that's ever come out of this gym."

Dray's battered heart felt better after Flint's statement. He and Flint had never been friends, but they had been friendly toward one another. "I appreciate it."

Flint nodded briefly then walked off.

Dray knocked once as he opened the door. "What a fucked-up mess," he said before Brick could start in on him.

"Sit," Brick ordered. He leaned his elbows on the desk and steepled his fingers. "What the fuck were you thinking taking pictures like that?"

Dray blew out a long breath. The idea that Brick, more than anyone, had seen those pictures of Vince's betrayal embarrassed and shamed him. "I didn't know. Vince must've had a hidden camera or something." He could see the disappointment in Brick's lined face and watery eyes. "I'm so sorry. I've tried for so long to hide who I really am because I knew this would happen."

Brick sat back in his chair. "I don't think I can fix this. You'll probably lose the UFC contract and most certainly the upcoming fight. If you want, we can lay low for a while and start back up in the underground circuit. You can rebuild your image with fans or take on a whole new persona."

Dray shook his head. "Have you heard what those people out front are yelling? They hate me." Although he knew it was his insecurities talking, he craved the attention and approval of his fans.

"They'll get over it eventually," Brick said.

"Yeah, maybe, but I'm not sure I will." Dray leaned forward and rested his forearms on his knees. "Even though

I knew this would probably happen if the truth came out, I wasn't prepared for the way it's making me feel." How did he explain how hurt he was by the public reaction? He'd been naïve to believe his fans had ever really cared for him. Evidently, they only cared for The Dragon, his cage persona. Yeah, he'd been stupid as fuck to think they actually cared about Dray Cruz.

* * * *

Lucky's friend, Sid, passed him a cigarette as they walked toward the gym after school. Most days he went home first to check on his mom, but after hearing the rumors about Dray in school, he knew he had to go to The Brick Yard. It had been three months since he'd overheard Dray and Vince in the shower and he hadn't uttered a word about it.

"What's up with the fag? Did you ever catch him checking out someone's ass?" Sid asked, taking the cigarette back.

"Dray's not like that." Friend or not, Lucky wouldn't let Sid bad-mouth Dray. It hadn't been Dray's fault Vince had fucking sold him out. He wondered how much a man's career was worth. Had Vince even warned Dray before selling the photos to the entertainment rag?

"You seem awfully defensive," Sid accused. "Is there something you want to tell me?"

"Fuck you." Lucky elbowed Sid in the stomach. "Dray's a damn good fighter, the best that's ever come out of The Brick Yard." He shrugged. "I just feel bad for him and Brick."

Sid stopped walking when they reached the mass of photographers and livid fans who had camped out in front of the gym. "I told Cassie I'd meet her at the diner. Later, dude."

"Yeah." Lucky ducked down the alley to the back door of the building and let himself in with his key. He passed by Brick's office, wondering if he should knock or get right to work. Although Brick was a tough old bastard, he suffered from high blood pressure on a good day, and no way was the hoopla surrounding Dray good for him.

"Brick?" Lucky knocked but didn't immediately enter.

"Later, kid," Brick yelled.

At least Brick had answered—it meant he was still alive. Lucky stowed his backpack in the storage room before getting to work by wiping down the exercise equipment. The members were supposed to do it after using them, but, like they did with the towels, one in four fighters thought they were too good to clean up after themselves.

"Did ya hear?" Flint asked as he jumped down from the fighting ring.

"About the pictures? Yeah." Lucky didn't want to talk about it to anyone but Brick.

"Two of his sponsors have already cut ties with him." Flint shook his head and nodded toward Brick's office. "They're in there trying to salvage the fight on Friday, but it doesn't look good. Half the people who bought tickets are demanding their money back, and the other half are excited to see the fag get the shit beat out of him. I'm telling ya, I've never heard of fans turning on a fighter this fast."

"Shit." Lucky picked up a few stray towels. "Talk to you later." As much as he usually hated the chore, escaping to the quiet of the laundry room sounded good. Before the news had broken, he'd been close to talking to Dray about being gay. Despite the realization that men definitely turned him on more than women, he didn't completely rule out messing around with either sex. He knew that made him bisexual and not gay, but it didn't make him straight either.

"I thought I might find you in here," a deep voice said from behind him.

Lucky turned to find Dray standing just inside the room. Dray's light-green eyes were normally breathtaking, but now they were red and swollen as if he'd broken down more than once that day.

Lucky dropped a towel into the washing machine. "I'm

32

sorry about what's going on."

"Yeah, well, that's my fault. I should've known not to trust Vince, but loneliness makes us do crazy things." Dray leaned back against the wall and crossed his arms over his muscular chest. "I'm leaving," he announced.

"What?" Lucky took a step toward Dray. "You mean you're going into hiding to get away from the reporters?"

Dray shook his head. "They canceled my fight on Friday and told me they didn't know where things would go from here, so I'm moving back to Kansas City."

"You can't just give up." Lucky gestured toward the front of the building. He couldn't imagine the UFC without Dray. Worse, he couldn't imagine The Brick Yard without him. "They'll get bored and go away if you give them some time. You've worked for years to get where you are. You can't just let them run you off."

Dray stared at the floor. "It's not the reporters or the sponsors that are running me off." He rubbed his eyes with the heels of his hands. "It's the fans. You should read some of the shit they've posted on the Internet. People wishing me dead. I get they're pissed, but, Christ, dead?" He ran his palms over his closely cropped hair. "I know some fighters might be okay with being hated by the fans, but I'm not one of them. If they're not behind me, I can't do this." He pushed off the wall. "I know I'm acting like a pussy, but the faster I can get outta here, the less likely The Brick Yard will be pulled down with my career."

"I'm sorry," Lucky said.

"Yeah, me too. Anyway, I wanted to ask you a favor."

"Anything." Lucky took a deep breath, trying like hell to keep his emotions in check.

"Take care of Brick. I love that old sonofabitch." Dray dug into his pocket and removed a slip of paper. "Here's the phone number to my cousin's tattoo shop. If anything happens, you can probably reach me there. If not, Berto can get you in touch with me."

"There's nothing that says you can't come back to see

Brick," Lucky pointed out.

Dray shook his head. "I can't stand to see the disappointment in his eyes. I know I fucked up." He met Lucky's gaze. "Do yourself a favor and don't make the same mistake I made."

Did Dray know? Lucky nodded.

"Sex, no matter who with, isn't worth giving up your dreams for. Remember that," Dray said before walking out of the room.

Lucky stared at the closed door long after Dray had gone, promising himself he'd never forget his idol's departing advice.

Chapter Two

Eight years later

"Dammit, boy!" Brick yelled. "Get your head out of your ass!"

Lucky blinked several times as Brick smeared more Vaseline over the newly opened cut on his left eyebrow. "I'm fine," he mumbled around the mouthguard. His opponent in the amateur match, Luke 'Lightning' Boone, had a better record and was higher ranked, but in Lucky's opinion, the guy's heart wasn't in it.

"The hell you are. We both know your power's in your fists. You can't use your best asset if you let this joker engage in dirty boxing."

Lightning was a clinch fighter, someone who preferred to hold his opponents too close to land punches. The prick was good at using his elbows to inflict injury, thus the cut above Lucky's eye.

"I'll finish him this round," Lucky declared. He needed the win. His record was good, but not great. Definitely not good enough to get the UFC's attention.

Brick slapped Lucky's chest before sending him back into the cage for round two. Lucky stared at Lightning and knew the next three minutes meant everything. Four more wins and he'd have a shot at a title match — something he wanted more than anything. He'd given up too much to not succeed in the damn sport.

"I'm taking this," he told Lightning.

Lightning smirked as much as the mouthguard allowed, but despite the attitude, the fire in his eyes had been snuffed at some point since the fight began.

Lucky waited for the referee to signal the start of round two. *Do it.* He took a deep breath then landed two power punches to the fucker's nose and an uppercut to his chin. Lightning's eyes rolled back and like a giant redwood, he toppled with a loud thud.

Lucky stared down at his opponent, wondering why the victory didn't feel as good as it should have. At twenty-four, he was already behind a lot of fighters due to the time he'd taken off to deal with his mom's legal shit and subsequent incarceration. Each knockout was a notch on his belt.

The referee bent over to assess Lightning's condition before signaling the end of the fight. Lightning's crew shoved Lucky out of their way as they raced to their fighter's side.

Lucky barely acknowledged the referee as his arm was lifted, signaling the clean win to the cheering fans. He needed the wins as much as he needed the peace fighting provided. As sick as it was, his passion for the sport had nothing to do with the fans or fame—it was all about the comfort he felt when he fought back against an opponent. He knew his reasons for getting in the cage were different than most of his challengers and he couldn't have cared less. No one, including Brick, needed to know that his desire to be hit was nearly as strong as his need to hit back.

Staring out at the crowd, Lucky couldn't help but see them as the people who had turned their backs on Dray— who was still the best fighter Lucky had ever followed. He refused to give those same people the power they'd held over Dray.

As Lucky watched Lightning's crew get him to his feet, he had the overwhelming feeling that he'd just beaten the last of Lightning's passion out of him. He stepped forward and held out his hand. They may have been opponents in the cage, but he knew Lightning was a good man, too good to be helped from the ring, bloody and defeated.

Lightning stared at Lucky's hand for several heartbeats

before taking the offered gesture. "Well done."

For some reason, Lucky felt the need to offer the man encouragement. "They don't call me Lucky for nothing." He knew it was a lie—he was a damn good fighter—and by the slight smile on Lightning's bloody face, he knew it, too.

* * * *

Dray put the DVD into the player, but held off on starting it. He knew what was on the disc, but he still didn't understand why Brick continued to send him copies of Lucky's cage matches. It was a sick hobby, but he couldn't stay away from it. No, that was a lie—one he'd told himself a million times. It wasn't the sport that still held him, but the fighter and the old man in the corner.

After moving his recliner closer to the fifty-inch television, he took his seat and pressed Play. The quality of the video wasn't great but good enough for him to get a decent look at Lucky. He still couldn't believe the muscular fighter on the screen was the same skinny teenager who'd once heard him fuck Vince in the shower. *Vince.* Dray shook his head. Falling in love with Vince had been the biggest mistake he'd ever made. Vince's betrayal had broken something in him that he doubted could be repaired—not that he hadn't tried at least twice a week since returning to Kansas City. His dick worked better than ever. It was his heart that was still stone cold.

His gaze was glued to the screen as Lucky disrobed. *Fuck.* The man's body was perfection. Dray stared at the creamy-white skin of Lucky's torso. The first time Brick had sent him a DVD, Dray had been surprised by Lucky's lack of ink. He wondered when Lucky had changed his mind about getting tattooed and why. Glancing down at his own arms and hands, he shook his head. There were few places on his body that didn't have art. Ink had always been his way of expressing his pain and after the life-altering affair with Vince, he'd gone crazy.

His eyebrows furrowed as he returned his attention to the fight just in time to see Lucky's opponent clock him with an elbow. "Get the fuck away from him," he yelled at the television, scooting to the edge of his chair.

The bell rang, signaling the end of the first round. During the minute between rounds, the camera only zoomed in on Brick and Lucky once and only for a few seconds. Still, he could see the anger on Brick's craggy face. He grinned, remembering what it felt like to be on the receiving end of Brick's sharp tongue. Lucky appeared indifferent to Brick's tirade, staring at his opponent instead.

"What're you thinking?" he asked Lucky, wishing he could get an answer to his question. He hadn't spoken to Lucky since the day he'd left him in the laundry room — not that he hadn't wanted to.

Lucky charged back into the ring with a determined expression on his battered face. Lucky's light-brown eyes zeroed in on Lightning, and Dray had no doubt the man was going down.

Lucky came out swinging as if he were possessed, landing three punches in quick succession, felling the taller man in seconds.

"Holy shit!" Dray yelled, jumping to his feet. He reached for the phone and called Brick.

"Did ya see it?" Brick answered without pleasantries.

"Yeah," Dray acknowledged while still watching the TV. "The ref's just called the fight."

"Keep watching," Brick urged, "and tell me what you see." He started to cough, prompting Dray to pull the phone away from his ear until he stopped.

The referee lifted Lucky's arm in a sign of victory, but Lucky's expression didn't change. Although the video didn't have sound, it wasn't hard to gauge the crowd's reaction to Lucky's win. *Christ.* The fan reaction had always been the high for Dray, but it didn't seem like Lucky even heard them. "What the fuck's wrong with him?"

"Wish I knew, but it's getting worse. He loves to fight, but

I can't get him to interact with the fans at all, and we both know the UFC loves fan favorites and winning records. Victories alone won't get him there. He might have a chance as a villain in the sport, but he won't even interact to earn that title. He's totally indifferent, and the fans know it."

"Yeah, I know all too well what part the fans play in the game." It was the loss of support from the crowd that had cost Dray his career.

Before Brick could answer, he was racked by another series of coughs.

"You sick?" Dray asked.

"I'll be fine," Brick replied. "I've had a damn chest cold for several weeks, but I'll get over it."

The hairs on the back of Dray's neck prickled. "You been to the doc?"

"Yeah, I got some antibiotics a week ago, but they haven't kicked in yet."

At Brick's age, pneumonia was the first thing to come to Dray's mind. "Maybe you should go back and have him check you out?"

"No time. Lucky's got another fight in two weeks, and I've gotta find a way to make him break out of his shell." Brick cleared his throat. "I'd hoped you'd talk to him. Give him some pointers."

Dray fell back to his chair and closed his eyes. He'd lusted after Lucky since Brick had sent him the first fight DVD nearly two years earlier. "I don't think that would be a good idea."

"How many fighters took the time to give you pointers when you were moving up in the ranks? Don't you think you owe Lucky the same treatment? He's got no one but me and that loser friend of his, who continues to tempt him with the darker side of this life."

Dray heard the reproach in Brick's voice loud and clear, but his attention was drawn to the bit about Lucky being tempted by the dark side. "Drugs?"

"Yeah. You'd think with his history, he'd stay away from

that shit, but I've caught him a couple times with glassy eyes between fights. He wouldn't tell me what he'd used, and nothing's shown up on his piss tests."

"Is he trying to ruin his career before it gets started?" Drugs had never been Dray's thing. He glanced down at his ink, knowing what he'd used to dull the pain. Suddenly, his attraction to Lucky took a back seat. "Hell. Give me a minute to find a piece of paper," he growled.

Tucking the phone between his shoulder and ear, he opened the junk drawer in the kitchen in search of a pen. "Goddammit," he cussed, coming up empty. "I can't find shit in this house. Just give him my number and tell him to call anytime."

"Thanks—" Brick's reply was cut short by another round of coughing.

Dray winced. "I'll do this on one condition. You have to promise you'll go back to the doctor."

"I will. Lucky could really use a friend beside that little fucker Sid," Brick said, his voice sounding wheezy.

Dray hung up and wondered what he'd agreed to. It had taken years to feel settled in Kansas City. The brutal hours he put in at his cousin's tattoo shop helped curb his urge to climb into a cage for the most part, but he knew deep inside, nothing would ever take the place of fighting. He could pound a bag for hours out in the barn and not assuage his raw desire to face off against an opponent. Even sex, as good as it felt, wasn't enough to satisfy him for long.

He'd planned to stay in that night, but with thoughts of Lucky churning around inside him, he changed his mind. There was a great bar in the city that always had a fresh supply of hungry men looking for a quick hookup. It wasn't the best way of getting Lucky off his mind, but it would have to do.

* * * *

Dray was leaning against a wall in the back of his favorite

40

bar, when his phone vibrated in his pocket. He glanced down at the twink giving him a decent blow job and pulled out his cell. *Shit.* He considered not answering Lucky's call, but decided he owed it to Brick.

"Hey," he answered, sticking a finger in his ear to block out the obnoxious music. "Can I call you right back?"

"Uhhh, sure," Lucky answered.

Dray ended the call before burying his fingers in the twink's hair. He held the younger man's head still while he fucked his throat, searching for a release that was just out of reach. Closing his eyes, he pictured Lucky's lips wrapped around his cock, and within seconds, he shot his load, coating the twink's throat.

Resting his head back against the wall, he reached for his zipper. "Thanks," he said, "but I need to go."

"What?" The twink got to his feet. "It's early."

"Yeah, but I've got a phone call to make." Dray felt bad that he didn't know anything about the guy. "What's your name?"

"Brandon." He dug into his back pocket and handed Dray a small, pale-blue card. "That's got my phone number and email address on it."

Dray glanced at the business card, printed simply with Brandon's name, phone number and email. *For fuck sake. How many of the damn things does Brandon pass out in a single evening?* He shoved it into his pocket to be polite but had no plan to use it.

With a smile, Dray kissed Brandon's cheek. "See you later."

Once he was in his pickup, he called Lucky back.

"Hey," Lucky answered. "I'm sorry. Did I wake you or something?"

After years of hiding who he was, Dray no longer attempted to lie. "I was getting a blow job."

"Oh, shit. I'm sorry," Lucky replied.

Dray found it interesting that Lucky didn't seem shocked or appalled by the confession. He'd had inklings that Lucky was gay—or at least bi—but he'd never followed up on the feeling. "No big deal. It wasn't that great."

Lucky laughed. "Now that's a damn shame."

"Tell me about it." Dray's nerves began to settle at the ease of the conversation. "I watched your last fight earlier. Good job. That uppercut is a killer."

"Thanks. Grappling is my weak point, but I've been working on it."

As Dray sat there, staring through the windshield at the front door of the club, he realized he had no idea how to get Lucky to open up to the crowd. "Let me ask you something. Do you enjoy fighting?"

"I love it," Lucky answered.

"All of it?" Dray pushed.

"Well, no. I like the training and the actual fighting, but once the bout's over…"

"You shut down?" Dray offered.

"No." Lucky sighed. "Not really shut down, but let down because it's over. Don't you dare tell Brick this, but most of the time, I couldn't give a shit if I win or lose. I know I have to win in order to get another match and earn a living, but it's the fighting that I crave. Standing there listening to the crowd does nothing for me."

It was as if Lucky were speaking a foreign language. Dray had never known a fighter who didn't get off on the fans that came with winning. "Without the crowd, you won't be able to fight at the level you deserve. I'm not saying you have to kiss their asses, but you need to at least try to smile and wave to them. Play up the win, get them fired up, and the UFC will take notice."

"You sound like Brick," Lucky grumbled.

"You should listen to him. Brick's the best, but he can't get you where you need to go. Only *you* can do that." Dray hoped he wasn't pissing Lucky off. "When's your next fight?"

"I've got Indianapolis in two weeks. Brick says there'll probably be another scout there from the UFC to watch me."

"I remember seeing you in the crowd when I was fighting. You were pumped, animated and always had a big smile on your face. When you get to Indianapolis, I want you to imagine you're one of the fans. After the fight, throw your arms up like you used to and cheer. Hell, it doesn't matter what you say, the crowd'll be so loud they won't hear you anyway. All they care about is that you're having as good a time as they are."

"I'll look stupid," Lucky argued.

"No you won't. Trust me." Dray hoped he was right. "In the meantime, I need you to make sure Brick sees a doctor about that cough."

"Yeah, that's some nasty shit. He spits stuff up all the time. Really gross."

Dray didn't like the sound of that. "Promise me you'll get him in there, no matter what you have to do to make it happen." He refused to tell Lucky what he was most afraid of. His uncle had died of lung cancer four years earlier, and Dray wouldn't wish that kind of death on his fiercest enemy. He tried to soothe his fear by telling himself that Brick had never been a smoker, but just as quickly, he was reminded of all the smoky arenas he'd fought in. "You'll let me know what the doctor says, right?"

"Me? Shouldn't you ask Brick to do that?"

"Brick won't tell me the truth and you know it," Dray pointed out.

"Yeah, you're probably right," Lucky agreed. "Okay, I'll call ya."

"I'd appreciate it. Talk to you later, and think about what I said."

"Of course I will."

"Good. Later." Dray hung up the phone and smiled. Lucky's voice was a lot deeper than he remembered. He sat back in his seat and opened the browser on his phone, wondering what the fans really thought of the fighter.

As soon as he typed Lucky Gunn into the search engine,

43

a series of pictures popped up, all of them either videos of Lucky's fights or candid shots of him with his arm around a woman. It didn't escape Dray's notice that a different woman seemed to be in each photograph, most of them with big tits and fake smiles.

He shook his head, knowing he was simply torturing himself for no other reason than to push thoughts of Lucky from his mind. How pitiful was he that he'd fallen in lust with a man on a screen?

A headline caught his eye, pulling his attention away from the bimbos. He clicked on a link titled 'The Ice Man Is Coming'. *What the hell?* A mixed martial arts enthusiast who'd attended several of Lucky's matches had written the article. It talked about the lack of emotion in Lucky, despite his winning record.

"Shit," Dray groaned, knowing the fan was right. The article went on to say that by the time Lucky made it to the pros, he'd be devoid of all emotion, giving the UFC and the spectators an Ice Man for a contender. It also questioned whether the fans and the industry were doing Lucky a favor by supporting him at all and begged Lucky to seek professional help.

The damn thing was written by someone who obviously seemed to care more about the man than the fighter, something that warmed Dray's heart. He considered reaching out to the author. Unfortunately, if the guy had followed the sport for long, he'd know exactly who Dray was and what had forced him out of the MMA world.

Dray turned the phone off and tossed it on the seat beside him. Before he could start his truck, the twink from earlier walked out of the bar alone. Dray rolled down his window. "Get in."

Brandon stopped walking and smiled. "Change your mind?"

"Something like that."

* * * *

Lucky dropped his phone onto the bed before swinging his legs over the side of the mattress. He walked three steps and opened the small refrigerator to retrieve a breakfast sandwich out of the pint-sized freezer.

"What're you doing? I thought we were going out," Sid said from the doorway.

"I'm over it," Lucky replied, closing the door of the microwave. He set the timer. "I think I'm gonna stick around here and work on my uppercut." The phone call with Dray had left him anxious, and he knew if he didn't do something to soothe his nerves, he'd do something to get himself into trouble.

"That sucks. It's one thing for you to still live in this rathole, but not even Brick expects you to train twenty-four hours a day," Sid argued.

"This isn't about Brick — or *you* — so drop it." Lucky opened the steamer trunk at the foot of his bed and withdrew a clean pair of workout shorts. Without waiting for Sid to leave, he stripped out of his jeans and T-shirt.

Sid's barb about the storage room where Lucky still lived bugged him, but he wouldn't give his buddy the satisfaction of discussing why he chose to stay at the gym instead of getting his own place. His bank account was healthy enough, but he couldn't bring himself to spend it. Instead, he continued to clean The Brick Yard and live on the small salary Brick could afford to pay him, which allowed him to save every cent of his winnings. It didn't seem to matter to anyone that the storage room was the only real home he'd ever known. The roach-infested apartments his mom had rented had never been home, simply because he'd never felt welcomed.

He scanned the room as he sat on the bed and reached for his shoes. Although Brick had eventually moved most of the old junk out to give Lucky more space, it was still tight, too tight for a man to call home, but it was.

"You're pathetic," Sid said, pulling a joint out of his coat pocket.

"Don't light that shit up in here," Lucky warned. It was one thing for Sid to get high but another for him to disrespect Brick by doing it inside the building.

Sid put the joint between his lips before retrieving his lighter. "You gonna stop me?"

What the hell? Does Sid have a death wish? Lucky got to his feet and stalked toward his friend, hands fisted at his sides. "You know what this place means to me, so, yeah…I'll stop you."

"This fighting shit has gone to your head." Sid spun around and walked out of the room. "Call me when you pull your head out of your ass."

Lucky watched from the doorway until Sid had slipped out of the back door. It was getting harder and harder to hold on to Sid, but who else did he have other than Brick? "Fuck!" He bent over and tied his shoes. The need to fight was so strong that he'd nearly punched his only real friend. The microwave beeped, but he was no longer in the mood to eat.

He left the safety of his room and looked around the dark, empty gym. *Christ.* He felt so incredibly alone. For a brief moment, he considered calling Briley. She wasn't what he considered a girlfriend, but she was fun to hang out with and more than willing to have sex whenever he needed it. *No.* Pussy definitely wasn't what he needed.

Instead of taping his knuckles, he grabbed a pair of black gloves. He was used to fighting bare, but the UFC required the thinly padded gloves to be worn during a match. Brick had told him he needed to get used to the UFC rules, but Lucky had resisted because he knew if he allowed himself to want the UFC too much, it would hurt that much more when it was taken away. So far, he'd done well to keep the other half of himself buried, but he also knew it would only take one time with the wrong man to destroy everything. It was the reason he'd never allowed himself to give in to his desires.

He started with the speed bag to warm up. The monotonous

rhythm always soothed him, allowing his mind to empty of everything that continued to press down on him. His waste of a mother was up for parole in a week and bad son or not, he prayed she didn't get it. *Thump. Thump. Thump.* The sound and movement mesmerized him as he concentrated on the black swinging bag.

The one and only time he'd tried to visit his mom in prison, she'd refused to see him. Just as well. He'd only gone in the first place because Sid had told him he should. Lucky didn't remember what had happened after he'd left the prison and met up with Sid. All he knew was that he'd woken in a hotel bed with three women, a hangover and an ashtray of marijuana roaches. Evidently, he'd been quite the stud—or so Sid had told him. By the time he'd arrived at the gym, looking like he'd been run over by the pussy train, Brick had been furious and had refused to speak to him for three days.

Lucky dropped his hands and took a step back. The speed bag wasn't doing it for him. He sat on one of the weight benches and wiped the sweat from his face and torso before taking his frustration out on the wall-mounted heavy bag. With each combination of punches, he began to feel his anxiety ebb.

Brick's health was a problem that Lucky had tried to ignore. It wasn't that he didn't care about the old man, just that he didn't want to face the possibility that something was seriously wrong. Brick was more than a boss, landlord or trainer, he was the only one to ever show him an ounce of love.

"Fuck!" Lucky yelled to the empty gym as he continued to beat the hell out of the bag.

Chapter Three

Lucky sat across the table from Briley, who was busy trying to decide what to order. He didn't bother with the menu since he never ordered from it. The cook and owner, Mac, was a sports nut who'd followed the fighters coming out of The Brick Yard for years, but he was more than that to Lucky. Brick may have been the only father figure he'd ever known, but Mac was like one of those grouchy uncles he saw on TV. Mac's Diner was right next door to the gym, so rarely a day went by when he didn't stop in to see Mac at least once.

"The usual?" Trish, the waitress, asked.

"Yeah." Lucky pulled his phone out of his pocket while Briley ordered. He still didn't know why he'd asked her to meet him. Probably something to do with the fact that he didn't want to be alone. "You mind if I step outside and make a call?"

Briley picked up her own phone and started scrolling through it, something that usually annoyed him. "Not at all."

Coat in hand, Lucky scooted out of the booth and headed for the door. He retrieved Dray's number and waited. It wasn't a call he wanted to make, but he couldn't put it off any longer.

"Hey," Dray answered.

"You gotta minute?" Lucky walked around the side of the building to shield himself from the brutally cold Chicago wind.

"I've got twenty of them until my next appointment. What's up?"

"I took Brick back to the doctor yesterday. According to him, the doc said it was bronchitis, but I've been around too many dirtbags to know when someone's lying to my face. So, I called the doctor this afternoon."

"Did you find out anything?" Dray asked.

"No, something about privacy laws."

"Shit."

"Yeah," Lucky agreed. He hadn't realized how much he needed to talk to Dray. Between the deep and raspy timbre of Dray's voice and his perfectly muscled body, Lucky hadn't stopped dreaming about Dray since finding him in the shower with Vince. At the time, Lucky had been too young to really get to know Dray, but they were both adults now, and he planned to take advantage of Dray's willingness to speak to him.

"You still there?" Dray asked.

"Yeah," Lucky replied. "I don't think there's anything I can do but watch him and wait for him to open up."

"The food's ready," Briley said, rounding the corner.

Lucky nodded. "Give me a sec."

She smiled and disappeared back around the side of the building.

"You with someone?" Dray asked.

"Yeah. I'm having dinner at Mac's with a friend." Lucky didn't feel the need to qualify his relationship with Briley. Hell, he didn't even know if they had a relationship. Briley was a cool chick who liked to fuck and cuddle on the couch as they watched movies. Never had he thought he'd be the kind of man to cuddle, but she'd shown him how comforting it was. He wasn't expected to talk or pour out what the hell was bothering him. All Briley wanted was for him to hold her.

"Christ, I haven't been to Mac's in years. Is it still as good?" Dray asked.

"Same old Mac's." Lucky grinned. Although Brick had kept him out of trouble and had given him a place to sleep during his teenage years, it had been Mac who'd fed him

49

most nights. He still remembered Mac knocking on the back door of the gym on the nights Lucky had slept over. He'd never been sure if Mac stopped by daily or if Brick had informed him when Lucky needed a place to sleep, but Mac had never failed to drop off leftovers. There'd been many times when Mac's generosity had been Lucky's only meal of the day.

"I'd tell you to say hi for me, but I doubt Mac would give a shit."

Lucky's eyebrows drew together at the troubled quality of Dray's voice. "You know that none of us think badly of you, right? I mean…what went down with the fans was one thing, but the folks around here thought of you as family."

Dray made a noise Lucky couldn't decipher. "I tried to tell Mac goodbye and he was so pissed he refused to talk to me."

"You shittin' me?" A combination of anger and disbelief filled Lucky. He couldn't believe Mac would do something like that, but he was sure as hell going to speak to him about it.

"No, but I don't blame him. He fed me like he did you." Dray chuckled. "You didn't think I knew about that, did ya?"

"*You're* the one who told Mac when I was spending the night in the storage room?" Lucky closed his eyes and turned toward the wall of the building. He had no doubt his emotions were clearly visible on his face.

Dray chuckled again. "No, that wasn't me. Brick always left the front window light on when you stayed over. It was different with me. The first time Mac gave me food was after I showed up at the gym to work and passed out from hunger before I could do my job. Brick marched me over to Mac's and bought me the first steak I'd ever eaten. Mac took one look at me, shook his head, and informed me that a diner has a lot of prepared food left over at the end of the night. He made it clear that I was to stop by before going home to pick up some of the food that would go to waste."

He sighed heavily. "I fed three people with that doggie bag. Thanks to Mac, me, my mom and my little brother Frankie never went to bed hungry."

Although Lucky felt better knowing he wasn't Mac's only charity case, he began to wonder if Jax, Brick's youngest employee, was also on the receiving end of Mac's generosity. An ache started in Lucky's chest at the thought of Jax needing a safe place to sleep and being unable to take refuge at the gym because Lucky was too afraid to move on. He knew from Brick that Jax's mother had taken off years ago. Maybe Jax needed the safety of the gym as much as Lucky had. "Has Brick told you about Jax?"

"Yeah, and Leon before that. Brick can't turn away someone in need," Dray replied.

Leon. Lucky remembered the skinny African American kid who used to sweep the gym and handle the laundry, but Leon had been a brainiac who'd earned a full-ride scholarship and had taken off for college as soon as he'd graduated high school. "What was the story with Leon?"

"Why don't you already know?" Dray asked.

"I don't know." Lucky felt like the biggest piece of shit in Chicago. "Tell me."

"Brick found him asleep behind the dumpster one morning. After that, Leon crashed on that piece-of-shit couch in Brick's apartment."

Lucky swallowed around the lump of self-hatred in his throat. He was almost afraid to ask about the new kid, but knew he had to do it. "And Jax?"

"His father likes to drink, gets mad and takes it out on Jax. He came to Brick to learn how to defend himself."

Lucky's nose burned as tears filled his eyes. He pounded his fist against the wall. He needed to get off the phone before Dray realized what a bastard he'd been to the kids. "Thanks for the information. I'll give you a call if anything changes with Brick."

"Hey," Dray said. "Anytime you need to talk, you can call me. It doesn't have to be about Brick."

"Thanks." Lucky didn't know what else to say.

"And now that you know the truth about Jax, pay it forward." Dray disconnected the call without another word.

Lucky wiped the back of his hand over his eyes before shoving the phone into his pocket. He went inside but didn't stop at his table. Instead, he walked straight to the kitchen. He found Mac standing at the grill, looking much younger than his fifty-plus years. "Dray said to tell you hi."

Mac turned around slowly and narrowed his eyes. "So he's not dead after all?"

"He said he came in here to tell you goodbye and you refused to speak to him." Lucky leaned back against the prep table and crossed his arms over his chest. Although Mac had done a lot of good in his life, Lucky wasn't sure he could forgive him for being a fucking bigot.

"Dray could've easily taken the UFC title, but instead of standing up to the assholes who wanted to bring him down, he tucked his tail between his legs and ran."

"The fans would've never accepted who he was," Lucky argued.

"We'll never know, will we? Fact is, he didn't care enough to try and make them accept him. He gave up because they hurt his feelings, and I can't stomach a quitter," Mac said. He returned his attention to the grill.

"It isn't easy to admit who you are, knowing the people you care about won't accept it," Lucky mumbled.

"Yeah, you keep telling yourself that, kid, and in the meantime, apologize to your *girlfriend* for making her eat alone." Mac glanced over his shoulder. "Now get the fuck outta my kitchen."

* * * *

Instead of going home with Briley, Lucky headed to the gym. As he'd thought, Jax was sitting in the laundry room doing his homework. "Hey," Lucky greeted from the doorway.

Jax glanced up from his history book.

Lucky had noticed the bruises on Jax's face before, but he'd wrongfully assumed they were from training. It made him wonder if Dray had ever taken the time to really see his bruises. Dray had always been nice to him, but he'd never spent real time with him. He gestured to the textbook. "History was the only class I enjoyed outside of gym and lunch."

"Yeah?" Jax grinned. "Well, it's kicking my ass," he admitted. "And I've got a big test tomorrow."

Lucky found another metal folding chair in the corner of the room and carried it over to the table. "Need some help studying?"

Jax shook his head. "That's okay. I know you're busy training and stuff."

"I'm not busy at the moment, so you should take advantage of it." Lucky smiled in an attempt to put Jax at ease. "Now, slide the book over, and if you get an A on this test, I'll teach you how to land an uppercut that'll knock an opponent on his ass."

Jax's big blue eyes rounded. "Really?"

Lucky shrugged. He'd planned to discuss Jax's father and living situation with the kid but decided at the last minute to get to know the younger man first. "Sure."

For the next several hours the two of them studied, only taking breaks long enough to fold towels. Lucky glanced at the clock on the back wall. "It's almost eleven." He stretched his arms over his head. "I think you got this."

Jax nodded and started to stuff his books into his backpack. "I appreciate your help."

Lucky got to his feet and pushed the chair in. "Are you going to head home or would you rather crash in Brick's office?"

Jax pursed his lips in thought. "Would Brick allow that?"

"Sure." Lucky made a split-second decision. "Actually, I'm planning to get my own place, so once I'm out, you can always stay in the storage room if you're too tired to go home after work. It's not perfect, but it's comfortable."

Jax's expression changed. "Brick told you, didn't he?"

Lucky shook his head. He wouldn't lie to the kid, but he wouldn't give Dray up either. "There's a reason I moved into that storage room in the first place. You're not the only one who's been afraid to go home at night."

"I don't want to talk about it," Jax mumbled, shouldering his pack.

"I can respect that, but if you change your mind, I'm here." Lucky picked up a stack of towels and waited for Jax to do the same. "And, for the record, I suck at math, so I can't help you there."

* * * *

After the phone call with Lucky, Dray lay awake for hours before finally reaching to the bedside table for his phone. It was nearly midnight on the East Coast, way too late to make the call, but he needed to talk to his baby brother. After their mother's death nearly four years earlier, Frankie had done his best to distance himself from Dray.

"What the hell, Dray?" Frankie answered.

"Sorry, I know it's late, but I can't seem to get ahold of you during the day." Dray knew it was a pathetic excuse, but it was the only one he was willing to give.

"That's because I work at an actual job," Frankie said.

Dray never knew what shamed his brother more, the fact that Dray was a tattoo artist or his sexuality, but Frankie always managed to make Dray feel inferior. "How's Florida?"

"Seriously? You called at eleven-fifty to talk about the fucking weather?" Frankie asked.

"No. Sorry." Dray took a deep breath. "I was just thinking about you, me and mom and how we had so little but so much at the same time."

"Are you drunk?"

54

"No." Dray was starting to get angry. "I just miss you. I've sent a couple emails, but you haven't replied, so I thought I'd take a chance and give you a call. You still dating Stella?"

Frankie snorted. "I haven't seen Stella in almost a year. Way to stay up to date, bro."

Dray bit his lip. It wasn't his fault that he didn't know whom his brother was currently fucking.

"What do you really want? Money?" Frankie asked.

"Have I ever asked you for anything?" Dray couldn't believe the man he was speaking to was the same sweet kid who used to look up to him. Hell, Dray had paid most of Frankie's college tuition.

"If it's not money, what is it?"

"Why do you hate me so much?" Dray finally asked. "Is it because I'm gay? Do I embarrass you?"

"I don't hate you. I don't know you enough to hate you. Once you started hanging out at that gym, you never had time for me or Mom. Then you started fighting and only came home long enough to throw money at us, like that was going to make up for you not being around. Then, you take off to Kansas City and didn't even come back to Chicago when Mom got sick. It was all on me, just like it's always been."

Dray sat up, shocked at Frankie's response. "Is that what you really think? I didn't even know Mom was sick. I spoke to her on the phone three times a week and she never once mentioned high blood pressure or chest pains. And, as for not being around, I was working my ass off, trying to become the best fighter I could be, so I could help Mom out financially. You may call it throwing money at her, but I was doing my best to help her out. You think I liked seeing her work so damn hard all the time? I thought if I made something of myself, I could give back an ounce of what she gave to me for so many years."

Frankie laughed. "Yeah, you made something of yourself all right. Mom may have talked to you until the end, but don't think for a moment that she wasn't just as embarrassed as I was about those pictures with you and that guy."

Dray swallowed several times in an attempt to keep his emotions in check. As much as he'd tried to deny it, the truth of his relationship with his brother was staring him in the face. "I'm sorry you feel like I did you wrong. Believe me, that wasn't my intention. I wanted to show you that you could rise above the neighborhood and make something of yourself if you put in the effort, but now I know you've only ever seen me as a failure." The truth hurt to say, and he waited a heartbeat for his brother to respond.

When Frankie remained silent, Dray knew it might very well be the last phone call he ever shared with his brother. "Right. I won't bother you again."

Dray hung up without another word from Frankie. He tossed the phone toward the nightstand, but heard it hit the carpeted floor. *Whatever.*

* * * *

After a sleepless night, Lucky knocked on Brick's office door. "You got a minute?"

"Yeah," Brick answered.

Lucky opened the door and stepped inside. Elbows propped on the desk, Brick ran his fingers through what was left of his white hair.

"What the fuck do you want? You should be training," Brick growled.

Lucky closed the door behind him. He was used to Brick's moods after so many years, but the man in front of him wasn't himself. "You feeling okay?"

Brick dropped his hands to the desk in exasperation. "Is there a reason you interrupted me?"

"I thought I'd let you know that I'm going out this morning to look for an apartment." Lucky sank onto the sofa, noticing the neatly folded blanket lying across the arm. "You should've kicked me out years ago."

"Why would I do that? I figured you'd leave when you

were ready," Brick answered before a coughing fit hit him.

Lucky didn't speak until Brick had regained control of his breathing. "You should've told me Jax needed a place to crash. Just like you should've told me about Leon."

Brick's gaze narrowed. "Did Dray open his fuckin' mouth?"

"Yeah, and in the process of telling me what you should have, he opened my eyes. I've been acting like a selfish bastard, and you let me." Lucky fucking hated the idea of moving out of his safe place, but he was an adult with enough money to get his own apartment. Jax wasn't as fortunate. Lucky got to his feet. "Anyway, I just wanted to let you know."

Brick growled under his breath, a sure sign he was frustrated as hell. "There's a one-bedroom apartment in my building for rent. I'll talk to the manager on your behalf if you're interested."

Lucky nodded. Brick's place was only two blocks from the gym. It was an older building with character and a small plot of grass in the courtyard for all the residents to share. He'd never been able to look out a window and see grass. "Okay. Yeah. I'd appreciate that."

Brick coughed again. "Fine. Now get your lazy ass out there and train. The Hammer isn't gonna lie down for you in the cage just because you've had a fucking epiphany about your life."

With a shake of his head, Lucky left the office. Brick was too goddamned stubborn for his own good. There was no fucking way the old man had bronchitis. Unfortunately, there wasn't much Lucky could do about it other than watch Brick and make sure he took care of himself.

He motioned for Hector, one of his sparring partners. "Let's go," he said, knowing the only way he'd feel better was to fight.

* * * *

Lucky carried the last of his boxes into his new apartment. He flipped on the light and grinned. The place had been fully furnished with clearance items from the local thrift store. He set the box down and sat on his twelve-dollar orange-and-gold-floral sofa. It looked like hell, but it was comfortable, probably more so than the mattress he'd dug out of the dumpster behind the building.

He leaned forward and pulled the box over. Staring down at the contents, he willed himself to reach inside and start reliving the memories of his childhood that were wrapped in yellowed newspaper. When he'd cleaned out his mom's apartment prior to her being sent away for distribution of a controlled substance — meth, of course — he'd packed up everything of value that she hadn't already sold or pawned and had shoved it under his bed at the gym.

With a deep breath, he reached in and withdrew a framed picture of his Grandma Gunn. He looked into the heavyset woman's eyes and wondered what she was like. Did she think about him or even know that he existed? His mom had been a runaway. Lucky knew that much, but he didn't know the circumstances behind her desire to flee with no money to the unkindness of a city the size of Chicago. Still, he couldn't believe the smiling woman in the photograph had forced her daughter out of the house.

He stood and carried the picture across the room. He placed it on the rickety dresser that doubled as a TV stand before stepping back to eye it again. As a child, he'd made up stories about the woman in the photo, praying that she'd swoop in and take him away from the life he'd been forced to live. Of course, she'd never come, never would.

The next item he pulled out of the box was a red-and-blue plastic truck. He smiled as he remembered the hours of enjoyment he'd gotten from the broken toy he'd found in the park. Using his forefinger, he spun the wheel he'd fashioned out of a metal orange juice lid that he'd also dug out of the garbage. When things had gotten rough at home, he'd taken his truck to the roof of the building and had spent hours running it back and forth over the hot surface.

Lucky glanced around the room. He wanted to set the truck out, but wondered if Sid or Briley would see it and think he was nuts for cherishing a broken toy. In the end, he decided to keep his treasure tucked safely in his box of memories.

The sound of his ringing phone finally pulled him out of his thoughts. He retrieved the cell from his pocket. "Hey."

"Brick told me you moved out of the gym," Dray said.

"Yeah." Lucky returned to the couch and stretched out as much as he could. "It feels weird," he confessed.

"I bet." Dray chuckled. "I remember the size of that storage room."

So what does it say about me that I'd much rather be back in my old space? Lucky decided to steer the conversation away from his new place. "How's the tattoo business?"

"Okay, I guess. I've been working more than I want, but I don't have anything else to do. I noticed you still don't have ink. What happened to change your mind?"

"Nothing. I haven't changed it. You just left before you could do it," Lucky confessed. He'd even considered asking Dray to do it when he'd fought in Kansas City a year earlier, but according to Brick, Dray had refused to see them.

"There're other artists in Chicago," Dray pointed out.

"I know, but you promised me a discount." Lucky hid behind the old agreement. "Maybe if I ever get another fight in Kansas City, you'll actually see me, and you can do one then?"

Dray was quiet for several moments. "You know why I had to turn down Brick's offer to see you fight when you were here, right?"

"Not really. Brick just said you weren't ready to see us again." Lucky scraped his teeth over his bottom lip. He didn't tell Dray how much it had hurt. How the pain of being turned away by Dray had been worse than the day he'd tried to visit his own mother.

"It wasn't that—not really." Dray sighed. "If I'd shown

up to that fight, I would've cast a shadow over your career. You've worked too damn hard for something like that to happen. The last thing you need is a photographer to snap a picture of you with the Fighting Fag."

Lucky hated the nickname the fans had given Dray after the affair with Vince had come out. He wanted to tell Dray he didn't give a fuck what the fans thought, but he couldn't. Although he held them in contempt for the way they'd treated Dray, Lucky knew the only shot he had of rising above the life he'd grown up in was through fighting. Still, as long as he kept his dick away from what it really wanted, no one could ever accuse him of being gay.

"Unless someone took a picture of the two of us making out, I think my career would be safe," Lucky replied.

Dray went quiet once more. "I'm not willing to take that chance... Not with you," he added after several heartbeats.

"So forget the fight. What if I borrow a car and drive down? Would you still give me that discount on the tat?" Lucky held his breath, waiting for Dray's answer.

Dray chuckled. "Maybe, but I'd suggest you wait for a break in your schedule. Depends on where you want the shamrock, but it'll take anywhere from a month to six weeks to completely heal."

Lucky couldn't believe Dray had remembered. "I'm over the idea of the shamrock."

"See, that's why getting a tattoo at sixteen isn't a good idea."

"What about you? You have tattoos you wish you didn't?" Lucky asked. He liked the lighter turn the conversation had taken.

"I did, but I've had most of them inked over," Dray answered. "You haven't seen me in a while. You may not recognize me anymore."

Lucky seriously doubted that. "Why? Did you grow out your hair or something?"

"Or something. The hair's the same, short as I can get it without shaving my head, but I'm showing a lot less skin these days. The ink's fairly solid from my collarbone to my ankles."

"Even your dick?" Lucky bit the inside of his cheek. *Fuck. Why the hell did I ask that?*

Dray laughed. "Hell no. I'm not that bad. I just meant full sleeves, chest, stomach and legs."

Lucky tried to imagine Dray's muscular body covered in tattoos. His cock stirred, liking the idea very much. His desire to flirt with Dray got the better of him. "I'd like to see that."

Dray made a choking noise.

"Sorry," Lucky mumbled. "I'm not very good at this."

"At what?"

"Flirting." Thank god, they were on the phone and not in the same room.

"You don't need to flirt to get my attention. Which's another reason I've stayed away." Dray made a noise, this one sounding more disgusted than the last. "Shit. I can't believe I just told you that."

Lucky's dick went rock-hard. "Are you saying you're attracted to me?"

"Doesn't matter. You're not in the position to do anything about it."

Lucky nodded, even though Dray couldn't see him. "I've never forgotten the advice you gave me that day before you left. I've shut out the side of me that wants what it can't have."

"And how's that going for you?" Dray asked, his tone lighter.

"Bearable, I guess. Fucking's fucking. It doesn't matter who I'm with if I can't have what I want."

"Trust me, Lucky, fucking Vince wasn't worth what I gave up."

"Yeah, that's what I keep telling myself whenever I think..." Lucky snapped his mouth shut. He'd almost confessed to thinking of Dray. "What about in KC? Have you found someone?"

"I've found a lot of someones, but like you said…fucking's fucking. No way in hell I'll ever trust someone again, so my cock's the only thing I'm willing to share."

Neither of them spoke for several moments. Lucky closed his eyes and listened to Dray breathe, imagining the two of them lying next to each other.

"I should let you go. I just wanted to see if you got moved into your new place okay," Dray said, ruining the moment.

"I'm in. That's about all I can say," Lucky replied. "By the way, the Indianapolis fight will be shown live online if you want to watch."

"I do," Dray answered immediately. "Remember to stand your ground in the cage. Own the fight from the moment you step inside."

"I will." Lucky felt warm at Dray's concern. "Night." He hung up the phone and clutched it in his hand as he stared up at the freshly painted ceiling. In that moment, he felt happier than he'd ever been. It didn't make sense, and he knew it would pass, but it had been the first real conversation he'd had where he could be himself. Did Dray have any idea what it had meant to him?

He closed his eyes and let the feeling wash over him. He'd promised himself that once his career was over, he'd be honest with those around him, but in the last few weeks, he'd gotten the distinct impression that those closest to him already knew his secret. What the hell did he do with that? Continue to pretend?

* * * *

Lucky had just finished changing into his street clothes when Jax came into the locker room. "Hey," he greeted.

Jax settled the stack of towels onto the shelf. "You got a minute?"

"Sure." Lucky finished tying his shoes. "What's up?" he asked when Jax didn't continue.

"Not here." Jax glanced at the handful of men in the room.

"Laundry room?"

"Okay." Lucky stood and grabbed the small backpack he'd picked up the previous day. It was the first time in his life he'd had to carry clothes to and from the gym, and he didn't like it at all. He entered the laundry room, expecting to help Jax with homework, but the expression on Jax's face told him something was wrong. Lucky wondered if Jax's dad had gone after him again. "Jax?"

Jax reached into one of the cupboards and pulled out a stained towel. "I found this in Brick's office. I went in there to empty the trash and the corner of this was sticking out of his bottom desk drawer."

Lucky took it from Jax and stared at it. There were spots covering both sides of the towel in varying shades between bright red and the dark, brownish red of old blood. It was obvious upon inspection that Brick had been coughing up blood for days, maybe weeks.

"What do you think it means?" Jax asked.

Lucky took a calming breath. "I don't know, but I'm damn sure gonna find out." He started to turn but stopped and glanced at Jax. "Thank you for showing me this."

"Do you think he'll be mad at me?"

Lucky shook his head. "I won't tell him how I got it." He left the laundry room and looked around the gym for Brick. When he didn't see the old bastard, he knocked on the office door.

"What?" Brick yelled.

Lucky walked into the office and threw the towel on Brick's desk before crossing his arms over his chest. "I need you to be honest with me."

Brick snatched the towel and shoved it back into his drawer. "You been snooping?"

"Doesn't matter," Lucky answered, refusing to give up Jax. "How sick are you?"

Brick took a sip of water. "Cancer. Stomach and lungs."

Lucky dropped into one of the chairs in front of Brick's desk. He bent over and rested his forearms on his knees, trying like hell to catch a breath. For over two months he'd watched Brick struggle with the damn cough. Yes, he'd pushed him to go to the doctor, but he'd known in his gut Brick had lied about the diagnosis and he'd done nothing. *Fuck!* He fisted his hands, trying to get his anger under control. "What're they doing about it?" he finally asked.

"Nothing," Brick replied. "And that's my choice, so don't start bitchin' about the doctor."

"What the hell? You're just going to give up?" Lucky pounded his fist on the desk. "What about this place? And Jax?" He tried to swallow, his throat thickening as he fought down the urge to hit someone. "What about me?"

"You'll be fine." Brick rubbed his face with his palm. "I'd planned to eventually talk to you and Dray about taking over the gym with the condition that you'll continue to watch over Jax and anyone who might come along after him."

Lucky thought of the bloody towel. "How long were you going to wait to tell someone?"

"If you're worried about your fight schedule, don't be. I should make it through the end of the season," Brick grumbled.

There were only three months left in the season. Was that all the time Brick had? Lucky shot to his feet. "Fuck you!" He walked to the door but couldn't make himself go through. He knew he wasn't angry with Brick, no matter how stupid the old man's statement had been. It was the situation that made him feel like he was about to explode. "Sorry," he said as he leaned his forehead against the door.

"I know," Brick replied. "I've been trying to figure out how to break it to you."

"Yeah, well, let me clue you in on something. Asking me if I care more about the fucking fight season than the man who's been the closest thing I've ever had to a real parent isn't it."

"I just wanted you to know that I can make it through the season," Brick said. "That's one thing I don't want you to worry about."

"I'm not." The cage was the furthest thing from his mind. "Are you going to call Dray?" When Brick didn't answer, Lucky shook his head. "You want me to do it, don't you?" Lucky guessed.

"I'd just fuck it up like I did with you."

The last thing in the world Lucky wanted to do was make the phone call to Dray. "I'll tell him," he conceded. Although there was a lot he still needed to discuss with Brick, Lucky wanted to get his head on straight first. "I'm going out for a while. Do you need anything?"

"Time."

"That's what treatment could've given you," Lucky snapped.

"Yeah," Brick agreed. "According to the doctor, I could've bought myself a month — two at most — but I would've been going through chemo and shit in the meantime." He shook his head. "That's not the way I wanna go."

Lucky sucked in a breath. "I guess I can understand that." Given the same diagnosis, he wasn't sure he wouldn't have made the same decision. "I'll go figure out what to tell Dray and check on you later."

"I don't need a damn babysitter," Brick said with a huff. "Just have your ass back in here at eight in the morning and be prepared to work. We've only got one more day of training before we leave for Indianapolis."

"Fuck the fight." Lucky stared at Brick. "The last thing you need to do is travel right now."

Brick narrowed his eyes. "If I gotta leave this world, I plan to go out a winner."

What the hell could Lucky say to that? "We'll see."

Chapter Four

Dray wiped the excess ink from the tramp stamp he'd just finished on a twenty-three-year-old woman named Amber. The young lady had a pretty ass, but the sight of it did absolutely nothing for him sexually, which was why her boyfriend had insisted Dray do the tat.

"Phone," Manny, one of the artists, said over the partition.

"Get a name and number and tell 'em I'll call them back," Dray replied without taking his eyes off the fresh ink. Tramp stamps, in general, weren't his favorite, but the intricate tree he'd designed for Amber was more a lower back piece. At first she'd thought it would be too big, but after discussing it with Dray, she'd finally agreed.

"It's gorgeous," Brad, Amber's boyfriend, commented.

"Yeah," Dray agreed.

"Hey, Dray, the guy on the phone said his name is Lucky and that you should call him as soon as possible."

Dray's gaze shot to Manny. "Did he sound upset?"

Manny nodded.

"Shit." Dray stopped admiring his own work and finished cleaning and bandaging the tattoo. "Manny'll give you a sheet for aftercare, but I assume you already know the drill." He pulled off his latex gloves and tossed them into the trash. Brad had been Dray's client for several years and had a myriad of tattoos on his body. Evidently, Brad wasn't bothered by Dray's out-and-proud status, but a lot of guys were. Dray didn't mind. He'd rather not work on the assholes anyway.

"Yeah, I'll make sure it's taken care of." Brad held out his hand. "You're the best, man."

"Thanks." Dray grabbed his phone off his worktable. "Sorry, but I need to return a call."

"Sure," Brad said, letting Dray go.

"Thanks," Amber called as Dray pushed open the door to the break room.

Dray grabbed a bottle of water out of the refrigerator and pressed speed dial.

"Hey, sorry for bothering you at work," Lucky answered.

"Don't worry about it. I was about done anyway." Dray dropped into one of the chairs that surrounded the small kitchen table they'd set up. "This about Brick?" It was the call he'd hoped would never come, but one he'd expected.

"Yeah. Jax found a bloody towel in Brick's bottom drawer. I confronted the old bastard, and he finally laid it all out. Cancer in his stomach and lungs. He's refused treatment because the chemo or radiation would only prolong his life for a short time instead of cure it," Lucky explained.

"Fuck!" Dray threw the half-full water bottle against the wall. "How long?"

"Hard to say, but Brick's determined to last through the rest of the season. I told him I didn't give a shit about the fights, and he informed me that he wanted to go out a winner."

Like always, there was a pen and pad of paper on the table, which all the artists used for doodling on their off moments. It was a nervous habit they all shared, and one Dray frequently used to rid himself of his excess energy while in the shop. "You're with him every day. What do you think?"

Lucky sighed. "I think he's strong enough to make the Indianapolis trip, but after that, my next fight isn't for another three weeks. With the amount of blood on that fucking towel…"

"Indianapolis will be his last," Dray surmised.

"Yeah, I think so." Lucky cleared his throat. "I put a call into Ray Bruno. He's got a winner-take-all tournament coming up next week. The weight classes are broad, but anyone can enter for five hundred bucks. The more entries, the more fights."

"Don't do it." Dray rubbed his hands over his bristly scalp. Ray Bruno's tournaments often turned into bloodbaths, pitting trained fighters against regular men who thought they were just as tough but weren't even in the same league as their skilled opponents.

"I can win," Lucky declared. "Not only will I need the release while dealing with this shit, but it's local, so I can give Brick the only thing he wants before he dies."

"And what happens if you don't win?" Dray asked. "What happens if you go against someone who fucks you up so bad your dream of going pro is over?"

"If some schmo in Bruno's tournament can fuck me up enough to put me out of the game, I don't deserve to go pro."

Dray added some shading to the portrait he'd drawn of Lucky. Even as a teenager, Lucky had been high-strung, only really settling down when he was in the ring or working one of the bags. Fighting for Lucky was like a drug, whereas it was the fan reaction that had always driven Dray. Although he didn't like it, he understood Lucky's need to do it. "Fuck," he groaned.

"There's something else," Lucky said. "Brick's leaving The Brick Yard to the two of us. He wants us to look after Jax and anyone else who comes along who needs it."

"What the fuck is he thinking? I can't just pick up and move back to Chicago. I've got a life here—a house, a job." Not to mention the fact that Kansas City was far enough away from Lucky not to pose a threat to the younger man's career.

Lucky was quiet for several moments before he exhaled. "I think he's worried about the kids, and this is his way of insuring they have somewhere to go. He's asking us to pay it forward."

Dray thought of the farmhouse he'd worked so hard on. It was still far from perfect, but it was his—or at least it would be in another twenty-one years after he'd paid off the mortgage. The house had filled the void left by Brick, Mac and, yes, Lucky, but lately, even his beloved home hadn't been enough to beat back the memories of his life in Chicago. He wondered if he should be honest with Lucky or if knowing how much Dray wanted him would put Lucky in a worse position.

Lucky made a noise that sounded suspiciously like a sob. "I can't do this alone," he finally said.

Motherfucker! Dray closed his eyes and shook his head, knowing he couldn't ignore the plea. He did a quick mental rundown of his upcoming appointments, savings account balance and people he could trust to watch his house, before relenting. "Okay. I need to take care of a few things, but I'll head that way in a few days. I'm not promising I'll stay for good, but I'll be there to help take care of Brick."

"Thanks," Lucky mumbled.

"In the meantime, keep me updated on what's going on." How the hell was Dray going to tell his cousin Berto that he had two days to find a replacement for him at the shop? "What about Indianapolis? You still gonna go?"

"Yes, but we'll be home on Sunday."

"Expect me on Sunday then," Dray said.

"Dray?" Lucky's voice was softer than Dray had ever heard it.

"Yeah?"

"I'm sorry. I know coming back here is probably the last thing you want to do and if I could handle the fights, the gym, Jax and Brick on my own, I would."

"I know," Dray replied. "I just don't want to cause problems for you, and I'm afraid that's exactly what's going to happen."

Lucky chuckled, but Dray could tell it was forced. "At least you'll be here to help me sort the shit out if it happens."

"If I fuck up your career, you may not want my help." Dray stared at the realistic drawing of Lucky under his fingers. He tapped the paper several times then pushed it away.

"Don't worry about my career, because I'm not sure I can fight without Brick," Lucky confessed.

"You can, and you will." As the realization of the situation sank in, Dray's hands started to shake. *Fuck!* He needed to get off the phone before he totally lost his fucking mind. "Hey, can I call you later?"

"Sure," Lucky replied.

"Thanks." Dray hung up and dropped his phone to the table before he threw it across the goddamn room. He sprang to his feet and kicked backward, sending the chair crashing against the wall. He couldn't imagine The Brick Yard without the man that had become its heart and soul. The old guilt came back full force. He shouldn't have walked out on Brick like he had. Running back to Kansas City had been a purely selfish move. After everything Brick had done for him, Dray had repaid him by turning his back on his mentor and the gym. He owed everything he was to Brick, and he knew in his gut it was time he stopped being a prick and paid it forward.

One thing he knew for sure, Lucky had the skill it took to become a champion. There were two kinds of fighters — those who learned and those who were born to the sport. In the cage, Lucky moved with a natural grace and single-mindedness that couldn't be taught, and one way or another, Dray was going to push Lucky into reaching for the stars he deserved to touch.

* * * *

Lucky studied Brick closely as they made their way through the parted crowd to the cage. The three-hour drive had definitely taken its toll on the older man, but Brick had refused to rest when they'd finally arrived at the hotel. Instead, Brick had demanded Lucky run through a series of warm-up drills and exercises until it was time to leave for the arena.

A woman with big tits pushed through the crowd and grabbed Lucky around the neck. "I love you!" she screamed, trying to kiss him as her giant breasts pressed against his chest.

In no mood for the unwanted attention, Lucky pushed her away from him. Unfortunately, he was already pumped and focused on the fight and the move threw her off balance. As the woman fell to the floor, the entire crowd started to boo.

Lucky immediately bent over and tried to help her to her feet. Unfortunately, the damage had already been done as far as the fans were concerned. *Shit.* He glanced over his shoulder at Brick then returned his attention to the woman. "You okay?"

"You're an asshole!" she yelled in his face, jerking her arm out of his hand.

"I'm sorry," he said, trying to apologize.

"Fuck off," she shot back.

His concentration obliterated, Lucky continued toward the cage. He had five minutes until he had to step inside, and his mind was so fucked, he doubted he could win. He thought he'd dealt with the Brick shit, but faced with the very real prospect of losing in front of the man who meant everything to him, he was hanging on by a thread. "Give me my phone." He held out his hand and waited for Brick to comply.

"What the fuck're you talking about?" Brick growled.

"Give me the goddamned phone!" Lucky felt like his world was crashing down around him.

With a loud curse of his own, Brick handed Lucky the phone. "Four minutes."

Lucky shrugged out of his robe as he waited for Dray to pick up. "Come on. Come on," he chanted.

"Hey," Dray answered. Lucky assumed Dray was already tuned into the fight because he could hear the roar of the crowd in the background.

"I can't do this," Lucky said in a rush. "I can't get up there. My head's all screwed up."

"Look up and to your left," Dray ordered.

Lucky didn't know what the hell Dray was talking about but he did as instructed. There, in the front row of the balcony, stood a tattooed god in a baseball hat. His eyes met Dray's.

"You can do this. Just breathe and don't let that fucker get too close to you."

"Come down," Lucky urged.

"No. You don't need me. You have Brick. Remember why you're doing this and fuckin' do it," Dray said before ending the call.

Lucky watched as Dray shoved the cell back into his pocket. "I can do this," he whispered as he turned to face Brick. "I can do this."

"You'd better fucking do it! That hotel room is costing me almost a hundred bucks." Brick gave Lucky a shove.

Lucky climbed the steps and entered the cage. He faced his opponent, Johnny 'The Hammer' Gains, as the referee set out the rules of the fight. *I can do this.* He glanced up at Dray once more and his need to fight slid into place.

* * * *

Arms resting on the railing in front of him, Dray let out a sigh of relief when the first round ended. So far, the match was a draw, but it was easy to see Lucky was finally getting warmed up while The Hammer was starting to wear out. He pulled out his phone and called Lucky.

"Not the time," Brick snapped into the phone.

"Tell Lucky to concentrate his blows on the left rib cage. The Hammer's protecting that area, so there's already damage." Dray stared down at Lucky as Brick reiterated Dray's instructions.

Lucky tilted his head back and looked straight at Dray then nodded. Dray put his phone away and took a moment to study the fans. The incident with the blonde still had the crowd in an uproar. *Shit!*

"Break the Ice Man!" one fan cried.

"The Ice Man is a cold bastard!" another screamed.

Dray watched as Lucky surged to his feet and turned in a circle to take in the catcalls. Dray saw the resolve to win in the clench of Lucky's jaw. "Oh shit." Dray had a feeling The Hammer was going down.

Lucky climbed back into the cage, snarling at several people in the crowd who dared to shout insults at him.

The bell rang and Lucky met The Hammer in the center of the cage. The two men danced around each other, landing punches here and there, but nothing that would win either of them the match. Dray could tell the catcalls were starting to get to Lucky when Lucky got sloppy, throwing power punches that missed their targets. "Fuck!"

The bell rang again, signaling the end of the second round. With only one left, Lucky had to pull his head out of his ass and focus on the fight instead of listening to the jerks in the arena.

The urge to call Lucky again was strong, but Dray held back. Instead, he tried to concentrate on the byplay between Lucky and Brick as a small cut on Lucky's forehead was attended to. Brick turned his head and started to cough. Lucky grabbed the sweat-soaked towel he'd used to wipe down and handed it to Brick before motioning for Dray to come down.

"Shit!" Dray excused himself as he made his way through the crowd, all the while keeping an eye on Brick. The coughing continued but Dray could tell Brick still had enough breath to argue with Lucky. Brick shook his head and pointed to the cage.

By the time Dray made it to Brick's side, Lucky was making his way into the cage. "I got him," Dray yelled loud enough for Lucky to hear.

Lucky turned back to The Hammer.

Dray squatted beside Brick, who'd already replaced Lucky on the stool. "You need a doctor?"

Brick shook his head and wiped the blood from his mouth.

"I need that boy to win," he gasped.

Dray kept his hand on Brick's shoulder as he stood. "Make it quick!" he yelled over the noise of the crowd.

In a surprise move, Lucky held his arms straight out, allowing The Hammer to land a series of punches to his jaw and stomach. The Hammer danced back, chuckling and shaking his head. Lucky stared at his opponent, watching him like a snake preparing to *bite*.

Dray's grip on Brick's shoulder tightened. "Do it," he said under his breath.

Striking fast and hard, Lucky drew his right arm back before throwing everything he had into a single punch to The Hammer's rib cage.

Although it shouldn't have been possible, Dray could have sworn he heard the sound of bones breaking as Lucky's fist connected.

The Hammer's eyes went wide as his legs gave out under him and he went down on his knees, hard. His mouth opened and closed several times as pain contorted his already ugly face.

The referee bent over to speak to The Hammer before motioning for the fighter's crew. Within moments, the fight was called and Lucky declared the victor. Lucky immediately climbed out of the cage. "How is he?"

"I'm fine, goddammit!" Brick got to his feet and reached up to run a hand over Lucky's sweaty hair. "Took you long enough, but you pulled it out. Good job."

Dray glanced at Brick, knowing from experience that the old man had just paid Lucky the only compliment he'd get regarding the match. "Let's get out of here," Dray said, motioning to the rowdy fans. They didn't appear pleased by the outcome, especially because The Hammer was still in the cage receiving medical attention.

Dray led the way with Brick behind him and Lucky bringing up the rear. He kept his head down, praying no one would recognize him while remaining vigilant of the crowd. One thing was certain, Lucky's new moniker was sealed. From that moment on, Lucky would be known as the Ice Man.

"Where're you parked?" Dray asked Lucky when they reached the lot. It was a chilly evening and they'd left the building without going back to the locker room to retrieve Lucky's clothes.

Lucky stripped off his gloves. "You have my keys?" he asked Brick.

Brick handed them over, along with Lucky's phone. The fact that Brick didn't complain about leaving the bag of equipment in the locker room said a lot. It seemed Dray wasn't the only one who had a bad feeling about the crowd.

"My truck's over there," Dray said, pointing to another lot. "Give me a minute, and I'll follow you." He jogged toward his truck, grateful the situation had been too chaotic for him to feel uncomfortable around two people he'd thought of daily but hadn't seen in years.

* * * *

Dray turned the television off when he heard a knock. He dropped the remote onto the king-size bed and moved to answer the door. Lucky, fresh from a shower, stood smiling at him. "Hey," Dray greeted, stepping back to let Lucky inside.

"Brick's asleep, so I thought I'd run downstairs to the bar for a drink. Wanna join me?" Lucky asked.

"Sure, just let me grab my wallet." Dray waited for Lucky to prop open the door with his shoulder before walking away to grab his money and room card. Lucky had offered to let Dray stay in their room, but no way in hell could he trust himself to share a queen-size bed with Lucky. He'd thanked Lucky but had politely refused the offer. "All set."

Lucky led the way into the hall and waited for Dray to join him. "So what made you decide to make the trip?"

Dray wasn't sure he could answer the question because truth be told, he wasn't sure he knew. He decided to go with Brick's illness as his excuse. "Just wanted to watch Brick in action once more."

Lucky pushed the elevator button. "Brick's had better nights. Sorry you had to see what you did."

"Don't be sorry. Despite everything, I saw the same fire in Brick's eyes as I did back when I was fighting." The elevator doors opened, and Dray entered. He felt oddly nervous when Lucky joined him in the enclosed space. "Good punch there at the end though, but I saw it coming. If The Hammer hadn't been so fucking sure of himself, he'd have seen it, too."

"Getting Brick out of there was the only thing I cared about," Lucky replied.

The doors opened and they stepped out into the lobby. Other than a few people standing in line to check in, there didn't seem to be anything going on. "Looks dead," Dray said.

"Thank God." Lucky took off toward the small bar. "I've had enough of people and their big mouths for one day."

Dray followed, trying in vain to keep his gaze off Lucky's ass. *Damn.* He felt his cock begin to harden and quickly averted his eyes, concentrating instead on the dark head of drying mahogany-colored hair in front of him and the broad shoulders that were so different than he remembered. Although he'd seen glimpses of the man Lucky would become years earlier, he'd had no idea the broody teenager would grow into the devastatingly handsome specimen in front of him.

Lucky walked to the back of the bar and slid into a booth. "This okay?"

"Yeah." Dray sat across from Lucky. He rested his hands on the table, trying like a motherfucker to figure out what to say next. Gone was the ease of their shared telephone conversations. He searched for something to say. *Oh. Fuck yeah.* "I brought my gun and ink, so after the tournament, if you want me to tat something for you, just let me know."

Lucky looked like he was about to say something but

turned his attention to the server who had stepped up beside him. "Shot of tequila and a Corona, both with lime," he ordered.

Dray nodded. "No tequila for me, just the Corona and the lime."

"Right up," the female server said with a smile. She lingered for just a moment, and Dray got the distinct impression she knew who Lucky was but was too shy to say so. She eventually turned and walked off without another word.

"I think she likes you," Dray commented. He didn't blame the woman. Despite the bruise on his jaw and a small bandaged cut, Lucky was damn hot. His eyes were the color of expensive cognac and rimmed with the longest red lashes Dray had ever seen.

Lucky shrugged and glanced toward the bar. "Didn't notice." He spun his cardboard coaster several times. "Brick's not going to last long, is he?"

Dray exhaled a ragged breath. "No, I don't think so. Although, my uncle got a lot worse towards the end." He fisted his hands, knowing what would come. After watching his uncle suffer so brutally, Dray wasn't sure he was prepared to go through it again. "Brick'll need oxygen before long. Then we'll probably need to call in hospice."

"I'll take care of him," Lucky declared.

"And I'll help you, but he'll need someone to come in and help him manage the pain." Dray didn't add that hospice would also be there to help Lucky deal with the end. Nor did he mention how horrible the end would be, because he knew from experience that in order for Brick to handle the pain, he'd have to be so heavily drugged he probably wouldn't be able to do anything but sleep. Lucky would spend days, possibly weeks, watching as Brick wasted away.

The waitress returned and set the drinks on the table. "Would you like to pay now or run a tab?"

Lucky upended the shot glass and downed the tequila.

He set the empty on her tray. "A tab is fine." He gestured to the glass. "And two more of those."

With a surprised expression, she nodded. "Okay."

Once they were alone again, Lucky took a swig of his beer. "How do we know when to do that?"

Dray swallowed a drink of his beer. "Do you know if he's still seeing a doctor?"

Lucky shook his head. "I don't know anything really. It's a wonder I got what little I did out of him."

Dray waited for their server to set down the shots and leave. "We can call them anytime, but I think it would be a good idea to get him back to the doctor first. He'll need to fill out an advanced healthcare directive while he's still able."

"What's that?" Lucky asked.

"Legal piece of paper that'll see that his wishes are carried out once he's unable to make decisions for himself." Dray took another gulp before continuing. "It won't be pleasant, but since he's refused treatment, it's necessary."

"I don't think Brick'll like a stranger in his house all the time." Lucky regarded him with red-rimmed eyes, whether from the tequila or the subject matter, Dray didn't know.

"Hospice will work with us. If we only want them to come for a few hours at a time, that's what they'll do. It all depends on us and how much we're able to do for him once it gets bad."

"I'd do anything," Lucky said.

Dray finally gave in to his desire and reached across the table to squeeze Lucky's hand. He stared at their hands when Lucky turned his over and threaded their fingers together. He'd never really noticed the difference in their skin color, but his own light-brown skin appeared even darker against Lucky's creamy white. He opened his mouth to point it out, but the waitress caught his attention. She was cleaning the table across from them, but her attention appeared to be on their clasped hands. *Shit.*

Dray tensed. If his earlier suspicion was right, the woman

knew who Lucky was. *Not good.* He thought fast. "I know Brick's been like a father to you, and I'll help you deal with the cancer any way I can."

Dray withdrew his touch. Lucky's expression changed, and it was obvious Dray had hurt his feelings. He wanted to tell Lucky the truth, that holding hands would inevitably lead to gossip. Worse, he'd enjoyed Lucky's warmth too much and could easily imagine Lucky's hand on his cock. *No.* He wouldn't let it happen. *No fucking way would he be Lucky's Vince.* He hadn't lied to Lucky. As long as he was needed to help care for Brick, he'd be at Lucky's side, but he couldn't stick around for the long haul. Lucky deserved his dream, and Dray would do everything he could to protect it.

"I know you will," Lucky mumbled.

In a move that was completely out of character for him, Dray reached for the last shot glass. He downed the contents. The burn of the alcohol was just what he'd needed. He'd hurt Lucky by pulling away, that much was more than obvious. *So be it. I'll be the asshole.*

* * * *

After stumbling back to the room he shared with Brick, Lucky kicked off his shoes. Unfortunately, the quieter he tried to be, the more noise he seemed to make.

"Boy, what the hell's wrong with you?" Brick asked, without turning on the light.

"Trying to be quiet," Lucky replied. "Go back to sleep." He eased his zipper down slowly.

"Don't let Dray get you into trouble." Brick rolled over.

Lucky stripped down to his underwear before sliding under the covers. Stretched out on his back with his hands clasped behind his head, he listened to each ragged breath coming from Brick's side of the room.

As he stared up at the blinking red light of the smoke detector, he tried to imagine working out at the gym without Brick. Sure, he'd spent years punching a bag after everyone had gone home for the day, but it wouldn't be the same knowing Brick wouldn't be there the next morning to check on him. It had been a habit Brick had gotten into after the first time he'd found Lucky bloody.

Lucky closed his eyes. He'd never been able to remember how he'd managed to get from his apartment to the Brick Yard as badly hurt as he'd been. All he knew was that he'd woken up in the storage room with Brick sitting in a chair beside him. It had been the first time in his life that he'd lain on a real mattress. The first time in his life he'd gotten a taste of what it would be like to grow up in a normal house.

Blinking away the tears, he turned his head to stare at the old man who had given him so much more than a place to work and train. In his own gruff way, Brick had shown Lucky firsthand what it felt like to be loved. A new resolve filled him as he promised to give back everything Brick had given him, tenfold. He would fight because he wanted Brick to see him as a winner before his time was up, but then he would do whatever he had to do to make sure Jax knew there was someone in the world who gave a shit whether he lived or died.

Chapter Five

"You want to go by the gym or should I take you home?" Lucky asked as they neared their neighborhood. The drive from Indianapolis, with Brick beside him and Dray following in his pickup, had been pure torture. He still didn't understand what had happened the previous night in the bar. When Dray had held his hand, Lucky had felt the heat between them, but it had been more than that. For possibly the first time in his life, he'd felt complete, and the goddamn homo inside him had wanted to pump his fist in the air. Unfortunately, the moment of fullness hadn't lasted and all too soon, Dray had withdrawn.

"Brick Yard," Brick replied.

It took a moment for the answer to filter through the shit in Lucky's brain but it sorted in time for him to take a left to the gym. He pulled into the parking lot but left the engine running. "I'm going to head home, but I'll be back in time for this afternoon's training."

Brick climbed out of the rented SUV but didn't shut the door immediately.

Lucky stared at the older man. "What?"

Brick shook his head. "Be careful."

"Of what?" Lucky asked, although he had an idea.

"Don't let your dick ruin everything you've worked for." Brick closed the door.

Dray parked beside Lucky and held up his hand. He leaned across the seat to roll down the passenger window. "You staying?"

Lucky shook his head. "I've got to get the rental back." They'd already decided Dray would sleep on Brick's foldout sofa while he was in town, so he chanced a request. "Would you mind following me?"

Dray's gaze went to the building. "You think Brick'll be okay without one of us here?"

"Flint's here, and school's almost out for Jax." Lucky nodded. "He'll be fine until we get back."

"Fuck. I can't believe Flint's still here." Dray chuckled, his smile wide.

Lucky bit his bottom lip. It was the first time in years he'd seen Dray's smile and it was breathtaking. "He's here. Flint likes working with the younger fighters."

Since Flint's fighting career had never really taken off, he'd decided to cut a deal with Brick to use the gym for private clients. Brick, being Brick, had agreed to let Flint do whatever he needed to do to make a living at a sport he loved.

"It'll be nice to see him again." Dray put his truck in reverse. "I'll follow you."

Lucky pulled out of the parking lot. He pictured Dray sleeping a floor above him and wondered how the hell he was going to keep himself in check. For eight years, he'd jacked off to memories of Dray's deep voice as Dray'd fucked Vince in the shower. Except in Lucky's fantasy, he was the one bending over for Dray. "Shit!"

Two miles from the gym, Lucky parked in front of the rental place. He jumped out and ran inside to drop off the keys. "All set," he said, climbing into Dray's truck.

"Where to?" Dray asked.

"Home," Lucky answered. "I'm starving, and I need to do a load of laundry."

Dray exited the parking lot. He cleared his throat and adjusted himself in the seat. "I've done nothing but think since I left you at Brick's door last night." He stopped at a red light and glanced at Lucky. "It's obvious we're into each other, so I won't pretend otherwise, but you need to know, I'm not going to act on that attraction."

Lucky held Dray's gaze until Dray broke eye contact

when the light turned green. "Why?" Lucky finally asked. He rubbed at the tightness in his chest.

"Because once it starts, we won't stop until someone finds out and it ruins your career," Dray stated in a matter-of-fact tone. "I won't do that to you, even if you beg me."

* * * *

After dropping off his luggage at Brick's, Dray bypassed Lucky's apartment and drove to the gym. He'd have normally just walked, but he wanted his truck in case Brick wasn't up to walking home at the end of the day.

Dray spent the first hour in the gym, talking to Flint, meeting Jax and several of the other members before finally joining Brick in the office. He shut the door behind him and dropped to the couch. Grinning, he ran his palm over the cracked avocado-green vinyl. "I can't believe you still have this."

"Why wouldn't I? It's still good and it wipes down easy. I can't tell you how many sweaty asses have been on that damn thing," Brick grumbled.

Dray laughed. Despite the years he'd been gone, it was nice to know Brick's sunny disposition hadn't changed. "I'll remember that the next time I come in after a workout without putting my pants on."

A coughing spell halted Brick's retort. Dray tensed for several moments before he leaned back and waited. He wanted to jump up and do something, but he knew that would only anger Brick. Not only that, but the old man had already hid his condition once, and Dray knew if he or Lucky started to hover, Brick would shut them out again.

Brick reached down and came back up with a stained towel as Dray averted his gaze. "Sorry," Brick mumbled after closing the drawer.

"Are you in pain?" Dray asked, needing to know.

Brick scratched his unshaven jaw. "I have pills."

"When do you go back to the doctor?" Dray hated to push

Brick with questions, but he didn't think Lucky would be able to ask them.

"I don't. I'm done."

Dray glared at Brick. As much as he loved the old man, the lies had to stop. "I know you don't want to think or talk about this shit, but it's happening." He'd kept his mouth shut while Lucky was around, but now that he was alone with Brick, he needed the truth. "How much weight have you lost? Fifteen pounds? More?"

Brick rested his forearms on the desk. "Why're you doing this? I'm dying, and I know it, so I don't need you to tell me I look like shit." He shook his head before opening the top drawer of his desk. He pulled out a plain manila folder and held it out. "I need you and Lucky to read over these and sign them. They have to be notarized, but you can get that done at the bank."

Dray retrieved the folder but couldn't bring himself to open it. "Is this your power-of-attorney paperwork?"

"Yeah, the Advanced Health Care Directive and a copy of my will," Brick replied.

Dray had known it was coming, but holding the proof, he just stared at the folder. He'd given the situation a lot of thought during the hours of driving. "I don't want Lucky's name on the directive."

"Why the hell not?"

Dray glanced at Brick. "Lucky doesn't need that shit weighing on him." Truthfully, he didn't think Lucky was strong enough to deal with what was coming, but he wouldn't verbalize it. "He needs to concentrate on the upcoming tournament he's registered for. He tell you about that?"

Brick nodded. "He needs the money. If he wins, he can make more in two weeks than he makes in a year on the circuit."

According to Lucky, he was fighting in the tournament for Brick's benefit. Dray couldn't help wondering who Lucky was lying to. "Is money a problem for him?"

If that were the case, Dray had some extra cash squirreled away. He'd much rather give it to Lucky than to have Lucky enter the bloodbath Ray Bruno was putting together. Despite Lucky's indifference to the fans, he was a damn good fighter and could probably win, but Dray never understood why skilled fighters entered the kind of underground tournaments that Bruno ran. Sure, there was money to be made, but Bruno's matches were often referred to as human cockfights. There were good amateur promoters out there, and even a few reputable underground matches to be found, but those didn't pay the kind of money Bruno's tournaments did, so men like Lucky were willing to take their chances.

"Lucky's mom's up for parole. He knows he's going to have to set her up in a place." Brick shrugged. "Alana's a fucking mess, always has been, but no matter how many times Lucky tries to tell himself he's over her, he always busts his ass to help when she asks for it."

"What'd she go in for?" Dray asked.

"It's her second time in. Both for distribution."

Dray wondered how Lucky would be able to deal with the tournament, Brick's failing health and his junkie mother. Dray stood and tossed the folder back on Brick's desk. "Lucky's got enough shit to deal with. Take his name off the power of attorney, and I'll sign it and get it notarized."

* * * *

After an easy workout and shower, Lucky grabbed his gym bag. He stopped at the laundry room to find Jax doing homework. "Hey."

Jax looked up and smiled. "I got my test back." He pulled a sheet of paper out of his backpack. "Take that!" he cried, slamming the test on the table.

Lucky grinned at the B-plus written in red. "Good job." He eyed Jax for several moments before gesturing with a wave of his hand. "Let's go. I think you deserve dinner at

Mac's."

Jax's big blue eyes lit up. "Really? What about showing me some moves?"

Lucky hadn't forgotten what he'd promised the kid in exchange for a good grade. "I believe the deal for showing you how to execute an uppercut was an A," he reminded Jax.

"Seriously?" Jax whined. "I got a fucking B plus, man."

"Yeah, and that's why I'm taking you to Mac's." Lucky pointed to the door. "Let's go." He grinned to himself, knowing he'd end up showing Jax a few moves, but first the kid needed to eat.

Jax caught up to Lucky halfway between The Brick Yard and Mac's. "I read that The Hammer suffered three broken ribs and a partially collapsed lung."

Lucky nodded. Brick had told him earlier on their way home from Indianapolis, but it wasn't something Lucky could dwell on. Every fighter knew what was at stake when he stepped into the cage. He opened the door to Mac's and waited for Jax to go inside.

"You almost lost that fight last night, boy," Mac yelled from the window cut into the wall between the counter and the kitchen.

Lucky ignored Mac and slid into his usual booth. "Order whatever you want," he told Jax.

"Anything?" Jax's eyebrows shot up toward his hairline.

"You earned it." Lucky sat sideways in the booth with his back against the wall. He needed to talk to Jax about Brick, but he wasn't sure how. "The usual," he told Trish when she came to the table.

"I'll have the rib eye, medium, with a double order of fries and a chocolate milkshake," Jax ordered.

"He'll have the rib eye with one order of fries and a side of green beans," Lucky amended. "But he can have the milkshake."

"Sure thing," Trish said prior to yelling their order across the diner to Mac.

"I like fries," Jax argued.

"Yeah, and you're gettin' fries, but you're also eating a vegetable." Lucky's diet consisted primarily of protein and vegetables. If Jax was serious about whipping his body into shape, he'd need to change his eating habits, but after finding out why Jax needed to learn to fight, he wasn't sure the kid wanted to make a career of it. Lucky decided to show Jax how to land an impressive uppercut, knowing a showdown between Jax and his father was inevitable.

"I met Dray today," Jax said.

Trish stopped at the table and set Jax's milkshake in front of him.

"Thanks." Jax smiled up Trish.

"No problem, sweetie." Trish walked off.

Jax took a sip and sighed. "Brick told me he used to fight professionally."

"Yeah. Dray was one of the best." Lucky took a drink of his orange juice. "He was known as The Dragon. Did he tell you that?"

Jax shook his head and smiled. "Do you think I can find something online about him?"

Lucky knew for a fact there were photos and two video clips, because he'd watched them multiple times over the years. "Probably." He heard a huff and glanced up just as Mac set two dinner plates on the table.

Mac stared down at Lucky's legs where they rested on the seat until Lucky got the hint and moved them. Sliding in beside Lucky, Mac scowled. "Dray's in town?"

Lucky nodded. "He came in to help out." He nudged Mac with his thigh and cast his gaze toward Jax.

Mac bit his bottom lip, and with a heavy sigh, climbed out of the booth. "Come and talk to me before you leave."

"Okay," Lucky agreed as he prepared to eat his dinner.

Several minutes after Mac had left, Jax set down his fork. "Is Brick gonna die?"

Lucky finished chewing a bite of steak, taking his time as he tried to come up with a good answer. Finally, once he'd swallowed, he took a deep breath and laid everything out. "Yeah. He's got cancer. We don't know how long he has, but our guess is a couple of months."

Jax's big eyes filled with tears but he sniffed and blinked them away. He pushed his plate away with half of his dinner left uneaten. "Is that why Dray's here?"

Lucky nodded. "Brick's leaving the gym to me and Dray, so you don't have to worry about it closing down."

"What about fighting? Are you still gonna have time for that?"

It was a question Lucky had asked himself a dozen times since talking to Brick. "I'm going to try, but in the end, The Brick Yard's more important than squaring off in a cage with an asshole week after week."

"But according to Brick, you've always wanted to be a fighter," Jax argued.

Lucky couldn't deny it. He'd always known fighting was his way out of the neighborhood. He didn't have the brains or the grades to go to college and working at a bullshit job just to make enough to scrape by each month wasn't the goal he'd set for himself. Once again, he thought of *The Great Gatsby*. It was the only book he'd ever owned, and the only one he'd read from cover to cover. Fuck, he'd read the damn thing so many times he'd practically memorized it.

"We'll have to wait and see what happens. It's possible. Depends on what Dray decides to do. He got out once, so I'm not sure if he's willing to come back permanently." Since his conversation with Dray earlier in the day, Lucky hadn't been able to think of anything else. Dray was into him—he'd said it himself—but he'd also said he wouldn't act on their mutual attraction. Of course Lucky knew why, and he understood Dray's reasoning, but he didn't believe a physical relationship between the two of them would be discovered. He trusted Dray not to talk, and he'd hid his true nature for years, so he doubted he'd give it away by his actions in public.

"Sit tight, and I'll get us a couple of to-go boxes while I

see what the hell Mac wants." Lucky slid out of the booth. He waited at the door to the kitchen until Mac waved him inside.

"You tell the kid?" Mac asked.

"Just now." Lucky leaned against the doorframe with his arms crossed over his chest. He knew Mac had watched the fight online, he'd already admitted as much. "Did you see Brick between the second and third round?"

"Yeah." Mac continued to clean the grill. "Didn't look good."

"It wasn't." Lucky took a deep breath. Mac was the only man who had the power to intimidate him. He was used to Brick's blustering, and although he knew Mac had a good heart, his opinion of the man had changed in the last few weeks. If Mac could cut Dray out of his life for disappointing him, what would he think of Lucky's decision to fight in Bruno's tournament? For days he'd gone back and forth on whether or not to fess up that he'd officially entered. *Christ.* He needed to just come clean because Mac would find out anyway, then there'd be hell to pay.

"I need to ask you a favor," Lucky began. "Brick wants to see me win something big before he dies, so I've entered Bruno's bullshit tournament. The problem is, I'm not sure Brick's well enough to train me, so I'm going to ask Dray to do it if Brick can't."

Mac turned around to face Lucky and narrowed his eyes.

Lucky held his hand up before Mac could chew him a new asshole. "It's already done, and I'm not withdrawing. What I'm asking from you is to sit with Brick if he needs it while Dray's with me at the gym or the fights."

"Does Brick know you entered one of Bruno's tournaments?" Mac asked.

"Yeah. He didn't try to stop me because he believes in me." Lucky felt his chest tighten. Brick had always believed in him.

"You really think you can win? Those fuckers fight dirty," Mac growled.

Lucky grinned. "I'm not opposed to giving what I get. They want to fight dirty? I'll give it right back to them."

"And if you get seriously injured? What happens then?"

"Then I get hurt fighting. We both know there're no guarantees in this business. Part of the thrill for me is knowing I'm putting my life on the line every time I step into the cage—knowing I'm the only one standing between me and pain."

Mac narrowed his eyes again. "You're a sick fuck if you're telling me you get off on putting your life on the line. That's not what the sport's about."

"Really? Because I can guarantee I'm not the only one who feels this way." Lucky took a moment to measure his words before continuing. "When I was a kid, I went to bed every night knowing it might be my last. My bitch of a mother had fucking tweakers in and out of our apartment at all hours doing that shit with her. I can't tell you how many times I had to intervene when one of them started beating her." He uncrossed his arms and fisted his hands at his sides. "I was beaten nearly to death by more than one junkie, and I told myself over and over that one day, I'd be the one in control."

"Have you told Brick that?"

"No, and I'm not sure why the fuck I just told you, so keep it to yourself."

Mac shook his head and sighed. "You've got something rotten inside you, boy, and if you don't find it and cut it out, it'll spoil the good parts of the man you are."

Lucky wouldn't lie to himself. Mac's words had hurt, but that didn't mean they weren't accurate. "What the hell do you think I've been trying to do for the last ten years? When I'm in the cage, I feel whole. Say what you want about my reason for doing it, but fighting is the only thing in this whole fucking world that I'm good at."

Mac continued to shake his head. "Don't build your life around something that could vanish in an instant. I never thought I'd say this to one of Brick's boys, but you may have the skill and drive to win, but it takes more than that. It takes the heart of a champion to be a great fighter, and you, boy, haven't found your heart."

Lucky took a step back. The air whooshed out of him as if Mac had just thrown a hard punch to his gut. Mac had always been one of his biggest supporters or at least he'd always thought so. *Fuck.* Maybe Mac was more like his mom than he'd ever realized. Could Mac see the bad boy inside him? Did Mac believe he was truly unworthy of becoming a champion? "Thanks for believing in me." He threw up his hands and walked out of the diner, leaving Jax to eat alone. With Brick dying and Mac turning on him, Lucky's world was getting smaller by the day.

* * * *

After Brick had gone to bed for the night, Dray headed downstairs and knocked on Lucky's door.

"Hang on a minute," Lucky called. It took several long moments but eventually the door opened. Lucky was dressed in nothing but a pair of gym shorts.

"Hey," Dray greeted. "Am I interrupting something?" He couldn't tell what it was but something seemed off. A vein in Lucky's forehead throbbed with the beat of his heart. It was something Dray had noticed when Lucky was in the cage, but it didn't fit with an evening at home.

Lucky stepped back, allowing Dray to enter the apartment. "I caught my arm on a broken piece of furniture I was trying to haul out of the dumpster downstairs." He held up his bandaged right forearm.

Dray reached for Lucky. "Is it bad?" The white gauze was spotted with blood. "Do you need to go to the hospital?"

"I'm fine." Lucky gestured to the couch before taking a seat on the opposite end. He turned on the television and began flipping through the channels. "Mac wants you to stop by the diner."

Dray glanced away from the TV. He'd given a lot of

thought as to how he would deal with seeing Mac again, but he'd never expected the old man to request a visit. "What's he want?"

"Fuck if I know." Lucky swung his bare feet onto the coffee table. "You'll have to go in alone though because right now, I don't care if I ever see that bastard again."

Dray moved to face Lucky. Despite Lucky's relaxed position, his body appeared anything but. He stared at Lucky's fisted hands. "What the hell happened?"

Jaws tightly clenched, Lucky shook his head.

"Talk to me." With Brick's health, the bullshit with the crowd the previous night and his rejection earlier in the day, Dray knew Lucky was strung tight. Being at odds with Mac was the last thing Lucky needed to deal with.

Lucky swallowed several times before jumping up from the couch. "Want a beer?"

"Sure." Dray reached down and removed his boots. "Did the two of you get into it over me?" he asked when Lucky stalked back into the room with that goddamn vein on his forehead throbbing again.

Lucky drank half the bottle then answered. "Mac's decided I don't have the heart of a champion."

Motherfucker. Dray knew what kind of damage a statement like that could do to a fighter. Before he could ask Lucky to explain further, Lucky started pacing the room.

"For the first fucking time in my life I really opened up to someone," Lucky spat. "And after seeing the inside of me, fucking Mac decides I'm not good enough." He stopped walking and hurled his bottle across the room. It hit the wall with a loud thud, but to Dray's surprise, it didn't break. Instead, it splattered the white paint with beer before falling unceremoniously to the floor. "I need to get outta here."

"No." Dray stood and put himself in front of the door. "You need to calm down first."

"Get out of my way," Lucky growled.

The pain was right there in Lucky's eyes. *Christ. What the hell had Mac done?* Dray reached out and grabbed Lucky by the shoulders. "You're practically naked. Think about what you're doing," Dray argued.

Lucky reached down and pushed his shorts to the floor. "Now I'm totally naked. Can I fucking go now?"

Dray closed his eyes and banged his head back against the door. He'd tried to do the right thing by pushing Lucky away, but as he watched Lucky fall apart, he saw a man who needed a lifeline. Dray reached out and wrapped his arms around Lucky's neck before pulling him close. He put his mouth to Lucky's ear. "I'm here," he whispered.

Lucky's entire body stiffened.

Dray knew what Lucky needed, what every man needed. "And I believe in you," he added.

Lucky's breath hitched. Several moments later he returned Dray's embrace. He didn't say anything, just held tight.

"We'll get you through this," Dray murmured, trying to soothe the man he cared so much about. It was more than respect for a fellow fighter. It was the lost expression he'd seen on Lucky's face. Dray remembered seeing that same damn look in his own eyes after he'd dropped out and had run to Kansas City. Yeah, that's exactly what he'd done. He'd dropped out of life for nearly six years until Brick had taken a chance and sent him a DVD of one of Lucky's fights. That had been two years ago. *Fuck.* Since watching that first video, he'd known he could help Lucky with his grappling skills and had done nothing about it.

Wielding a tattoo gun was peaceful and a way to pay the bills, but his passion had always been and would always be MMA. He might not agree with the way Lucky dealt with the fans, but Mac was wrong. Like Dray, most fighters fought for the glory, the fan worship and the money they could make. Lucky didn't seem to care about any of that. For Lucky, the fight itself was the prize. Pitting his own skills against an opponent's was the thrill, and the sweat he earned after a hard-fought bout the reward.

Lucky had given Dray back his passion, and Dray would

be damned if he'd let Mac or anyone else try to fuck with Lucky. Mac was a kind man to kids in need, but he was also just a man. Sure, with age came wisdom, but there were also a lot of old idiots out there, spreading shit they had no business spreading.

"The only one who knows whether or not you have the heart of a champion is you, and don't you *ever* let someone try to tell you different," Dray said, his mouth brushing against Lucky's ear. He lowered his head and placed a soft kiss on the pale skin of Lucky's neck.

Lucky dipped his chin. When their mouths met for the first time, Dray sighed. *Fuck.* He'd spent years wondering what Lucky would taste like and the answer was beer. He grinned before delving his tongue into Lucky's mouth once more. He ran his hands lower and worshipped Lucky's muscular physique with each touch. It surprised him that after waiting so long to finally have Lucky in his arms, he had no desire to rush it. On the nights when he'd lain in bed and fantasized about making love to Lucky, their coupling had always been rough and raw, two athletes going at each other with an unquenchable thirst. But, as he gave the hard cheeks of Lucky's ass a gentle squeeze, he felt the vulnerability radiating off his confused fighter.

Dray broke the kiss and stared into Lucky's eyes. "I promised myself I wouldn't do this."

"Because of Vince?" Lucky asked.

Dray nodded. "Vince outed me on purpose, and you have to know I would never do that, but I don't want to take the chance that we'll slip up. You deserve your dreams, and I want to be the kind of man who will walk away so you can achieve them."

"My dreams?" Lucky huffed. "I'm not sure my dreams are the same as everyone else's. I need to fight, but I also want to make Brick proud. In order to do that, I have to win."

The statement confused Dray. "You don't care if you win?"

Lucky shrugged. "It's nice to win, but it isn't why I fight."

"So why do you fight?" Dray asked. He couldn't help but think the answer to that question was the key to Lucky.

"Because I *need* it." Lucky shook his head. "I can't tell you why because I don't know." He pressed his forehead against Dray's. "But I also need you. You make me feel normal, and I've never really had that."

Dray closed his eyes, wondering how he was supposed to resist taking what he wanted when it was right in front of him. He knew how Lucky felt because standing with Lucky in his arms was like coming home, which should have been ridiculous, but it was true. "This could be a huge mistake."

Lucky's gaze went to Dray's swollen lips. "I'm the king of mistakes, but this doesn't seem like one to me."

It didn't to Dray either, so he nodded. "Okay." He reached for Lucky's hand and pulled him toward the bedroom and to his delight, Lucky didn't resist.

Chapter Six

While Lucky watched Dray undress, he couldn't stop himself from palming his own cock. He'd witnessed an entire parade of big-chested women disrobe for him, but he'd never had a man stand beside his bed and hold his gaze while slowly peeling off his clothes. As Dray's muscular, tattooed body was revealed, he knew he'd trade all the fucks he'd ever had for this one moment.

Dray's chest was covered in short black hair. Lucky had never seen Dray with chest hair because Brick always demanded his fighters either shave or wax, but Dray had been out from under Brick's thumb for years and it showed. He gestured to the blank skin over Dray's heart. "How come there's no ink there?"

"The skin over a man's heart is sacred, meant only for the one whose soul is bound to the one getting the tattoo." Dray ran a hand over his pecs. "You like a man with hair?" he asked, as if reading Lucky's mind.

Lucky knew the time would come when he'd have to admit he was a virgin when it came to being with a man, but he'd hoped he would have more time to prepare for it. "I like what I see and since you're the only man I've ever had strip for me, I guess my answer would have to be yes."

Dray's black eyebrows drew together in confusion. "The only man?"

"Yeah. I thought I'd told you that I'd listened to your advice."

"You did, but I guess I didn't realize that meant you'd never been with a man," Dray replied, hooking his thumbs into the waistband of his briefs.

Lucky's gaze shifted from the hold Dray had on his underwear to the man's green eyes. "I only ever wanted you."

Dray jolted as if Lucky had slapped him. He stood stock-still for several moments before pushing his underwear down.

Lucky couldn't help but stare at the impressive dark-skinned cock in front of him. *Holy fuck.* He squeezed his dick harder in an effort to keep himself from reaching for Dray's. Although Dray's shaft was lined with thick veins, they weren't as visible through the skin as Lucky's. Why would they be? Dray was a bronze-skinned god, and Lucky was a pale, freckled Irish kid.

Dray moved slowly, climbing onto the mattress like a wild animal readying his stomach for a meal. He hovered over Lucky for a minute before dipping his head down to take Lucky's crown in his mouth.

"Christ," Lucky groaned once his dick was enveloped in the warmth of Dray's mouth. He'd had hundreds of blow jobs in his life, but watching Dray's lips wrapped around him did something to him that no woman had ever managed to accomplish. Dray made him feel at peace with himself for the first time in his goddamn life.

Lucky parted his legs and rested his hand on the back of Dray's head, feeling the thick bristle of Dray's short hair against his palm. He moaned again, trying to convey the way Dray was making him feel, but gave up and simply said it. "Never like this," he said. "Never."

Dray moved to lie on the bed between Lucky's spread legs and met his gaze. Those gorgeous green eyes captured Lucky's attention as Dray continued to suck him like a fucking pro. Dray released Lucky's cock, wrapped his hand around it and went to work licking and sucking his balls.

Pre-cum slid down the length of Lucky's cock, and Dray used it to ease his hand as it moved up and down. As embarrassed as Lucky was to admit it, he was going to blow before he even got the chance to touch Dray's impressive erection. "I'm gonna come," he warned.

Dray grunted and slid his tongue up the shaft, licking pre-cum as he went. With a devilish grin, he captured the crown between his lips and eased Lucky's cock down his throat.

Lucky fisted the blanket in his free hand. "Fuck!" he yelled, loud enough for the neighbors to hear. He pressed against the back of Dray's head and surged upward, coming in Dray's mouth.

Dray backed off a bit and swallowed Lucky's seed. He performed the action like he'd done it a hundred times before. For some reason, instead of being elated that he was finally with Dray like he'd always wanted, he felt jealous of the men who'd taught Dray how to suck a dick.

Lucky swung his arm over his face, shielding his eyes from Dray while he tried to work his feelings out.

Dray crawled up to lay on top of Lucky's body. He kissed Lucky's jaw and neck several times before he spoke. "Where'd you go?"

"You're good at that," Lucky answered. "Guess I'm just thinking about who you practiced on."

Dray rolled off Lucky, and Lucky immediately felt chilled.

"I'm not a virgin. You knew that," Dray growled. "I put everything I had into making your first time a good one."

Yeah. Lucky knew that. He uncovered his eyes and stared up at the ceiling. "It was better than good," he confessed. He turned his head to the side to look at Dray. "Don't pay attention to me. I'm being a jealous asshole who can't stop thinking about all the men you've been with."

Dray propped his head up on his hand and used his free arm to pull Lucky closer to him. "And you don't think I've wondered how many cunts you've eaten and fucked over the years? Just because you've never been with a man doesn't mean I don't feel jealous of the women you've been with."

"I'm having a hard time dealing with the fact that they've had what I've always dreamed of," Lucky tried to explain.

Dray leaned over and buried his face against Lucky's neck. "I'm sorry, but there's nothing I can do about my past."

"I know." Lucky rolled to his side and reached between them to touch Dray's cock for the first time. "Ignore me."

Dray shook his head and draped Lucky's thigh over his own. "Not possible." He kissed Lucky, soft and sweet, before pulling back. "Tell me what you want."

"Everything," Lucky replied. "As long as it's with you."

Dray ran his hand down Lucky's back to the swell of his butt. "Have you ever played with your ass?"

Lucky stared at Dray without admitting to anything.

"There's nothing to be embarrassed about." Dray lifted his fingers to his mouth and spit on them. "Making yourself feel good is perfectly natural." He touched Lucky's hole.

"Yeah? Then why do I have to hide it? Why do I have to pretend to be someone I'm not?" Lucky hitched his thigh higher around Dray's waist.

"You know why." Dray circled Lucky's pucker several times. "But you haven't answered my question?" He touched the pad of his finger to Lucky's hole.

"Yeah," Lucky admitted. "I have stuff."

Dray licked his lips. "Where?"

"In a box under the bed," Lucky confessed, pushing back against Dray's finger.

"Get it," Dray instructed. "Condoms?"

"In the canister on the bedside table." Although he'd loved the feel of Dray touching him, Lucky did as asked and climbed off the bed to retrieve the small shoebox that contained his secret identity. He opened the box and quickly turned the picture of Dray face down in the bottom. "What do you want out of it, just the lube?"

Dray shook his head and held out his hand. "I want it all."

With a sigh, Lucky gave Dray the bottle of lube and two toys, one to stimulate his prostate and one that resembled a big brown dick. "That's it," he said and quickly put the lid back on the box.

Dray's eyes narrowed. "No it isn't."

"That's it!" Lucky snapped. He'd already shared all that he was prepared for. He shoved the box back under the bed before rejoining Dray.

The corner of Dray's mouth lifted in a half-smile. "Okay." He stretched out and waited. "Have you changed your mind?"

"No." Lucky hadn't, but he suddenly felt incredibly raw and exposed.

Dray lifted the dildo. "Interesting color choice. The one in my bedside drawer's much paler." He made a point of glancing at Lucky's growing erection.

Truth was, after seeing Dray's dick, Lucky's dildo was darker, but it was still closer to Dray's Hispanic skin color than the pinkish-tan ones he'd found. "You have one?"

"Sure." Dray grinned again. "Like I said, it's perfectly natural."

Lucky stretched out beside Dray, feeling much better.

"When's the last time you used this?" Dray wrapped his hand around the dildo's girth, no doubt comparing the fake to the real thing.

"A few days ago, after Brick told me about the cancer and I talked to you on the phone." When Dray's grin grew into a full-out smile, Lucky groaned. "You don't have to look so damn smug."

"Yeah, I do." Dray set the toys on the old milk crate beside the bed then opened the bottle of lube. "How do you want to do this, stomach or back?"

Lucky thought about it for a moment. He wanted to watch, but at the same time, he knew he'd be embarrassed the first time. Without saying a word, he rolled over and tucked his legs under him, putting his butt on full display. He quickly discovered it wasn't the position that embarrassed him but the exposure.

Dray sat up and scooted closer. He ran his palm over the cheeks of Lucky's ass before upending the bottle of lube. Cool liquid dripped down Lucky's crack, prompting an all-over body shiver.

Dray chuckled. "Let me warm that up for you."

Lucky thanked the stars above when Dray did just that by running his fingers up and down the crack of Lucky's ass. "Oh, yeah, that's working."

"Someday soon I'm gonna take the time to eat this ass, but I need to bury myself inside you too bad for that now." Dray circled Lucky's hole with his thumb several times before pressing inside.

Lucky moaned at the invasion.

After fucking Lucky for several minutes with his thumb he removed it.

"Don't stop."

"Patience."

Lucky heard the lid of the lube click shut then Dray's touch returned, only instead of a thumb, he got first one finger then another. Thinking of his neighbors, Lucky buried his face in the pillow and groaned.

"Am I hurting you?" Dray asked.

Lucky shook his head but didn't speak, couldn't speak as Dray continued to pump his fingers in and out. For years, he'd told himself that fucking a woman was all he'd needed to satiate his lust, but at that moment, he knew the truth. Women had been a tolerable distraction, but his body had been made to feel a man's dick sliding in and out of him.

"Do you think you're ready for me?"

If the amount of pre-cum running down his dick was any indication, Lucky's body was more than ready. "Mmm hmm," he managed to get out.

Dray reached over and grabbed a condom. Seconds later, Lucky felt the blunt head pressed to his hole. With one hand resting on the small of Lucky's back, Dray pushed inside.

Reminding himself to breathe, Lucky planted his hands on the mattress and rose up enough to rock back. Pain rippled up Lucky's spine when his hole stretched around Dray's shaft. He gripped the sheet in his hands and slowly impaled himself further.

"Take it," Dray growled when he steadied Lucky's hips and surged in to the hilt.

Lucky sucked in a gasp of air when the burn gave way to pure, unadulterated pleasure. "Christ!" He swiveled his hips, needing more, embracing the part of himself he'd denied for too long.

"Give me a sec," Dray ground out, and Lucky could hear him breathing heavily.

Lucky smiled into the pillow, feeling his heated breath against his face. The idea that Dray could be close to losing control just by being inside him thrilled him. He used every ounce of reserve he had to stay still, praying Dray pulled himself together in quick order.

When Dray finally retreated before pushing back inside, Lucky groaned into his pillow. He'd no doubt woken his neighbors with his earlier cry of pleasure but that didn't mean he needed to give them a thrust-by-thrust commentary of the best fucking sex he'd ever experienced. He buried his face. "Yeah, pound it. Fuck my ass."

Although he'd come only thirty minutes earlier, Lucky wanted to be touched. He reached a hand underneath him and wrapped it around his length. Hell yeah, he was ready to come again. He'd never considered himself a stud in bed, but he'd always been proud of himself for being able to go twice in the same night, but it hadn't even been a fucking hour and he was ready. He suddenly felt sorry for all the women he'd ever tried to please.

"I'm ready when you are," Lucky panted, paying particular attention to the sensitive spot just below the crown. Pleasure shot up his dick from his balls as he grew closer and closer to climax.

"I don't want to stop, but I can't hold back any longer." Dray pounded into Lucky's ass so hard Lucky was in danger of banging his head against the headboard.

"Unless this is the last time you plan to fuck me, I'm coming with or without you," Lucky declared, unable to hold on any longer.

Dray draped his torso over Lucky's back and cried out his release. "Fuck!"

"Yes!" Lucky agreed loud enough to wake the dead, or in his case, the neighbors. No doubt he'd be kicked out of his apartment within a month of moving in.

Dray kissed the back of Lucky's neck before pulling out. "I have a feeling that's not going to be the last time."

Lucky panted as he tried like hell to catch his breath. The smell of cum was thick in the room, and he doubted he'd ever inhaled anything sexier. "Hope not."

* * * *

Dray stared up at the ceiling long after Lucky had drifted off to sleep. He knew he needed to get back upstairs to Brick in case he was needed, but he wanted a few more minutes of sharing Lucky's warmth.

He rolled to his side and stared at Lucky's profile and tried to figure out how he could leave if it came to that. There was something so vulnerable about the man beside him, and when he'd seen Lucky lose it earlier, he hadn't been able to stop himself. All his good intentions had flown out of the window when faced with the very real possibility that one more emotional upset could send Lucky over the edge. When Lucky had told him about his need to feel normal, Dray had known exactly what he meant.

Earlier, Lucky had asked him about the empty patch of skin over his heart, Dray hadn't known what to say, so he'd given him a half-truth. He hadn't confessed that in the last few years, he'd thought of inking Lucky's name there. Despite the fact that he and Lucky could never have a public relationship, he knew whom his soul was tied to. It was utterly ridiculous. Other than a handful of phone conversations and watching videos of Lucky for hours upon hours, Dray barely knew the man Lucky had become.

Without warning, Lucky moved to wrap himself around Dray. "All I ever wanted," he mumbled and settled back to sleep.

Dray rested his hand on the back of Lucky's head and held him for several minutes before placing a kiss on Lucky's lips. "I need to go," he finally said.

"No," Lucky replied without opening his eyes.

"Brick might need me. Besides, I haven't slept on a mattress this bad since I was a kid." Dray wasn't joking. He didn't know how the hell Lucky could sleep on it.

Lucky tightened his hold. "If you leave, you'll never come back."

Dray relaxed, hoping Lucky would loosen his grip. He knew Lucky was wrong, because he would be back tomorrow and the next day and the next—until Brick passed. Even if all he could do was offer Lucky comfort in secret, Dray would be there for him, and when the time came and Lucky was ready to resume his career, Dray would step back and allow Lucky the dream he deserved.

* * * *

Lucky glanced at Dray as they jogged side by side on the eighteen-mile trail that wound its way along Lake Michigan. It felt nice to have someone to run with for a change, even better because it was a gorgeous day. He'd been surprised when Dray had asked him to get out of the gym for a while. "So why'd you wanna run here?"

"It used to be my favorite place to clear my head before a fight." Dray returned Lucky's glance. "And I want to talk to you about Flint."

"Flint?" Lucky had noticed Dray spending time with Flint that morning, the morning after the best fucking night of Lucky's life.

"I think he should go with you to the tournament. He can keep an eye on Brick and step in if Brick doesn't last the entire tournament," Dray explained, his breathing still even after almost six miles of nonstop running.

Lucky slowed. He didn't want to think about Brick not

lasting through the tournament. Even worse, he didn't want Flint as a backup trainer. "Why can't you do it?"

Dray snapped his fingers and motioned for Lucky to catch up. Once Lucky was beside him, Dray spoke. "Bruno knows who I am, and he's got a big mouth. Even if I wear a hat and try to fly under the radar, word will get out."

"So? I know you think you being in my corner will somehow paint me as gay, too, in the public eye, but I don't agree. I know almost nothing about my opponents' trainers. The focus is always on the fighters, and even if someone had a gay trainer, I don't think that would be newsworthy."

"I won't take that chance," Dray replied.

"But you're the best fighter I've ever known, and if something happens to Brick, I'll need you there." A muscle clenched in Dray's jaw, and Lucky knew he was getting to him. "Without you there, I'll likely withdraw from the match because I'll be too worried about Brick. You're the only one who'd be able to verbally kick my ass enough to get me to go on."

They ran in silence for several moments before Dray spoke. "Flint's in your corner with Brick, but I'll be in the building. If I feel I'm really needed, I'll step in. Otherwise, I'll stay in the shadows."

Lucky didn't like it, but he knew it was the best he was going to get out of Dray. "Fine." They still hadn't talked about their night, and the thought that it would never happen again worried him. "You coming by tonight after Brick goes to bed?"

Dray nodded.

Lucky grinned to himself. He ran the next eight miles thinking about having sex with Dray again.

Once they reached the end of the trail, Lucky stopped and retrieved a water bottle out of his backpack. He continued to walk beside Dray, keeping his muscles warm while he rehydrated. A soft mewing caught his attention. "Did you hear that?"

Dray lowered his bottle. "Huh?"

The sound came again and Lucky realized it was coming from a tall patch of weeds. He walked over to investigate. "Oh, shit." He stared down at the emaciated black-and-white kitten. The poor fella looked like he could barely raise his head. Without a thought, he bent over and picked up the tiny body. He turned toward Dray and held it out. "You think someone just dumped it?"

"I don't know, but be careful handling it. Might have some kind of disease," Dray replied, stepping closer. He stared at the kitten stretched out in Lucky's palms. "I don't think it's going to make it."

The kitten lifted his head and mewed.

"He'll make it," Lucky said, smiling down at the helpless creature. "He's a fighter."

* * * *

With a towel wrapped around the kitten, Lucky curled up in the corner of the couch and held a tiny bottle of milk replacer to the cat's mouth. He couldn't wipe the smile from his face as the kitten greedily sucked, getting more around her mouth than down her throat. "You need a name."

According to the veterinarian, the kitten was female, four to five weeks old. She'd been severely malnourished and full of worms, but the vet had given her medicine for the worms and assured Lucky that as long as she was fed regularly, she should pull through.

He'd made Dray go with him to the pet store to stock up on supplies, including a litter box, milk replacement, a tiny bottle with extra nipples and a small stuffed animal. The last was something the vet had recommended. Evidently, kittens liked to cuddle when they slept. He had to take the vet's word for it because he'd never had a pet—unless, of course, he considered the rats and cockroaches he'd grown up with.

Lucky ran his finger against the soft pad of one of the white paws. He had no idea how to go about naming something, but he didn't want to rush it. He knew a name stayed with you for the rest of your life, so it needed to be special, needed to be right.

He heard the knock he'd been expecting. "Come in," Lucky called.

Dray used the spare key Lucky had given him and entered the apartment. He shut the door and smiled down at Lucky. "How's it going?"

Lucky wiped the kitten's mouth with a corner of the towel before resettling the bottle in its mouth. "Good. We're trying to come up with a name for her."

Dray pointed to the kitchen. "Mind if I have a beer?"

"Not if you bring me one, too," Lucky replied. He tore his gaze away from the kitten to watch Dray walk across the living room to the kitchen. There was something in the hunch of Dray's shoulders and the set of his jaw that bothered Lucky. "How's Brick?"

Dray opened the fridge, removed two bottles, and closed it. "He's having a hard time this evening. Told me I could use his bed from now on because he's found he sleeps better if he sits up in his recliner." He passed a beer to Lucky before sitting on the sofa beside him. "I told him I'd take him back to the doctor as soon as he can get an appointment. I think he needs to be put on oxygen—or at least have it available to him."

"What? He seemed fine this morning. Well, not fine, but not bad enough to need oxygen." Lucky wondered if Dray was being an alarmist. He knew from talking to Dray that the time would come when Brick's lungs wouldn't be able to draw in enough breath, but it was too soon for that.

Dray stretched his arm across the back of the couch and brushed his fingertips across Lucky's neck. "He's been hiding shit. I don't think he would've confessed if I hadn't walked in on him gasping for air after one of his coughing spells." He leaned in and kissed the spot he'd just touched. "I'm sorry, Lucky, but he's failing."

Lucky stared down at the kitten, needing something other

than Brick to focus on. He pulled the bottle away, realizing it was empty, and set it on the coffee table. "She's a fighter," he mumbled. He glanced at Dray. "Do you think it'd be wrong to name her Gatsby?"

"Why would it be wrong?" Dray asked.

"It's a boy name." Lucky wiped the kitten's face with the towel. He lifted the sweet little thing to his cheek and rubbed against her soft black-and-white fur. "I want her to be happy with the name I give her."

"Does the name Gatsby mean something to you?"

"Yeah."

"Then how could she ask for more than that?" Dray petted the kitten's side with the back of his index finger.

"Hey, Gatsby," Lucky crooned. "I don't really know how to take care of you, but I'll figure it out." He kissed Gatsby's head. "Promise."

Chapter Seven

After searching the rest of the gym for Lucky, Dray made his way to the laundry room. He stopped outside the open door when he spotted two people bent over the old table that had probably been there since Brick had bought the place.

Lucky scratched his head. "Hell, that can't be right." He bit his bottom lip as he ran the eraser end of his pencil over the sheet of paper in front of him.

"Told ya," Jax said. "I think Mr. Gregory throws those stupid story problems in just to fuck with us."

"I doubt that's the reason. I never had to take one of those college entrance exams, but I heard they were pretty tough. Most likely Mr. Gregory is trying to teach you something you'll need to know in the future." Lucky blew on the paper, sending small bits of pink rubber to the floor. "Okay, there's seventy-five dollars to divide between three people, but the second person gets twice as much as the first person, but five dollars more than the third person. Find out how much each individual is to be paid."

Both Jax and Lucky continued to stare at the paper for several moments before Lucky let out a growl. "I hate math."

"Yeah," Jax agreed.

"Need some help?" Dray asked from the doorway. He hated to butt in, but math had never been easy for Lucky. He had a feeling Lucky was helping Jax more to find out how the kid got the black eye than to do his homework.

Lucky sighed and leaned back in the chipped metal chair. "Hell yes." He slid the paper across the table toward Dray.

"You both know Brick would have a fit if he heard you cussing like that," Dray said as an aside. He read the problem through twice. "You have a piece of scratch paper?"

"We have to show our work," Jax said.

"Okay, but there's nothing that says you can't copy the problem onto your worksheet after you've figured it out." Dray held out a hand and waited for Jax to tear a sheet out of his spiral notebook. "This is algebra, yeah?"

Jax nodded.

"Right, so let's start with the first person. We'll call his share of the money x. The second guy gets twice as much, so that'll be 2x. Follow me so far?" Dray wrote *x plus 2x* on the paper.

Both Jax and Lucky nodded.

Dray broke the problem down for them. He watched Lucky and Jax closely after each step to make sure they were following him.

"So, x equals sixteen," Jax proclaimed.

"That's right. Now all you have to do is plug the sixteen into the formula in place of the x," Dray explained.

While Jax finished the problem, Lucky reached for Jax's notebook. He tore out another sheet before handing it to Dray. "Give us another problem like this one." He stretched out and tapped his pencil against Jax's hand. "I'll race ya."

Jax rolled his eyes. "Give me a minute to finish this one first."

"Whatever." Lucky returned his attention to Dray. "Were you looking for me?"

"I thought I'd put you through a few drills and show you some grappling moves that worked well for me, but what you're doing is more important." Dray gestured to the pile of books next to Jax. "Come and find me once you're finished here."

"Algebra's the last thing I have to do. You mind if I watch the two of you?" Jax asked.

"Sure thing." Dray thumped Jax on the back. "In the meantime, I'm going to find Flint."

Dray walked out of the room without giving in to his desire to kiss Lucky. They'd only just started seeing each other, and he was already tired of having to check his natural instincts. He spotted Flint working with Beck, a local cop who used the facilities to stay in shape. "Got a minute?"

Flint pulled off his gloves and said something to Beck that Dray didn't catch. He turned to face Dray. "What's up?"

Dray motioned for Flint to step farther away from the cop. Although, maybe Beck was exactly who he should be talking to instead of Flint.

"Brick okay?" Flint asked.

"He's at home resting." Dray glanced at Beck. "How trustworthy is he?"

"Beck?" Flint looked over his shoulder. "He's a good guy. Why?"

"Did you see Jax?" Maybe Dray was wrong and Jax had received the black eye during training, but his gut told him that wasn't the case.

"I did. He said he got in a fight at school," Flint said.

"You believe him?" Dray didn't know Jax well enough to make the call. He didn't get the feeling that Jax had trouble in school but anything was possible.

"Hard to say. Sometimes, when kids catch hell at home, they take their frustrations out on someone weaker." Flint shrugged. "I've seen Brick try to question him about bruises before, and Jax shut down completely and stayed away from the gym for nearly a week until his face started to heal. Since then, we don't question him, but he knows we're here if he wants to talk or needs help."

Dray didn't quite understand that philosophy. Sure, it was important to give Jax a refuge, but something should be done about it if Jax's dad was beating him. "Have you ever talked to Beck about it?"

Flint shook his head. "The one and only time Brick suggested Jax report the abuse, Jax threatened to run away. I guess Brick feels it's better to keep Jax safe and fed here than to take the chance of Jax being alone on the streets."

Dray growled as he scrubbed his palms over his bristly hair. "I can't stand the thought of sitting on my hands when I know he's not safe in that house."

"You and me both," Flint replied.

"Are we done for tonight?" Beck asked as he walked toward them.

"No. One second," Flint said over his shoulder. He returned his attention to Dray. "Do you remember how bad Lucky was in the beginning? Hell, that boy'd come in here black and blue and so swollen he was barely recognizable, but he kept coming back. He's the man he is today because of this place. I figure Brick must know what he's doing."

"Yeah." Dray gestured to Beck. "Go on back to work."

Flint nodded.

Dray watched the two men spar for several moments before heading toward Brick's office. Flint's reminder of Lucky's bruises felt like a punch to the gut. He'd seen the evidence of abuse on Lucky back then, but he'd been too wrapped up in training and climbing the ranks to pay Lucky the attention he'd deserved.

As he entered Brick's office, Dray swore to himself he wouldn't make the same mistake with Jax.

* * * *

Lucky sat across from Dray as the waiter placed the large pizza with everything on it in the center of the table. He needed to talk to Dray about Mac because as much as he enjoyed eating out, nowhere was as good as Mac's.

The waiter stepped away, and Dray leveled Lucky with a look. "What?" Lucky asked.

"Tell me what happened to Jax," Dray said.

Lucky lifted two thick Chicago-style slices from the pan and set them on his plate. "I think you already know what happened."

"Did he tell you about it?" Dray asked.

"Nope. Didn't need to." Lucky shook red pepper flakes onto his pizza before reaching for the parmesan cheese. "I don't want to talk about it."

Ignoring their dinner, Dray leaned his tattooed forearms on the table. "What would you have done if Brick or Flint had called the cops on your mom?"

Lucky closed his eyes, trying to drive the memories from his mind. "I survived because of The Brick Yard. If someone there had betrayed me by going to the cops, I'd probably be either dead or in prison right now. I always knew if I'd wanted help I could've gone to one of my teachers or Brick, but as twisted as it probably sounds, I couldn't abandon my mom. She's always been fucked up, but she's kind of like a chameleon in that she mimics whatever man she's with. There were times when she'd find men who were decent to her and me." He opened his eyes and stared at Dray, wondering if Dray had the slightest idea what he was talking about. "They made up for the losers that hung around most of the time."

"So you did have some good?" Dray asked, finally relaxing enough to reach for a slice of pizza.

Lucky chewed the bite of food in his mouth until he could swallow. "Yeah. There was this one guy, Ben or Brett, or something like that. He took me to the zoo. He said he wanted to give my mom a break for the afternoon." He smiled, remembering the fun he'd had that warm summer day. It was the first time he'd been to the zoo, and he'd been fascinated by the exotic animals. "Mom screwed it up though because when Ben brought me home, she was there wasted with another guy." He took a deep breath. "Even though that was the last time I saw him, I still have the memories of that day, so I guess it was worth it."

Dray started to reach across the table but pulled back before he could touch Lucky. "I'm sorry. That sucks."

"I don't see it that way. There were a lot of kids in the neighborhood who hadn't been to the zoo. I always saw myself as lucky for getting the chance. Besides, if my mom hadn't screwed up that day, she'd have done it the next no doubt. She's a junkie. Always has been and always will be. That's something I've had to come to terms with. People don't change just because you love 'em."

"Maybe not, but moms are supposed to love and protect. It doesn't sound like your mom did much of that."

Lucky stuck another big bite into his mouth instead of answering. He didn't want to talk about his mom or her deadbeat boyfriends. The fact was, when he'd been younger, he'd been at the mercy of a drug addict who hadn't cared enough to be a mother to him. All the talking in the world wasn't going to change that. Thankfully, he'd found Brick, Flint, Mac and even Dray when he'd needed them the most. He'd learned to be a man by watching how the men at the gym treated each other. That's what he needed to make sure was available to Jax. If the police got involved, they'd put Jax into foster care, and even though Lucky had never been forced to endure the life of a kid in the system, he'd heard plenty of horror stories.

Dray seemed to study Lucky for several moments before breaking eye contact. "I hope you and Brick know what you're doing with Jax. I'll stay out of it for now, but it twists me up to know someone's beating on him."

"I'll keep an eye on him," Lucky said around a mouthful of food.

"Good." Dray started to eat in earnest.

Lucky wondered if he should bring up Mac but decided against it. There would be time, and he'd had enough heart to heart for the day.

* * * *

Out of the corner of his eye, Dray watched Brick scream last-minute instructions to Lucky. The crowd was different from the fans in Indianapolis. In the dark and dirty warehouse Ray Bruno had secured for the tournament, the audience acted more like feral cats than human beings. The place reeked of onions, which he knew from experience was body odor and whatever had died in the warehouse before the cage had been constructed.

Worse, instead of hiring off-duty cops to handle the crowd, Bruno had gone cheap and pulled his own guys in. *Stupid fuck.* He overheard the jerk beside him talking on his cell phone.

"Yeah, give me two hundred on the Ice Man," the guy said. "That fucker's gonna tear this place up!"

Dray's gaze went back to Lucky, who was jumping in place just outside the cage and shadowboxing with a determination on his face that didn't bode well for his opponent. It was obvious Lucky was pumped, and Dray knew the crowd had little to do with it. It was also obvious the Ice Man didn't have fans in attendance—at least not ones who would openly cheer for him. He glanced at the pinhead beside him. Lucky may not have had the hearts of the crowd, but they definitely knew who was going to win.

Lucky climbed into the bright-white cage. Unlike a lot of promoters, Bruno chose the color white specifically to showcase the crimson that would spill from the fighters throughout the tournament. By the time a winner was declared, the entire floor of the cage would be red with blood.

The bell rang and Lucky stepped up to his no-name opponent. The son of a bitch had been taunting Lucky for the last ten minutes. Lucky said something to his competitor and stood his ground.

Lucky threw a single punch, aimed at the asshole's nose, and the jerk who'd been full of himself only seconds earlier fell flat on his back, out cold.

"Yeah!" Dray cried, pumping his fist in the air. He turned to the pinhead. "That's the way to do it!" he shouted in excitement.

Smiling from ear to ear, the pinhead retrieved the phone from his pocket and started dialing.

Dray leaned back against the wall and crossed his arms.

He couldn't stop grinning as the referee lifted Lucky's arm over his head. Lucky still had one more match before they could go home and Dray could show him just how proud he was.

Lucky stepped out of the cage and immediately went to Brick's side. He wrapped an arm around the old man and disappeared into the crowd with Flint following. Dray waited, praying that Brick was okay. He dug out his phone and held it in his hand, waiting for a call.

Instead of a call, Flint appeared in front of Dray. "Lucky wants you. He's in the locker room."

Dray nodded, pulled his baseball cap lower on his forehead and followed Flint out of the main part of the building and down one of the darkened hallways. "Is it Brick?"

Flint shrugged. "I guess so. Brick keeps telling Lucky he's fine, but Lucky keeps arguing the point." He glanced over his shoulder at Dray. "I think they're both wrong."

"How's that?" Dray asked as Flint stopped in front of a door.

"Brick's the same as he was earlier today. Nothing's changed. I think the real problem is Lucky. I think he's so focused on Brick that he can't concentrate on anything else. This last match wasn't a big deal because the guy was a fucking joke, but the pretenders will be weeded out within the next two days."

Dray took a deep breath. "Is this a shared room?"

Flint snorted. "It's more like a closet, and no. Lucky worked that into his deal with Bruno. He didn't want anyone around if Brick had trouble."

"Okay. Keep an eye on the door and don't let anyone in," Dray instructed. He entered the room to find Flint's description accurate. There was barely space for three chairs, a small cooler and Brick's bag of supplies.

Brick and Lucky both looked up at him from their seated positions, but it was Brick who spoke. "Would you tell this wiseass that I'm perfectly capable of being out there?"

Before Dray answered, he took a moment to study the rise and fall of the old man's chest. By the exaggerated breaths and tinge of blue on Brick's lips, it was obvious he was having a hard time, but Flint had been right, Brick wasn't any worse than he'd been before the fight. Dray put his hand on Brick's shoulder. "Maybe Lucky wouldn't be as worried if you'd calm the fuck down. He knows what he has to do, so you screaming at him, especially in your condition, isn't doing either of you any good."

Brick glowered up at Dray. "You telling me how to do my job now?"

Dray released his hold on Brick's shoulder and held his hands up. "Don't listen to me, and keep doing whatever the fuck you want, but don't be surprised when you have to deal with Lucky and his mood after every goddamn fight." He knew he sounded harsh, but so did Brick, and he'd learned from the best.

Dray swung his attention to Lucky. "Good drop on the asshole out there. Why don't you do yourself a favor and keep your mind in the cage instead of worrying about Brick. I'm here. Flint's here. Let *us* worry about Brick."

Brick huffed and Lucky opened his mouth to argue, but Dray continued without giving him a chance. "You've got a whole fucking room of people out there who are just waiting for you to fall."

Lucky stared up at Dray like he was crazy. "Did you not just see me take that fucker down with one punch?"

"Yeah, I saw it, but that asshole looked like a desk jockey who had five hundred bucks he wanted to piss away—not a trained fighter." It wasn't the whole truth, the guy did have a nice body, but nothing like Lucky's. "Who's next for you?"

"Depends on who wins the Braun versus Triple Threat fight," Lucky replied.

"Triple Threat? Are you kidding?" Dray had fought Triple Threat nearly nine years earlier. "I can't believe that fat bastard's still around."

"He doesn't compete much anymore, mostly tournaments like this," Lucky explained. "Still, he's got nearly fifty pounds on me."

"More, from what I remember." Dray jerked his thumb toward the door. "I'd better get back out there, but I'll give you a piece of advice. If you go up against Triple Threat, he's always had a weak chin."

"I've already told him that," Brick grumbled.

Dray looked at Lucky and Lucky gave a slight shake of his head, indicating Brick hadn't said anything. "Okay, well, I'll get outta here then."

"Thanks for coming back," Lucky said.

Dray glanced over his shoulder, wondering if Lucky meant back to town or back to the locker room. By the warmth in Lucky's eyes, Dray understood it was both. "Sure thing."

* * * *

The following night, Dray, Lucky and Gatsby were cuddled on the sofa, going over rough footage of the fight Flint had taken, when someone knocked on the door. Dray glanced at Lucky. "You expecting company?"

Lucky pressed his lips against Dray's neck before handing over the kitten. "Nope. I'll get rid of them." He stood and stepped over Dray's legs to the door. "Briley," he said in a surprised tone.

Dray looked over his shoulder to see a young woman standing in front of Lucky. He recognized the name as a friend Lucky had mentioned several times on the phone, but by the way Briley was smiling at Lucky, Dray knew they'd been more than friends.

"What's up?" Lucky asked.

Briley popped her head inside and spotted the kitten. "Oh my god," she squealed, moving toward Gatsby.

Dray had two choices, hand the kitten over or allow Briley to grab Gatsby out of his lap. He chose the first option. "Her name's Gatsby."

"Gatsby?" Briley echoed and rolled her eyes before turning them on Lucky. "You and that dumb book."

"It's not a dumb book." Lucky shut the door. He picked up his empty beer bottle off the table. "You want another?" he asked Dray.

Dray really didn't, but he hoped accepting would let Briley know he wasn't planning to leave anytime soon. He stared at Briley, who rubbed faces with the kitten. He hated to admit it but she was pretty, and not the kind of fake pretty which pissed him off even more. The jealousy crept up on him, and he needed like hell to beat it back. He and Lucky had talked briefly about the fact that they'd both had an active sex life before they'd gotten together, but talking about it and actually meeting one of Lucky's lovers was different. "Sure," he finally told Lucky.

"You're Dray?" she asked.

"Yeah."

With Gatsby snuggled under her chin, Briley turned her attention to the TV. "This from last night?"

"Yeah," Dray repeated as Lucky opened the refrigerator.

Briley waited for Lucky to come back into the room. "How'd you do?"

"Won both," Lucky replied, handing Dray a beer. He took a seat on the sofa, although on the opposite end from Dray. "The first one was a piece of cake, but the second wasn't as easy. Dray and I were just trying to figure out what went wrong."

Briley glanced at the screen again. "You let him get you in a clench," she said like it was the most obvious thing in the world.

Dray hid his grin behind the mouth of his bottle. He'd tried to tell Lucky last night that Triple Threat almost beat him with the clench. As good a fighter as Lucky was, he sucked at the wrestling aspect when it happened.

"Shut up, Briley," Lucky shot back.

Dray was surprised by the outburst, but even more so

when Briley just laughed. *Damn.* Not only was the girl pretty but nice, too, and it was obvious she could hold her own with Lucky. *Sonofabitch!* Never in his life had Dray been jealous of a woman.

Briley swayed back and forth, holding Gatsby in her hands. "You'd better be nice or I'll take this little honey home with me."

"Over my dead body," Lucky said, getting to his feet.

Briley smirked and nodded toward the television. "If you fight like that tomorrow night, taking your cat won't be a problem."

Lucky exhaled. "Did you come by just to torment me?"

"Oh shit! I forgot why I came over." She handed Gatsby back to Dray. "I just saw Sid at Jerry's Place. He's really messed up, and he was starting to get mouthy." She bit her plump bottom lip. "I thought you'd want to know."

"Hell," Lucky groaned. He closed his eyes and winced. "Yeah. I'd better go get him home."

Briley gave Lucky a soft kiss on the lips. "You're too good to him, and everyone knows it, including him."

Lucky shrugged. "Sid's always been there for me."

"I know," she said, moving to the door. "It was nice to meet you, Dray."

"You, too," Dray returned.

"Bye, doll." She waved at Lucky on her way out the door.

"You want some help with Sid?" Dray asked. He settled Gatsby on the couch beside him before standing.

"You mind? Depending on how bad he is, it might not be easy getting him out of there," Lucky said as he grabbed his sneakers.

"I don't mind." Dray pulled his coat on. He knew Brick believed Sid was pulling Lucky down, so he wanted to see for himself what kind of bullshit Sid was involved in. Once Lucky had his coat on, Dray wrapped his arms around Lucky's waist. Although it wasn't the time, he couldn't help but wonder just how close Briley and Lucky were. "Do you love her?"

Lucky's eyebrows drew together. "Briley?"

For some reason Lucky's response made Dray angry. "Who the hell do you think I'm talking about?"

Lucky broke eye contact. "She's a friend."

Dray could tell by the way the two had interacted that Lucky had told the truth, but he also knew there was more to it, and the green-eyed monster was ready for a fight. "Do you fuck her?"

"God, Dray. Do I ask you about all the guys you fuck?" Lucky shot back.

"I barely remember the *men* I fuck," he replied, putting emphasis on the word men. "I certainly don't consider them friends."

Lucky poked Dray in the chest. "You're the one who told me to bury who I am."

Yeah, I did do that. Dray took a step back. "Let's go get Sid."

Lucky didn't move. "I get lonely sometimes and when I do, I usually call Briley," he confessed.

Dray knew all about loneliness. Guilt filled him. He had no right to make Lucky feel bad about seeking solace in someone else, but he couldn't keep the bitterness out of his voice when he said, "I'm here for now, so there's no reason for you to call her. Do you understand what I'm saying?"

Lucky nodded. "How long *are* you going to be here? Have you decided whether or not you're going to help me with The Brick Yard after…?"

"Hiding my sexuality hasn't been my way since I moved to Kansas City, and, to be honest, I'm not sure how long I can do it."

"I understand." Lucky zipped his coat. "Let's go."

* * * *

Lucky entered Jerry's Place, a small neighborhood dive bar, and scanned the room. Sid was by the old-fashioned jukebox talking to Jimmy Black, a known dealer. "Fuck."

"Yeah, I see him," Dray said from behind.

Lucky glanced over his shoulder. "You know who that is?"

"His name? No. What they're doing? Hell yes."

"Wait here," Lucky said before making his way across the bar. He stopped several feet away from Sid. Jimmy was a paranoid asshole who wouldn't think twice about pulling a knife if he felt cornered. Lucky waited for Sid and Jimmy to look his way. He nodded once. "Jimmy."

Jimmy sniffed and rubbed his nose. "You want something?"

"No, I need to talk to Sid," Lucky replied.

"Oh?" Sid let out a harsh bark of laughter. "I've left you three fucking messages in the past week, and you haven't bothered to pick up the damn phone."

"I'm here now." Lucky rested his hands on his hips and stared at Sid, willing his friend to send the dealer away. He could tell by the blown pupils in Sid's eyes that he'd already sampled quite a bit of Jimmy's product. Briley had been right to worry. "Sid."

With an exaggerated sigh, Sid looked at Jimmy. "I'll catch up with you later."

"Yeah, whatever, man." Jimmy quirked his lip at Lucky before walking away.

Once Jimmy had left, Lucky stepped closer to his friend. He knew from experience that he couldn't push Sid, so he tried a different route. "I'm sorry I haven't called you back. This shit with Brick and the tournament has really been fucking with my head."

"You sure it doesn't have something to do with the tattooed fag over there? What's he doing back anyway?" Sid asked.

Lucky curled his hands into tight fists. Sid had never liked Dray, but the harsh criticism was out of line. "Dray's here to help me with Brick and the gym."

"Are you sure that's all it is?"

"Sid." Lucky moved until he was within striking distance.

He'd never given Sid a reason to question his sexuality, so he wasn't sure what the fuck his friend was talking about.

Sid held up his hands in mock surrender. "Just seems off that he shows up and you forget about everyone else."

"That's not true. I've seen Briley, and I've spent most of my time at the gym, preparing for the tournament." Lucky hated the half-truth, but protecting what he had with Dray was worth it.

"Yeah, that's what I wanted to talk to you about. I need some cash, so I thought you could give me some inside scoop on the fighters."

Lucky knew exactly what Sid needed money for, and he wasn't about to give him the information he wanted. As he stared at his friend, his heart sank. When they'd been teenagers, they'd both smoked pot on occasion. Well, Sid had smoked more than occasionally, but it hadn't been a problem. Things hadn't started going bad until Sid had dropped out of high school two months before graduation and had gone to work at a chicken-processing plant. Lucky still couldn't put his finger on it, but Sid had changed since then. Maybe it had something to do with the men Sid hung out with at work or the escalation of his drug use from pot to the harder, more expensive shit he used almost daily.

"If you need cash, the last thing you should be doing is gambling."

"You asshole!" Sid yelled. "After all I've done for you, I'm just asking for a fucking favor."

"No, you're asking me to help you buy drugs, and I'm not gonna do that!" Lucky shouted back. He sobered when he noticed several people turn toward them. He took a deep breath. "I hate to see you like this, and it kills me to know you won't let me help you."

"I don't need your help," Sid growled. "What I need is for you to stop treating me like you're so much better than I am. Newsflash, your mom's a fucking meth-head whore."

Lucky wrapped his hand around Sid's scrawny neck and slammed him against the wall. "This has nothing to do with my mom," he ground out between clenched jaws.

Sid stared at Lucky and shook his head. "It has *everything* to do with her. You're just too blind to see it." He put his hands on Lucky's chest and pushed. "Get outta here, Lucky. Go back to your gym, your tattooed freak and your joke of a career."

Lucky's breath hitched. He released his hold on Sid but didn't immediately move back. The expression on Sid's face said it all. How many times had Lucky seen the same look on his mom's face? He knew it had nothing to do with drugs. Sid had given up on a better life. He'd accepted where he'd come from and refused to want more. "If you ever need me, you have my number."

Lucky turned and walked away. It was the hardest thing he'd ever done, but he couldn't travel back down that road. Dealing with his mom's shit had nearly broken him, and he knew he couldn't survive it again. It was hard to love someone more than they loved themselves.

"You okay?" Dray asked when Lucky reached him.

"He's lost," Lucky mumbled, not willing to say more.

"Looks that way," Dray agreed. "Why haven't you cut him loose?"

"I owe him, and he reminds me of that every time something like this happens." Lucky wasn't the kind of man to give up on people. Hell, his mom was the perfect example of that.

"Why do you owe him?"

Lucky pushed open the door. Once on the sidewalk, he glanced at Dray. "Sid never gave a shit what my mom did or how many bruises I had on any given day." He shrugged. "He was always there for me."

"I'm glad that you had that, but you can't let someone try to pull you down just because they were nice to you fifteen years ago. I know I'm an outsider in this situation, but it doesn't seem like he's been much of a friend to you for a long time."

Lucky shrugged again. He didn't expect Dray or anyone

else to understand, because there were times he still didn't understand why the hell he put up with Sid's shit. "I can't turn my back on him. I'll never treat someone the way I was treated."

Dray took a step toward Lucky and reached out, but stopped short of touching him when the bar door opened and several people exited. Instead, Dray shoved his hands into the front pockets of his jeans. "That's what makes you the person you are, but I'd hate to see someone use that loyalty against you."

Lucky was starting to come to the same conclusion, but he hated himself for even thinking about tossing Sid to the curb. "Go on back to Brick's. I'm gonna hit the gym for a while."

"It's almost ten," Dray reminded Lucky.

"I do my best thinking when the place is dark." Not for the first time, Lucky wished he could crawl back into the bed that had helped him survive a lifetime of fucked-up shit. He felt his throat tighten and his nose burn and quickly turned away. "Would you stop by and check on Gatsby?"

"Sure." Dray put a hand on Lucky's shoulder. "You sure you don't want some company? If you need your space at the gym, I can wait at your place for you."

Lucky shook his head. The way he felt, it would take hours in the gym to get his head on straight. "Thanks, but this is going to take some time. It's how I deal."

After several moments, Dray started toward the apartment. "Don't wear yourself out. You have to fight again tomorrow night."

"Yeah." Lucky took off toward The Brick Yard and soon his jog became a sprint. By the time he reached the back door, his hands were shaking with the need to pound his fists against something other than Sid's face. He pulled out his keys and stepped into the darkness. The light in the front of the gym hadn't been on, so he assumed Jax wasn't spending the night. *Good.* He'd work out his anger then sleep in his old room.

Crossing to the speed bag, he pulled off his shirt and dropped it to the floor before reaching for the tape.

"Lucky?"

He turned toward Jax's voice but couldn't see him in the shadows. "Hey," Lucky said. "I didn't think you were around."

"I just got here." Jax's voice sounded thick. "Can I ask you something?"

"Sure." Lucky tore off a long piece of white tape. He started wrapping his knuckles, but when Jax's question didn't come, he looked back to the shadowy figure in the doorway. "Jax?"

"Do you know where I can buy a gun?" Jax asked in a voice so soft and vulnerable it broke Lucky's heart.

Dropping the tape, Lucky moved. There was only one reason Jax would ask that particular question. He turned on the hallway light and took a step back. "Christ!"

Jax turned his head. "He wouldn't stop," he mumbled. "He'll never stop."

Lucky's breath froze in his chest. Jax's face was so badly beaten, Lucky barely recognized him. The anger that had overwhelmed him earlier flared to life again tenfold. "What's your address?"

Jax shook his head. "I can't tell you."

"You have to." Lucky rested his hands on Jax's thin shoulders. "The only other choice is to call the police."

"No, no cops. They'll take me away."

God, Lucky thought. Jax was just like he'd been. "Better the monster you know," he said, reading Jax's thoughts. "So, give me your address."

Jax's tongue ran over the cut on his lip that looked bad enough for stitches. "You'll get into trouble."

Lucky wrapped his arms around the sixteen year old. He thought of the many times he'd been on the receiving end of a fist as a boy and had wished he'd had someone who would stand up for him. Jax was right. Lucky could get into a hell of a lot of trouble for teaching Jax's dad a lesson, but Jax deserved to know he had someone who'd watch his back. He dug out his phone and handed it to Jax. "Take pictures of your face and anywhere else he hurt you." He met Jax's gaze. "Anywhere," he emphasized, not knowing whether Jax's abuse delved into a sexual nature. "If your old man calls the cops, show 'em the pictures."

Jax stared at the phone for several moments before giving in and rattling off his address. "His name's Steve, and he was wasted when I ran out, so he may be passed out by now." He dug into his pocket and removed a single key on a chain. He thrust it out to Lucky. "If he doesn't answer, use this."

Again, Lucky's heart clenched. "Okay."

Chapter Eight

Lucky pounded his fist against the door for the fourth time. He had the key in his pocket, but he'd cooled down enough to realize what would happen to him if he kicked Steve's ass inside his own home. Seeking justice for Jax was one thing, but ending the night behind bars wouldn't help Jax, Brick or him.

He raised his hand to beat against the wood once more, but before his fist could connect, the door swung open. A muscular man wearing nothing but a T-shirt and a pair of boxers stood in front of him. *Shit.* Jax's dad was at least six-five and although he looked soft around the middle, it was obvious he was stronger than shit by the size of his muscular arms.

"Who the fuck're you?" Steve slurred.

Lucky knew the best chance he had was a surprise attack, so he grabbed Steve's shirt, yanked him out of the apartment and landed a power punch to the man's nose. Taken off guard, Steve stumbled back. Lucky didn't waste time with words as he continued to deliver punches to Steve's face and stomach.

"What the fuck!" Steve yelled loud enough to wake the entire building.

Lucky lifted his leg and delivered a kick to Steve's gut. The bigger man toppled to the floor, and Lucky placed a knee on his chest, keeping the asshole on the ground. He added as much of his weight as he dared and spit in Steve's face. "If you ever lay a hand on Jax again, I'll kill you."

"Mind your own goddamn business!" Steve said.

Lucky wrapped his hand around Steve's throat and

prepared to deliver another blow. A door two apartments down opened. A middle-aged man popped his head out and stared at Lucky.

Still pinning Steve to the floor, Lucky scowled. "This man beat his son so bad the boy's face is unrecognizable," he stated. "Just enacting a bit of vigilante justice."

After a quick glance at Steve, the neighbor met Lucky's gaze. He gave Lucky a sharp nod before going back inside.

"Even your neighbors know you're a piece of shit who likes to beat on an innocent kid." Lucky narrowed his eyes and bent lower. "I have photos of what you did to Jax, so here's what's going to happen. Tomorrow, I'm going to bring Jax over when you go to work, and we're going to pack his shit. From there, it'll be up to him whether or not he ever sees your sorry ass again." He leaned in until Steve's entire focus was on Lucky's face. "Don't fuck with me on this. You won't win."

"What are you, some kind of pervert? If you think I'm just going to let my boy go with you, you're crazy."

Lucky landed another vicious punch before answering. "The only interest I have in Jax is making sure the last two years of his childhood are spent unafraid. I wasn't there for the first sixteen years, but I'll be there for the last two." Lucky got to his feet. "You're a stupid sonofabitch, because you have the kind of son a man can be proud of, and you threw it away. If you cooperate and leave him the hell alone, you'll still be able to draw your government assistance. If you force the issue and call the cops, I'll show them the pictures and they'll put Jax into the system." He leaned down, putting his face even closer to Jax's dad's. "No Jax, no free money. Get where I'm coming from?"

Steve shook his head. "Take him. He's a nagging little bitch anyway."

The words sliced through Lucky because they were so close to the way his mom used to talk to him. Each time he'd asked his mom for money to pay the rent and utility bills, she'd start in about how selfish he was. Once Brick had given him a job, Lucky had done his best to juggle the utility payments enough to keep them on month after month.

"Someday, Jax is going to be stronger than you are. You'd better pray he's forgiven you by then," Lucky said before walking away.

* * * *

Dray was sitting on the couch watching television when he heard Brick rustling around in his room. He got up and knocked on Brick's door. "Everything okay?"

"I'm thirsty, and I spilled the glass of water you put in here earlier."

Dray opened the door to find Brick trying to mop up the water with several bloody tissues. "Leave that. I'll grab a towel. You want more water or would you rather have tea?"

"Tea'd be nice if we have some of that lemon juice left to put in it."

Dray fought a grin. "I bought real lemons at the store, so I'll cut one of those up for you."

"Why the hell'd you do that? Those plastic lemons filled with juice are good enough for me. I've been using those since before you were born," Brick said.

"I was trying to do something nice for you, you grouchy sonofabitch." Dray opened the small linen closet outside the bathroom and retrieved a hand towel. He stepped back into Brick's room long enough to toss Brick the towel. "You get what's on the table, but leave the floor for me."

"I'm not helpless," Brick grumbled.

"No, but you don't need to be crawling around on the floor either." Dray shook his head as he strode to the kitchen. Brick was stubborn on a good day—on a bad day, he was nearly impossible to deal with. Dray knew he should be more patient. For a man like Brick, asking for or accepting help was a sign of weakness. Dray promised himself he'd keep that in mind whenever Brick's temper flared.

He reached for a lemon out of the bowl on the counter but stopped himself. From personal experience, he knew real lemon juice tasted different from the kind that came out of the stupid plastic lemon. Sure it was better, but it was still different. Maybe Brick needed the normality of something as simple as a glass of tea. He set the lemon back in the bowl. He found the plastic lemon easily enough and shook it. There appeared to be enough for one or two more glasses, so he put it on his mental grocery list for next time he went to the store.

After making Brick's drink, he entered the bedroom to find Brick staring at a framed picture that Dray had never seen. It was a sepia photograph of a large family. He knew nothing about Brick's family, so he took a chance. "Is that your folks?"

Brick nodded and pointed toward a toddler in the arms of a plump woman. "That's me right there, and that gorgeous woman holding me is my mom." He ran his fingertip over the image. "I don't remember her. This and an old patchwork blanket were the only things she left with me when she dropped me off at the orphanage."

Dray leaned in to get a better look at the picture. There were five other children in the photograph besides Brick. "Did something happen to them?"

Brick sighed. "From what I understand, my father was killed in some kind of accident at work." He met Dray's gaze. "This was during the Great Depression, so there was no government funding to help families who needed it. My mom didn't have much choice but to give me up. As you can see, I was much younger than the rest of my brothers and sisters. I guess my mother hoped they could help her enough financially to keep them, but I was a liability." He shrugged as if it were something he had come to terms with.

"Were you adopted out to another family?" Dray asked, his heart breaking for his old friend.

"No. When I was thirteen, the orphanage let me go to find my own way."

"At thirteen?" Dray couldn't imagine.

"It was a different time. I managed to get a job in a brick factory. That's where my last name came from. The nuns who ran the orphanage knew my first name but not my last. The owner of the factory who took me in and gave me a chance, he said I needed a last name, so he gave me Brick." Brick chuckled. "Not very original, but I loved it because it was given to me by a very hard but caring man."

Dray was fascinated. Although the story was heartbreaking, it was a glimpse into the man beside him. He was ashamed of the fact that he'd never asked Brick about his family or life. "And your family? Did you ever see them again?"

"I didn't know their last name, so I had no way of looking them up." The corners of Brick's lips lifted in a semi-smile. "I could have dozens of nieces and nephews running around the neighborhood, and I'd never know it. That's why I decided to do what I could when needed."

"How long did you work at the factory?" Dray asked, moving to sit on the edge of Brick's bed.

Brick tilted his head back and scratched his chin. "Let's see. The factory closed down in 1963, so I guess I was around twenty-nine? By that time, the owner, Mr. Clausen, and his wife had all but claimed me as a son because she'd been unable to have children. Mrs. Clausen had developed bad asthma and her doctor told her she needed to move to a warmer, dryer climate. Mr. Clausen had been an amateur boxer in his early years, and he loved to teach me everything he knew."

Brick smiled, the first real smile Dray had seen since he'd been back. "I was good." He winked at Dray. "Mr. Clausen saw that my real passion was in the gym and not the factory, so when he decided it was time to move to Arizona, he closed the factory and gave me the building and as much money as he could spare as a loan, and The Brick Yard was born."

"Why didn't I know any of this?" Dray asked before

the answer came to him. "I'm sorry that I've been so self-absorbed."

"Don't be sorry about that. Growing up, you were so intent on following your dreams while still trying to take care of your family that you barely had time to eat and sleep," Brick said.

"I can't believe the gym used to be an actual brickyard." Dray shook his head. "Does Lucky know that story?"

"Naw. I'm too busy to sit around and tell stories about the way things used to be." Brick coughed, and Dray handed him a tissue.

"That's probably enough for tonight, but I want to hear more," Dray said.

Brick nodded as he spat into the tissue. "I'm tired anyway."

Dray gestured to the monitor he'd picked up earlier in the day. "Don't fuck around with that again. I'm going to go down and wait for Lucky to get home, but I want to be able to hear you if you need me."

Brick's eyebrows furrowed. "Where's Lucky?"

"He had a run-in with Sid, so he took off to the gym to work through his anger," Dray explained.

"Keep a close eye on him. This'll get too much for him eventually, and I don't want him turning to Sid for ways to cope. Keep him in the cage, and he'll make it through this," Brick said.

Dray thought of his earlier conversation with Lucky. "Do you have any idea of why Lucky feels he needs to fight? We talked about it, but he claimed he didn't know why he needed it so much."

"Don't know what's in the boy's brain. Just know he goes into the cage antsy and comes out calm. He was beat pretty good as a kid. I've always thought it was his way of fighting back. Now, he may not realize that, but it's not my place or yours to try to analyze him. The important thing is since he's been fighting in the cage, he hasn't been in nearly as many fights outside of it, especially since you've been back," Brick said.

"I didn't realize he'd been getting into bar brawls." Dray wondered if hanging with Sid had anything to do with it. If so, it was yet another reason Lucky should cut Sid out of his life.

"I don't know if they're bar brawls, but if he goes too long between fights, he shows up at the gym and it's obvious he's gone several rounds with someone. I've had to stitch him up twice in the last five years because he won't go near a hospital."

"Why's he afraid of hospitals?" Dray asked.

"I think it's a holdover from his childhood. You can't imagine the shit I've seen him use to close a wound — tape, strips of dirty rags, glue." Brick coughed again, but it didn't last long. "He'd panic if I mentioned taking him to the emergency room, so I learned to just patch him up right — even if that meant stitching him up myself."

"Shit." The more Dray learned of Lucky's childhood, the more he wanted to give him something good in his life. He noticed Brick's eyes drooping and realized he'd spent far more time questioning the old man then he'd intended. "Get some sleep. I'll check on Lucky and see you in the morning."

"Let me know if he needs anything," Brick mumbled.

Dray quietly left the apartment and let himself into Lucky's place. He still couldn't get over the story Brick had told him about his childhood. No wonder Brick was so quick to help the string of needy kids that managed to find their way to the gym. He silently thanked Mr. Clausen, the man who'd obviously started it all.

* * * *

Dray turned on the bedside lamp when Gatsby jumped off the bed and raced into the living room. He heard Lucky murmuring to the kitten before coming into the room. "Hey."

Lucky, who was still holding Gatsby, set the kitten on the floor. "I thought you were staying at Brick's."

Dray folded the blankets back on Lucky's side of the bed. He pointed to the monitor. "I wanted to be here in case you needed me."

Lucky undressed and slid into bed beside Dray. He curled around Dray's body and sighed. "How's he doing?"

"As well as can be expected. He told me about his childhood." Dray ran his hand down Lucky's back. "It was quite a story. I think you need to ask him about it."

"Why can't you just tell me?" Lucky asked.

"Because I think it'll mean more coming from him. It explains a lot." Dray noticed the split knuckles and bruises on Lucky's hand. He still didn't know what had gone on between Lucky and Sid at the bar, but it had taken everything he'd had to let Lucky go to the gym without him. "Did you work out your anger?"

"Sort of." Lucky kissed Dray's neck. "Jax came into the gym. His dad worked him over pretty good tonight."

Dray stilled. "Did you call the police?"

"No."

"We have to call them. What if something more serious happens next time?" Dray had been luckier than most kids who'd wandered into The Brick Yard needing a job. His home life had been pure shit, but it was more a case of circumstances. His mom had never raised a hand to him, even when he had been too small to fight back.

Dray lifted the battered knuckles to his lips and placed soft kisses over the wounds. Brick had let it slip that on more than one occasion, he'd found Lucky in the gym passed out from a night spent beating the bags, trying to fight the demons that threatened to destroy him. Dray pressed his cheek against the back of Lucky's hand.

"I went to see Jax's dad," Lucky replied.

"Lucky, no. Do you have any idea how much trouble you could get in?" Dray understood Lucky's anger toward Jax's dad, but he also knew the kind of damage Lucky's fists could do. Losing Lucky to the cage was one thing, but losing him to jail was another.

"I don't think he'll go to the cops, but I've got pictures of Jax, so if he does, he'll be in for one hell of a fight." Lucky kissed Dray's neck again. "I'm glad you're here."

Dray turned onto his side and pressed his cock against Lucky's. He wanted to tell Lucky he'd always be here, and it would be the truth. After giving it a lot of thought, he'd decided the last thing Lucky needed was to worry about The Brick Yard. If Lucky continued to move up in the ranks, the UFC would start seriously scouting him. Brick's hope that the gym would be a place for future fighters and kids who needed a way out of the neighborhood couldn't be ignored.

Staring into Lucky's eyes, Dray knew it wasn't only the street kids he'd be preserving The Brick Yard for. The rundown brick building that housed four other storefronts, including Mac's, was Lucky's home. "I've decided to manage the gym. That way you can concentrate on training and fighting."

Lucky broke away enough to lean up on his elbow. "You've decided to stay?"

Dray nodded. He worried his bottom lip with his teeth, wondering if he should share more. Lucky wouldn't truly be his until he'd gone as far as his career would take him, but Dray knew he wouldn't be able to push Lucky away when, and if, Lucky needed him. "Once you're traveling, we won't see much of each other, but when you do come home, I'll be around."

Lucky reached for Dray's semi-hard cock. "In that case, I'll come home often."

Dray closed his eyes as Lucky began to stroke him. He knew what life was like on the road and how important it was to train full time year round. Lucky would be home for a few months a year, at most. He didn't want to think about Lucky having sex with anyone else, but he was a realist. The adrenaline produced during a match made most fighters horny as hell afterward. Trading promises that they'd remain faithful would be setting each other up to fail. It simply wasn't possible for Lucky to be surrounded by beautiful women and not fall back into his old patterns. When Dray had been on the circuit, he'd had it easier because he'd had Vince, who everyone around them had thought was his best friend. The lesson he'd learned from Vince had forever changed the way Dray looked at relationships. He wanted to tell Lucky that, as much as the thought killed Dray, he needed to stick to women. It would be too easy for a one-night stand to betray Lucky's secret.

Lucky released Dray's cock and moved to run his fingers between the cheeks of Dray's ass. When he pressed against Dray's hole, Dray couldn't help himself. He pushed back, letting Lucky know without words what he wanted. The two of them had fucked numerous times over the last few days, and he'd been surprised to find he enjoyed receiving pleasure as much as giving it. Without a word, Dray rolled and reached for the bottle of lube. With his back to Lucky, Dray held the slick up.

Lucky ground his erection against the crack of Dray's ass as he took the bottle. "I've been thinking of this all day," he whispered in Dray's ear.

Dray slid his legs apart, bending his right leg toward his chest. Before Dray, Lucky had never fucked a man, so Dray hadn't known what to expect the first time it had happened. He'd been pleasantly surprised by how confident Lucky had been with the whole process. It wasn't until afterward that Lucky had confessed that although it was his first time with a man, it wasn't his first time doing anal. As ridiculous as it was, Dray's jealousy again flared at the news, but he'd swallowed the hurtful words that had been on the tip of his tongue and had given Lucky the moment. For his part, Lucky had been supremely content and had curled his body so tightly around Dray afterward, Dray hadn't had a choice but to fight the green-eyed monster back.

Lucky's lubed finger began to circle Dray's puckered hole.

"Being inside you is the closest I've ever come to heaven," he whispered in Dray's ear.

Dray groaned when he felt the head of Lucky's erection press against him. "Let me roll over," he said, pulling away from Lucky. He moved to lie on his back and opened his legs. "I want to hold you," he explained.

Lucky looked surprised at the request. "Yeah?"

Staring up into Lucky's big brown eyes, Dray nodded. *Damn.* It would be easy to get used to seeing the soft expression on Lucky's handsome face each day, but he knew it was an unrealistic expectation. At most, he'd be a shelter in the storm for Lucky in the years to come. At worst, he'd be nothing at all.

"Thank you," Lucky said. He started to say more but shook his head instead. Taking a deep breath, he reached for the bottle of lube again. He coated his cock and scooted closer, insinuating himself between Dray's legs.

Dray hooked his forearms under his knees and brought his thighs against his chest. It was obvious the change in position had Lucky nervous, something Dray found incredibly endearing. Deciding to help Lucky out, he reached down and guided the head of Lucky's dick toward his hole. Lucky hadn't taken much time in stretching him, so Dray warned, "Just go slow."

Licking his lips, Lucky pushed inside Dray with infinite care.

"Christ, you're good at this," Dray groaned as Lucky slid forward. He'd only bottomed a few times before Lucky because the men he'd been with hadn't given a shit whether or not their entry was painful. The fact that Lucky cared enough to take his time showed in the pure pleasure that ran through Dray during the invasion.

"I have an excellent teacher." Buried to the hilt, Lucky swiveled his hips. He braced his hands on the backs of Dray's thighs as he slid out before surging back inside.

As good as Lucky's length felt moving in and out of him, Dray's attention didn't wander from Lucky's face. Of all the men Dray had been with over the years, never had he seen a more expressive set of eyes. He doubted Lucky would ever be able to lie to him because no matter what came out of the gorgeous man's mouth, Dray would always be able to read his eyes.

At the moment, Lucky's gaze spoke volumes, and Dray's heart leaped. *Don't fall in love with me.* He broke the heaviness of the moment by reaching down to feel Lucky's cock as it continued to pump inside him. The way the skin of his hole thinned to stretch around Lucky's girth turned him on. "Fuck, babe, you're killing me."

Lucky moaned and surged in harder. "No, I'm not. I'm imprinting myself on you."

Dray wanted to tell Lucky he already had, but he was too close to coming. He reached for his shaft and wrapped his hand around it just as Lucky let out a series of grunts, signaling his own journey to climax. *God.* He loved that Lucky didn't try to hide the way Dray's body made him feel.

"Fill me," Dray said, finally finding his voice. "Give me everything you have." He jacked himself harder and faster, mimicking Lucky's thrusts.

"Yes. Oh fuck yes," Lucky groaned, grinding against Dray's ass.

Warm seed shot from Dray's cock to splash onto his stomach as he cried out his release. He swore he felt the beat of his own heart in the length of his shaft. He pulled Lucky into a deep, erotic kiss, trying to tell Lucky without words how good they were together. Within a few days, Lucky had become the best lover Dray had ever had. He wasn't sure if that said a lot about him or Lucky, but he was fully sated, so he'd take either as a win.

Settling beside Dray, Lucky rested his head on Dray's shoulder. He was silent for several moments before letting out a long sigh. "I tried to get Jax to come home with me, but he insisted on staying at the gym after we got him cleaned up." He shrugged. "He has several small cuts on his face, but I put some Steri-Strips on them, so they shouldn't scar."

Dray held Lucky close, loving the way Lucky's five o'clock shadow rasped against his skin. It was real and masculine and reminded him once again how much he cared for the man in his arms.

* * * *

Dray held the phone to his ear as he watched Jax's apartment building from the safety of his truck.

"It's about time you called, asshole," Berto answered.

"Sorry. Things have been hectic around here." Dray sat up straight when a man emerged from the building across the street, but relaxed when he saw no visible signs of bruising.

"How's Brick?"

"Fading fast." Dray took a drink of his water before setting it back in the cup holder. "It looks like you're going to have to find someone to fill my spot. After being here, I've decided to stay after Brick passes and run the gym."

"Fuck. What about the house?" Berto asked.

Dray hated the thought of giving up his beloved farmhouse, but he could always use the proceeds to find something in Chicago. He knew he wouldn't be able to afford anything half as nice as the farm, but surely he could find something with a small yard at least. "I'm going to have to sell it."

"Are you sure about all this? Is the gym worth giving up everything you've worked for?"

"Yeah." Dray surprised himself for blurting out the answer before he'd given himself a chance to think about it first. It wasn't as if he were giving up his job and home without considering the pros and cons, just that the pros far outweighed the cons. "Brick's built something special here, and without my help, Lucky'll have to give up fighting."

"So. You gave it up and came out okay. What's to say Lucky won't do the same?" Berto asked.

Dray rubbed his forehead while deciding how much to

confess to his cousin. The family knew why he'd stopped fighting, so they'd never brought it up. "I was wrong to quit when I did." He blew out a breath. It was the first time he'd ever admitted to anyone that he'd made a mistake in leaving Chicago. "I was ashamed when people found out what I was and instead of standing up for myself, I ran. I see now what a mistake that was. Not only did I let myself down, but I think I hurt the people who believed in me the most."

"Cut yourself some slack. Those fans were brutal in the way they talked about you," Berto said.

"Yeah, they were, but I think I left some of my self-respect in the cage when I took off like I did," Dray explained.

"So what's that mean? You're going to help Lucky become champion to spite the fans?"

"Hell no. I just think I might be able to get back some of what I lost if I do the right thing and make sure the gym stays open. Not sure if you know this, but Brick's helped a lot of kids over the years." Dray knew he'd never have children of his own, but by doing his best to fill Brick's shoes, maybe he could make a difference in the lives of kids like Jax and Lucky.

"What about the tattooing? You're damn good. It'd be a shame to waste that talent," Berto said.

"To be honest, I don't know. After things settle down, I may see if I can rent a chair in one of the local shops for some extra money." *Shit.* Even though Dray had said it as if it were no big deal, his hands itched to hold a tattoo gun again. When he put ink to skin, everything around him disappeared except the art. It was the zone he missed the most.

"Sounds like you've got it all figured out, bro. I hope you get out of it more than what you're giving up."

"Me too," Dray agreed. "I'll make the drive down as soon as I can to get the house emptied and up on the market. In the meantime, if you run across anyone looking to buy, give them my number."

"Will do, although, you might want to consider renting the place out until you know how things are going to develop there."

Dray had already thought of that but had decided against it. "Nope. If I'm going to do this, I need to commit to it one hundred percent."

"Whatever. I have a customer waiting, so if that's all, I'll let you go," Berto said.

"Yeah, that's all for now. Tell everyone hi for me," Dray said before hanging up. He missed the whacked-out crew who worked in Berto's shop, but none of them were as easy to look at as Lucky.

Movement off to his left caught his attention a few minutes later. "Bingo." Carrying a brown paper sack, full of liquor no doubt, Jax's dad appeared thoroughly beaten to shit. The way he held his free hand protectively over his right rib cage told Dray that Lucky hadn't spared the older man's torso from the ass whooping either. "Good."

Satisfied that Jax's dad planned to go right on drinking himself to death instead of calling the cops, Dray started the truck.

* * * *

Lucky faced Dray in the training ring, listening intently to Dray's directions.

"You can't let the assholes get you into a clench. No matter what." Dray turned to the side and kicked out, his foot coming within inches of Lucky's stomach. "Use your strengths. Your hands are your best asset, but your legs are your best bet for keeping those fuckers from getting too close. You'll have to watch them carefully, read their faces, if you're going to use your kicks successfully without getting hurt."

Lucky nodded. It wasn't like he hadn't been told a million times to use his legs to keep an opponent at bay, but his past always clouded the advice. Even standing within the safety of the gym, the three-inch long, one-inch wide scar on his calf seemed to burn as he remembered a night that still seemed like it had happened yesterday. He turned his back on Dray and climbed out of the ring. "Be back," he said over his shoulder as he headed for the locker room.

Struggling to catch a breath, Lucky rushed into a stall. He shut the door and pressed a hand to his heaving chest. Normally, he'd have gone into the storage room, but Jax was still in bed due to the sore nature of his battered body. Alone, Lucky rested his sweaty forehead against the cool door and fought back the memories. It wasn't like a vicious attack by one of his mom's strung-out boyfriends had been unusual. Yet, for some reason, the beating and subsequent punishment had changed him more than any other.

Lucky awoke to the sound of his mom crying out in pain. He heard the loud voice of a man, and willed himself to be strong. He was only eight and way too small to go up against one of the junkies his mom had allowed into the house, but he couldn't listen to his mom's cries without doing something. He slowly crept from his bed and peered into the living room.

His mom was cowering in the corner with her hands held up defensively. Her whacked-out boyfriend landed another punch to her already battered face.

"Momma." Lucky charged toward the asshole beating her. He used all his strength to pound his small fists against the man's back, praying it would be enough to save his mom.

With a growl, the man reached back and grabbed a handful of Lucky's hair. "Piss off, you little bastard!"

The boyfriend flung Lucky across the room as if he were nothing more than a momentary distraction. Lucky landed with a thud, his head slamming against the wall. He stared up at the ceiling for several precious seconds while he tried to keep himself from passing out. His mom's screams came again, and Lucky knew the man wouldn't stop until he'd killed her.

Lucky used the wall to steady himself and slowly got to his feet. Tears began to run down his cheeks when he realized what he had to do. He knew the punishment for being a bad boy. Making his way into the kitchen, he accepted his fate. The important thing was saving his mom. He slid open the drawer and pulled out a serrated knife. Let it be sharp enough, *he prayed as he prepared himself to do the unthinkable.*

Armed, he took a deep breath before running as fast as he could toward his mom's boyfriend.

"Watch out, Carl!" his mom screamed and pointed to Lucky.

It was the first time Lucky had ever heard the man's name, and as he raised the knife over his head, he knew he'd never forget the betrayal he'd just been handed by his own mother.

The warning was enough for Carl to spin around and plow his fist into Lucky's face before the knife connected with Carl's dark skin.

The force of the punch knocked Lucky backward, landing him on his ass. He immediately pressed his cupped hand to his nose, knowing he'd get into trouble if he got blood on the already stained carpeting. He squeezed his eyes shut, willing himself not to cry because he knew it would only get him into more trouble.

When he felt a hand wrap around his ankle, he automatically kicked out, thinking it was Carl.

"You little fucker! What've I told you about kicking!" his mother yelled. "For that, we're going to teach you a lesson you'll never forget."

When the next part of the memory hit him, a soft sob forced its way out of his tortured throat.

"Lucky?" Dray's deep voice called from outside the stall.

Lucky wiped his hands down his face, trying to rid himself of the tears that had snuck up on him. "I'll be out in a minute." He turned and gathered a length of toilet paper to blow his nose. There was no way he could hide the fact he'd just been a crying pussy. Dray had obviously heard the sob that had escaped him.

After several minutes, Lucky took a deep breath and stepped out of the stall. He found Dray leaning against the closed locker room door, arms crossed over his chest and feet crossed at the ankles.

"It's locked," Dray announced, gesturing behind his back.

"I thought we might talk a minute about what's going on."

"Nothing's going on. I just needed a minute."

"Bullshit," Dray replied. "Something's bothering you."

"Just demons." Lucky glanced at the large clock on the wall. "We need to get ready to leave."

Dray didn't move. Instead, he opened his arms and waited.

It was the first time Dray had initiated any kind of romantic contact at the gym, and Lucky was more than surprised at the offered gesture of comfort. He stepped into Dray's embrace. "I can't talk about it," he said, trying to ward off further questions.

"Is it something I said?" Dray asked, running his hands up and down Lucky's back.

Lucky shook his head. "I told you, just demons from the past." He moved in for a kiss, sweeping his tongue between Dray's parted lips. He tried to lose himself in the moment of passion, tried to push the memories of his stoned mother helping her equally high boyfriend prove a point about kicking people. He tried to forget using toilet paper and Scotch tape to bandage a wound that should have been medically treated.

Dray broke the kiss and stared into Lucky's eyes. "Sure you're okay to fight?"

Lucky grinned. "Fighting's exactly what I need to do."

Dray licked his lips as he studied Lucky. "You know you can tell me anything, right? I won't judge you for your past."

Lucky did know that. "Yeah." The reason he couldn't tell Dray had nothing to do with trust. If people, including Brick and Dray, had any idea of what had gone on in his home growing up, they would think he was a fool for helping his mom throughout the years. With her getting out of prison soon, Lucky had no doubt he'd end up helping her again, and he didn't want the people he cared about most looking down on him for it.

* * * *

Dray knocked on the office door before stepping inside. He found Brick stretched out on the old sofa. "You feeling okay?"

Brick removed the wet washcloth from his face and glanced at Dray. "My stomach's acting up."

Dray noticed the trash can next to the couch and cocked his head to the side. Brick hadn't eaten enough to feed a bird, so he couldn't help but wonder what the older man had to even throw up. He stepped forward and, as much as he hated to, peered into the wastebasket. "Fuck!" He stumbled back and clasped a hand over his mouth as he fought to settle his own stomach. *Blood.* Fucking blood coated the scraps of paper in the trash. "Goddammit, Brick!"

Dray moved the can of blood and kneeled beside Brick. "We need to get you to the hospital."

Brick shook his head. "Lucky won't fight if he knows."

Dray didn't know which he wanted more, to strangle the old man or wrap his arms around him. He settled on pressing his forehead against Brick's temple. "You're a hell of a lot more important to Lucky than a fight."

"I'm going to be gone soon," Brick said. "Fighting's his future. I'm his past."

"Don't fucking start with that shit, Brick. If you continue to try and hide how bad you're feeling, you're not allowing Lucky the time he needs to prepare himself."

Brick stared up at Dray. "I was talking to a friend the other day about what'll happen at the end, and he said I needed to pray it doesn't get that far." He grabbed the front of Dray's T-shirt. "I want you to promise me you won't let me suffer."

It took a few moments for Dray to figure out what Brick was asking. When he did, he reared back. *Holy fuck.* His heart plummeted at what Brick had asked him to do. The nausea he'd felt earlier at the sight of the trash can returned in full force only for a much different reason. "You want me

146

to kill you?"

Brick shook his head. "No, I just want you to help me die."

"Just?" Dray fought to keep his anger under control. "No fucking way," he spat, getting to his feet. He'd seen firsthand with his uncle what happened in the days leading up to death, but even knowing what he did, he couldn't imagine helping Brick end his life. He pointed his finger at Brick. "And don't you fucking dare ask Lucky to help you either. It would destroy him, and you know it."

Brick turned his head, breaking eye contact. "I'm not going to the fight. Tell Lucky I'm tired or something, and remind him to listen to Flint."

Dray rubbed the heels of his hands against his eyes. As angry as he was, he couldn't ignore the fucking problem that sat in the can between him and Brick. "Will you let me take you to the hospital after he leaves?"

"Only long enough to get something for the throwing up," Brick said. "I'm not staying."

Dray headed for the office door. "I'll be back."

While searching for Lucky, Dray tried to calm himself. No way in hell would Lucky leave for a fight if he knew what was going on in Brick's office. He eventually found Lucky leaning against the doorframe of the storage room. "There you are."

Lucky glanced over his shoulder. "You looking for me?"

"Yeah. Brick's not feeling well, so I'm gonna take him back to the apartment." Dray put a hand on Lucky's shoulder. "He said to tell you to listen to Flint."

"He's not coming?" Lucky asked.

"Not for this one. I think he's overexerted himself." Dray couldn't meet Lucky's eyes because of the half-truth, so he looked around Lucky to Jax. "How're you feeling today?"

Jax shrugged. "Fine," he mumbled.

"Liar," Lucky said. He gestured to the sixteen year old. "He's so sore he can hardly move. I was offering to cook him some soup."

Jax pointed to his split lip that was so swollen he could barely open it. "Not eating."

"Don't worry about it," Dray soothed. "I'll get him to eat something before I take care of Brick. You just go and knock the fuck out of those assholes." He thought of the episode earlier in the locker room. The sounds he'd heard from behind the stall door had broken his heart. He didn't know what demons were plaguing Lucky or why, but their training session had sparked it. He'd gone over and over it, and he still hadn't figured it out. As wrong as it seemed, he knew the answer was the key to the darkness that had locked Lucky away for so many years. Against his better judgment, he pushed. "Remember what I told you. You have to kick as well as throw punches."

"I'll do what I have to do to win," Lucky growled before pushing by Dray.

Dray watched Lucky walk away. Even though he now knew the trigger, he still wasn't sure what it meant or what he could do about it.

* * * *

Head down, Lucky stared at his bruised and swollen knuckles as Flint drove him home. Although he'd won both fights, thus continuing in the tournament, the victories had felt hollower than ever. He wasn't sure if his earlier mood was still affecting him or if winning his first fight without Brick in his corner had soured the wins.

"You did good," Flint said, turning a corner. "Brick'll be proud of you."

"I guess," Lucky answered. Bottom line for Brick was winning, but Dray wasn't so easily pleased. Lucky knew Flint hadn't taken the time to shoot video, so, hopefully, Dray wouldn't know that Lucky hadn't kicked either of his opponents during either fight. He lifted his head to stare out of the passenger window. "Did Brick talk to you about training me after he's gone?"

"Yeah, he mentioned it, but I told him it wasn't his decision. It was yours." Flint double-parked in front of Lucky's building. "I know this thing with Brick's got your head out of it right now, but when you're ready, and if you want me, I'll be there."

Lucky liked Flint well enough, but he also thought the ex-fighter was unbelievably good with the young teenagers who came into The Brick Yard for lessons. "The problem is, if I pull you away from your young homies, they'll hunt me down and kick my ass. Flint style," he added.

"I might be able to do both," Flint argued. "Anyway, the offer's out there if you need me."

Lucky opened the car door. "See ya later."

"Yeah, see ya," Flint called out through the open window as Lucky crossed the sidewalk.

Lucky used his key and entered the building without looking back even though he knew Flint was waiting to make sure he made it safely inside. Lucky bypassed the temperamental elevator and hiked up the stairs to his apartment. Letting himself in, he whistled for Gatsby, but his four-legged friend didn't come. "Dray?" he called, taking off his sweatshirt.

When he received no answer, he continued to the bedroom. He needed a shower, but before he gave in to his desire to wash the sweat and blood from his body, he opened his gym bag and called Dray.

"Hey," Dray answered, his voice soft and low.

"You upstairs?" Lucky toed off his athletic shoes.

"Yeah. You home?"

"Just getting ready to hop into the shower. Want me to leave the door unlocked?" Lucky pushed his warm-up pants and underwear to the floor.

"Ummm," Dray began. He sighed deeply. "Why don't you come up after your shower instead?"

The odd request put Lucky on edge. "Why? How's Brick?"

"He's asleep, but he's still not feeling well, so I don't want to go far."

Lucky wondered how one flight down could be considered far unless Dray was truly concerned that Brick might need something and not be able to call out, because so far the baby monitor had worked perfectly. He looked down at his chest. As much as he wanted to run up to see what was really going on with Brick, he couldn't do it without washing first. "I'll be up in ten minutes."

"See you then." Dray hung up without another word.

Lucky stared at his phone. More worried than ever, he wasted no time in the shower. Lately, Dray had ended all their calls with the same phrase, "Can't wait to see you." What had changed, he wondered?

He continued to stew over Dray's parting words as he dressed in an old, comfortable pair of gray sweatpants and a faded red Brick Yard T-shirt. He slipped on a pair of flip-flops before running upstairs to Brick's apartment. He tried the doorknob, but found it locked. He knocked softly, trying not to wake Brick.

The door opened to a disheveled-looking Dray. The pale-green eyes that had always drawn Lucky's attention appeared to be slightly swollen and red-rimmed as if he'd been crying.

Lucky knew Dray wasn't the kind of man who cried without a damn good reason. Fear filled him as he looked around Dray to Brick's empty chair. "You okay?" Lucky followed Dray into the living room, wondering what had happened.

Dray sank onto the couch and picked up a beer. "I had to take Brick to the ER. They pumped some fluids and anti-nausea medicine into him, but he refused to let them keep him."

Lucky looked toward the closed bedroom door. He dropped down beside Dray. "What'd they say?"

Dray bit his lower lip as his eyes filled with tears. He swallowed several times. "He's got a week. Maybe two." He shook his head. "He was vomiting blood, but that seems to have stopped for the moment. More important, he's not eating."

"He's giving up?" Lucky asked, his own eyes starting to water.

Dray scooted closer and wrapped his arms around Lucky. "It's not that he's giving up. It's part of the process. One of the last stages. The hospital thinks it's time we called hospice."

Lucky pulled away from Dray and sprang to his feet. "They're wrong. I just talked to him today, and he seemed weaker but not on his deathbed."

Dray stood and walked toward Lucky. "He's not leaving us tomorrow," he said, no doubt trying to soothe him. "We just need to really prepare for it."

Lucky took a step back. His short nails bit into his palms when he clenched his hands into bruising fists. He felt like someone had lit a match to his temper as sweat began to drip down his face. "Stop." He wasn't angry with Dray, but a rage he hadn't felt in years was building within him. After another glance at Brick's door, he turned his back on Dray. "I'm sorry, but I need to go."

"Don't." Dray grabbed Lucky's shoulder in an attempt to still him. "You need to talk about what you're feeling. Running away isn't the way to handle this." He stepped closer and started to wrap his arm around Lucky's waist.

"I know you're trying to help, but I need to do this on my own. At least for now." His anger was palpable and the last thing he needed was for it to spill over onto Dray.

Dray kissed Lucky's neck. "Take your phone with you and call if you need me."

"I'll stop by my apartment and grab the phone, but you probably won't hear from me tonight," Lucky said before pulling away to open the door.

Chapter Nine

After checking Lucky's apartment, Dray drove the few blocks to the gym. The last time he'd been upset, Lucky had gone to The Brick Yard to work off his anger. Dray prayed that was where he'd find him because other than home or work, he didn't know where else Lucky went when he was troubled.

He let himself in through the back door and started turning on lights. It was nearly seven in the morning anyway, the usual time Brick opened the place. He searched the gym, Brick's office, the locker room and finally, he opened the storage room door.

Jax was sitting in a chair beside the twin-size bed where Lucky was stretched out. He quickly put his finger to his battered lip and got to his feet. He motioned for Dray to precede him out of the room.

Dray nodded in acknowledgment, but before leaving, he moved closer to Lucky. He swallowed the bile rising in his throat at the sight of the man he'd grown to care so deeply for. There were two nasty-looking cuts on the right side of Lucky's face—one above his eye and one on his cheekbone—but it wasn't just the lacerations that disturbed Dray. The entire right half of Lucky's face was bruised and swollen. He glanced back toward Jax with a questioning expression. He'd seen Lucky after his fight the previous night and knew the injuries hadn't been sustained in the cage.

Jax, once again, pointed toward the open area of the gym.

Tearing himself away from Lucky, Dray followed Jax. "What the hell happened to him?"

"I don't know," Jax said. "I heard someone banging on the front door." He swallowed several times. "I thought my dad had found me, so I snuck out of my room to use the phone in Brick's office, but then I heard someone calling my name." He glanced up at Dray. "My dad never uses my name, so I knew it wasn't him."

"It was Lucky," Dray surmised.

"Yeah, I unlocked the door and helped him inside." Jax shook his head. "He was really drunk and bleeding." He took a deep breath, no doubt remembering the episode. "I wanted to call you, but he wouldn't let me. He kept saying bad boys get what they deserve." Tears filled his eyes. "I thought he was talking about me, but then he started going on about his mom and Brick and how Brick was going to die because Lucky didn't deserve anything good in his life."

Dray pulled Jax into his arms, more for himself than to soothe the younger man. "It'll be okay. Lucky's having a hard time dealing with Brick's cancer." He pressed his cheek to the side of Jax's head. He wondered who'd given Lucky the beating. More importantly, why had Lucky allowed it?

Jax pushed against Dray's chest. "I can't breathe."

Shit. Dray hadn't realized how tight his hold had become. He released Jax. "Why don't you run down to Mac's and get something to eat while I see what I can do for Lucky?" He dug a few bills out of his pocket and handed them over.

"You don't hafta…" Jax began.

"Take it." Dray withdrew a twenty and handed that over as well. "Bring Lucky and me back one of Mac's ham-and-cheese omelets and a double order of wheat toast." He glanced at the storage room. "I'll make a pot of coffee and try to sober Lucky up before you get back."

Jax looked like he wanted to say something more, but turned toward the door. He simply nodded and walked away.

Dray went to Brick's office to make coffee. He thought about Brick back at the apartment, and Lucky in the storage room. Knowing he couldn't be in two different places at the same time, he pulled out his phone.

"Yeah?" Flint answered.

"It's Dray. I need you to swing by the apartment and stay with Brick for a few hours." He carried the coffee pot to the locker room.

"Of course. What's up?"

Dray wasn't sure how much to tell Flint, but he decided Flint had a right to know about Brick's condition. "I took him to the emergency room last night. It's not good. I'm going to call hospice today and see what can be done to make him more comfortable."

"Shit." Flint sighed. "Fuck!"

Yeah, Dray knew exactly how Flint felt. He rinsed and filled the pot while Flint continued to digest the information. "Anyway," he began when Flint took a break from cussing. "I need you to go over there while I deal with a situation here at the gym."

"What's up at the gym?" Flint asked.

Dray scraped his teeth across his bottom lip. Although Flint had a right to know what was going on with Lucky too, he hated to betray Lucky's trust. "Lucky's not dealing with Brick's condition very well," he settled on. He realized he hadn't even asked Lucky how the matches the previous night had turned out. "When does he fight again?"

"Tomorrow," Flint replied. "That crazy sonofabitch knocked out both opponents in the first round last night."

From what he'd seen of Lucky's face, Dray wasn't certain Lucky would be able to continue in the tournament. He'd keep the information to himself until he'd had a chance to assess Lucky's condition. Pouring the water in the machine, he set the coffee to brew. "You'll need to swing by and get a key."

"Yeah, no problem. I'm on my way out the door now."

"Thanks." After hanging up, Dray shoved the phone back into his pocket as he held a cup under the dripping brew. The moment the cup was full, he did a quick switch with the pot. Coffee in hand, he went to the storage room.

Taking the chair beside Lucky's bed, Dray set the cup on the small table. He reached out and brushed his fingertips over the worst of the bruises on Lucky's face. The skin was swollen, scraped and an intense shade of purple. "Lucky?" As much as he hated to wake the sleeping man, he had to make sure Lucky didn't need to go to the hospital. The beating he'd taken had been bad.

Lucky groaned and rolled away from Dray.

"Lucky?" Dray tried again. "I need you to wake up and look at me."

"No," Lucky finally answered, pulling the blanket over his head.

"I brought you a cup of coffee." Dray struggled with what to say. "Who did that to you, and why the hell did ya let 'em?"

When Lucky didn't reply, Dray growled his frustration. The noise that erupted from Dray's throat did what words couldn't. Lucky rolled to his back and lowered the blanket. "I'm fine. Sore and hungover, but I'll live." He seemed to realize what he'd said and closed his eyes. "Fuck. I can't believe it's happening." He opened his eyes again and stared at Dray. "I don't want to continue the tournament. With training and the fights, I'll be so busy, I won't have time to be with Brick."

Dray swallowed around the thick lump of emotion lodged in his throat. He nodded in understanding. "You want me to call Bruno?"

"You don't need to. I told him last night," Lucky admitted. "As I suspected, he didn't take the news well."

Dray automatically curled his hands into fists as he got to his feet. "Bruno's thugs did that to you?" The thought of Lucky being beaten by the five no-necked giants that guarded Bruno sent Dray into a tailspin. "I'm gonna fucking kill him."

"No." Lucky started to shake his head but winced and settled back down. "This happened later."

"How?" Dray was starting to lose patience.

"Doesn't matter now." Lucky placed his palm on his forehead before slowly sitting up. "Fuck." He blinked several times. "I could use that coffee and about twenty aspirin."

Dray left the room and quickly retrieved a bottle of pain relievers and the first-aid kit from Brick's office. He was torn between backing off and getting more answers. Even if he didn't question Lucky further on who'd hurt him, there was one answer he had to have. Dray returned to the storage room. He sat on the edge of the mattress beside Lucky and held out the bottle. "Why'd you come here instead of home to me?"

Lucky scowled. "It wasn't that I didn't want to be with you." He reached for his coffee. After taking more aspirin than was necessary, he gazed around the room. "This is my safe place. Always has been." He lifted the cup to his lips, looking contemplative. Lowering his coffee, he stared at Dray. "I didn't come to you last night because I knew you'd try to make me feel better, and I didn't want to feel better. I've got a lot of bad shit in my head right now, and I don't wanna do or say something that'll make you think less of me."

Dray eased the cup out of Lucky's hand and set it aside. "I've told you, there's nothing you can tell me that'll make me think less of you. I understand you have demons—we all do—and I'm not going to guilt you into sharing them with me, but I need you to know that monsters are only scary until you turn on the light."

Lucky's eyebrows drew together. He was obviously thinking about what Dray had said. "Thanks," he mumbled. "Maybe someday."

Dray opened the first-aid kit. "You need some butterfly bandages on those cuts, and we'll have to think of something to tell Brick."

* * * *

"Damn," Brick wheezed when Lucky stepped into the apartment. "I thought Flint said you won both fights?"

"I did." Lucky sat on the couch across from Brick's recliner. He nodded an acknowledgment at Flint, who was sitting on the opposite end of the sofa. "Flint did a good job."

"Yeah? So why the hell do you look like you've been run over?" Brick asked before a coughing fit overtook him.

Lucky winced at the wet sound of Brick's breathing as his gaze slid to the oxygen tank half-hidden behind Brick's chair. "One of the bastards fought dirty." He hoped Brick believed him. No way could he tell Brick what had really happened. "Does he need that?" He looked at Flint and pointed to the tank.

"He's got the mask tucked beside him. He'll use it if he needs to bad enough," Flint explained.

Brick lifted a trash can and spit into its depths. "I'm fine," he growled when he caught Lucky staring at him. "Now let's talk about your face."

"I'm fine." Although Lucky would rather have told Brick the news in private, he knew he'd have to eventually discuss it with Flint anyway. "I've decided not to go on with the tournament. I don't like the way it's being run. Bruno's got featherweights matched up against heavyweights." It wasn't the truth, of course, but telling Brick he was going to quit because he wanted to spend more time with him wouldn't have gone over well. He knew Brick wanted to see him win, but from the sound of things, Brick may not even be alive by the time the tournament came to an end. Losing the last days with Brick for nothing wasn't something he was willing to do.

"But you've got a real chance at winning," Brick argued.

"I also have a real shot at getting seriously hurt," Lucky countered. "I think I'd rather take a few weeks off. I'll get back into the regulated fights once you're better."

Brick's eyes filled with tears. "You know I'm not going to get better, son, don't you?"

Throat tight, Lucky couldn't believe Brick had called him son. He glanced at Flint to find he and Brick weren't the only ones in the room trying to swallow tears. "We'll see," he finally replied. "In the meantime, Dray and I'll take turns sitting with you and running the gym."

"I can help, too," Flint cut in. "With Jax there to clean up, one person can handle the actual running of the place."

"Thanks." Lucky would have to look into the financial stability of the gym. Brick had owned the place since the sixties, so, unless he'd taken out a second mortgage, he was positive it was free and clear, but he needed to know what the profit margin was. He'd like to start paying Jax a better salary so the kid could get an apartment or save for college if he decided to go. He sat back on the couch. There were so many things he needed to think about without allowing the ghosts from his past to interfere.

Brick slowly got to his feet. "I'm gonna go lie down for a while."

Lucky started to get up to help, but a quick, subtle shake of Flint's head told him to stay where he was. He waited for Brick to disappear into his room and shut the door before turning to Flint. "What?"

"He doesn't want help. Believe me. I got my ass chewed earlier for offering to get him a glass of that vitamin supplement shit the doctor said he should drink." Flint rubbed his palms back and forth over his knees. "What's the real reason you're dropping the tournament? Is it Brick—or whoever did that to your face?"

"Brick," Lucky confirmed. "I don't doubt I could win, but at what cost?" He shook his head. "I'd rather spend the time with that old fucker in the next room. There'll be other tournaments."

"So what's the real story on your face?" Flint asked.

Lucky shook his head again. "Just a fight."

Flint stretched his arms over his head and yawned. "You gonna be here long? I think I'll run over to the gym and give Dray a break."

Lucky was dead on his feet. "Yeah. I'll stretch out here on the couch and try to get some more sleep."

Flint stood and mussed Lucky's hair. "Call me if you need anything, even if it's just to talk."

"Sure." Lucky had known Flint for years, but the two of them had never been close. Still, looking up at the brown-haired man, Lucky felt something stir in his chest. Maybe by the end of the whole shitty ordeal, he could count Flint as a friend. It felt good, especially since his friends seemed to be dropping like flies recently.

* * * *

Dray pushed a small cart up and down the aisles of the drugstore as he waited for one of Brick's prescriptions, which was bullshit. No way should it take them thirty minutes to fill the fucking thing. He knew pharmacy techs prolonged the wait just to make customers do exactly what he was doing.

He stopped the cart in front of a display of toys and grinned. Unable to resist, he grabbed the colorful box and put it in his cart among the other crap he didn't really need, except the chocolate-covered cherries. Those he needed.

"Refill for Tony Brick is ready," a voice said over the speakers.

Dray made his way to the back of the store, stopping only to put a giant plastic container of peppermint puff ball thingies into his cart.

The cashier at the pharmacy desk stared down her nose at Dray's cart of shit. "You'll have to pay for that up front."

Dray rolled his eyes. "Whatever." He handed the woman money for the high blood pressure medicine, one of Brick's routine medications.

The clerk glanced at his cart again. "You have kids?"

Dray looked at his haul. "No," he replied sheepishly. He understood why she thought that, but almost everything in his cart was meant to make Lucky smile. He accepted his change and shoved the small white pharmacy bag into his coat pocket before pushing his merchandise to the front counter to wait in yet another line.

By the time he'd left the store and picked up dinner, it was almost eight o'clock. He could've made the trip much quicker if he hadn't been so picky about his pizza. The small pizzeria was outside the neighborhood, but well worth driving the extra few miles. Unlike most people in Chicago, Dray didn't care for deep-dish pizza. Nope. He liked thin-crusted, brick-oven-baked pizza. He wasn't sure which Lucky preferred, but hopefully Lucky would be so hungry he wouldn't care.

Dray let himself into Lucky's apartment. He turned on the light and set the pizza and beer on the coffee table before going back down to the truck for the other goodies he'd purchased at the drugstore. He stashed the sacks next to the dresser that held the television. Pulling out his phone, he texted Lucky.

Hey. Is Brick in bed?

Yeah. Just a few minutes ago. Where R U?

Dray grinned. *Downstairs.*

I'll find Gatsby and be down.

Dray set his phone on the counter and put the twelve-pack of beer in the refrigerator. He was in the process of plating the pizza when the door opened. Lucky came into the apartment, looking worn out, bruised and without his furry friend. "Where's Gatsby?"

Lucky dropped his keys onto the coffee table. "She's curled up beside Brick." He sighed. "Do animals know when people are sick?"

"Sure. I think they smell it or something." Dray carried the plates into the living room. "Want a beer?"

Lucky made a face and shook his head. "Water's fine for

me." He toed his shoes off and set them inside the bedroom while Dray retrieved a bottle of water and a beer from the fridge. "When I went into Brick's room to look for Gatsby, Brick had his oxygen mask on."

Dray paused in the process of handing Lucky his water. He hadn't been to Brick's place since he'd left earlier that morning. Although he'd spoken to the hospice nurse and she'd told him she'd arranged for the delivery of two oxygen tanks, he hadn't thought Brick would use them. "Is he sleeping better?"

"Yeah, seems like it." Lucky set the baby monitor on the coffee table before joining Dray on the couch. "I'm still not sure if I trust this thing. If I don't hear him in the next twenty minutes or so, I'll have to go back up and check on him." He reached for a slice. "Thanks for the pizza. I'm starving."

Dray noticed how Lucky had purposely sat on the right side of the sofa so the bruised half of his face was hidden from Dray's view. "Good. Eat up."

Lucky took a bite and moaned. "Fuck, that's good."

Grinning, Dray started to open his beer but changed his mind at the last moment. He stood, put the bottle back into the refrigerator and removed a bottle of water. It was obvious Lucky wasn't drinking because he'd had too much the previous night, but Dray knew it would be all too easy for both of them to fall into the habit of getting drunk every night to deal with the pain of Brick's illness.

"You don't have to do that," Lucky said when Dray sat back down.

"I might want to kiss you later." Dray shrugged.

Lucky leaned over and kissed Dray's neck. "I'd like that." He sat back. "As long as you don't mind looking at my ugly mug."

Dray still wanted to know how the beating had happened and by whom, but he wouldn't push. He grinned. "You'll heal."

"For now," Lucky said. "I got a call from Bruno. He's still pissed that I'm pulling out of the tournament, something about screwing up the odds."

"You think Bruno will come after you?" Dray wouldn't put it past the asshole to make an example out of Lucky.

"Don't know. Don't care." Lucky moved his head from side to side, brushing his lips across Dray's neck as he spoke.

Dray hadn't wanted Lucky in the tournament to begin with, but he knew Lucky needed to do something other than sit at Brick's bedside watching him deteriorate. "You'll still need to keep up with your training."

"It'll wait." Lucky pressed his face against Dray's neck.

"You, of all people should know that's not true. At least go into the gym for a few hours a day to keep your stamina up. You being in Brick's face all the time isn't going to do either of you any good."

"Fine," Lucky mumbled.

Dray dropped the subject and tilted his head to the side when Lucky began to lick the tattoo that inched above the neckline of his T-shirt. "You know, there are some people who're turned off by my ink."

"Yeah, crazy people," Lucky murmured. "You've always been the sexiest man I've ever known."

Pizza forgotten, Dray sat back on the couch and pulled Lucky into his arms. "I have something for you."

"You do?" Lucky moved to straddle Dray's lap. He wiggled his ass. "Is it big?" he asked.

Dray rested his hands on Lucky's hips. *Christ.* It would be so easy to lower his zipper, push down Lucky's sweats and plow the sweet ass that tormented him. He took several deep breaths and reminded himself they had all night to fuck. Before that, though, he wanted to hear Lucky laugh. Stupid maybe, but he truly believed laughter could heal wounds medicine couldn't.

Lucky continued grinding his ass against Dray's hardening cock.

Despite his body crying foul, Dray did his best to still Lucky's hips. "You'll get that present later. First, I wanna have some fun. I want to see you smile."

"Oh, we'll have fun." Lucky reached down and pulled Dray's T-shirt up over his head and off.

Dray closed his eyes as he gave himself over to Lucky's touch. He loved the feel of Lucky's fingers as they ran over his abs and through the short hair on his chest. *Damn. I'm a weak sonofabitch.*

Lucky reached for Dray's zipper and slowly began to lower it. "I want to suck you." He licked Dray's left pec, running the flat of his tongue across the empty patch of skin. "I wanna taste your cum in my mouth."

Hell yeah. Dray lifted his hips when Lucky tugged on the soft denim waistband. His plan to force fun on Lucky went out the fucking window for the moment.

Lucky pushed the coffee table back before sliding off the couch. "This" — he ran his tongue over the crown of Dray's erection — "is the only thing that got me through the day."

Holding his cock by the base, Dray painted Lucky's lips with pre-cum. "Me too," he agreed, loving the way his slick desire made Lucky's lips glisten. It wasn't the entire truth, but he knew it was what Lucky needed to hear. For him, sex with Lucky was a product of simply being around him. He didn't spend time with Lucky just to get him into bed. Although sex with Lucky was better than anything he'd ever had, he'd found it soothing that he could let his guard down around him. He'd built a fortress around his heart after the Vince fiasco, and he welcomed the chipping of the stone Lucky accomplished each time they were together.

Lucky sucked Dray's length into his mouth and for the next several minutes, Dray could think of nothing but the warmth that surrounded him. Lucky backed off and kissed his way down Dray's dick to his balls.

"Fuck," Dray groaned when Lucky began sucking on his sac. He allowed Lucky time to play and tease him, but eventually, Dray's body demanded more. He gently pushed Lucky away from his balls before guiding his dick back to Lucky's mouth. "Suck it."

Lucky wrapped his lips around Dray's length.

"Suck me deeper," Dray growled, thrusting up into Lucky's mouth. The contractions of Lucky's throat as he gagged sent a shiver up Dray's spine. The squeeze to his cock nearly toppled him over the edge. "Fuck, yeah."

Lucky looked up at Dray and nodded, silently asking for more.

Dray gave it to him. He held Lucky's head still and began to fuck in and out, feeding a bit more down Lucky's throat with each thrust. Lucky gagged several more times, but eventually took Dray's length like a pro. "Fuck! I can't…" he panted. His entire body vibrated as he fought like hell to hold on, but it was a losing battle. "I'm coming." The first volley of cum shot from his dick with so much force, Lucky had to back off. Dray watched as he filled Lucky's mouth with his seed. He groaned when a small amount of cum escaped Lucky's lips and dripped down his chin.

Lucky pulled back and wiped a hand over his chin, a wide grin on his swollen lips. "That was intense."

Dray ran his hand up and down his chest several times as he studied Lucky. "Stand up," he ordered, wanting to give Lucky the same attention he'd just received.

It wasn't until Lucky stood that Dray noticed the cum splattered on Lucky's stomach and chest. "Fuck." Dray ran his fingers through the milky-white fluid. He glanced up at Lucky. "You enjoyed that more than I thought."

"I love touching you," Lucky confessed, looking embarrassed.

Dray licked a path through a rope of seed and groaned as Lucky's taste exploded on his tongue. He greedily cleaned Lucky's skin until there was nothing left. "Best. Dinner. Ever," he proclaimed.

* * * *

After a quick shower, Lucky entered the living room to find Dray sitting cross-legged on the floor with his back against the couch. "Brick okay?"

"Yeah. When I went up to check on him, he was sleeping with his oxygen mask on, so he must've given in at some point. I put the monitor next to his bed, and I heard him coughing a few minutes ago, so that's working okay."

"Good." Lucky moved closer. On the coffee table in front of Dray sat a game that brought tears to Lucky's eyes. "That's…" He swallowed around the lump in his throat and tried again to get the words out. "That's Rock 'em Sock 'em Robots."

"Yeah." Dray continued to fiddle with setting up the childish game. "I thought maybe you could take your frustrations out on this since you won't be fighting for the next few weeks." He secured the red robot's head into place.

Lucky dropped down on the opposite side of the table. "I remember seeing these in the store when I was younger." His gaze flicked to Dray. "I don't know how to play though."

"It's not hard. Just follow my lead." Dray grabbed the plastic controller and placed his thumbs on the buttons. "You just try to knock my head off," he said as he started pushing the buttons in succession. Within moments, the blue head of Lucky's robot popped up. "Get it?"

Lucky nodded and mimicked Dray's hand position. He chuckled as the excitement shot through him. "When I was in school, I heard kids talking about this game, but I never thought I'd actually get to play it."

"On the count of three. Ready?" Dray asked, grinning.

"Yeah." Lucky's heart beat faster as he waited. The second he heard the word three, he came out swinging, working his thumbs as fast as he could. It was over too quickly when both heads sprang up.

"That's it?" Dray stared at the bobbing heads. "I thought it'd be a lot more fun."

Lucky agreed, but he didn't want to say that. The fact Dray had purchased the game meant more than the game ever would. As far back as he could remember, he'd never been given a toy as a gift. "Probably is to six or seven year olds."

Dray crossed his arms over his bare chest and shook his head. "That sucks." He got to his feet and went to the sacks beside the TV. Carrying one of the bags to the sofa, Dray sat back down. "Let's see, we have Battleship, a deck of cards, Super Elastic Bubble Plastic or Silly String." He looked up and waggled his eyebrows. "And a shitload of candy." He dumped the sack on the floor. "Take your pick."

"The bubble thing first," Lucky answered, getting excited all over again. He reached for a can of Silly String. "I'm gonna take this to the gym with me tomorrow and sneak up on Jax when he's in the laundry room." He chuckled. "I can't wait to see his face."

Dray held up two packages. "Which color do you want? I've got purple or red."

"Purple," Lucky replied, reaching for it. He turned the package over and stared at the illustrated directions before ripping it open. Following the instructions, he squeezed a glob of black-looking goo onto the end of the short straw and blew as hard as he could. The goo shot off his straw and landed on Dray's upper chest. "Oops."

With a shake of his head, Dray smiled and picked the glob off his skin. "I don't think you're supposed to blow that hard."

"Give me a break. I've never done this," Lucky said, adding more goo to the end of his straw. His second attempt was better, but the bubble barely reached the size of a dime before it popped and deflated.

Dray made a noise, and Lucky looked up to see a bubble the size of a plum at the end of Dray's straw.

"You suck." Lucky returned his attention to his own straw. He may have to go through the entire tube, but he was going to fucking make a goddamn bubble if it killed him.

"On occasion," Dray replied. He eased the bubble off his straw, sealed it, then set it on the table.

Show off. Lucky eyed the bubble. He gestured to the sack

still next to the TV. "What else did ya get?"

"Just stupid movies out of the clearance bin. Comedies. I thought we could use some mindless fun in the next week or so." Dray loaded another blob to his straw.

Lucky concentrated on his own bubble creation. He blew a steady stream of air into the straw and as his bubble expanded excitement filled him. He began to tap his free hand against the table to get Dray's attention. When he looked up, he realized he hadn't needed the thumping. Dray was staring straight at him. Not the bubble at the end of his straw, but him. Deciding not to press his luck, Lucky stopped blowing when his creation was a tad larger than Dray's. He eased it off the plastic tube and carefully sealed it. "There," he said with a hint of arrogance.

Dray clapped his hands three times. "You're the champ."

"Yes I am." Lucky got to his feet and danced back and forth from foot to foot with his arms raised in the air.

"If you get cocky, we'll end up spending the rest of the night seeing who can outdo the other," Dray said. He smiled. "But I do love to see you in a good mood, so losing's worth it."

"Okay, so if we played Battleship next and I plastered a smile on my face the whole time, you'd let me win?" Lucky asked.

"I didn't say that. I just said it's worth losing to see you happy."

Lucky's smile fell as he felt the emotion behind Dray's statement. He dropped the straw to the table and moved around to stand beside Dray. Holding out his hand, he waited for Dray to take the offered gesture. Neither of them talked about their feelings, but he realized that everything Dray had done that evening was proclaiming the way he felt, loud and clear. The pizza, the candy, the games and the movies were meant to convey what Dray couldn't say, and Lucky had finally heard him. "Come to bed with me."

Dray looked toward the ceiling. "First, I should check on Brick again." He took Lucky's offered hand and got to his feet. "You wanna come?"

Lucky nodded. The more he saw Brick in his weakened condition, the more real the predicted outcome became. The first time he'd watched Brick bring the oxygen mask to his face when he'd thought Lucky hadn't been in the room had been gut-wrenching. Dray had tried to tell him Brick was sicker than he was pretending, but Lucky hadn't believed it. In that moment, however, when he'd watched Brick desperately struggle to draw in a full breath, he'd known the truth. The man who had given him the only parental love he'd ever known was leaving him.

Chapter Ten

"This is getting old!" Jax wailed.

Lucky was still laughing when he dropped the empty can of Silly String in the trashcan. It was the third time in a week and a half that he'd managed to sneak up on Jax for an attack. "Hang on," he told Jax. "Let me get a picture of you." He withdrew his phone, but Jax charged toward him.

"Don't you dare!" Jax yelled, trying to get to Lucky's phone.

"Nope." Lucky easily evaded the sixteen year old.

Covered from head to toe in bright pink strands of foam, Jax gave up and began to pull the shit out of his hair. "I hope you know you're cleaning up this mess," Jax pouted.

"I'll clean it up. I always do." Lucky snapped several pictures of Jax. He would never forget the look of surprise on Jax's face the first time he'd snuck into the laundry room and hit him with the initial blast of the pink string. At first he'd thought Jax was pissed, but soon they'd both been laughing their asses off.

"Hey, Lucky," Flint called from the doorway.

"You gotta see these," Lucky said, holding up his phone.

Flint smiled at the photos as Lucky scrolled through. "There's a woman here to see you. Says she's your mother."

Lucky's entire mood changed from one breath to the next. *No. No. No.* He wanted to scream to the world that he wasn't ready to deal with his mom's typical bullshit. Not yet. Not now. He considered sneaking out the back door of the gym, but he knew if she wanted something from him, she wouldn't stop until she got it. "Where is she?"

"Standing by the front door." Flint wiped the sweat off

his forehead with the back of his hand. "You want me to tell her you left?"

Lucky shook his head. He didn't want to lie to her, but he wouldn't taint The Brick Yard either. "I'll be at Mac's if anyone needs me."

"Are you sure?" Flint asked. "You don't look so good, man."

"She won't leave until she gets what she's come for." Lucky pulled out his wallet and checked to see how much money he had. Not much, but he'd give her all of it if she'd go away. He glanced back at Jax, who was still picking pink strands off his shirt. "Sorry, but it might be a while before I can clean this up."

Jax bit his bottom lip and looked around. "Don't worry. I'll do it."

Lucky turned to leave the room, but Jax stopped him.

"You want me to come with you?" Jax asked.

Lucky wanted to say yes because nothing good ever happened when he was alone with his mom, but he couldn't drag Jax into his bullshit. He walked back over and gave Jax's forehead a quick peck. "Thanks, but I don't want you anywhere near her."

Lucky spotted his mom from across the gym. It never ceased to amaze him how small she actually was now that he was grown. As a kid, the sight of her looming over him with anger in her eyes had scared the shit out of him. Dray spoke of demons and monsters, but it was his own mother's face that haunted Lucky's nightmares.

The closer he got to his mom, the more different she looked. She seemed to hold herself straighter and her eyes appeared normal. Her fiery red hair was clean and pulled back into a ponytail.

"Mom," Lucky said once he was close enough. He still wasn't sure why he bothered calling the woman *mom* since she'd never been a real mother, but calling her by her given name of Alana seemed wrong as well.

"I wanted to come by and let you know I'm out and to

apologize for not seeing you when you came to visit. I've been working a program, and I wanted to make sure I could stay clean before I saw you again," Alana said. She took a step toward Lucky and lifted her palm to his face. "What have you done to yourself?"

Lucky pulled his head back, breaking the connection between them. "Are you hungry?"

Alana nodded.

Lucky opened the door of the gym and gestured for his mom to turn left. They walked to Mac's in silence. Once they were seated in his regular booth, he felt more at ease. He hadn't been in Mac's since the argument about Dray, but at that moment, he needed the comfort of the diner more than he needed to hold on to the anger he felt toward its owner. "Order whatever you want."

Alana began to scan the menu. "I'm staying at a halfway house. Hopefully, I'll be able to make the transition this time without slipping back into my old ways."

"That's good, Mom." Lucky sat with his back to the wall, thrumming his fingers on the table.

Connie, one of the lunch-hour waitresses, stopped at the table. "Hey, Lucky." She glanced up from her tablet. "Wow. I take it you finally lost a fight?"

Lucky didn't bother answering the question. "I'll have a double bacon cheeseburger, fries and a Coke."

"Really?" Connie's jaw dropped. "I've never known you to order anything off the menu."

Lucky shrugged. "Trying something different." He didn't tell her that after the fight he'd had with Mac, he doubted the owner would want to cook him his usual meal of steak and grilled vegetables.

Connie looked to Alana. "What can I get you?"

"I'll have the hot beef sandwich with mashed potatoes and a glass of water," Alana said before replacing her menu.

After Connie had left, Alana started talking again. "Anyway, I'll be at the halfway house for another two months. Hopefully, I'll be able to get a job and find another apartment."

Lucky continued to nod, but he looked everywhere except at his mom. It wasn't that he didn't believe she would stay clean for a change, he simply found he didn't care. No, that wasn't completely true. The more Alana talked about making a new life for herself, the angrier he became.

A plate landed in front of him with a clatter.

Lucky's gaze shot up to see Mac's scowling face.

"What the fuck're you doing eating that shit?" Mac asked.

"You made it. You calling your own food shit?" Lucky asked. Even to himself he sounded like a smart-ass teenager.

Mac leaned against the table and put his face a few inches from Lucky's. "You know what I'm talking about," he growled.

Lucky flicked his fingers toward Alana. "Mac, I'd like you to meet Alana Gunn, my mother. Mom, this is Mac, the man who made sure I didn't go to bed hungry when there was nothing in our house to eat because you'd bartered the food stamps for booze and drugs." He said it in a rush before pushing Mac out of his way. He dug into his wallet and pulled out every bill he had and tossed them on the table. "Take the cost of the meal out of it and keep the rest," he told his mom.

Lucky had just made it outside when a large hand clamped onto his shoulder. He spun around to find Mac staring at him. "I'm not in the mood."

"Yeah, I figured that out all on my own." Mac released his hold on Lucky. "Does your mood have something to do with your mom showing up?"

Lucky rolled his eyes. "What do you think? She's going on and on about being clean and how her life is going to be so much different now. Hell, she even said something about getting a fucking job that didn't involve her spreading her legs or dealing dope to schoolkids." His throat started to tighten but he forced the anguish down. His mom didn't deserve his tears.

Mac's expression softened. "I think the best thing you can

do is to wish her well and send her on her way."

"Yeah." Lucky looked through the window to see his mom calmly eating her lunch. "I want to hate her."

"Of course you do." Mac waved Lucky to the side of the building. "I think it's time we talked about a few things."

"Don't you need to cook?" Lucky wasn't looking forward to another talk with Mac. The last one had nearly destroyed him.

Mac continued to walk until they reached the back of the diner. He motioned for Lucky to have a seat on one of the old milk crates as he sat on another. Forearms resting on his knees, Mac leaned forward and stared at the crumbling asphalt under his feet. "I had a son," he began.

That announcement caught Lucky's attention. "Had?"

Mac nodded. "I was a shitty father—too young, I suppose. I didn't marry his mom because the thought of being tied down didn't appeal to me." He took off the white knit hat he always wore and crumpled it in his hands. "I saw Jimmy from time to time, nothing that he could count on, mind ya, but I was around." He glanced up and met Lucky's gaze. "He joined a gang when he was thirteen. His mom tried to tell me that it was my responsibility to set him straight, but I was too busy fucking up my own life to give him advice. I figured he'd grow out of the thug way of life eventually, but he didn't make it that far. He was killed in a drive-by a month before his fifteenth birthday."

"Shit," Lucky mumbled.

"I didn't tell you so you'd feel sorry for me," Mac said. "I don't deserve your pity or anyone else's. I certainly don't deserve your praise for feedin' ya. We all have to pay for the mistakes we've made along the way, and me giving out leftovers is one way I do that. I ride your ass all the time because I don't want you to make the same mistakes I made with my boy. When I see you fucking up, I wanna set you on the right path, even if I have to push your ass."

"The shit that you said to me the last time we talked really got to me," Lucky admitted. "I guess I always thought of you and Brick as being on my side." He kicked at a chunk of asphalt. "When you told me you no longer believed in me, it hurt."

"Yeah, I know it did, but you gotta know it has nothing to do with believing in you. Just the opposite really. Damn it, kid, I care what happens to you." Mac scrubbed at his face with his palms. "I don't think fighting's the right path for you anymore, and I couldn't live with myself if I just let you continue down that road and something serious happened to you or someone else."

"But fighting's what I love to do," Lucky argued.

Mac shoved his hat back on his head before reaching over to grab Lucky's wrists. "I need you to do one thing for me. Search your soul, and figure out why you love to fight. I'm not talking about the bullshit you hand Brick and everyone else. I'm asking you to dig deep and come up with the real answer."

"You say that like you already know." Lucky pulled his hands back, breaking the contact.

"I think I do, but what I think doesn't matter. You've gotta come up with your own truth." Mac got to his feet. "I'd better get back. No doubt Connie's fixing to skin me alive."

"Mac?" Lucky called out before Mac could disappear.

"Yeah?"

"How'd you come to own this place?" After the story Mac had told, Lucky had a hard time understanding how the man had gone from being a worthless father to owning his own diner.

Mac grinned. "You don't think Dray was the first person Brick helped, do ya?" He walked back into the diner with a smug grin on his face.

Left stupefied by Mac's parting words, Lucky slowly shook his head. Was there anyone in their section of the city that Brick hadn't saved in one way or another? He rested his head against the wall and stared up at the sliver of sky he could see between the buildings. "What the fuck?" he asked God. "Why the hell're you taking away the one angel this neighborhood has?"

* * * *

Lucky entered Brick's apartment to find Brick and Dray watching old videos of Dray's UFC matches. "Hey." He dropped his gym bag on the floor and took off his shoes. It had been a while since he'd watched Dray fight. In the beginning, when Brick had been trying to teach Lucky proper skills, he'd used the videos as training guides.

"Sit down and learn something," Brick wheezed.

Lucky joined Dray on the couch, his gaze riveted on the television. Brick had always been right about Dray's skills. They were perfect. Watching Dray land punches and kicks in equal measure had Lucky involuntarily rubbing the scar on his calf through his thin sweatpants.

"You sore?" Dray asked.

"Huh?" Lucky wasn't sure what Dray was talking about. "I'm fine."

Dray gestured to Lucky's leg. "So what's up with your calf?"

Lucky jerked his hand away. "I'm fine. Just a habit."

"There," Brick said. "Did you see that combination?"

"Sorry. I missed it," Lucky replied.

"Well pay attention!" Brick's yell was followed by a series of coughs.

Lucky used the time to get up and scoop Gatsby out of Brick's lap. He kissed the kitten's head. "Did you feed her?" he asked Dray.

Dray nodded. "I wasn't sure what time you'd be here, so I fed her about an hour ago." He pointed to Lucky's leg. "So what's the deal with the leg?"

"Nothing." Lucky carried Gatsby into the kitchen. He looked into the pot on the stove. "Can I have some of this chili?"

"Sure, but I have to warn you, Flint made it and dropped it by." Dray chuckled. "Despite that, it was pretty damn good."

Lucky set Gatsby down and spooned up a bowl. He added a healthy dose of hot sauce and grabbed a bottle of water before going back into the living room. He'd been trying to figure out a way to tell Brick and Dray about his day, so he decided to just spit it out. "My mom came by the gym today," he announced.

For the first time since Lucky had come into the apartment, Brick tore his gaze away from the television. He reached for the remote and turned off the set. "What'd you say?"

"Mom came to the gym. Evidently she's clean and sober and ready to be a decent person for the first time in her miserable life." Lucky concentrated on his dinner, so he couldn't see Brick's or Dray's reaction, but he didn't have to wait long.

"I don't want that bitch in my gym," Brick declared.

"I know. I took her to Mac's to get something to eat," Lucky said around a bite of chili.

"So why're you eating now?" Dray asked.

"Because I didn't stay long enough to touch my food." Lucky glanced at Dray. He wanted to talk to Dray about his discussion with Mac, but not in front of Brick. "Anyway," he began, returning to his dinner, "Mom's staying at a halfway house for the next two months. She didn't ask for it, but I have a feeling she's going to want money. I gave her what I had, but she'll be back."

"Don't give her a dime more." Brick turned his gaze on Lucky. "You don't owe her anything."

Lucky shrugged. It was a long-running argument between them, and although he understood Brick's position, Lucky had been trained since birth to put his mother's needs before his own. It was a hard habit to break, even if he understood how unhealthy it was. Forget cigarettes, booze and drugs. He was addicted to pain—the kind of pain that only a mother could dole out.

Appetite gone, he stood and carried his bowl to the kitchen. He scraped the uneaten chili into the garbage before washing his dish and putting it back into the cupboard. He jumped when he felt a warm hand on his lower back and glanced over his shoulder to see Dray. "Hey."

"You okay?" Dray asked.

"Tired." It wasn't exactly a lie. He was tired of everything, and what he really needed was to fight. Pulling out of the tournament suddenly felt like a very bad idea. He'd done it to spend time with Brick, but he was quickly figuring out that he needed that release to keep sane. "I think I'll go back to the gym for a while and work the speed bag."

Dray settled his hands on Lucky's hips and pressed against his back. "Why don't we go for a run instead? I could use some exercise."

"What about Brick?" Lucky turned to face Dray.

"We'll turn the fight back on. Brick'll never miss us." Dray gave Lucky a soft kiss, slipping his tongue inside for the briefest moment.

Lucky licked his lips. "Okay, but I want to stop by the gym afterward to check on Jax."

"I'll get changed." Dray kissed Lucky again before walking out of the kitchen.

Lucky waited long enough for his erection to subside prior to re-entering the living room. "Dray and I are going for a run," he told Brick. "You need anything?"

Brick looked up at Lucky. "Do you know what you're doing?" he asked, his voice thick with emotion.

Lucky wasn't sure what Brick was asking, but it didn't really matter. "No," he answered honestly. "I have no fucking idea what I'm doing."

* * * *

After a five-mile run, Dray felt the burn in his calf muscles as he walked alongside Lucky toward The Brick Yard. He glanced up and saw a light on in Mac's apartment over the diner. "I was surprised to hear you took your mom to Mac's. I thought the two of you weren't speaking."

Lucky lifted the bottom of his T-shirt and wiped the sweat from his face, taking special care with the bruises and scrapes. "I guess we worked it out." He lowered his shirt. "Did you know Brick helped Mac get this place?"

Dray shook his head.

"Yeah," Lucky confirmed. "I wonder how many other people Brick's helped through the years. Maybe Mac can give us some names, so we can call them for Brick's funeral. I think Brick would like knowing his boys were there to send him off." He stopped walking when they were outside the door to the gym. "What kind of fucked-up world do we live in when someone as good as Brick dies while someone as evil as my mother is given a second chance at life?" He blew out a long breath. "Sorry. I just don't know how to feel about her."

"I can understand that." Dray sat on the sidewalk, resting his back against the building, hoping he could get Lucky to keep talking. "I would imagine it's nice to see your mom clean and sober for a change, but you're angry that it happened now instead of years ago."

"Yeah, maybe." Lucky didn't sit, instead he started to pace back and forth in front of Dray. "She always told me that bad people get what they deserve." He tilted his head back and let out a growl of frustration that echoed against the brick buildings.

Dray remembered what Jax had told him about Lucky's mumblings on the night of his beating. "Bad people or bad boys?"

Lucky's entire body jerked as if Dray had just delivered a knockout blow. After several moments, he stared daggers at Dray. "I'm not done running. Why don't you go in and check on Jax?"

Lucky took off at a dead run before Dray could get to his feet. "Fuck!" Dray growled. As he watched Lucky pound down the sidewalk, Dray swore he could see the ghost of a small boy chasing him.

Once Lucky had rounded the corner, Dray pulled out

his keys and unlocked the front door. He glanced at the light that Lucky must've left on when he'd closed the gym earlier. Whether Lucky wanted to realize it or not, he'd already begun to slip into Brick's shoes.

"Jax?" Dray called. He didn't want to frighten the kid, and he had no doubt Jax had heard the door open.

"Hey." Jax came out of the laundry room. "Is something wrong with Brick?" he asked, worry in his voice.

"No. I went for a run with Lucky, so I thought I'd stop by and check on you. You're not still working, are you?" Dray asked, walking across the expansive two-story space of the gym.

"Homework." Jax leaned against the doorframe. "Lucky attacked me with Silly String earlier." He chuckled. "It took me forever to get it cleaned up, which put me behind schedule." He wandered back to the scarred table. "Chemistry." He groaned. "Sucks!"

Dray walked into the room and sat on the corner of the table. "Sorry, can't help you." With the exception of math, he'd barely made it through high school because he'd been so immersed in training that he'd cared about little else.

"Yeah, neither can God evidently, because I've been begging him all evening." Jax tapped the end of his pencil against the thick textbook. "Is Lucky okay?"

"He's working through shit, but he'll be fine," Dray said, knowing Jax had his own problems to deal with. "Has your dad been around?"

Jax shook his head. "He doesn't know about this place. I saw him waiting for me outside school yesterday, but I spotted him and used the exit out the back."

Dray had given Jax's situation a lot of thought. Legally, Jax's father could go to the cops and get his son back, but according to Lucky, he didn't think Jax's dad would do that. However, the fact that The Brick Yard was harboring a runaway could get Brick, Lucky and Dray in trouble with the authorities. It was a fucked-up situation, but one Brick had been willing to risk everything on for years. The answer to the problem was to become a foster parent to Jax, but that process required extensive background checks. He studied his tattoo-covered arms. For the first time in his life, he worried what another person might think of his ink. Would the foster care officials take one look at his tatted-up skin and deem him unworthy? Then, of course, there was the gay thing. The fact that he didn't even have a home in Chicago. *Christ.* There was no way in fuck they'd let him be a foster parent.

"Well, until I can figure something else out, just keep your eyes open," Dray finally said.

"Yeah, I get ya." Jax glanced back at his book. "Lucky's mom seemed nice to me, but I could tell by the way he reacted to her that she isn't. It made me wonder what other people see when they look at my dad."

"Appearances can be deceiving, that's for sure," Dray agreed. He pointed to Jax's homework. "You almost finished?"

Jax looked at the page in front of him. "Six more problems to answer."

"Is that the last of it?" Dray stood.

"Yep. Don't worry. I plan to go to bed the minute I'm done."

"Good deal." Dray moved toward the door. "I'll lock the front door when I leave, but Lucky's still out there somewhere, so don't freak if he shows up again."

"You want me to call you if he does?" Jax asked.

"Yeah. That'd be great." Dray studied the gym as he passed through. Brick had done what he could to maintain the place, but the building was old and in need of basic updates. He blew out a breath when he tried to imagine how much it would cost to replace the windows. As far as he knew, other than the big front window, which had been replaced in the early eighties, the rest of the windows were original to the building. The cost would be astronomical, but he bet it would be a hell of a lot easier to heat the place.

After locking the door, Dray took a deep breath and

headed toward the diner. He wasn't looking forward to seeing Mac again after so many years, but he knew it was time.

A rush of memories assaulted Dray the moment he stepped into Mac's—the first steak Brick had ordered for him, the first time he'd taken Vince out to eat and the last night he'd tried to talk to Mac. *Fuck.* Mac had gutted him by refusing to speak to him.

Dray hadn't realized how long he'd been standing just inside the door until Mac appeared carrying a plate loaded with a double bacon cheeseburger and spinach.

"Sit." Mac slammed the plate onto the table of Dray's favorite booth.

Dray pushed past his unease and made his way through the empty diner toward the table. He wasn't sure why it surprised him that Mac had remembered his usual meal. Hell, he'd ordered the same damn thing almost daily for years before he'd taken off. He made a mental note to find out Mac's secret for cooking spinach because no matter how many times he'd attempted to duplicate it, it never tasted like Mac's.

Reaching the booth, Dray stood in front of his old friend. "I need to talk to you."

"It's about fucking time." Mac sat down.

Great. Mac wasn't going to make it easy for him. Dray slid in before turning the plate to suit his attack on the burger. "Brick's fading fast. Originally, I thought he had a few months, but it's looking like a few weeks at best."

"Shit." Mac rubbed his hand over the back of his neck, dislodging his customary white knit hat. "I knew it had to be something bad to get you in here again, but that's not what I expected."

"What *did* you expect?" Dray felt his temper rising and didn't try to push it down. The diner was empty, and he was frustrated with Lucky. Yes, a good old-fashioned argument might be just what he needed at the moment. "We both know what happened last time I came in here."

"I haven't forgotten." Mac leaned his forearms on the table. "I remember clearly how fast you walked away from the people who'd treated you like family."

Dray paused with the cheeseburger halfway to his mouth. "Are you seriously trying to tell me your attitude back then had more to do with the fact I was leaving than me being gay?"

"Don't go putting words in my mouth, boy," Mac said. "You were one of the best, and you could've overcome that bullshit everyone was spouting if you'd held your head high, but you gave up. You just walked away from your career, Brick, Lucky and, yeah, me. Brick and I were there for you when you needed us growing up, yet you couldn't run away from us fast enough when your career hit a bump in the road."

"A bump in the road? I had people wanting me dead. *Dead.*" Dray set his burger down before pushing his plate away. "I grew up with nothing, but I worked my ass off to make something of myself. I gave them everything I had in me except that one part, and when they found out, they wanted me dead. Do you have any idea what that did to me?"

"Don't forget, you're talking to a black man. I pass people on the street every day who would just as soon spit on me as look at me and all because of the color of my skin," Mac said without raising his voice. "So, yeah, I understand what it feels like to be judged for something you can't do a damn thing about, but that doesn't mean it's okay to drop out and run off. I've learned over the years that the best way to get back at the bigoted assholes is to look them in the eyes, smile and tell them to have a nice day, which is what you should have done. You taking off the way you did just proved to those fans that you weren't worthy of their respect."

Dray couldn't argue because he knew Mac was right. Vince had definitely betrayed him, but shit like that happened to people all the time. Yes, Vince's betrayal was headline news, but Dray was beginning to see how he'd hurt the people he'd left behind. It wasn't just Brick, Lucky and Mac he'd hurt, but his mom and brother. "I fucked up," he finally confessed.

"Yep," Mac agreed.

"Not much I can do about it now," Dray said.

"You're wrong about that. You can make up for it by doing right by Brick."

Dray stilled. Had Brick talked to Mac about his final wishes? "I can't help him die if that's what you're getting at. I won't."

"What the fuck're you talking about? Taking care of Lucky, Jax and The Brick Yard is how you can make it up to Brick. What's this shit about helping him die?" Mac asked.

Dray shook his head. "Nothing." He needed to change the subject. "I've decided to stay after Brick dies. I'm going to help with The Brick Yard, which should give Lucky the time to train and travel." He knew what Mac thought of Lucky fighting, so he sat back and waited.

"Sounds like you and Lucky are getting closer."

"We are," Dray agreed.

"If you care about him, you'll keep him outta that cage." Mac pushed the plate of food back toward Dray.

Dray stared down at the cold hamburger. "He needs to fight."

"No, he *needs* to deal with his past. When he steps into that cage, he's fighting himself, and if you haven't realized that, you're not as close as you think."

* * * *

After only a few hours of sleep, Lucky shuffled into his kitchen to find Dray leaning against the counter, staring at the coffee pot. He wrapped his arms around Dray's waist. "Can't you make that brew any faster?"

Dray reached back and slapped Lucky's ass. "I wish."

Lucky rested his chin on Dray's shoulder. After a punishing run and a few rounds with the heavy bag, he'd returned to his apartment to find Dray sound asleep in his bed. He'd taken a shower and joined Dray under the covers. Dray had curled around him, but that was it. For the first time since they'd been together, they hadn't had sex. "Are you mad at me?"

"No. Why would I be?" Dray withdrew mugs from the cupboard.

"Because of the way I acted last night." Lucky kissed the tattooed skin between Dray's shoulder blades. "We didn't have sex."

Dray poured two cups of coffee before turning around, leaving the coffee on the counter. He palmed Lucky's ass and pulled him closer. "We don't have to fuck every time we're together. You had a bad night, and I thought maybe it would be better to just hold you."

"I don't understand. Why would you want to sleep with me if you didn't wanna fuck?" Lucky knew he probably sounded crass, but he needed to know.

Dray stared at Lucky, his mouth set in a thin line. "What kind of asshole do you think I am?"

Lucky took a step back, unsure how to take Dray's obvious anger. "I don't think you're an asshole."

"Then why…?" Dray sighed. "You really don't get it, do you?"

"Evidently not, because I can't figure out why the fuck you're mad at me all of a sudden," Lucky said.

"Because I care for you. This isn't just about sex for me, but I can see you feel differently." Dray turned his back on Lucky and lifted his cup to his lips. "If that's all you're after, that's fine, but you should have said something before now."

Lucky's chest felt tight as he tried to comprehend Dray's words. "You care about me?"

Dray punched the cabinet door in front of him, cracking the cheap wood from top to bottom. "Fuck!" He shook his head and several drops of blood splattered onto the floor.

Lucky rushed forward and grabbed a dish towel. "Did

you break it?"

Dray took the towel from Lucky and wrapped it around his hand. "Don't worry about it." He pushed past Lucky and left the apartment without putting a shirt on.

Lucky stood in the middle of the kitchen, wondering what in the hell he'd just done.

Chapter Eleven

Dray was working his frustration out on the heavy bag with Jax sitting on a stool nearby. With his hand fucked up, he was forced to stick to his legs and his left hand, but he was slowly bringing his blood pressure down. It seemed he and Lucky had something else in common.

"Why'd you quit?" Jax asked.

Dray glanced at Jax. "Didn't Brick tell you?"

Jax shook his head. "He said you had some personal problems."

"The fans found out I'm gay and turned their backs on me. Once the fans turned, so did the UFC and my sponsors." Dray kicked the bag several times, switching from foot to foot.

When Jax remained quiet, Dray was suddenly afraid he'd lost the respect of the teenager. He stopped and faced Jax. "Does that bother you?"

Jax shook his head. "Why would it? Men are sexy." He gestured to Dray's bandaged hand. "How'd that happen?" he asked as if his confession were no big deal.

"Got pissed and punched the kitchen cupboard." Dray frowned. "I wouldn't recommend it."

"I'll remember that. What made you so mad?" Jax asked.

"Do you always ask so many questions?" Dray left Jax sitting by the heavy bag and went over to the speed bag. Using only his left hand, he started a rhythm.

"I'm not trying to be nosey or anything," Jax said, setting his stool down before climbing onto it. "I need to tell you something, and I need to make sure it's not going to make you even madder."

"You can tell me anything," Dray said, not taking his eyes off the bag.

"That night Lucky came here and he was so beat up, he said something that I didn't understand at the time, but I've been thinking about it, and I think you should know."

The mention of Lucky's name got Dray's full attention. "What'd he say?"

Jax shifted on his stool, clearly uncomfortable. "I think he thought I was you, because he said I was his world, the only man he'd ever wanted, but that he couldn't have me because he didn't deserve me. Then he went on about being a bad boy."

Speed bag forgotten, Dray dropped his arms to his sides. Although he'd suspected Lucky cared more than he'd let on, it was Lucky's incoherent mumblings to Jax that sealed Lucky's fate, as far as Dray was concerned. Knowing what he did now, there was no way in hell he was going to let Lucky push him away.

Jax climbed off the stool and stood. "Why does Lucky think he's so bad?"

"I don't know. I'm sure it has something to do with his mom though." Dray picked up a towel and wiped the sweat from his head and chest. He still didn't know what haunted Lucky, but he knew the biggest and baddest monster in Lucky's closet was his own mother. "I don't suppose you know what her name is?"

"Alana. I heard Flint call her that after Lucky left with her."

Dray remembered Lucky saying his mom was living at a halfway house. He didn't know how many were in the area, but it was worth looking for her.

* * * *

Although he'd never set eyes on Alana Gunn, Dray knew who she was the moment she walked out of the house. "Alana?"

187

Stopping abruptly, Alana stared at Dray with fear in her eyes. "I don't do that anymore."

Dray ground his teeth. "I'm not a fucking dealer," he growled. "I want to talk to you about Lucky."

"Does he owe you money?"

Dray tried his best to control his temper. "No. I'm a friend of his." He scanned the rundown neighborhood. "Is there somewhere we could go to talk?"

Alana bit her upper lip before pointing to a small bench at the side of the house. "I have to catch the bus in twenty minutes."

Twenty minutes wouldn't give him enough time to figure out what the hell the monster in front of him had done to her son, but it was better than nothing. "Okay." He followed her around the side of the house and sat down. "I know you're trying to straighten your life out, but I'm worried about Lucky. A close friend of his, Brick, is dying, and Lucky's not taking it well. It seems to be bringing up some bad memories for him, and I thought maybe you'd be willing to help me understand what's going on in his head."

Alana set her purse on her lap and withdrew a pack of cigarettes. "Don't bother trying to understand him. Lucky's always been screwed up." She lit a cigarette and inhaled deeply before blowing out a stream of smoke. "When he was young, he used to purposely do things to make me angry."

"Like what?" *Ask for food?* The longer Dray sat next to the woman, the more he grew to hate her.

"Cry nonstop, for one." She sighed. "He'd do anything to get my attention. Once, he flushed an entire bag of pills down the toilet." Shaking her head, she took another puff. "Needless to say, he didn't do that more than once."

"Why? What did you do to him?" Dray asked, although he wasn't sure he wanted to know.

"Me? I didn't do anything. I tried disciplining him once when he was little and a neighbor saw me, said she'd call social services if she ever saw me hit him again. I couldn't have that because I needed the welfare check." Alana snorted. "After that, I made him punish himself. Bad boys need to be punished, but I didn't need to go to jail for it or lose my food stamps."

Bile rose in his throat as he fought the urge to hit the bitch. Never in his life had he hit a woman nor had he been tempted, but at that moment, he wanted to feel his fist smash against the woman's face. He fought to control his anger as he shoved his hands into his pockets. "How did he punish himself?"

Alana dropped the half-smoked cigarette and crushed it under her shoe. "I need to catch my bus."

Dray jumped in front of her, blocking her path. "Not until you tell me how you made him punish himself."

She scowled up at him. "Why should I? So you can look down your nose at me? I did the best I could. Raising a kid like him wasn't easy."

"You're garbage," Dray said. "Even sober, you're garbage." He jabbed his finger toward her. "Stay the fuck away from him." He strode away from Alana, hoping he'd never see her spiteful face again. He still didn't know the full story of Lucky's past, but he had a much better idea of why Lucky found the idea of someone wanting to spend time with him for something other than sex so alien. Lucky didn't seem to recognize love when it was being directed at him, and Dray had no doubt it was because he hadn't been shown an ounce of it as a child.

The problem was, how did he show someone who'd never felt loved that he loved him? He'd stupidly believed he'd been doing a damn good job of telling Lucky without words how he felt, but he'd obviously been mistaken. Sadly, the way things were between them, Dray wasn't even certain Lucky would believe him if he came right out and declared his feelings. Nope. He needed to find another way.

* * * *

Lucky was sitting beside Brick's bed, watching the old man sleep, when the door behind him opened. He glanced over his shoulder to see Dray's handsome face.

"Can I talk to you?" Dray whispered.

Lucky gave Gatsby's tiny black-and-white head a gentle scratch before following Dray out of the room. He hadn't spoken to Dray since that morning and wasn't sure if he should ask about Dray's injured hand or not. "What's up?"

"Jax is coming over to sit with Brick. Flint's closing up the gym, and you and I are going out," Dray announced.

"Out? Out where?" Lucky was in his usual garb of faded sweats and a T-shirt.

"I'm hungry for seafood."

Lucky sighed. He knew he wasn't dressed for a restaurant nicer than Mac's. "I'll have to change."

"Okay. Can you be ready in fifteen minutes?" Dray asked.

"Twenty?" Lucky winced. "I need a shower."

Dray grinned. "Okay, twenty, but bring a coat. We're going to Milwaukee."

"What the hell're we going to Milwaukee for?" Lucky knew of several good seafood places in Chicago. The drive to Milwaukee would be a waste of gas.

"Because I feel like getting out of the city for a while. It's a nice evening, so I thought we'd go for a drive. Don't worry about it. Just go get your shower."

Lucky got the feeling he was starting to piss Dray off again. He'd worried over their morning exchange all day, and although he still wasn't sure what he'd said to anger Dray, he certainly didn't want to do it again. "Whatever," he said, backing off.

* * * *

Once Dray had passed the worst of the traffic, he turned on the radio. "What kind of music do you like?"

"I'm not picky. I usually listen to rock, but Brick blasts the old shit, so I'm used to that, too."

"Country?" Dray didn't really like it, but he thought he'd throw Lucky a curveball.

"Fuck no." Lucky started to laugh. "Do you?"

"Not a chance." Dray held out his bandaged hand. "Take that off for me."

"Why?" Lucky asked.

"Because I want to hold your hand." Dray glanced at Lucky. "In case I didn't make it clear back at Brick's, this is a date."

Lucky licked his lips. "A date?"

"Yeah." Dray waited for Lucky to unwrap the elastic bandage. He wanted to talk to Lucky about the meeting he'd had with his mom, but tonight was about showing Lucky he had genuine feelings for him because as much as he'd tried to deny it, he had them.

Lucky dropped the bandage onto the seat before examining the smaller piece of gauze taped to Dray's knuckles. "Is it bad?"

Dray shook his head. "You can probably take it off. It was bleeding when I wrapped it up, and I didn't want to get it on the bandage."

Lucky wrinkled his nose. "No thanks."

Dray spread his hand out and waited. It was obvious Lucky wasn't going to make the date easy, but Dray decided to cut him some slack. Although Lucky had dated women for years, it was his first date with a man.

Eventually, Lucky sighed and threaded his fingers through Dray's. "You gonna try and grab my boob next?" Lucky joked.

Dray squeezed Lucky's hand. "Let's get something straight. You're not a woman. I don't think of you as a woman, and I sure as hell don't want to treat you the way I would a woman."

Lucky cleared his throat. "Sorry. I guess I'm nervous, which is completely stupid, but I don't know how to act." He sighed heavily. "Fucking, I know." With his free hand he gestured around the cab of the truck. "I guess I've never really dated. I fuck." He said the last two words so quietly Dray barely heard them.

"What about Briley? You were having dinner with her when I called that time," Dray pointed out, his jealousy flaring.

"Briley's cool. We hang out, but I'd never consider meeting her at the bar or at Mac's to be a date. It's not like that with us. We have fun together and she likes my cock. That's all there is to it."

"Well, this is a date. This is me trying to show you that we're not just friends with benefits. That every time we're together, whether it's at a restaurant, bar or just your apartment, it's a date because being with you means more to me than having sex."

Eyes closed, Lucky shook his head vehemently and released Dray's hand. "You can't care about me like that. I won't let you."

"Why? Because you think you're a bad boy?"

Lucky gasped. "Why would you say something like that to me?"

"I know you think you're a bad boy for some reason, because that's what you told Jax the night you showed up at the gym after getting the shit beat out of you. So tell me, did you purposely go out and look for a fight or did something else happen?" Dray had a strong feeling he knew, but the truth was so fucking messed up, he prayed he was wrong.

"Stop it!" Lucky yelled. "You want to go on a stupid date, we'll go, but don't try to analyze me."

Dray bit his tongue for another ten minutes. Letting his anger get the better of him wouldn't do either of them any good. It didn't matter that Lucky's defensive response was clearly a way to keep others at arm's-length. Dray knew he'd been stupid to set wheels in motion before nailing down the relationship he felt he and Lucky had developed. *Fuck!* He exited the highway without a word, stopping at the first fast food joint he spotted. "What do you want?" he asked as he drove up to the drive-thru speaker.

"What're we doing?" Lucky asked.

"Well, since you don't give a fuck about this date, I don't see a reason to drive all the way to Milwaukee, but I'm starving, so I'm going to get something to eat and head back. Now, what the hell do you want?" Dray tapped his fingers on the steering wheel as the guy on the other end of the speaker barked at him.

"Nothing," Lucky mumbled.

"Whatever." Dray stuck his head out of the window. "A double cheeseburger meal with a Coke." He dug his wallet out of his back pocket then drove around the building.

"Why're you being such an asshole about this?" Lucky asked as soon as Dray was handed his food and had rolled up the window. "I'm just trying to save you."

"Why the hell're you trying to save me? I don't need you to save me, I need you to—" Dray bit his tongue.

"I'm not a good person," Lucky mumbled. "People who care about me end up disappointed or dying."

The anger drained out of Dray. He parked under a shade tree in the back of the lot. Food forgotten, he unbuckled and turned in the seat to face Lucky. "Brick's cancer has absolutely nothing to do with you. Your mom's drug and alcohol abuse has nothing to do with you. She's a fucking bitch of a loser because that's who she is in her soul. I don't know for a fact, but I'm going to guess since your dad was a dealer, she was fucking up her life before she ever got pregnant with you." He rested his elbow on the back of the seat. "Now, who else's life have you fucked up?"

"Sid's fucked up."

"Yeah, you're right. Are you going to tell me you're responsible for his mistakes, too?" Dray lifted his hand and touched the shell of Lucky's ear. "You have to stop blaming yourself for the pain around you."

"Pain's all I know."

"I bet Brick wouldn't agree with that. Neither would I. Don't forget, I know what you did for Jax, and I know you gave up on winning a shitload of money in that tournament so you could spend more time with Brick." Dray tugged on Lucky's ear until Lucky looked at him. "I know how you make me feel when you hold me at night. Believe me. I'm a hard man to get close to after what happened with Vince, but you did it."

Lucky bit his bottom lip and jerked his head around to stare out of the passenger window. "Aren't you the one who told me to bury that part of myself?"

Dray *had* told Lucky that, but he'd thought they'd moved beyond it. "Maybe I was wrong. Vince's betrayal took everything from me, including my heart for a while. When I said I'd be here for you to come home to between fights, did you think I just meant I'd be ready for a no-strings fuck?"

Lucky nodded but didn't say a word.

Dray counted to ten to give himself time to cool down before answering. He started the truck and pulled out of the parking lot. "I'm too goddamned old to be your fuck buddy, so if that's all you want, all you think you deserve, we'll end it — because I deserve more than being relegated to that particular role."

* * * *

On the highway heading back to Chicago, Lucky felt like he couldn't breathe. The thought of ending things with Dray was almost more than he could bear because Dray was the only thing keeping him together.

He hadn't been loved as a child and more often than not, his mom had blamed him for all that was wrong in her life. He wasn't a complete moron. He'd heard how important it was for a child's mental health to form attachments at a young age, but the thought of opening a part of himself that had never seen the light of day scared the fuck out of him. He had strong feelings for Brick and if he was honest with himself, for Mac, too, but they'd both continued to tell him he wasn't good enough at this or that. The one and only place he'd ever been good enough was in the cage.

And, stupidly, he'd even considered giving that part of himself up over the last few days. What the hell had he been thinking?

Lucky chanced a quick glance at Dray. He knew Dray hadn't fully meant what he'd said. Dray was the kind of man who pushed, hoping to get the outcome he wanted. Yeah, Dray was definitely trying to push him into opening that dark part of himself. The problem was, Dray had no idea what he was really asking for.

With a sigh of exasperation, Lucky scrubbed his hands over his face. He wanted to run away, to climb back into the cage where he felt nothing but his fists hitting flesh, where winning was a good thing and losing meant he'd suffered for being bad. He knew the rules of the cage, understood them. Life outside sucked because emotions were too confusing. "I think I'll start training tomorrow to get ready for the fight in St. Louis."

Dray turned off the radio. "I went to see your mom earlier."

Lucky froze. *No.* The last thing he wanted was for his mom's poison to leak out and infect one of the few people he gave a shit about.

"What did she mean when she said that she made you punish yourself?"

The scar on Lucky's calf began to burn again and a split-second later, he was thrust back to his childhood. "I'm not allowed to talk about that."

"Fuck!" Dray jerked the truck to the right and off the highway, tires screeching. "You *are* allowed to talk about it. You *have* to talk about it." He unbuckled and leaned over the center console. "What happened to you was the worst form of abuse I've ever heard of, and a person doesn't just deal with shit like that on their own."

"I'm fine," Lucky replied. His voice sounded cold, even to him.

"You're not fine, baby." Dray grabbed Lucky's chin and turned his head to face him. He stared with tears in his eyes at the healing bruises on the side of Lucky's face. "Tell me how this happened."

Lucky clenched his jaws, remembering the hard smack of the brick wall each time he'd slammed his face against it. He could tell by the expression on Dray's face that he'd already figured it out, so why the fuck did he have to say it?

Dray's cell phone rang, breaking the silence in the cab. He glanced down and swore. "Fuck. It's Jax."

Lucky's heart began to hammer. "Answer it."

"Hey," Dray said, picking up the phone. "Slow down," he told Jax. "Is Flint there?" He settled back into his seat and reached back to put his seat belt on. "Okay, call Flint and have him call the hospice nurse—her number's on the fridge. When Flint gets there, you need to go back to the gym." He shook his head. "No, don't argue about this. The last thing Brick would want is for someone to find you there and notify your dad." He licked his lips as he continued to listen. "We're about forty minutes away. Yeah." Dray closed his eyes. "Just make him as comfortable as you can until Flint gets there. I'm sorry, Jax. I swear I didn't think…"

Lucky felt the tears running down his face and quickly wiped them away.

"We'll be there as soon as we can." Dray hung up the phone before he pulled back onto the highway. He held out his hand. "I know you're mad at me, but I need you right now."

Lucky nodded and held Dray's hand. "What's going on?"

"Brick's throwing up blood again. The nurse said it could happen when he got closer to the end, but I didn't expect it so soon." Dray lifted Lucky's hand to his mouth and kissed it. "I did this. I put Jax in a position he isn't prepared to deal with, and I'm not sure I'll ever be able to forgive myself for it."

Lucky heard the words, but he knew the truth. Dray had tried to give Lucky something special because he'd talked to Alana and felt sorry for him. And here they were, miles from home, and Brick was paying the price for Dray's kindness.

* * * *

Still holding Lucky's hand, Dray ran up the stairs. He stopped at Brick's door and looked at Lucky. There were so many things he wanted to say, so many things they needed to work through, but it wasn't the time. Lucky had all but shut down completely on the drive into Chicago.

"I know I've got really shitty timing, but I need you to know that I love you," Dray said. "And I don't care what you think you've done in the past or how you see yourself. My feelings aren't going to change. Because I've seen the way you treat Jax and Brick, and the fact that you can cry at all tells me you're worth every ounce of feeling I have for you."

Lucky shook his head.

Dray gave him a quick kiss. "Now, let's put this discussion on the back burner and take care of the man who's saved both of our lives."

Lucky didn't say anything, but he didn't pull his hand away when they entered the apartment either. Flint was at the kitchen sink with the water running.

"Hey," Dray said, getting Flint's attention.

Flint glanced over his shoulder. "The nurse is with him. He's stopped throwing up for now." He lifted a portion of the bloody sheet. "I didn't want to run downstairs to the laundry room, so I thought I'd wash it out up here, but it's not working."

Lucky gently pushed Flint out of the way. "I'll do it."

Flint took a step back and glanced at Dray.

Dray shook his head, letting Flint know not to argue with Lucky.

"I've given Mr. Brick a shot of morphine. He's sleeping now, but he told me he doesn't want me here," the nurse informed them. "Even though his body's shutting down, he appears to be of sound mind, so I have to follow his wishes."

Dray nodded in understanding. "What should we do?"

"Make sure he stays propped up as much as possible. Actually, he'd probably be more comfortable in his chair, but he wouldn't listen to me." She eyed Flint, Dray and Lucky. "If the three of you can manage to carry him in there, he'll rest a lot easier."

"Okay," Dray agreed.

"I know Sylvia showed you how to give morphine injections if he needs them, but you might want to show whoever else is staying with him," she said.

Dray thought about Brick's request to help him die and quickly shut the door on that thought. "Thank you."

She handed Dray a business card. "If you need me, call me. Even if it's just to talk."

Dray glanced at the card. "Thanks, Janice. I appreciate you rushing over."

Janice squeezed Dray's arm. "I know this isn't easy to hear, but it helps them pass if they know you're ready for it. I know it sounds crazy, but patients tend to hold on for their family, even through the pain."

Sylvia, the nurse he'd met a week earlier, had told him pretty much the same thing. "Yeah." The problem was, he wasn't ready to let go of Brick, and he knew for a fact Lucky wasn't ready either.

* * * *

Wincing, Lucky scooted out of Dray's comforting embrace to rub his back. The damn metal bar under the foldout sofa's thin mattress had been torture all night long. He was in the process of sitting up when he noticed Brick's eyes were open and staring right at him. "Morning," he whispered, trying not to wake Dray.

Brick's gaze swung between Lucky and Dray. "He's a good man," Brick rasped.

"Yeah," Lucky agreed. He knew he'd been caught in a

198

compromising position but wasn't sure what to say or how much to admit.

Brick lifted the oxygen mask to his mouth for several moments before speaking again. "I knew, but I didn't want you to make the same mistake Dray did. Was I wrong to bring him back here?"

Wearing only his underwear, Lucky reached for his jeans on the floor. "He's good for the gym."

"But is he good for you?" Brick asked, his voice barely audible.

Lucky stood and pulled his jeans up. "I'm not good for him." He walked over and kneeled beside Brick's recliner. He swallowed around the lump in his throat. "Are you disappointed in me?"

Brick lifted a shaking hand and laid it on top of Lucky's head. "I've never been disappointed in you, son. Don't you know that?"

Lucky ducked down and rested his forehead on Brick's leg as tears began to run down his cheeks. *Christ.* He'd cried more in the last two weeks than he had in his entire life. Why the fuck couldn't he get his emotions under control? He reached up and pressed Brick's hand tighter to the back of his head, needing the closeness.

"I doubt Jax'll be back. I scared him last night, so I can't blame him, but I need you to look out for him, and I need you to make sure he knows that I love him, just like I love all you boys."

Snot dripped from Lucky's nose as he fought to keep it together. He nodded but held onto Brick's hand even tighter. "I don't want you to go."

"I don't want to go," Brick said, his voice fading even more, "but I need you to wake up Dray and call Flint and Mac."

"I'm awake," Dray said. "I'll make the calls."

"One of you, put on one of my tapes for me," Brick ordered.

Lucky wiped the wetness from his face while he did what

Brick wanted. He found a DVD from one of his first big fights and slid it into the player. He glanced toward the bed, but Dray was no longer there. "Let's see if you remember this one," he told Brick as he returned to sit beside the chair.

Brick started to chuckle when a nineteen-year-old Lucky filled the screen. Unfortunately, his mirth was cut short with a coughing fit.

Lucky jumped up and urged Brick to put the oxygen mask back on. "Do you need a shot?"

Brick shook his head. "I want to be awake."

Lucky handed the remote to Brick. "I'll be right back."

Brick didn't look away from the television, but he nodded in understanding.

Lucky found Dray in the kitchen, staring out of the small window at the building across the alley.

"Yeah," Dray said into the phone. "Anything's fine." He must have sensed Lucky behind him because he turned before ending the call. "See ya in a bit." He hung up and set the cell on the counter. "Mac's gonna bring over some food in case more people stop by."

"That's nice." Lucky wanted to walk into Dray's embrace and never let go, but he couldn't make himself move. "You think today's the day?"

"Maybe. For sure by the weekend." Dray used the back of his hand to dry his eyes and cheeks. "I'm gonna run down and pick Jax up. We'll just close the gym for now."

"Brick said he doubted Jax would be willing to come back. I guess Brick freaked him out last night," Lucky said.

"I'm sure Jax was freaked, but that doesn't mean he doesn't want the chance to say goodbye."

Lucky shuffled his feet, feeling uneasy, like his body needed to move but his brain wasn't even in the same room. He didn't want to say goodbye to Brick. He wasn't ready.

"I heard what you said to Brick about you not being good for me, and I want you to know that's not true. I'm a better man for knowing you." Dray picked up his keys from the counter. "I'll be back as soon as I can. Are you going to be all right until Flint gets here?"

"I'm fine," Lucky lied. He needed a moment to think about what Dray had just told him.

Dray stopped in front of Lucky, reached up to grab Lucky behind the neck and pulled him close. He pressed his lips against Lucky's ear and spoke. "Brick needs to believe you're going to be okay without him."

Lucky shook his head. "I won't be."

"Maybe not at first, but you'll get there," Dray whispered.

"But what if you get tired of putting up with my shit?" Lucky asked. Next to Brick's death, it was Lucky's greatest fear.

"I'm not going anywhere. You can try like hell to push me away, but I'm as stubborn as that old man in there when it comes to not giving up on you," Dray whispered.

Chapter Twelve

Dray stood outside on the fire escape as Mac smoked a cigarette, simply because he couldn't stand to see Lucky fall apart any longer. The mood inside the apartment was depressing, and it had been that way for the last two days. The longer it went on, the more he began to curse himself for not putting Brick out of his misery. According to Sylvia, it was a matter of hours, but she'd said that almost every time she'd stopped by.

The situation had gotten so bad Jax had asked to go back to the gym. It seemed even Jax couldn't take being around the broken man who'd refused to leave Brick's side.

"I'm worried about Lucky. He hasn't eaten a damn thing in two days," Dray said.

"He'll eat when he's ready," Mac replied before putting his cigarette out against the railing and flicking the butt to the alley below.

"I need a favor," Dray began. "Jax's dad has been showing up at the school looking for him. Eventually, I think we're going to have to bring the authorities in, but before that happens, I wonder if you'd consider becoming a foster parent."

Mac shook his head. "I fucked up with my own kid. I can't do it again."

Mac had told Dray about his son the previous day, but that didn't stop Dray from believing Mac deserved a second chance. "Jax needs you," Dray said.

"No, Jax needs *you*," Mac pointed out.

"Look at me. Do I really look like the kind of man they're going to find suitable to care for a teenage boy? Forget the fact that I'm covered in ink. What do you think they're going to say when they find out I'm gay?" Dray argued.

"Gay people become foster parents all the time. You just need to believe in yourself. Get off your ass and do what needs to be done."

Dray grunted. "Why're you being such a bastard about this?"

"Because Lucky's not the only one who's in need of a little redemption."

The window opened and Lucky stuck his head out. "Brick wants you, Dray."

Dray stared at Mac for another moment. He wanted to tell Mac that he'd let people down once before and falling short again would break him, but he kept his fears to himself and crawled back through the window. He followed Lucky to Brick's bedroom, where they'd carried Brick a few hours earlier.

"Why don't you get something to eat?" Dray urged Lucky.

"I'm fine."

"Go eat," Brick ordered as much as his weakened condition would allow. "I want to talk to Dray alone."

Lucky scooped Gatsby up and left the bedroom, looking like he'd been kicked.

Dray leaned over the bed and kissed Brick's forehead. "How's the pain?"

"Bad," Brick replied. "But no morphine."

"You've always been a stubborn sonofabitch." Dray sat down in the chair Lucky had carried in earlier.

Brick slid the mask off his face long enough to say, "Lucky."

"I know." Dray took a calming breath. "I'll help him get through it." He wasn't sure how he was going to get through to Lucky, but he wouldn't be pushed away.

"I have pictures in my desk. I need you to get them before Lucky finds them." It seemed to take Brick forever to get the words out, and once he had, Dray wasn't sure he understood them.

"What kind of pictures?" Dray asked.

Brick glanced toward the door. "He gets bruised a lot. I thought it was his mom, but it kept happening after she'd gone to prison. I have pictures." He reached for Dray's hand and squeezed. "I need you to find them and destroy them."

Dray nodded. "Alana told me she forced him to punish himself as a child. Do you think he's still doing it?"

Tears filled Brick's eyes. "He's a good boy."

"I know," Dray agreed.

"Take care of him."

"I will," Dray promised.

A knock sounded at the door and Lucky stuck his head inside. "Brick? Leon's on the phone. He'd like to talk to you for a minute."

"Yeah." Brick waved his fingers, asking for the phone.

With a shake of his head, Dray stood and kissed Brick on the forehead once more. "I'll see ya later, old man." He stepped out of the room and waited to see if Lucky would follow him.

When Lucky appeared in the doorway, Dray smiled. "I'm going to run down and check on Jax," Dray said, looking around. "Where'd Mac go?"

"Trish called. Jose didn't show up, so he had to go down to the diner, but he said he'd be back as soon as he got things settled."

Alone for the first time in almost two days, Dray took the opportunity to wrap his arms around Lucky. "Did you eat something?"

Lucky shook his head. "I tried earlier, but it didn't stay down." He pressed his cheek against Dray's shoulder. "This is worse than I thought it'd be."

Dray held him tighter. "I know, babe. I wish I could make it easier." Guilt settled in his gut. He could have made it easier, still could, if only he were strong enough to do what Brick had asked of him. "You want me to stay until either Flint or Mac get back?"

Lucky kissed Dray's neck. "I'm fine. I'll sit with Brick."

Christ. Despite everything going on around them, Dray wanted to bury his cock deep inside Lucky. He yearned to lose himself in Lucky's arms. To lose the heartache if only for a few minutes. He wanted to tell Lucky he loved him again, but Lucky didn't look like he could handle anything else at the moment. Instead, he cupped Lucky's face and leaned in for a deep kiss.

Lucky opened immediately, but pulled away before Dray was ready. "I need to get back to Brick."

And I need to find an envelope of pictures, Dray reminded himself. "Okay. I have my phone, so call if you need me or if anything changes." Lucky stared at Dray with an expression Dray couldn't read. "Lucky? Are you okay?"

"You should probably say goodbye to him, in case he's gone before you're done at the gym," Lucky said.

"I know he can go anytime. That's why I say goodbye to him every time I leave the room, but I'm worried about Jax," Dray replied.

"Hang on." Lucky walked into the kitchen, and Dray could hear cupboard doors opening and closing. When he came back into the living room, he held out a bag.

"What's this?" Dray asked, opening the sack.

Lucky walked over to the couch and picked up Gatsby from the pillow she'd made a nest in. He gave the growing kitten a kiss on the top of the head then held her out. "Ask Jax if he can watch Gatsby for me."

Dray didn't know that he'd ever loved Lucky more than he did at that moment. He knew how much comfort Gatsby had offered Lucky in the previous hours, and for him to share his security blanket with Jax was the mark of a good man. Why couldn't Lucky see that?

"I'm sure Jax'll love to watch Gatsby," Dray said, taking the cat from Lucky.

Lucky nodded and rubbed the kitten's ears. "I'll see you later."

Dray waited for Lucky to disappear back into Brick's room before tucking Gatsby more securely under his arm and leaving the apartment.

* * * *

Dray left Jax to play with the kitten while he began the task of going through Brick's desk. He couldn't believe the crap he had to sift through. Who knew Brick was such a goddamn packrat? He came across a pile of receipts and pulled one out. It was a rent receipt and not for The Brick Yard.

Looking around the desktop, he found the folder that contained Brick's will. He'd signed the damn thing, even had a copy, but he'd never taken the time to read it. Sure, it was irresponsible of him, but Brick had already told him he and Lucky would get The Brick Yard. He flipped through the thick packet of papers and was soon lost in legal speak. The one thing he understood was he and Lucky, no middle name, Gunn would inherit the legal holdings of Anthony Brick.

Shaking his head, he tossed the paperwork onto the desk and continued his search. It took him almost twenty minutes of digging through the drawers, but he finally came up with a large manila envelope marked L.

Dray sat back in the chair and stared at the photographic evidence Brick had gathered. The pictures were all different sizes and apparently in no order, so he started going through them one at a time. Each bruise shown in the photograph was circled in red. On the back, Brick had written the date and, in some cases, a short explanation. Lucky varied in age between eight and his current age. No doubt if Brick were healthy, Lucky's latest bruises would also be included.

"Fuuuck," Dray drew out.

He shoved the pictures back into the envelope, wondering what the hell to do with them. Brick wanted them destroyed, but if that were the case, why'd he take them and document Lucky's injuries in the first place? A thought occurred to him. Lucky had had Jax take pictures of his bruises after the most recent beating from his father. Had Brick taken them in case Alana sent the cops to his door?

As far as Dray knew, Lucky was the youngest kid Brick had ever taken under his protective wing. Hell, even he remembered the first day Lucky had shown up at The Brick Yard. Dray had already started fighting in amateur matches, so he'd been heavily into training at the time.

It had been a bitterly cold Chicago winter day and most schools in the city had been closed because of it. Lucky had been looking in the front window, something he'd done for months without coming in. For some reason, Brick had decided he'd given Lucky enough time to come in on his own and had gone after him.

One look at the near-frozen boy and Brick had struck a deal. Lucky could hang out at the gym anytime he wanted, but he'd need to do some chores around the place, for which he'd be paid in cash. Dray had known from experience that it hadn't been cheap labor Brick had been after. *Christ*. Dray wondered, not for the first time, just how many lives Brick had saved over the years.

Dray's phone rang, and he immediately tensed. He pulled the cell out of his pocket and swiped his finger over the screen. "Hey."

"You need to get over here," Flint said.

"Is he gone?" Dray asked the question he feared most. Although he'd prepared himself for the news, it still hurt.

"Yeah, and so is Lucky. From the amount of blood on Brick's bed, I'd say he started vomiting again, died, and Lucky freaked out."

Confused, Dray shook his head. "Are you telling me Lucky took Brick somewhere?"

"No, I'm telling you Brick's still in his bed, but he was alone when I got here. I'm assuming Lucky left after Brick died, but I don't know for sure."

"Yes, you do. Lucky wouldn't have left Brick's side otherwise." An eerie calm passed over Dray at the news of Brick's death. He'd been prepared for it, and although he knew the realization would hit him eventually, for the moment his thoughts were on Lucky.

"Maybe Lucky's on his way there. Could be something he didn't want to tell you over the phone," Flint offered.

"Yeah, maybe." Dray stared at the envelope in his hand. "Call Mac and then call either Sylvia or Janice. I'll tell Jax and wait around for a few minutes to see if Lucky shows up." His gaze landed on the will. He'd have to call Brick's attorney as well, but there was no rush. Brick had already taken care of his funeral arrangements.

"Okay," Flint agreed.

Dray hung up and tried Lucky's cell, but as predicted, the call went to voicemail. "Hey, babe. I need you to call me."

Before he could stop himself, he upended the metal trash can that had to be an antique and dumped everything on the floor. After setting it in the middle of the room, he dropped the photos inside. It only took a moment to locate an old book of matches in Brick's drawer and within seconds, the photographic evidence of Lucky's past started to burn. It took poking around to separate the pictures and several more matches, but eventually, the photos were reduced to a pile of ash.

"Is something burning?" Jax asked, throwing the door open. His gaze landed on the trash can in the center of the room. "What's that?"

Dray shook his head. "The past."

* * * *

Dray rinsed the bloody washcloth in a bowl of warm water. He'd held off calling the funeral home because Jax had asked to say a final goodbye, and there was no way in hell he'd let the kid into Brick's room the way it had been. He'd immediately stripped the sheets and Brick's clothes before giving the old man a sponge bath.

It had been over an hour since he'd left the message on Lucky's phone, and so far, no word. "He loved you so much," he told Brick. "But I'm worried about him."

Dray had been torn between seeing to Brick and looking for Lucky, but he knew it wouldn't have been fair to ask anyone else to take care of Brick. He owed it to the old man to take charge of the situation and see that it was handled properly. After the funeral home picked up the body, he could try to find Lucky.

Once Brick had been cleaned, Dray found an old Brick Yard T-shirt. He borrowed a page from an old cable show he used to watch about a funeral home and split the shirt up the back in order to put it on Brick. Pulling a pair of sweatpants onto Brick was the hardest part, and he was exhausted by the time he'd finished the task. He used a fresh sheet to cover Brick from feet to chest and arranged his hands at his sides.

Dray stared down at the man who had meant so much to so many. "You look good," he whispered, his throat tight with emotion. He hadn't allowed himself a chance to cry because he had a feeling if he started, he wouldn't stop, and with Lucky still missing, he had other things he needed to take care of. He brushed the white wisps of Brick's hair across his balding head before leaning down to place one last kiss on Brick's forehead. "I love you."

* * * *

Dray stopped into Jerry's Place to see if Lucky was drowning his pain, but the only one he recognized was Sid, sitting on a stool at the bar. He walked over and leaned against the scarred wooden surface. "You seen Lucky?"

Sid shook his head, his pupils dilated. "Haven't seen him."

As much as Dray hated to talk to the stoned asshole, he needed answers. "Where's he usually go if he's upset?"

"I don't know."

"How can you not know? You've been his best friend since he was a goddamn kid." Dray took a deep breath. Pissing

Sid off wouldn't get him what he needed. "I'm gonna guess it'll be the same place he went when he was young."

Sid shrugged and took a drink of his beer. "He used to hang out on the roof of his building, but they don't live there anymore, man."

It wasn't much, but it was the only lead Dray had. "Address?"

Sid scratched his greasy hair. "I don't remember the address, but it's that apartment building across the street from that salvage place that takes the junk metal."

"Keen's?" Dray asked.

"Yeah, that's it. So, why're you looking for him?" Sid asked.

"Brick died, and Lucky took off. I'm worried about him," Dray replied.

Sid snorted. "Don't worry about him. Lucky always manages to take care of himself." He stared down at his empty glass. "He doesn't need anyone."

"That's not true." Dray couldn't stand the little weasel, but he knew Lucky loved the guy like a brother or at least he had at one time. "Do me a favor. If you ever decide to pull yourself together and get clean, come by The Brick Yard, and I'll see what I can do to help you out."

Sid curled his lip. "I don't need you."

"No, you don't, but I think you need Lucky—and I also think he needs you." Dray slapped his hand against the bar. "If you happen to see Lucky, tell him to call me."

"Yeah, whatever."

Dray left the bar and jumped into his truck. He drove the ten blocks to Keen's Salvage and parked in front of the rundown building across the street. Staring up, he wondered why the city hadn't had the building condemned years ago.

"Please don't be here," Dray mumbled as he made his way into the building. The dark stairwell smelled of urine and other things he didn't want to think about. The building was only four floors, so it didn't take long to reach the ladder that led to the roof. He shoved open the hatch and studied the floor for several moments, trying to determine how stable the damn thing was.

A noise off to the left caught his attention. He stepped up the last few rungs and climbed onto the roof. He heard the sound again and walked toward it. "Lucky?"

He didn't see Lucky immediately, but he eventually caught sight of a sneaker peeking out from behind one of the heating vents. Glad that he'd finally found Lucky, he walked over, bracing himself for what he might find.

Lucky was curled into a ball, his face buried against his knees. Dray's gaze went to the dried blood on Lucky's hands and arms. *Shit!* Without a word, he sat down. Lucky hadn't bothered to lift his head, so Dray simply put his arm around him and waited. He knew there were no words that could make Lucky forget what he'd so obviously witnessed.

Dray leaned his head on Lucky's shoulder and for the first time since Flint's call earlier that day, he cried. What started as a trickle of tears soon became a torrent, soaking his face and Lucky's T-shirt.

When Lucky finally moved, it wasn't to wrap his arms around Dray. Instead, as if in slow motion, he threw himself forward, bashing his face against the roof.

"What the fuck, Lucky?" Dray scrambled to grab Lucky before he could do it again. "Stop." He wrapped his arms around Lucky's chest and tried to hold him still, but Lucky started to fight his way out of Dray's grasp, continually slamming his forehead against the rough texture of the roof.

Lucky's elbow connected with Dray's eye, knocking him back. Shaken, Dray touched his fingertips to his brow bone, knowing the skin had split but trying to determine how bad the cut was.

"See? I told you. I'm bad!" Lucky yelled, turning to look at Dray for the first time.

Blood streamed down Lucky's face from a three-inch cut to his forehead. The fresh blood, combined with the dried blood covering Lucky's hands and T-shirt stole Dray's breath from his lungs. He pressed one hand to his chest and the other to his eye. He needed to get Lucky to the hospital, but he knew Lucky would never admit he needed help. Lying sucked, but it had to be done. "I think I need to go to the emergency room. I think you broke something."

Lucky wiped the blood away from his eyes and kneeled beside Dray with an anguished expression. "I didn't mean..."

"I know," Dray whispered. He shrugged out of his coat before pulling his shirt over his head. Five stories up, the cold wind stung his skin, but he was starting to really worry about the wound on Lucky's forehead. "Press this against your cut," he instructed.

"I'm fine."

"The hell you are!" Dray wiped his own blood from his face. "I need you to help me, but you're not going to be able to do shit for me if you pass out before you get me to the ER." It was a weak excuse, but Lucky was so out of it, Dray prayed he wouldn't realize it. He slowly lifted his hands and gently pressed the T-shirt against Lucky's forehead. Stretching it out, he tied the material behind Lucky's head. "There, now you look like a ninja warrior."

Lucky continued to stare at Dray. "I-I..."

"What, babe?" Dray cupped Lucky's face and kissed him. "Talk to me."

Lucky's gaze zeroed in on the cut above Dray's eye. "Nothing. Let's get you to a doctor."

* * * *

With Dray right behind him, Lucky unlocked his apartment, but before he pushed the door open, he stared at the ceiling, to the spot in front of Brick's place. Once again, the guilt overwhelmed him. "I can't do this. I can't be here."

Strong arms wrapped around Lucky's waist. "Wait right here. Just give me five minutes to grab us a change of clothes and we'll go to a hotel for the night."

Lucky nodded. "Yeah." He sighed, glancing toward Brick's apartment again. "I need to go up."

"Wait for me, and I'll go with you."

"I need to do it by myself." Lucky lifted a hand and ran his fingers over the bandage. He should've known he couldn't take Dray to the ER without being pulled in himself. He'd received three times the number of stitches Dray had and would probably be paying the hospital for the next two years.

"Okay. I'll come up after I pack a few things."

Lucky tried to give Dray a smile, but he knew it came out looking more like a grimace. He didn't wait for Dray to go inside the apartment before he headed back to the stairs. By the time he reached Brick's, the guilt had swallowed him whole.

It took several moments of fumbling, but he managed to unlock Brick's door. Stepping inside the quiet living room, he shoved the keys back into his pocket as he walked toward the crime scene. Brick had given Lucky a second chance at life, so when Brick had asked Lucky for a favor, how the hell could Lucky turn him down? Brick had never asked for anything in exchange for the safety of the storage room, the training, the job and the friendship.

The door to Brick's room was already open, so all Lucky had to do was step inside. He was surprised to find the bed neatly made with fresh sheets and blankets. There was no sign of the blood that had erupted from Brick's mouth, prompting Lucky to give in and inject the older man with enough morphine to kill him.

A whoosh of air escaped him as he slid to the floor. He'd killed Brick. It was a secret he'd have to keep for the rest of his life, one that would no doubt destroy him in the end.

Lucky heard the sound of a throat clearing moments before he felt Dray's warmth wrap around him. Dray rested his chin on Lucky's shoulder. "Brick asked you, didn't he?"

"Huh?" Lucky's heartbeat sped up at the question.

"He asked you to help him die. I didn't think of it earlier

because I was so focused on finding you, but walking in here, seeing you sitting here, I knew." Dray pressed his lips against Lucky's neck. "He asked me, but I wasn't strong enough. I made him promise not to ask that of you. Goddammit! I hate that I'm suddenly so fucking angry with him, and he's not even here to yell at."

"I told him I couldn't do it, but the longer I sat in here and watched him fight for each breath, I figured when the time came, I'd give him what he'd asked for. I didn't tell him I would because I wasn't positive I could go through with it, and I didn't want him to see it coming. I loaded the syringe this morning." Lucky didn't bother wiping the tears as they fell. "When he started to vomit again, I knew I couldn't hold off any longer." He grabbed Dray's hands and pulled them tighter around him. "He went pretty fast after that, and he gave me what I like to believe was a smile before he died."

"Oh, baby." Dray continued to place soft kisses on Lucky's neck. "I'm sorry this is causing you so much pain, but I need you to know that I think you did the right thing. Thank you for being stronger than I am. Thank you for helping the man we both loved go a little easier."

Lucky sat there for a long time, happy to be in Dray's arms. "When I was eight, one of my mom's boyfriends was beating her. I tried to help, but he knocked me back. I was so afraid he'd kill her. So I went into the kitchen and got a knife, intent on getting him away from her any way I could." He took a deep breath. He'd never told the story to anyone. "My mom warned him and he turned and knocked me to the ground, broke my nose, blacked my eye, but that wasn't enough for them."

Dray stopped kissing Lucky's neck. "What happened, babe?"

Lucky wasn't sure why he was so afraid to tell Dray what he'd done. Dray already knew that his mom had forced him to punish himself as a child, so what had happened next shouldn't come as a big surprise.

"I kicked them when they were trying to overpower me, but I wasn't strong enough to get them away. It only took a second for mom's boyfriend to incapacitate me. Mom handed me the knife and told me bad boys need to be punished. I already knew that, because it was a phrase she said almost every day of my life." Instead of explaining what he'd done, he pulled up the leg of his jeans and directed one of Dray's hands to run over the scar on his calf. "It took two tries before it was deep enough to satisfy Mom," he confessed.

"Christ." Dray's hand curled into a fist. "I noticed the scar before, but you have so many from fighting. I had an idea your aversion to kicking stemmed from your childhood, but I had no idea it was that bad. Promise me you won't ever talk to that woman again."

"She's my mom," Lucky said. "I didn't make things easy on her."

"Fuck that. My mom had two kids to raise, no fucking man to help her out and no money to feed us, but she never once raised a hand to us." Dray pushed against Lucky's shoulders until Lucky was forced to turn around. Dray leaned forward. "I'm going to say something that's going to piss you off, but I need you to understand I'm saying it because I love you."

Each time Dray said those words to Lucky his heart clenched. They were starting to get easier to hear, but he still didn't believe them. "What?"

"She didn't love you. I don't know how that was possible, whether it was the drugs or something in her past, but I'm telling you now, there's no way in hell that woman could have loved you and still done the things she did to you."

Lucky let Dray's words sink in. He'd always suspected his mom didn't love him, but he'd never been able to fully admit it to himself.

"You need to go see someone, a doctor or counselor—someone who can help you deal with the shit your mom put in your head." Dray ran his hand down the side of

Lucky's face. "Because, babe, you're everything to me, and I need you to see that you're a good, kindhearted man who would do anything for the people around him."

Lucky squeezed his eyes closed. "The only place I'm good is in the cage."

"No. That's not true. When you told me what Mac said to you, I nearly flipped my shit, but I had a talk with him the other day, and he explained the entire conversation, and I think I agree with him."

Lucky opened his eyes and stared at Dray. "You agree with Mac?"

Dray held up his hand. "I don't agree with all of it. You do have the heart of a champion. I'm just not sure the cage is the best place for you. You've suffered a lifetime of abuse. Choosing a career that involves hurting and being hurt isn't the healthiest thing for you, in my opinion. I think your heart and your skills can be better put to use at The Brick Yard, and I truly believe Brick felt the same way. I think that's why he left the place to us. He wants you and me to carry his legacy to the next generation of boys who come into the gym, looking for a safe place."

Lucky didn't know what to say. He wanted the gym to be that kind of place for kids like him, but he couldn't imagine a life outside the cage.

"Tell me you'll let me get you some help? You need to talk to someone." Dray continued to push.

"I'm talking to you. I don't trust anyone else," Lucky finally admitted.

"Will you?" Dray asked. "Will you open up to me and talk about the ghosts that chase you?"

The last thing he wanted was to poison Dray with his past, but he didn't want to lose him either. Selfish or not, he wanted Dray even if he didn't deserve him. "If I do, will you stay?"

Dray smiled. "I'm not going anywhere unless it's with you." He got to his feet and held out his hand.

"What about your house?" Lucky asked. Dray had told

him all about the little farm where he lived.

"I bought that house when I needed to feel grounded to something, and I think it served its purpose, but now things are different. *You* ground me. The Brick Yard grounds me. I didn't realize when I left that I was leaving more than my career behind. I thought the best thing for everyone was for me to get as far away from Chicago as possible, but I was wrong." Dray glanced at his outstretched hand. "Come on."

Lucky took the offered gesture and allowed Dray to help him stand. "We can stay downstairs if you think that's for the best," he conceded.

"Not yet. For now, we'll go to a hotel." Dray flashed Lucky that sexy grin of his. "I wanted to fuck you the last time we were in a hotel room together, but I couldn't work up the nerve to make my move. Hopefully, this time I'll get lucky."

Chapter Thirteen

With a towel wrapped around his waist, Dray opened the door to the bathroom and stepped into the hotel room. Lucky was already under the covers, his hair slightly damp from his earlier shower. "What're you watching?"

Lucky shrugged. "Just flipping."

Dray checked the locks on the door before turning off the light in the small entryway. He didn't take Lucky's silence personally. He knew there was a lot going on in Lucky's head, and the emotional drain for both of them had taken its toll.

Dropping the towel, he slid into bed and lay on his back. He stared up, watching the shadows thrown by the television dance across the popcorn ceiling.

"Dray?"

"Yeah?" Dray responded, turning his attention to Lucky.

"Would you hold me?"

With a groan, Dray immediately wrapped Lucky in his arms. "I'm so glad you asked. It kills me to see you hurting and not touch you."

"Don't ever be afraid to touch me," Lucky mumbled against Dray's chest.

Dray closed his eyes, content for the moment to hold the man he loved.

"Talk to me. Tell me what's next," Lucky said.

Dray rubbed his chin across the top of Lucky's head. "I'll need to go by the funeral home tomorrow. Brick already handled the arrangements, but the final details like when they can schedule the services and stuff need to be dealt with. Mac's already started to make calls, but I'll find Brick's address book and make sure he didn't miss anyone."

"What can I do?"

Dray wasn't sure how much Lucky would be able to handle, so he tried to think of a few simple tasks that would need to be taken care of that would still make Lucky feel like he was helping. "Well, the lawyer will have to be notified, and we'll have to pick out some clothes for Brick and take them by the funeral home. Do you think you're up to that?"

"Yeah. Brick already told me, no suit." Lucky looked up at Dray and grinned.

Dray smiled back. "Sweatpants and a Brick Yard T-shirt?"

"Yeah, that sounds right," Lucky agreed as a yawn escaped him.

They settled in, and Dray was almost asleep when he felt Lucky move. "You comfortable?"

"I'm good." Lucky kissed Dray's chest. "Did you work things out with Mac?"

Unsure why Lucky had been thinking of Mac, Dray ran his hand down Lucky's back. "For the most part."

"I don't understand why he got so mad at you for not fighting but he wants me to stop. I mean, I know you were better than I am, but I'm not too old to learn."

"It has nothing to do with your skill level. Like I told you on the roof, we worry that the fighting's keeping you from dealing with your past. Mac may be crazy about the sport, but he cares more about you. You know Mac. He's big on the whole path-in-life analogy. He said I let a little pothole in the road scare me into taking the easier path. With you, he sees one clear path and one that's so wrecked with pitfalls that he's not sure you'll survive it."

Lucky rolled to his back. "What two paths? I have fighting. I've never thought of doing anything else."

Dray sighed. Although he knew Lucky didn't mean to do it, his words hurt. "You don't even want to consider me and The Brick Yard a path?"

Lucky turned his head to look at Dray. "I thought you said if I was on the road fighting, I could come home to you?"

"I did." Dray took a deep breath. "But that was before I figured out how much I love you. I'm not saying I'd turn you away, but I don't think I can hide what I feel for you, so maybe it would be better if we're not together at all."

"No," Lucky said, shaking his head.

"Our relationship is bound to get out, and I won't be your Vince," Dray argued. "I won't drag you down. I've told you that before."

"You're nothing like Vince," Lucky shot back.

"No, I'm not, but the result will be the same." Dray pulled Lucky into his arms. "But it's more than that. I know the time commitment involved in taking your career to the next level, and I don't want to spend my days and nights without you while you're traveling around the country. That's not the kind of life I want."

"What kind of life do you want?" Lucky asked.

Dray closed his eyes and allowed himself to dream. "Thanks to some pushing from Mac, I want to become a licensed foster parent, so I can legally help kids like Jax." He glanced at Lucky, unsure how Lucky would take the next part of his dream. "I'd like to make some changes at the gym."

"What changes?"

"I'd like to open it up to more kids. Adult membership is dwindling anyway. With all the fancy athletic clubs opening up, fewer people are interested in working out at an old-school setting." The more Dray talked about it, the more he liked the idea.

"What'll we do for money? Without paying members, we'll drive the place into the ground."

Dray smiled. He liked that Lucky included himself in the plan. He doubted Lucky had even realized he'd done it. "We can apply for grants, but I also think there's more to Brick's estate than the gym. We already know he owns Mac's diner, but I found a bunch of rent receipts. I'm not sure, but I think he owns your apartment building."

"No way. He would've said something."

"Would he?" Dray ran his hand down Lucky's spine to land on his ass. "I think we can pay it forward while still keeping our heads above water, but I don't think I can do it without you. It'll be a lot of work and probably a lot of heartache, so, yeah, I'll need you with me."

"I'll think about it."

Dray wondered why the hell Lucky needed to think about it. "Are you saying you're not sure a life with me is worth giving up the cage?"

"No." Lucky pulled away and leaned up on one elbow. "I'm not sure I'm the best person to be around the kids."

"Are you joking?" Dray ran his palm down Lucky's cheek. "You're the perfect person because you won't pass judgment when they come in with bruises or empty stomachs. Because, babe, despite your childhood, you've grown into a man they can look up to."

Lucky seemed thoughtful for several moments before leaning down to seal his mouth over Dray's.

Dray opened to Lucky's kiss. He wouldn't push Lucky further for now, but he wouldn't give up either.

"I need you," Lucky whispered against Dray's lips.

"What do you need?" Dray asked.

"I need you to fuck me."

"No." Dray refused to let Lucky's request hurt him. "Now, ask me to make love to you." They'd done it before, many times, actually, but it was important to him that Lucky acknowledge it.

Lucky's eyebrows rose to disappear under the bandage on his forehead. "What's the difference?"

Dray moved to lie on top of Lucky. "Fucking's a physical act. Making love can only happen between two people who love each other." He held his breath. Lucky had never verbally reciprocated his feelings, and he prayed Lucky would take the lifeline he'd just thrown out.

Lucky licked his lips and swallowed several times before answering. "Okay."

"Okay what?"

"I need you to make love to me."

Dray smiled. Although Lucky hadn't come out and declared his feelings, for the first time he'd actually acknowledged that he had them. Dray climbed off the bed and dug around in his bag for the bottle of lube. "Missionary," he said when Lucky started to roll onto his stomach.

Chuckling, Lucky moved back to his original position. "You're being bossy."

Dray crawled onto the bed to kneel between Lucky's legs. "I'm practicing." He set the lube aside and took some time kissing and licking Lucky's muscled torso, paying particular attention to the pale, tawny nipples he loved to torture with his teeth and tongue.

"Fuck," Lucky moaned.

Dray released the nipple between his teeth and scooted down on the bed. He rubbed the crown of Lucky's cock against his lips before circling the circumference with his tongue. "Tell me what you want." He tapped the tip of his tongue against the slit on Dray's cockhead.

"Touch me, eat me…fuck, I don't care. It all feels so good when you do it," Lucky crooned.

Dray took Lucky's length as far down into his throat as he could then pulled back, repeating the action several times. He reached over and grabbed the bottle of lube. Staring into Lucky's eyes, Dray coated his fingers.

Lucky slid his feet up the mattress, spreading his legs wider apart to give Dray access to his ass.

Unable to resist, Dray leaned down and swiped his tongue across Lucky's hole, tasting the perfume left over from the hotel soap Lucky had used earlier. Each flick of his tongue seemed to drive Lucky's lust higher.

"Oh fuck. Need you in me," Lucky panted.

"Not yet. I'm enjoying myself too much," Dray replied. He watched closely as he pushed his finger inside Lucky's ass. The sight of the puckered skin opening to accept his touch fascinated him. How many others had he been with, and he'd never taken the time to marvel at something so incredibly amazing.

Soon, Dray slid another finger inside. "The way your body accepts mine is beautiful," he mumbled.

"Give me your cock," Lucky begged. "I need it."

Dray withdrew his fingers and moved back up to a kneeling position. He stared down at Lucky while applying lube to his shaft. "Stay with me," he whispered. He set the bottle aside and positioned himself at Lucky's entrance. "Make a difference with me."

Lucky bit his bottom lip but didn't reply to the plea.

Dray knew Lucky still didn't believe he could make a difference in the lives of others, but there was little else he could say to convince him. With a slight shake of his head, he let it go for the moment. Pushing inside, he again watched as Lucky's body stretched to accommodate him. "Fuck," he growled.

Lucky sat up enough to grab the back of Dray's neck. He pulled Dray down and draped his legs over Dray's shoulders. The new position allowed Dray to drive in deeper, with the added bonus of bringing them close enough to kiss.

Dray wasted no time fucking Lucky's mouth with his tongue as his dick began to slide in and out of Lucky's ass. He pushed his arms under Lucky's back and curled his hands around Lucky's shoulders to hold him in place when he began to fuck harder. Each thrust of his hips prompted a moan from Lucky. Grunting into the kiss, Dray swiveled his hips, grinding Lucky's cock between them.

The sharp intake of breath combined with the squeeze of Lucky's body and the sudden warmth against Dray's skin signaled Lucky's climax. "Love me!" Lucky howled as his body continued to jerk with the force of his orgasm.

"Always," Dray promised, driving deep several times before giving in to his own desire to come. He collapsed on top of Lucky, shrugging Lucky's legs off his shoulders as he struggled to catch his breath. They would both need to shower again, but for the moment, he wanted his softening dick to stay inside Lucky for as long as possible. He buried his face against Lucky's neck, inhaling the scent he'd grown to associate with a sense of home and love.

* * * *

Dray wiped the tears from his eyes as he went in search of Lucky. He wasn't surprised to finally find him in the storage room with Jax, but what the two of them were doing did surprise him. "Why does it smell like chocolate in here?"

Lucky smiled. "I'm showing Jax how to make a cup of chocolate cake in the microwave."

With the manila envelope still tucked under his arm, he leaned against the doorjamb. "I can't believe Brick let you have chocolate cake."

"He didn't *let* me have a lot of things, but that doesn't mean I didn't have them," Lucky said. He pointed to the envelope. "What's that?"

"Something I want to talk to you about." Dray moved to sit on the corner of the twin bed where Jax slept. He opened the envelope and gently removed a stack of eight-by-ten photographs. "I found these in Brick's desk."

Dray didn't say anything about finding an envelope that Brick had kept of Jax's injuries, but unlike the one of Lucky's, Dray hadn't burned Jax's in case there still came a time when he needed it. He held the first photograph up. It was a much, much younger Brick standing with his arm slung over a boy's shoulders. "Benjamin Hooks, 1968. Brick has scrawled at the bottom, died in Vietnam May 15th, 1971." He set that picture on the bed before holding up another one. "Robert Scarponi, 1974." Dray added that one to the pile. He picked up one of his favorites. "Makenzie Jefferson, better known as Mac, 1978."

"Dude, let me see that." Jax took the photograph out of Dray's hand. "I can't believe Mac's mom gave him a girl's name."

"If you know what's good for you, I wouldn't tease him about it," Lucky warned.

"This whole pile is kids Brick's helped. I'd like to frame them and find somewhere in the gym to hang them." Dray spread the others out on the mattress, pulling three out to lay on top. "Do you remember taking these?"

The microwave dinged, and Lucky stepped away long enough to remove the old coffee cup from inside. He hunted around in the basket on the makeshift counter before handing a spoon and the cup to Jax. "Eat up."

Jax lifted the cup to his nose. "I can't believe how good this smells. Now that you showed me how to make it, I may have to treat myself every night."

"No you won't," Lucky argued. He turned his attention back to the photo of himself. "Didn't you take this one of me and Brick?" he asked Dray.

"Yeah. I remember thinking it was weird when Brick asked me to do it. I'd never taken a picture in my life, but he gave me the camera, showed me how to use it and grabbed you for the shot. I guess I didn't ask why he wanted it at the time because I was so honored to touch his beloved camera in the first place." Dray gestured to the stack of pictures. "He's helped so many of us."

"We should frame them and put them out during the memorial," Jax suggested.

"Good idea. You and Lucky want to tackle that project while I finish in Brick's office?" Dray asked.

Jax and Lucky glanced at each other before Lucky shrugged. "Sure."

"After I finish this," Jax said around a mouthful of chocolate cake.

Dray noticed the shadow that seemed to have enveloped Lucky in the last minute or so. Maybe he shouldn't have asked Lucky to buy the frames. What if he didn't have the money for something like that? Instead of embarrassing Lucky in front of Jax, he decided to call him out. "Jax, you finish eating. Lucky, I could use your help in the office for a minute before you go."

"Okay." Lucky got to his feet and followed Dray out of the door. "Make sure you wash that mug as soon as you're finished. Roaches are the last thing we need in here."

Dray waited until he closed Brick's door before turning to face Lucky. "What's going on in that handsome head of yours?"

"Huh?"

Dray grabbed Lucky's hand and led him over to the sofa. "Something about those pictures is bothering you, and I want you to tell me what it is."

Lucky shrugged. "I don't know. I mean, I knew I wasn't the first person Brick had helped, but I had no idea there'd been so many. Brick made me feel special, and now I'm thinking I was just fooling myself, because I bet Brick made all of them believe that."

Although Dray understood how Lucky could have come to that conclusion, he didn't agree. "First of all, you are special. Other than leaving Mac the diner and apartment over it, Brick left everything else to you and me. That means out of all the boys he's helped throughout the years, he knew you and I would keep his legacy going. That says a lot about the kind of man he believed you to be."

"Maybe," Lucky mumbled.

"Here's something else to consider. I know that Brick's attention made me feel special. Could you possibly begrudge any of those kids the same attention? That's the beauty of what Brick did. He never seemed to run out of special." Dray gathered Lucky into his arms. "You're it for me, but I'll still do my best to make a difference in Jax's life or any kid who comes after him, because I had a fantastic old man in my life who showed me it was possible for me to feel special."

Lucky nudged Dray's ribs with his elbow. "Now you're just trying to make me feel like a jerk for being jealous of all those pictures."

"I'm not trying to do that. I just want you to figure out that love is endless because the more you give, the more you have to give."

Lucky raised one eyebrow. "Did you read that on a fortune cookie?"

Dray shook his head. "Nope, I guess I just realized it when I found that envelope. Brick loved you, but he also loved me, Mac, Flint, Jax and the thirty-one people that came before us. I once asked him why he'd never married, and he told me he'd never felt the need. I didn't push it at the time, but now I think he had all he ever wanted by taking care of kids just like him. That's what I want, which is why I'm ready to do whatever's necessary to legally take in kids who could use the help, but I need you to be on the same page because I can't do it without you."

Lucky stared at Dray for several moments before nodding. "Just tell me what you want me to do."

* * * *

Lucky pulled at the collar on the white dress shirt Dray had insisted he buy. As uncomfortable as he was in the suit, it was nothing compared to the unease he felt as friends of Brick's stepped up one by one to shake his hand and offer condolences. He felt like an imposter, knowing the receiving line was usually reserved for family of the deceased.

A short, middle-aged man released Dray's hand and reached for Lucky's. "I'm sorry for your loss."

Lucky had learned what to say from listening to Dray over and over. "Thank you. How'd you know Brick?" He stared, trying to imagine a younger face because he figured the guy in front of him was also on one of the tables lined with photographs.

"He gave me my first job, nearly thirty years ago." The older gentleman smiled as if remembering his youth. "Brick rescued me from a group of bullies. He hauled me into The Brick Yard and taught me everything I needed to know about defending myself."

The story made Lucky smile. "Yelling at you the entire time, no doubt."

The man laughed. "You know it." He glanced toward the closed casket. "I imagine he was ornery up until the last moment."

Lucky's smile faltered, his throat growing thick with emotion for the first time since he'd arrived. He'd purposely avoided looking at the coffin just for that reason. "Actually, at the very end, he was…" *Fuck.* He tried to get his emotions under control as he recalled his final memory of Brick. "At peace," he finished.

Suddenly, he felt like the air had been sucked from the room. He offered the man an apologetic smile. "Excuse me."

Without waiting for a response, Lucky stepped away from the line of people and pushed open the side door of the small funeral home chapel. He stopped in his tracks when he came face to face with the shiny black hearse. "Goddammit!" he screamed, as loud as his lungs would allow.

Lucky heard the door open behind him. He glanced over his shoulder, expecting to see Dray, but he was surprised to find Jax standing behind him. "Hey." Lucky quickly pulled out the white cotton handkerchief Dray had given him earlier in the day, and wiped his eyes as he turned to face Jax.

Jax moved closer. "I know this isn't cool, but…" He threw his arms around Lucky's chest and hugged him.

Lucky held Jax as the two of them quietly mourned the loss of their friend. There was nothing he could say that would make Jax feel better and they both knew it, so instead, he gave the teenager the one thing he had to give.

"I wish I had a dad like him," Jax said, his breath hitching with each word.

"Me too," Lucky agreed, petting Jax's shaggy hair as he continued to hold him. "Although, I guess we're both lucky

Brick didn't have his own family because then he wouldn't have been available to help so many of us."

Jax nodded.

Lucky thought of Jax and the teenagers who'd come before him, and knew which path he needed to take. "Dray wants to turn The Brick Yard into a place where kids can come if they'd like help."

"Yeah?" Jax pulled back slightly and looked up at Lucky. "What do you think?"

"I think the biggest thank you we can give Brick is to continue his legacy. I wouldn't even be here if it weren't for him and the gym."

"Did your dad hit you, too?" Jax asked.

"I didn't really have a dad," Lucky confessed, "but I had a mom who made me believe horrible things about myself."

"Why?"

"I don't know," Lucky admitted. "I'm still working through it. I doubt I'll ever understand why she felt I wasn't good enough, just like you're probably trying to figure out why your dad treated you the way he did." Lucky released Jax and wiped his face before blowing his nose. When he noticed Jax was in the same predicament, he pulled a wad of tissues out of his suit pocket and handed them over. "I'm not very good at talking about stuff, but if you need someone to listen, I'm here."

Jax wiped his nose. "There's a freshman at my school that I'd like to bring by the gym. I've never talked to him, but he has the same look in his eyes that I used to see in my own before I met you and Brick."

To hear that he'd had even a small part in helping Jax filled Lucky with pride. "Bring him by. Dray's going to see if he can qualify to become a foster parent. That way, he can legally keep kids safe."

"What about you?" Jax asked. "Don't you want to become a foster parent?"

Lucky shoved his hands in his pants' pockets. "I'm a mess. I wouldn't be a good mentor for anyone."

"Are you shittin' me?"

Lucky fingered the row of stitches on his forehead. He couldn't tell Jax about all the ways he'd punished himself over the years because he didn't want to admit just how screwed up he was. "No. Like I said, my past is too fucked up."

Jax dipped his head and stared down at the parking lot. "If all that happened when you were my age and you're still fucked up, what chance do I have?" He glanced up at Lucky. "Will I always be fucked up, too?"

A noise drew his attention, and Lucky caught sight of Dray. He stared at Dray, still trying to figure out what Dray saw in him that he didn't see in himself. How could he try to help the kids that came into The Brick Yard if he couldn't help himself?

"Not if you talk to someone," Dray said, answering Jax's question.

Jax spun around to face Dray. "Can you find someone for Lucky to talk to, too?"

Dray shrugged. "That's up to Lucky."

Lucky couldn't take his eyes off Dray because in that moment, he knew he'd fallen hopelessly in love. He knew he owed it to Dray to become a man worthy of the love Dray gave. He'd always felt talking to someone about his past would make him weak, but he owed it to Dray and kids like Jax to get better. "I could maybe talk to someone," he agreed.

Jax looked back at Lucky. "Really?"

Lucky nodded. "Yeah. Really."

Jax hugged Lucky again, and Lucky watched as Dray mouthed the words, "I love you."

* * * *

Dray tossed the magazine back onto the waiting room table and got to his feet. His stomach in knots, he began to pace the small space. What if pushing Lucky into the appointment had been the wrong thing to do? What if digging up the past ended up hurting the man he loved even more?

The phone in his pocket began to vibrate. He pulled it out and swiped his finger across the glass before putting it to his ear. "Hey."

"How'd it go?" Mac asked.

"I don't know yet. He's still in there." Dray blew out a breath. "I'm worried though."

"Don't be. He's where he needs to be."

"I hope so." Dray glanced at his watch. "Is that the only reason you called?"

"No. That gal from the state was by, asked me a million and one questions and had me fill out some paperwork. I had no idea giving you a reference for your application would be so damn complicated. I thought I could tell them you were a good guy despite your fucked-up tattoos and call it good."

Dray chuckled. The application process hadn't been an easy one and he still had twenty-four hours of training left, but becoming a foster parent to Jax would be worth it.

The door leading to the psychiatrist's office opened and a puffy-eyed Lucky walked out. "He's done. I'll talk to you later. Thanks for talking to Mrs. Gaines for me."

"No problem," Mac replied before hanging up.

Dray shoved his phone back into his pocket. "You okay?"

Lucky nodded. "He wants to see me a couple times a week for now."

"Okay. Did you take into consideration our trip to Kansas City when you made another appointment?" Dray asked.

"Yeah." Lucky gestured to the closed office door. "He's a smart man."

"Oh yeah? That's good." Dray led Lucky to the door with a hand on his back.

"He told me I'm a lucky man to have someone like you who loves me so much." Lucky grinned at Dray over his shoulder. "I told you, smart man."

Crossing the parking lot toward Dray's truck, Lucky cleared his throat. "Do you still have your tattoo supplies with you?"

"At the apartment," Dray confirmed. "Why? You finally figure out what you want?"

"I've been giving it a lot of thought. I want to do something for Brick, but I haven't been able to figure out what." Lucky dug a piece of paper out of his pocket but held it clutched in his hand. "I talked to Dr. Sherman about it, and how I wanted to honor Brick with something as beautiful as he was. Dr. Sherman asked me a bunch of questions and then recited this quote to me." He shrugged before handing the paper to Dray. "I knew as soon as I heard it, it would be a fitting tribute."

Dray stopped beside the pickup and unfolded the paper. "'When a great man dies, for years the light he leaves behind him, lies on the paths of men.'" He nodded, knowing it truly did fit Brick. "That's beautiful. Who wrote it?"

"That's the best part. Henry Wadsworth Longfellow wrote it, so people will read it and think I'm smart. It's a win-win for me."

Laughing, Dray leaned in and gave Lucky a deep kiss. "I'm surprised you're in such a good mood. I thought the session might be hard on you."

"It was for a while, but after I told Dr. Sherman a bunch of my shit, he said he believes he can help me." Lucky opened the truck door. "It gave me hope, and that's what I came here for."

Dray climbed behind the steering wheel and started the engine. "I'm proud of you."

"I haven't done anything yet," Lucky argued.

"Yes, you have." Dray reached over and squeezed Lucky's hand. "You've just taken the first step in bringing a gym full of troubled teens hope."

Chapter Fourteen

"What're you doing?" Dray asked Lucky.

"Checking in with Jax." Lucky held his phone to his ear. He hated that they couldn't bring Jax along on their trip to Kansas City to pick up Dray's stuff.

"You just called him two hours ago," Dray reminded him. "And we're almost there."

"I know," Lucky said.

"Hey," Jax answered. "I'm still here."

Lucky chuckled. "I forgot to tell you. I left a plastic container of shredded baked chicken. Gatsby likes it mixed with her canned food in the evening."

"No shit," Jax replied. "Is it just for Gatsby or can I have some, too?"

"The shredded stuff's for the cat, but I also left several grilled breasts in wrapped foil for you." Lucky glanced at Dray and rolled his eyes. "Did you really think I'd feed Gatsby better than you?"

"It crossed my mind. I know how much you love that cat," Jax said.

"Not as much as I love you." Lucky slapped his hand over his mouth. He couldn't believe he'd just blurted that out. He felt Dray's hand on his thigh. Panicking, he tried to backtrack. "I mean, you know, I care enough to feed you." He winced at the way he knew that had sounded. "Shit. I mean—"

"It's okay, Lucky. I know what you meant," Jax said, but Lucky could tell by Jax's tone that he didn't see at all.

Why is it so hard for me to admit what I feel? Lucky chewed his bottom lip for a moment. "I do love you, Jax. I'm not good at saying stuff like that, but don't ever doubt it."

Jax was quiet for several moments. "Me too," he said in a voice so soft that Lucky barely heard it.

Lucky released the breath he'd been holding. "Okay. Enough of the mushy shit. Give my kitty some extra snuggles for me."

Jax laughed. "How is it that neither of us are comfortable showing affection for people, but we have no problem giving it to Gatsby?"

Lucky grinned. "I don't know. Maybe because we know Gatsby doesn't judge us for who we are. As long as we take care of her, she loves us."

"You might be right," Jax agreed.

"Yeah." Lucky realized the truck was slowing and glanced around. A white, two-story farmhouse came into view at the end of a long gravel driveway. "I think we're here," he told Jax. "I'll call you later."

"Sure thing. Have fun," Jax replied before hanging up.

Lucky set the phone in the console and leaned forward to get a better view of the house through the trees. "This is your place?"

"Yep," Dray said with obvious pride in his voice as he pulled to a stop.

Lucky opened his door and climbed out of the pickup. He'd never owned a house, never even lived in anything other than an apartment, so he couldn't imagine having so much space to move around in. "How're you going to go from a place like this to my apartment?"

Dray led Lucky up several steps to stand on the deep front porch. "What do you see?"

"Huh?" Lucky wasn't sure what Dray was asking until he followed Dray's line of sight. "You mean the rocking chair?"

"*The* rocking chair. *One.* When we get back, I want to use the profit from this place for a down payment on buy a house in Chicago that'll work for us. If we're lucky, we'll find something with either a porch or a deck where we can put *two* rocking chairs. Now, does that answer your question?"

"Really? You want to buy a house in Chicago?" Lucky's stomach fluttered at the idea.

"Yeah. Chicago's expensive, so it probably won't be anything as big as this, but we should be able to find something nice enough for us, Jax and maybe one or two other foster kids." Dray unlocked the front door before pushing it open.

Lucky followed Dray inside, still shocked at Dray's plans. He gaped at the dark polished woodwork in the entryway. "Dray."

"Yeah, I love it, too." Dray picked up a basket of mail and started sorting through it. The basket was huge, reminding Lucky just how long Dray had been away from his home. "Feel free to look around," Dray said, opening a large envelope.

Lucky wandered into the living room, taking in the large brick fireplace and comfortable-looking leather chair beside it. He glanced around at the other furniture in the room and quickly came to the conclusion that only one piece of furniture was used on a regular basis. Just like the porch, Dray's house was a home of one. Lucky started to feel better about Dray making the move to Chicago. At least in the city, he'd never again be alone if Lucky had anything to say about it.

* * * *

Dray tossed a pack of thick steaks into the grocery cart as his cell phone started vibrating in his pocket. He moved his cart to the side of the aisle before answering the call. "Hey."

"I know tonight's special and all, but would it be okay if I brought that kid, Luke, to dinner?" Jax asked.

Dray glanced at the three big T-bones in his cart and winced at the thought of buying another, but Jax had been talking about Luke for months. "I guess so. It's your

235

celebration dinner after all."

"Thanks. Luke's not looking so good today. You'll see it as soon as you meet him. It's like he's giving up. His eyes look kinda dead," Jax said.

"You don't have to explain your reasons for bringing him home with you. I trust you. If you think the boy needs our help, bring him." Dray steered the shopping cart with one hand as he made his way back to the butcher counter.

"Cool. I'm gonna go find him then. Are you still coming by the school to officially update my address and guardian info?"

"Yeah. I'm at the store now. I'll run this stuff home then be over to take care of that. You want a ride home?" Dray asked as he took a number at the meat counter. He couldn't believe the ink was barely dry on Jax's foster placement with him, and Jax was already recruiting more kids.

"I don't know yet. It depends on Luke and whether or not I can convince him to come to dinner. If I'm at the office when you're ready to leave, that means I'm riding home. If not, I'll be home as soon as I can with Luke in tow."

"Sounds good." The butcher called Dray's ticket number. "I have to go."

"Right. Love you, Dray."

Dray grinned. Since the day of Lucky and Jax's weird, stilted conversation about using the word love, Dray had noticed they all said it a lot more often. "Love you, kid."

* * * *

Lucky felt as if he'd accomplished something by the time he walked into the apartment. He'd managed to buy most of the gifts on his list, and Thanksgiving was still three days away. It wasn't like he was always so ahead of the game, but the upcoming Christmas would be his first with a real family. In the past, he'd exchanged gifts with Briley, Sid, Mac and Brick, but those presents had usually either been generic non-personal items or, in Brick's case, something he'd heard Brick had needed that he wouldn't have bought for himself.

After shrugging out of his coat, Lucky did the responsible thing and hung it in the closet. BD, or Before Dray, Lucky would've tossed the coat on the couch, but after months of keeping the apartment clean for the foster system's surprise home visits, he'd changed a few of his usual habits.

"Lucky?" Dray called from the kitchen.

"Yep." Lucky noticed the small dining table, which had once belonged to Brick, was set for four. Evidently, they were having company.

"Did you have a good day?" Dray asked when Lucky entered the kitchen.

"A great day." Lucky wrapped his arms around Dray from behind. "Is Mac coming to dinner?"

Dray shook his head. "Jax brought Luke home. Why don't you go say hello, then we need to talk."

Lucky pressed a kiss to Dray's neck. "Something wrong?"

"You'll see. Go say hi," Dray ordered.

Lucky moved to insinuate himself between Dray's chest and the kitchen counter. It was his first look at Dray's face and it was immediately obvious the man he loved was pissed about something. "Dray? What's going on?"

Dray's jaw ticked as he continued to avoid Lucky's gaze. "We need to move to a bigger place."

"I thought we were going to look for houses in the spring." Lucky couldn't figure out what had happened to sour Dray's mood. Earlier in the day, Dray had been on top of the world after getting the paperwork for Jax's official placement in their home.

"That was before I met Luke," Dray said. "And as far as I'm concerned, now that he's here, he's not going anywhere."

Shit. "Okay," Lucky agreed. "Then we'll start looking for houses tomorrow. We'll have to take a day or two off for Thanksgiving, but we'll find something as soon as we can."

Dray settled his hands on Lucky's hips. "I need to ask you something, but I hate to because I don't want to drag up a bunch of shit from your past."

"Ask." Lucky prepared himself for what was to come.

"How did Brick convince you to let him take pictures of your bruises and stuff when you first came to The Brick Yard?" Dray asked.

Lucky stiffened. "How'd you know about those?"

Dray sighed. "Brick kept an envelope in his desk. He asked me to burn it before he died because he didn't want you to be the one to find it."

"Just like the one he had on Jax," Lucky said. *Fuck*. Why hadn't he realized there'd been one of him too? He'd known when Brick had taken the pictures why he'd done it, because he'd explained it at the time. "I think you gotta just be honest with Luke. Brick explained to me that a lot of adults don't believe kids when they say they're abused, so having proof of injuries would go a long way if the police ever showed up at The Brick Yard. He made it sound like it was to protect him more than me, and I was a kid who'd had kindness handed to me for the first time. I'd have done anything Brick asked me to."

"Are you mad that I didn't tell you about the pictures?" Dray asked.

Lucky shook his head. "No. I'd have done the same thing. I didn't think of it until now, but my first reaction when I saw Jax's bruises the last time his father beat on him was to take pictures of his injuries." There was a certain amount of comfort in knowing Brick had trained him to carry on the legacy without even realizing he was doing it.

Dray retrieved his phone from the counter before pressing it into Lucky's palm. "Would you try to talk Luke into letting you take pictures of his bruises? I'd ask Jax to do it, but I'm not sure he's ready for that."

"Sure." Lucky gave Dray a deep kiss before leaving the kitchen. He still wasn't sure why he deserved such a good man, but he definitely had one.

Lucky knocked on Jax's closed bedroom door. "Jax?"

The door swung open. "Hey." Jax stepped back and

ushered Lucky inside. "Luke, this is my foster dad, Lucky."

"You're the fighter," Luke said from his position at the foot of Jax's bed.

Lucky sat on the desk chair. It only took a moment for him to understand why Dray had reacted the way he had. Not only was Luke skin and bones, but he had a healing black eye and a few jagged scars visible on his arms below his short-sleeved T-shirt. "Jax, why don't you go help Dray in the kitchen?"

Jax exchanged a knowing look with Lucky before turning to Luke. "Will you be cool here with Lucky for a few minutes?"

Luke shrugged one bony shoulder. "I guess."

It was obvious to Lucky that Luke didn't trust him, but he hoped he'd eventually earn it. He waited until Jax left the room, pleased when Jax read the situation well enough to leave the bedroom door open. "To answer your question, I was a fighter, but then I realized my fighting had nothing to do with enjoyment and everything to do with my childhood." He leaned forward, resting his forearms on his knees, and gave Luke a brief summary of his life.

"That stuff really happen to you?" Luke asked when Lucky had finished.

"Yep. Jax, too. Did he tell you that?" Lucky asked.

Luke shrugged again. "Some. He mostly talked about what happened after he ran away from his dad."

Lucky nodded. Jax still had trouble talking about the actual abuse he'd suffered at the hands of his father, but he was getting better with therapy. "Can I be honest with you?"

"I guess."

"You remind me of me, so I hope I'm not overstepping when I ask this, but who's hurting you?" Lucky asked.

Luke's hands curled into fists on his lap. He broke eye contact and appeared to battle with himself for several moments. "My mom mostly," he mumbled. "She hates me. She tells me all the time that I look like the man who raped her, and she needs to cut the devil out of me."

Lucky swallowed several times in an attempt to keep his emotions in check, but his eyes filled with tears regardless. "Are there other children in the house?"

Luke shook his head. "We're staying with one of her boyfriends now. He's got a couple kids, but he doesn't have visitation rights."

A red flag went up for Lucky. "Do you know why he doesn't get to see them?"

"He did time for beating his ex." Luke finally met Lucky's gaze. "They sound like the perfect couple, right?"

"Yeah, match made in heaven." Lucky studied Luke for a moment, trying to figure out if Luke would be open to the idea of leaving his mom. "What would you say if I told you it might be possible for you to come and live with us?"

"Like Jax?" Luke asked.

"Yeah. We'll have to go through the proper channels, but from what I see, I think it can be done if you're ready for that kind of thing." Lucky pulled Dray's phone out of his pocket. "You'd have to let one of us take pictures of your injuries or let us take you to the hospital though."

Luke chuckled. "I've been to the hospital enough times that they practically know me by name."

That announcement surprised Lucky. "Really? Your mom took you to the emergency room?"

"It was either that or let me die." Luke lifted his threadbare T-shirt and pointed to several prominent scars. "This one punctured my lung. That was the first time she took me. She told them I'd joined a gang." He shook his head. "I didn't contradict her at the time because I didn't really know what else to do. What I didn't know was that she'd use that excuse to continue." He ran his fingertips over a long scar on his stomach. "This one wasn't bad enough to do permanent damage, but it was deep enough that I almost bled to death before she could get me to the ER."

Bile rose in Lucky's throat as he took in the myriad scars littering Luke's torso. He didn't doubt the boy's story.

Social services did what they could when they were alerted to a problem, but there were so many fucking kids to help that they didn't go looking unless someone filed a report. He held up the camera. "You mind?"

Luke bit his bottom lip as he dropped his gaze and shook his head.

Lucky took a deep breath before snapping several pictures. "Are there more?"

Luke stood and started to take his shirt off, but Lucky stopped him. "No. Just lift it up for me," Lucky said. He knew he had to be careful when dealing with abused kids, especially because he was in a relationship with another man. There were far too many people in government positions who would readily misconstrue Lucky's motives for having a young teenage boy strip, even if only from the waist up.

Luke turned around and lifted his shirt.

Lucky gasped at the sight of the crisscrossing scars. A few of the cuts appeared to be freshly made. "When's the last time you went to the hospital?"

"Almost two years ago," Luke said. "The hospital started asking questions that Mom was uncomfortable with, so she made it a point not to cut me as deep after that. I guess I should be grateful."

Lucky steadied his hands enough to take a couple of pictures. "There's nothing about those wounds to be grateful for. With your permission, after dinner, I'll ask Dray to call the social worker assigned to Jax. If we can't get clearance for you to stay here tonight, I've got a few places available where you can hide until we get the legal shit worked out. One thing I'm sure of. If you don't want to go back to your mom's house, all you have to do is ask for help."

Luke released his hold on his T-shirt and let it fall back into place. "I don't want to be just another fucked-up kid in the system." His eyes brimmed with tears by the time Lucky finished. "Thank you."

"Don't thank me. Thank Brick." Lucky pointed to a copy

of the picture that hung on the wall of The Brick Yard. It was the one with Brick's arm slung over Jax's shoulder. "He may not be the man that started it all, but he obviously learned from the best and passed that gift on to me, Dray, Jax and a whole bunch of other people."

"Sounds like you're continuing that for him," Luke said, moving closer to the photograph on the wall.

"We're sure as hell going to try."

* * * *

Dray felt anxious as he waited for Lucky, Jax and Luke to arrive at the house. It wasn't the biggest house they'd seen, but there was something about it, besides the fact that it was only a few miles from the gym, that had called to Dray when he'd spotted the 'For Sale' sign on his way home from the Department of Children and Family Services.

"The basement appears dry," Steve, Dray's realtor, said as he shut the door to the downstairs.

"Yeah, that's one of the main reasons I think this'll work for us. Eventually, we'll be able to finish it off and add more bedrooms." Dray walked over to the old tiled fireplace. The house had been built in the twenties, so a top-to-bottom inspection would be vital. "Do you know if this is in working condition?"

Steve looked at the listing sheet. "It says it is."

Dray nodded. The house definitely needed some work, but aside from replacing a few boards on the porch, painting, reworking the kitchen to make it flow better and refinishing the floor, the house had good bones. The windows were relatively new, along with the roof.

Dray heard laughter outside and smiled. "I think they're here."

The sound of footsteps on the porch steps had Dray moving that way. Before he could reach it, the front door opened.

"We're here," Jax called into the empty house.

Dray leaned against the arched doorway that led into the large living room and waited. He didn't want to influence Lucky by immediately blurting out how perfect the house could be for them. Instead, he continued to wait as Lucky wandered through several of the rooms before meeting back up with Dray in the living room. "What do you think?"

Lucky stared at the fireplace before turning to meet Dray's gaze. Tears dripped down his face. "It's perfect."

Dray let out a sigh of relief. "I'm glad you think so. There are four bedrooms, but they're all about the same size, so no spacious master for us."

"Does it have an attached bathroom?" Lucky asked.

"Yeah. It's small with just a toilet, sink and walk-in shower, but at least we wouldn't have to share with the boys," Dray said.

Lucky returned his attention to the fireplace. "I never thought I'd have one of those." He wiped his eyes on the sleeve of his coat. "Do you think the front porch is big enough for a couple of rockers?"

"Absolutely." Dray moved to wrap his arms around Lucky. "The boys can both have their own rooms, and we'll still have one available in case we need it down the road. Plus, the basement can eventually be finished to add more space, if it comes to that."

"You don't have to sell me on this place," Lucky whispered against Dray's lips. "I was sold as soon as we drove up and I saw the yard and the porch."

"So, I think we should put in a strong offer. Steve said it's been empty for a couple of months, which means we might be able to knock a little off the asking price, but it's already cheaper than what we'd planned on spending." Dray was ready to give the owners more if necessary to procure the house. In his heart, he knew he'd do whatever it took to give Lucky, Jax and Luke the home they deserved.

* * * *

"You got the next one cut?" Dray asked, holding out his hand.

"Yep." Luke passed Dray another tile. "I'm getting good at this shit."

Dray chuckled. "You've had plenty of practice." They'd been in the house for a little less than a year, and he was finally getting to the master bathroom renovation. The first thing they'd tackled after buying the house had been the kitchen, and Luke had proved to be a very adept assistant.

"Is Jax coming home for Christmas?" Luke asked.

"That's the plan. He has to work until the twenty-third, but then he's off until just after New Year's." Dray couldn't wait to see Jax. He'd tried to be understanding when Jax had applied to colleges in California, but he couldn't help but feel Jax was running away from Chicago for the wrong reasons. After talking it over with Lucky, they'd decided to support Jax's decision, but that didn't mean he had to like it.

The house phone rang and Dray glanced toward Luke. "You mind getting that?"

"Sure." Luke stood and brushed the ceramic dust from his jeans before crossing to the bedside table. "Hello?"

Dray watched as the color drained from Luke's face. "Who is it?"

"Okay. Yeah, I'll tell him." Luke hung up the phone. "That was Lucky. He sounds like he's losing it. He wants you."

Dray was on his feet, rushing out of the torn-up bathroom before Luke could finish saying Lucky's name. "What's happened?"

Luke shook his head. "I don't know. He was talking really fast and he was crying, but he said he was outside Jerry's Place and something about it was all his fault."

Panic filled Dray as he raced toward the front door. "Stay here and bring the dog inside," he ordered Luke. "I'll call you as soon as I can."

Dray hated it when Lucky went anywhere near that fucking dive bar because the only reason he did was to see

Sid. When he turned onto the block, the first thing he saw was flashing red and blue lights. *No. No. No.* He double-parked a block away from the bar, not giving a shit if he got a ticket.

A crowd of cops and paramedics surrounded something in the alley. "Lucky?" Dray called.

A female police officer turned to regard Dray. "You know this guy?"

Dray nodded. "I haven't seen him yet, but I got a call from my partner asking me to come down."

"He won't let us anywhere near the body," she said.

"Body?" Dray questioned.

"Yeah. Looks to be an overdose. The owner found him and went inside to phone it in, but whoever that guy is, got to him before the police could."

Dray did his best to push past the circle without getting himself arrested. "Excuse me," he said, until he finally had a visual. His heart dropped when he caught sight of Lucky, cradling an obviously dead junkie. It had been a couple of years since Dray had set eyes on Sid, but he had no doubt the emaciated man was Lucky's ex-best friend.

"Lucky," Dray said, moving slowly toward the man he loved.

Lucky raised his head. "It's my fault. He called me last night, but I blew him off. I went by his place today to see if I could find him, but he doesn't even live there anymore."

Dray kneeled beside Lucky and wiped his tear-stained cheek. "You need to let these people take care of Sid."

"It's my fault," Lucky repeated.

"No, baby, it's not. We both know Sid could have reached out to either one of us if he needed help." Dray carefully slid his arms under Sid's cold body. "Let me hand him off to the paramedics, then I'll take you home."

"Why would you do that? I couldn't save my best friend. How am I supposed to save a bunch of kids?" Lucky asked without loosening his grip on Sid.

"One at a time," Dray reminded Lucky.

Epilogue

Three years later

In his usual booth, Lucky leaned back against the wall and shook his head at Briley. "Haven't you figured out yet what causes that?"

Briley looked down at her baby bump. "Evidently not."

Lucky loved spending time with Briley, her husband and their two kids, but damn. Three kids in less than four years was insane. "Tell me you're gonna name this one after me."

"Uhhh, that would be a no." Briley threw the paper wrapper from her straw at him before opening her notebook. "So I wanted to go over the final details for the fundraiser with you."

"Okay." Fundraisers were Lucky's least favorite thing, but they were unavoidable. Like several people in their neighborhood, Briley had stepped forward to offer her help once The Brick Yard had officially become a youth center. Not only did she tutor at the center twice a week, but she also helped with the yearly citywide fundraiser that had become quite a popular charity with local musicians.

"So, the tickets have already sold out," she said.

"That's great." Lucky didn't understand why Briley didn't look happy. At two hundred bucks a pop, he couldn't have asked for more. He'd thought Briley and the other volunteers were crazy when they'd suggested upping the price of the concert tickets, but they'd assured him that with the lineup they'd secured, two hundred bucks was a steal.

"Well, yes and no. I've been looking, and I've found

a bigger venue that we can get. The only problem is it's downtown."

"No." Lucky shook his head. "We've always had the concert at The Brick Yard. It won't be the same anywhere else." Since expanding the gym to include the space between the original gym and Mac's Diner, there was plenty of room to hold the fifteen-hundred spots they'd allowed for.

"I know, but we could sell more tickets if we moved to a bigger venue. The important thing is raising money."

"No, the important thing is letting those kids know they matter to this city. Seeing those musicians come to their little neighborhood goes a long way in showing them that." Lucky crossed his arms. "I appreciate what you're trying to do, but some things are more important than money."

Briley sighed. "You're so goddamn stubborn."

"You're right, I am—something else I inherited from Brick." He grinned and took a sip of his milkshake. "What's next?"

"The bar area. On the diagram, you have it clear in the back, but it needs to be closer to the stage."

"Why? The kids stand in front of the stage. It's bad enough that we have to have alcohol at all at this thing, but putting it right next to a crowd of teenagers is a recipe for disaster." Again, Lucky understood that grown-ups didn't want to spend a fortune on a concert without enjoying a beer or two, but if the gym didn't need the new roof and central air unit so badly, he would have put a stop to it.

"How about a compromise?" Briley pointed her pencil at the gym layout and tapped a section near the middle of the open space. "What about along this wall? It should be behind the space reserved for the kids, while still being close enough that the paying customers can get to it easily."

Lucky lifted his hand. "Whatever."

Briley's eyebrows shot up. "Dang. That was easy enough. You're getting soft."

"Am not," Lucky argued. "Just tired of this shit. Jax should be showing up any time, and I want to be next door to welcome him home."

Briley's face lit up with a huge smile. "Is he home for the whole summer?"

"He's here for good. He's decided to transfer to the University of Chicago." Lucky was so fucking proud of Jax and happy that after four years away, Jax had finally decided to come back to Chicago to earn his Master's degree.

"What? Is he tired of all that California sunshine?" Briley asked.

Lucky shrugged. "I don't know what changed his mind, but he said they had a great program here, and he was ready to be home." He didn't care why Jax was returning, just that he'd have the kid back. "We done here?"

"Yeah." Briley closed her binder. "Don't forget, pre-concert mixer with the bands and press at six on Friday."

Lucky slid out of the booth. "I'll be there, but I'm not wearing a goddamn suit like you made me wear last year. I looked like an idiot."

"You looked hot," Briley countered.

"Yeah, and that drummer from Midnight Breeze pinched my ass. I thought Dray was going to kill the guy." Lucky grinned. He had to admit, he loved Dray's jealous streak. *Damn.* It made him horny just thinking about the way Dray had gone after the guy. He started to reconsider the suit but shut that thought down. "No, no suit."

Lucky could still hear Briley's giggle as he left the diner. He went next door, to the most recent addition to the gym. It was called Sid's Room. The teenagers who came into the center after school were required to stop at Sid's Room first to make sure their homework was finished before they could indulge in the other activities The Brick Yard had to offer. For those who needed tutoring, a steady stream of retirees were always on hand to help. He'd been amazed at the response from the community when he'd put word out that the center was looking for volunteers. They had retired accountants, bankers, computer programmers and just about everything in between.

Lucky waved to Tonya, a fourteen-year-old girl who was new to the center. "How's it going?"

"Good, Mr. Gunn," she replied, before going back to her math book.

Lucky shook his head. He doubted he'd ever get used to being called Mr. Gunn, but Dray insisted on it. According to the love of his life, the kids needed the boundaries, and they needed to learn to respect those who treated them with respect. It sounded like a bunch of bullshit to Lucky, but he wasn't about to argue over something so trivial.

He passed through the first addition they'd made to the gym. The space had once been a tea shop, but when the business had finally gone under, Dray and Lucky had decided to take it over and turn it into a food pantry of sorts. Dray had spent months going to damn near every restaurant, food distributor, bakery and grocery store in the city asking for any help. The Brick Yard currently had a van that traveled the streets during the late-night hours to pick up surplus food. The result had become a decent food pantry, something Lucky would have appreciated when he'd been young and digging through the garbage for something to eat.

When Lucky felt the memories start to encroach on his mood, he touched his thumb to the silver ring on his left ring finger. A present from Dray—one that meant they were together forever.

Lucky entered the gym and looked around. Dray was across the room, instructing three teenage boys on grappling moves. He walked over and waited until he got Dray's attention.

"What's up?" Dray called.

Lucky pointed to his watch. "What time's Jax coming?"

Dray glanced up at the oversized clock on the wall. "Any time."

Lucky gestured to the office, and Dray nodded. He glanced around the large open space. Without looking at the check-in roster, he'd guess they had about thirty-five kids in-house at the moment, but it was still early. As far as he was concerned, there could be a hundred teenagers roaming the place and it wouldn't be enough, because he knew there were thousands out there who needed a place like The Brick Yard.

* * * *

Dray watched Lucky disappear into the office and grinned to himself. It still surprised him how quickly Lucky had taken to the overall running of the place. Despite his constant bitching about it, Lucky was fantastic at the business aspect, seeing that bills were paid on time, collecting the rent checks from the two apartment buildings they'd inherited, along with the numerous retail shops that leased space from them. Not only did Lucky handle the money, but he also spent a lot of time filling out grant forms and talking to potential supporters.

"Can I try that hold on Cameron?" Pete asked.

Dray returned his attention to his class. "Sure, but go easy."

Pete was their newest foster son and had only been with them for five months. So far, Pete had adjusted well to their growing household, although they'd quickly discovered he'd started hoarding food under his bed. Dray and Lucky had sat Pete down and promised him that *never*, while living under their roof, would he go hungry. The situation had improved after that and eventually, the smells coming from Pete's room had dissipated. Dray chuckled just thinking about it. They'd been sure a rat or something had died inside the wall. It hadn't been until Lucky had got out a hammer to knock a hole in the drywall that Pete had confessed.

Dray watched Pete perform a perfect Boston Crab hold on Cameron. "Easy," he warned, knowing Pete was stronger than his opponent. He glanced at the clock again, wishing

Jax would get his ass to the gym. He'd missed that boy like crazy while he'd been away, but he hadn't tried to hold him back. Jax had grown into a damn fine young man. His grades were excellent, and he seemed to settle easily into the rules Lucky and Dray had put in place when he'd come to live with them. Dray just wished he could say the same for Luke, not that Luke was a bad kid, because nothing could be further from the truth. Luke simply acted out on occasion, but Dray suspected, like Lucky, Luke had trouble dealing with his demons from the past.

Luke's story still tore at Dray's heart, and he did his best to shower Luke with love without becoming clingy. It helped that a year after Luke had come to live with them, he'd brought home a boxer puppy they'd named Moby.

For months, Lucky and Luke had worked with that damn dog and by the time they'd finished, Moby was an absolute joy to have around. Dray grinned. He'd discovered that an evening spent on the couch with Lucky and Moby snuggled against him was the closest thing he'd ever found to heaven.

Dray felt pressure against his calf and glanced down to find Gatsby. "Hey." He bent and scooped the cat into his arms. Gatsby had officially become the guardian of The Brick Yard. After Moby had moved into the house, Gatsby had decided having the run of the gym was a hell of a lot better than being chased under the bed twenty times a day. He rubbed Gatsby's ears. "It seems we're both anxious for Jax to get here."

Dray barely had a chance to get the words out when the front door opened and Jax stepped inside. Dray released Gatsby before crossing the gym. He wrapped his arms around Jax and buried his face against Jax's neck. "It's been too long since you've been home."

Shit. Dray hated to cry in front of all the kids, but, damn, he'd missed his boy. He pulled back and bracketed Jax's head with his hands. "You look good."

"I feel good," Jax replied, a huge smile on his face. "How's Lucky?"

Dray nodded. "Getting better all the time." Although Lucky's appointments with Dr. Sherman had gone from a couple of times a week to every other week, both Lucky and the doctor had agreed that continued therapy was for the best. "At least he doesn't punish himself anymore." He smiled. "Now he just picks a fight with me if he's really angry with himself over something."

"And how're you dealing with that?" Jax asked, worry in his tone.

"I'm okay with it for now. Like I said, he's getting better all the time. I usually just let him bluster and then apologize for whatever I didn't do and take him to bed."

"TMI, Dad," Jax replied.

Dray leaned in and kissed Jax's forehead. Jax didn't call him Dad very often, but every time he did, it warmed Dray's heart. "God, it's good to have you home."

"So where is Lucky?" Jax asked.

"Office. He'll never say it, but I think he feels closer to Brick in there." Dray released Jax and took a step back.

"He should. That damn desk chair still has Brick's sweat stains on it."

Before Jax could head toward the office, Dray whistled to get Pete's attention. "I want you to meet someone," he told Pete. With a hand on Pete's shoulder, Dray gestured to Jax. "This is Jax. Jax, this is Pete, the next UFC champion to come out of The Brick Yard."

* * * *

Stepping into Brick's office, Lucky sighed. Unlike the rest of the gym, nothing had changed in there, except he, Dray and Jax had given the space a thorough cleaning. He sat behind the desk and powered up the laptop. Another small change that he prayed Brick would have approved of. He scrolled through his emails, bypassing the lottery wins, penis enlargement promises and limited time offers. He growled as he marked the offending items as spam.

A particular email caught his attention and he smiled. It had been months since he'd heard from his biggest critic. Although Chad no longer called him the Ice Man, he did continue to criticize Lucky for giving up on his career. He opened the email and began to read.

Hey UnLucky,

Just saw your picture in the paper. Why didn't I know you were running a gym for kids? I mean, don't get me wrong, it's a noble thing you're doing, but what the hell? If you'd stuck with it, you could've been with the UFC by now. Seriously, are a bunch of street kids worth giving up your dream?

Chad

Chuckling, Lucky fired back a reply. A few years ago, Chad's email would've pissed him off, but he wasn't the same man he used to be.

Chum,

Sorry you don't have anyone else to pick on lately. Maybe you'll get lucky and another asshole who irritates you will soon join the ranks. And, just to clarify, I'm living my dream. The children I help give me more peace of mind in one day than the cage could have given me in a lifetime.

I wish you the best of luck, as always.

Lucky

He pressed Send before sitting back in the chair, feeling incredibly pleased with himself. He heard a cheer go up in the gym and jumped out of his chair. Without bothering to shut down the computer, he rushed out of the office. "Jax!"

The tall, handsome man who turned a brilliant smile on Lucky was a stark contrast from the skinny kid with a mop of blond curls who'd first come into The Brick Yard. Lucky's strides slowed as he wove his way through the crowd who'd surrounded Jax.

When he finally reached the kid who'd helped save his life, Lucky was filled with a sense of pride. Despite his childhood, Jax had overcome his demons a lot sooner than Lucky had—not that Lucky wasn't still working on it. He threw his arms around Jax and held him for several heartbeats. "We've missed you."

"I've missed you, too." Jax pulled back and studied the gym. "When did you replace the windows?"

Lucky walked Jax toward the office. "Last spring, but enough about the gym, I want to talk about you."

"What about me?"

Lucky directed Jax to the couch before sitting beside him. Like all the furniture in the office, the couch was the same piece of vinyl shit Brick had used, but Lucky and Dray couldn't bring themselves to replace it.

"As much as I love the fact that you're moving back, I want to know why," Lucky said. Since receiving word from Dray that Jax was returning to Chicago, a niggle of worry had begun to creep its way into Lucky's head. What if something was wrong with Dray, and Jax was coming back to help him get through it? As irrational as it sounded, Lucky had a hard time believing his happiness would last. It was something he'd tried time and time again to work out with Dr. Sherman, but that constant threat was always in the back of his mind.

"It's time." Jax shrugged. "I went out to Cali because I thought it was important that I experienced a different way of living, but something happened that made me realize this is where I'm supposed to be."

"What happened?" Lucky touched his thumb to the silver band, silently gathering strength.

"I was sitting at this outdoor café with a group of friends, and I saw a little girl and her mom rooting through a trash can." Eyes filled with tears, Jax looked at Lucky. "I ran inside the café, ordered a couple of sandwiches and offered them to the girl and her mom. They thanked me, but they looked at me suspiciously, and when I got back to the table, the people I considered my friends were laughing at me." Jax cleared his throat. "I decided I'd rather be back here with the people who know me and love me anyway."

Although he hated to hear how much Jax's experience had hurt him, Lucky was happy to know Jax's change in plans hadn't been anything to do with Dray. "You are loved," he told Jax, reaching for his hand.

"Should I be jealous?" Dray asked from the doorway.

Jax chuckled. "You know Lucky only has eyes for you, and gross, Lucky's like my dad, you pervert."

Dray leaned against the doorjamb and crossed his arms over his chest. "I changed the sheets on your bed in the storage room," he told Jax.

"My bed? You mean you don't have anyone staying in the storage room?" Jax asked, releasing Lucky.

"Not since we bought the house." Dray flicked a glance at Lucky. "Although sometimes Lucky sneaks in there to take a nap during the day."

Lucky wouldn't deny going into the storage room, but he rarely went in there to nap. There were times, especially after a particularly bad day or session with Dr. Sherman, that the safety and memories the room held were the only things that helped him pull himself together.

From behind Dray, Gatsby slunk into the office. "You've got someone else who wants to say hi," Lucky said.

Jax lifted the black-and-white cat into his arms. "Shit, I've missed you," he said, rubbing his face against Gatsby's head.

Dray dropped onto the sofa next to Lucky. "I need you to do me a favor."

Lucky rolled his eyes. He had a good idea what that favor would be. "What?"

"Go by the school and pick up Luke?" Dray asked. "He had to stay after to make up that test and missed the school bus."

Lucky groaned. "Why don't you do it?"

"Because I promised the new boys that I'd show them how to hit the speed bag," Dray replied.

"I can show them," Lucky argued.

Dray sighed and kissed Lucky's cheek. "I love you, babe, but we both know you don't have the patience needed to teach a group of eleven and twelve-year-old boys how to fight."

Grumbling, Lucky got to his feet. As much as he hated to admit it, Dray was right. Learning to use the gym's equipment had come so easy to Lucky that he couldn't understand why someone needed to be shown the same damn thing over and over before they got it.

Dray dug the van keys out of his pocket and tossed them to Lucky. "Thanks, babe."

"You owe me," Lucky called as he left the office. He planned to collect as soon as he was alone with Dray in their master bedroom. At the moment, they only had two boys under their care, so it wasn't that hard for him and Dray to find alone-time together. Of course that might all change in the next few weeks. He'd noticed a boy around twelve hanging out in front of the gym. The kid had yet to come inside, but it was obvious the boy needed help.

The minute Lucky stepped outside, he spotted the kid leaning against the corner of the building. "Hey."

"I'm just standing here," the boy replied.

"Why?" Lucky asked. "You should go on in and get something to eat. Dray's getting ready to work with a few of the others on the punching bags. You might learn something." He slowly approached the boy as he spoke, praying he wouldn't scare him away.

The boy looked down at his ratty sneakers. "I thought you had to go through the homework area before you could get something to eat."

"What's your name?" Lucky knew if he could at least get that much information, he'd be able to track the boy down if necessary, to check up on him.

"Dylan," the boy mumbled.

"What's your last name?" Lucky prodded for the rest of it.

"Sheets. It's a stupid name."

Lucky grinned and pointed to himself. "I'm Lucky Gunn."

Dylan's eyebrows rose. "No shit? That's a cool name."

Lucky chuckled. "Glad you think so." He hooked a thumb over his shoulder at the door. He had a good idea why Dylan was afraid to step foot inside The Brick Yard. "So why don't you want to go into Sid's Room? School not your thing?"

Dylan shook his head. "School's lame." He licked his lips.

"You hungry?" Lucky asked.

After several moments, Dylan broke eye contact and nodded.

"Then go on in. Tell whoever tries to stop you that Lucky said it was okay to come in and get something to eat. After your belly's full, stay and hang out for a while." He hoped Dylan would still be there when he returned from picking up Luke, but if not, at least he'd know the kid had eaten.

"They'll really let me in?" Dylan asked.

"Yep. I promise." Lucky crossed his heart with his index finger.

"Thanks."

"As far as I'm concerned, you can come back every day if you need to, but I'll eventually want to talk to you about why you think school's so lame." Lucky had a feeling Dylan had either never attended school or had stopped going because of something going on at home. It wasn't until he'd taken over running the gym that he'd realized just how many kids were in dire situations.

When Dylan didn't immediately head toward the door, Lucky realized the kid was waiting until he didn't have an audience. *Okay then.* Lucky clapped his hands together. "I've got to pick up one of my foster sons at school, but I'll be back later if you need anything."

"Lucky," Dylan called as Lucky headed toward the van.

"Yeah?"

"I'm not sure why you're being so nice, but thank you."

Lucky swallowed around the lump in his throat and nodded. "Anytime, Dylan." He climbed into the van, hoping he'd see Dylan again. There were certain kids he seemed to form an instant connection to, and Dylan was one of them. He had no idea what Dylan's story was, but as Lucky pulled away from the curb, he vowed to do everything he could to help the boy.

As Lucky drove to the special high school Luke attended, he kept a close eye on the sidewalks. The area of town where Luke studied advanced math and science also happened to be the part of town Lucky's mom had moved to. He'd only seen her a couple of times since she'd been released from prison, and the last time he'd spotted her coming out of a neighborhood liquor store, she appeared to be back to her old habits.

There had been a time, before Dray, Jax and Dr. Sherman had saved him, that he would have let the guilt of his mother's relapse drive him to hurt himself, but that time was over. He'd come to terms with his mother's addictions and although it had taken years of therapy, he'd finally realized he wasn't responsible for her actions.

He pulled up in front of the school to find Luke talking to a girl. "Test. Right." Lucky leaned on the horn until he got Luke's attention.

Luke leaned over and gave the girl a kiss before jogging to the van. "Hey, thanks," he said, climbing inside.

"Who's that?" Lucky asked.

"Who?"

"Don't." Lucky glanced at the pretty brown-haired girl still standing by the tree, staring at Luke.

"Oh, that's Jen."

"Is Jen the reason you missed the bus?" Lucky asked as he turned and headed back to the gym.

Luke started in on a rambling story about how he'd stayed after school to finish a test and happened to run into Jen after he got out of class. Evidently, it was pure coincidence that Jen was still there when he'd walked out of the school.

Lucky chuckled and shook his head. He wasn't even thirty yet, so why the hell did a seventeen-year-old boy think he didn't know what was up? "Stop by the office later and pick up some condoms."

"Seriously, dude, that's embarrassing," Luke said, resting his head against the window.

"You wanna know what else is embarrassing? Having to tell that nice girl's dad that you knocked his daughter up because you were too much of a pussy to wrap it up."

Luke groaned and hid his face in his hands.

Lucky grinned, feeling quite pleased with himself all the way back to the gym. "Oh, Jax is here," he told Luke as they walked across the parking lot. "Family dinner at seven. Be there."

"Cool."

The minute they entered the building, Luke took off toward Sid's Room to check in, and Lucky walked toward the sexiest man on the planet. Shirt off and chest shiny with sweat, Dray had an entire crowd of girls watching him demonstrate the speed bag. "Of course he does," he mumbled. His gaze went to the cheesy shamrock tattoo over Dray's heart. *Sorry, girls, he's mine.*

"Showing off for your admirers?" Lucky asked Dray.

Dray grinned. "I don't encourage it."

Lucky ran his gaze over Dray's sculpted chest. "Maybe you should put your shirt back." He longed to pull Dray into his arms and feel that powerful body against him, but even though they occasionally gave each other quick kisses with the kids around, they never engaged in full-out public displays of affection.

"I would, but that Tennison kid puked all over it after I made him run laps around the gym for swearing," Dray replied.

Lucky took a step back. "That's gross."

"Tell me about it."

Lucky studied the room. He didn't see Dylan, but The Brick Yard had grown so large, there were plenty of places to hang out other than the open gym. "You know that boy who's been hanging around outside?"

"You mean the one who reminds me of you?" Dray wiped the sweat from his chest with a towel.

Lucky rolled his eyes. Other than the fact that Dylan hung around outside The Brick Yard, they looked absolutely nothing alike. Lucky was a pale redhead with more freckles than he could count, and Dylan looked to be a mix of white and either black or Mexican. His light-brown skin wasn't enough to make a positive identification and his eyes were so pale they appeared gold in the sunlight. Whatever Dylan's heritage, the mix was absolutely breathtaking.

"Yeah," Lucky finally replied. "I spoke to him outside before I left to pick up Luke. I told him to come on in and get something to eat. At first he didn't want to because evidently people have informed him that they have to stop by Sid's Room before they're allowed to enjoy the rest of the center. I got the feeling he doesn't go to school and that's what was keeping him away."

"Seriously?" Dray tossed the towel toward one of the hampers sprinkled around the room.

"Yeah. From the look of him, he's not eating well, so I told him to come on in and get something for dinner." Lucky rubbed the back of his neck. "You know I can't let this go until this has being taken care of, right?"

Dray reached out and ran his thumb lightly over Lucky's lips. "You wouldn't be the man I love if you did."

Lucky kissed the pad of Dray's thumb. "Cool. I'm going to see if I can find him."

"Don't scare him away," Dray warned.

"I won't." Lucky did another loop around the large open space of the gym before entering the pantry area. He didn't see him in the room, but that didn't mean he hadn't been there. "Louis," he called, getting one of the few paid staff member's attention.

"Yeah, boss?"

"Have you see a young man with pale-brown eyes come in here?" Lucky asked.

Louis nodded. "He fell asleep on the table before he could

finish the food I gave him. Jax woke him and told him he had a bed he could use." He shrugged. "The boy said you told him he could come in and eat."

"I did." Lucky slapped Louis on the back. "Although I don't plan to announce it, I've decided to change the policy. From now on, feed anyone who comes in who's in need of a meal. It doesn't matter if they go through Sid's Room or straight here."

"Okay," Louis replied.

"Thanks." Lucky took off toward the storage room, but before he could reach it, he saw Jax walking in his direction. "Did you get Dylan settled in the storage room?"

Jax shook his head. "As soon as I opened the door to the room, he got a scared look on his face and took off before I could stop him. I don't know what spooked him, but something definitely did. You know him?"

"He's been hanging around outside for the last week or so. I finally convinced him to come in and get something to eat." Lucky sighed as he ran his fingers through his hair. "If he was spooked, I doubt he'll be back."

"You want me to go look for him? He's only been gone for about ten minutes. He's probably still close by," Jax said.

"I'll do it. Do me a favor and ask Louis to make up a couple sandwiches. I'll take them with me in case I can't get him to come back here." Although it was almost time for him to get home to make dinner for the rest of his family, Lucky wouldn't be able to sit down at the table without knowing Dylan was safe.

"Sure thing. If you find him, ask him to stay in the storage room. I can sleep on the couch in the office or at home. It's not a big deal."

"Thanks." Lucky gestured toward the pantry. "Go get the food while I find Dray."

"Right." Jax jogged off without another word.

Lucky smiled at the teenagers who greeted him as he passed. Whether he wanted to admit it or not, he was much better with the kids one-on-one. No, that wasn't true either. He seemed to do best with the boys and girls who came from the worst situations. Maybe it was his ability to understand the haunted look in their eyes or perhaps it was that he knew deep down they were probably as fucked-up as he was. Whatever the reason, he'd always felt the best thing he had to offer The Brick Yard was his understanding of situations so screwed up a normal person wouldn't begin to know how to relate.

"Did you find him?" Dray asked when Lucky drew near.

Lucky shook his head. "Evidently he fell asleep at the table. Jax woke him and told him he could get some sleep in the back, but when Jax opened the door to the storage room, he freaked and took off."

"You going out to look for him?"

"Yeah. Jax is grabbing some food for me to take with me. Sorry, babe, but I think you'll end up cooking dinner tonight or have Luke do it. He's not the best cook in the world, but he can handle spaghetti."

Dray leaned in and brushed his lips across Lucky's. "Be careful out there."

"Yeah." Lucky saw Jax coming toward them with a white plastic grocery sack in his hand. "Gotta go." He gave Dray a quick kiss before taking the bag from Jax. "It's not exactly the homecoming I wanted you to have," he told Jax.

Jax bumped his elbow against Lucky. "It's the best kind of homecoming because this is the reason I wanted to come back. What you do here is important. No, more than that. It's life changing."

Lucky shrugged. He'd never been good with compliments because he'd never understood the motivation behind them.

As Lucky left the gym, he stared up at the brick facade and wondered how one building could make such a difference in the lives of so many. It had certainly changed his. He kissed his fingers before pressing them to the dirty wall. He'd wandered into the gym looking for a place to shelter himself from the cold and had found a home and family.

"I'll miss you forever, Brick," he whispered before going in search of Dylan.

Coming Soon

Book two in the Brick Yard series

Defender

Excerpt

Chapter One

The sweat that dripped down Jax Hurly's forehead stung his eyes, but he refused to stop long enough to wipe it away. His foster dads were due home any moment, and their decree that the lawn be cut that afternoon, or Luke would be benched for his big game, wasn't an idle threat.

Jax was going to kick Luke's ass for taking off with his girlfriend instead of doing what he'd been told. It would serve Luke right to miss that damn game, but Jax couldn't let that happen. It wasn't that baseball was everything to his foster brother or that after a rough start in high school, Luke had managed to graduate with decent grades. Nope, it was the fact that baseball was Luke's ticket out, and after the life the kid had led before coming to live with them, Luke deserved it.

Jax cut the engine. He was drenched in sweat and feeling a bit lightheaded, but it was done. He took a moment to survey the job he'd accomplished in half the time it usually took and sighed in relief. The yard looked like crap, so Lucky and Dray would totally buy the fact that Luke had taken care of the weekly chore on his own.

Jax quickly sprayed the mower down with the garden hose then put it back into the shed. Task complete, he raced into the house with only minutes to spare. "Taking a shower," he informed his youngest foster brother, Pete as he passed through the family room.

"Dray just called and said they were stopping to pick up

fried chicken on their way home," Pete returned.

The news that he had a few extra minutes didn't slow Jax's pace as he headed to his makeshift apartment in the basement, while firing off a text to Luke

U owe me BIG

Jax had already stepped into the shower when he heard his phone ping with an incoming text. He needed to have a serious talk with his brother. As much as Jax liked Luke's girlfriend, Jen, she wasn't worth defying the laws set forth by their foster parents. Dray and Lucky only had a few rules—honesty always, do your part at home and stay in school—and they expected them to be followed.

Jax rinsed the shampoo from his hair as he wondered whether Luke would be able to handle his classes at Elmhurst College. It wasn't the coursework Jax worried about. Luke was smart if he put his mind to it, but Luke also had a tendency to get sidetracked by bullshit.

Just as Jax began drying off, Lucky called down the stairs. "Dinner."

"Be right there." Jax hung his towel on the back of the bathroom door. He read the text from Luke as he walked naked across the unfinished basement.

I've got trouble. Deal with Dray and Lucky for me.

"Shit." There had been times over the summer that Jax had wondered why he'd decided to come home to get his graduate degree from University of Illinois instead of staying in California. Then Luke would get himself into trouble and it would all become clear. Jax was needed at home. Lucky and Dray had their hands full with the center they ran for kids and looking after Pete, and since Jax had been the one to bring Luke into the family, he felt a certain amount of responsibility toward the reckless jerk.

By the time he made it upstairs, Pete, Dray and Lucky

were already seated at the table with their plates filled. "Sorry I'm late." Jax sat in his usual spot.

"Nice try on the yard, but you made the mistake of putting the mower away," Dray said without looking up from his food.

Jax winced. "Don't get mad at Luke. He was getting ready to do it when Jen stopped by. Not sure what's going on, but she seemed upset."

"He cheat on her again?" Lucky asked, his gaze intense on Jax.

Jax shrugged. "Don't know. One minute they were in the front yard talking and the next they were driving away in her car." He selected a breast and a thigh from the bucket. "You're not going to pull him from the game, are you?"

"Not your problem, son," Dray warned in that deep voice he used if one of them was in trouble.

Jax had spent the previous four years obtaining his psychology degree at the University of Southern California, so he'd been away from home for a while, and knew he should trust his foster parents to do the right thing. Lucky and Dray had saved the lives of three boys, including him, by bringing them into their home, so Jax knew they weren't going to punish Luke for the hell of it.

"You think I'm wrong?" Dray asked after several moments of silence.

Jax wiped his hands with a paper napkin. He might have been closing in on twenty-three years old, but he was still living under Dray's roof, so he needed to remember to keep his tone respectful. "I don't disagree that he needs to be punished, but making him sit out the game hurts all of us. We've been planning the picnic around the game for weeks, and it's the last one of the season, which means it may be the last time we get to spend more than an hour with him."

"Elmhurst is only a half an hour away," Dray reminded Jax.

"Yeah, but he's living on campus, so he'll be too wrapped up in himself to come home," Pete chimed in.

Dray's attention swung to the youngest member of the family. "You ganging up on me, too?"

Pete grinned, flashing white teeth that seemed too big for his mouth. "I don't know, is it helping?"

"Why don't we just wait and see what Luke has to say for himself before we hand down judgement." Lucky rose from the table. "In the meantime, I'm going to take a couple pieces of this chicken and get outta here for a while."

Jax watched in silence as Lucky wrapped up two legs, a thigh and two of the leftover rolls. He didn't need to ask who the extra food was for. Several months earlier, Lucky had tried to help a young boy named Dylan, but the kid had run away from the shelter, and Lucky had been looking for him ever since.

"I've got my phone, so text when Luke shows up." Lucky bent to give Dray a quick kiss before walking out of the house.

Jax stared at the closed door for several moments. "Is he okay?"

"He'll be fine once he finds Dylan. Mac stopped by the center to tell us another crack house was torched last night and since we still don't know where Dylan's staying, Lucky's worried."

Jax didn't blame Lucky. The first day Lucky had followed Dylan, he'd been led to an abandoned building where, unfortunately, Dylan had given Lucky the slip.

Dray pushed back from the table. "You're on kitchen duty, Pete." He glanced at Jax. "I need to talk to you."

Jax reached out and mussed Pete's dark brown hair. "You got this, squirt?"

"Got it."

Satisfied, Jax followed Dray out of the kitchen to the large family room. "What's up?"

"Do you have an appointment with Dr. Sherman this week?"

"Thursday morning. Why?" Since his return to Chicago from California, Jax had started seeing his old psychiatrist every other week.

"I need you to do me a favor and mention Lucky's obsession with Dylan to Dr. Sherman," Dray said. "I woke up at three o'clock this morning, and Lucky was nowhere to be found. He got in at nearly five, just two hours before we had to be at the center."

Shit. From the worry lines etched around Dray's dark eyes, Jax surmised it wasn't the first time Lucky had woken in the middle of the night to search for Dylan. He hated to ask, but he needed to know if his foster dad was sinking back into his old ways of dealing with stress. "Is he hurting himself again?"

Dray shook his head. "Not yet, but he picks a fight with me damn near every day." He sighed as he rubbed his eyes with the heels of his hands. "I promised him I wouldn't call Sherman, but I thought maybe if you mentioned it during your session, it would seem normal."

"Right." Jax would do anything to help Lucky. "Is that all or was there something you needed to tell me about the center?"

"Ruben's girlfriend kicked him out so he's staying in the back room until he can find another place."

The news didn't surprise Jax. Ruben's girlfriend had been a nightmare since the two had gotten together a year ago, but, despite his lack of skills in picking women, Ruben was a smart guy. "Good for him."

Dray chuckled. "Yeah, that's what I told him. Anyway, he's agreed to lock up while he's staying there, so you can make an early night of it for a while."

That was the best news Jax had heard all week. As much as he loved working with the kids at The Brick Yard, a few nights spent around the television with the family sounded great. Plus, he had an early meeting with his graduate school advisor. "Sounds good. Classes start in a few weeks, so I could use a break before I have to juggle both working at the center and my classes." He felt his pocket to make sure he had his keys and his phone. "Talk to you later."

"Jax," Dray called. "Yeah?"

"I know you think I'm too hard on Luke, but I worry about him," Dray said.

Jax shook his head. "You wouldn't be you if you didn't." He smiled. "But I wouldn't be much of a brother if I didn't stick up for him either."

Dray grinned. "I know."

* * * *

Jax was stopped at a light when activity in the alley to his right caught his attention. "Christ!" He pulled his old Toyota into the first parking spot he saw before jumping out of the car. "What the fuck're you doing?"

Two teenage boys stopped kicking a small dog and turned his way. "Beat it," one of them yelled.

Jax pulled out his phone. "You've got two seconds to clear out or I'll call the cops on your asses." Now that he was closer, he recognized the punks. He'd only seen them a few times when he'd been home at Christmas the previous year, but Dray had pointed them out to Jax and had asked him to watch them. It hadn't taken long for Jax to figure out why the two kids had needed a set of eyes on them at all times while in The Brick Yard. Kids were rarely banned from the center, but the two in front of him had pushed Lucky and Dray beyond their limits the day they'd ganged up on a much smaller boy and had beaten him severely. There wasn't a doubt in Jax's mind that Lucky still felt guilty for the incident. The Brick Yard was supposed to be a safety zone, so something like that happening had been heartbreaking. Last he'd heard, Frankie and James had been sent to juvenile detention for the beating, but Jax had no idea how long it had been since their release.

Frankie started to reach for the dog, but there was no way Jax would let them out of the alley with the abused animal. "The dog's mine now."

"The hell it is." James, the older of the pair, puffed out his scrawny chest and took a step toward Jax.

Jax stared into a pair of lifeless black eyes. *Shark eyes.* His initial reaction to the evil he saw staring back at him was to withdraw, but he'd spent his entire childhood being afraid, and no matter what, he wasn't going to leave that alley without the dog. He glanced at the blood staining James' right hand and wondered how much damage he'd done to the dog. "I recognize you from The Brick Yard, and I'm sure you recognize me."

"What about it?" James asked, his voice devoid of emotion.

"I know your names. All it would take is a phone call to the cops to get the two of you locked up again. Now, get out of here before my finger starts pressing buttons." Jax's thumb hovered over his screen pad. He hadn't continued with his mixed martial arts training after Brick had died, but he still remembered how to kick ass, and even if Frankie and James were underage, Jax would do what was necessary to defend himself and the helpless dog.

Frankie backed away from the injured animal. "Let's get out of here."

James moved as if he were preparing to rush Jax, but changed his mind at the last moment and slid past him. "Fucking dog's not worth puttin' up with your shit, but you'd better watch your back."

An uneasy feeling crept its way up Jax's spine as he watched them leave the alley. He doubted it would be his last run in with James. Jax turned his attention to the whimpering dog. Upon closer inspection, what he'd taken to be a full-grown dog was nothing more than a big pup. *Shit.*

"Hey, boy," he cooed in a gentle tone. He knew better than to reach for the dog prior to assessing its temperament.

Predictably, the abused puppy growled, lifted its bloody head from the pavement then snapped in Jax's direction. It was a clear warning to back off.

Traumatizing the dog even more didn't sit well with Jax, but the little guy needed medical attention. He tapped his forefinger on the edge of his phone several times as he warred with himself. If he called home, Dray would tell him to call the cops or the Humane Society, but if he phoned Lucky there was the possibility that he'd distract Lucky from his obsession with Dylan, and while that wasn't great news for Dylan, it was the best thing for Lucky's mental well-being. Decision made, he pulled Lucky up in his contacts.

Phone pressed to his ear, Jax waited four rings before Lucky answered.

"You find Luke?" Lucky asked.

"No, but I've got another problem. Do you remember those kids who beat up Jason Trager?" While he spoke, Jax swung his gaze from the mouth of the alley back to the dog.

"James and Frankie. Yeah, I remember them. Why?"

"Well, I caught them torturing a puppy about three blocks from The Brick Yard. Unfortunately, the pup's in no mood to be touched, so I thought maybe you could come by and help me out."

"How bad's the dog? It's Saturday, but the vet clinic is open until three, which means we only have an hour to get the puppy there and get him seen," Lucky explained.

"I don't know how seriously it's injured, but its bleeding from a cut or something on its head and its eyes seem damn near swollen shut. I know I've never seen anything like it. I tried to get close, but it had enough strength to growl and snap." Jax heard a low sound coming from the other end of the phone and realized it was Lucky's own growl.

"Do you still have that blanket in your car from last week's game?" Lucky asked.

"No, Pete dripped mustard on it, so I took it inside to wash it." Jax glanced around the alley. "What about using my T-shirt?"

"Better than nothing. Set it next to the dog's nose for a few minutes. If it remains calm, do your best to gently wrap it around its muzzle. It might growl, but from the sound of it, I doubt it has enough strength to do serious damage. I'm still about ten minutes away, so if you can do it, I think I should just meet you at the clinic."

"Right. You want me to call the vet and warn them I'm coming?" Jax wasn't afraid of dogs, but the puppy appeared to be a Rottweiler Shepard mix, and he'd heard more than one horror story involving both breeds.

"I'll do it. I'll tell them the situation, and maybe they'll take pity on us."

The tightening in Jax's chest loosened a smidge. If Lucky was planning to pay for treatment, it meant he was already making plans to take the pup home. *God bless Lucky's big heart.* "Okay."

"Call me if you need me," Lucky ordered before hanging up.

Jax shoved the phone into his back pocket before pulling his T-shirt off. The pup didn't move when Jax dropped the shirt next to his face, which either meant the dog didn't mind Jax's scent or the pup was too weak to do anything about it. Jax wasn't sure which option he preferred.

"Okay, boy, I'm going to get you some help if you'll let me." After a quick prayer, he lightly touched the dog's lower back, the farthest point from the dog's mouth, and waited for a reaction. Not a sound came from the injured animal. He eased his hand up the dog's side.

"That's a good boy." Despite Lucky's suggestion, Jax didn't think wrapping the pup's muzzle was necessary after all. Instead, he used his shirt to wrap around the dog. "I'm going to pick you up now, but I promise I'm not going to hurt you."

Jax moved slowly, continuing to talk in gentle tones as he carefully lifted the pup from the ground and into his arms. Aside from a few faint whimpers, the dog didn't seem to have any fight left in him. *Not good.* Wasting no time, Jax carried the injured animal out of the alley to his car.

* * * *

Jax sat next to Lucky in the otherwise empty waiting

room. The receptionist had locked up and was currently filing as Lucky and Jax waited for word on the puppy. "If she makes it, do you think Dray'll let us bring her home?"

"I don't know. Depending on what the doc's doing in there, we may have to sell the house to pay the vet bill." Lucky tossed the magazine he'd been flipping through onto the table. "I can't stop thinking about those boys. What if we gave up on them too early?"

Jax couldn't believe Lucky was doubting himself. "Seriously? James and Frankie terrorized the other kids at the center. It's supposed to be a safe place for them. You did what you needed to do to make sure it stayed that way."

Lucky blew out a long breath. "Maybe I'll track them down. See if there's anything I can do to help them. Just because I don't feel right about having them at The Brick Yard, doesn't mean they don't need guidance."

"I can't imagine where I would've ended up if it hadn't been for you, Dray and Brick, but that doesn't mean you can save everyone." Jax leaned closer. "I stood not five feet from James, and I can promise you, I saw nothing in him worthy of your time or your compassion, and I don't say that lightly." He reached over and squeezed Lucky's hand. "We've all been worried about you lately. This thing with Dylan isn't healthy, but if you promise to let James go, I'll help you look for Dylan."

Lucky appeared surprised by Jax's vehemence. "What happened in that alley? Did James threaten you?"

If anyone else had asked him the question, Jax would have been offended. After all, James was five or six years younger and at least forty pounds lighter than him. Fortunately, Jax knew Lucky's heart was in the right place. "It has nothing to do with what he said. It's more a gut feeling. I know you believe that every troubled kid is worth saving, and that's why I love you, but, sadly, I think there are people in this world who are born evil, and in my opinion, James is one of them."

Lucky remained silent for several moments before slowly

nodding. "Okay. I promise I won't go searching for James, but I can't promise anything if we happen to cross paths."

"Thanks." Jax didn't like it, but there wasn't much he could do short of following Lucky around all the time. Unfortunately, the sinking feeling in his gut worried him. He prayed it wasn't a premonition of things to come.

"Now, about this dog," Lucky began. "What're we going to name her?"

All Play & No Work

Excerpt

Chapter One

Nate Gills looked out the passenger window at the Rocky Mountains. It was beautiful country, but he was ready to get the hell out of this truck. It seemed like he hadn't really had a home since he left Chicago to help his friends, the Good brothers in Nebraska.

He looked over at the hunk of a man driving. Rio was like a wet dream, the best bits from all his fantasy men rolled into one. At least he now had a family. Rio and their other partner Ryan meant the world to Nate. They may have only been together for a month, but damn, what a month.

Thinking of Ryan had him depressed again. He sighed and crossed his arms, putting his expensive Italian loafers on the dash. Feeling Rio's hand cup his cheek he turned his head.

"What's wrong, baby?" Rio asked, trying to keep one eye on the winding mountain road.

"I'm tired of this damn truck and I miss Ryan." Nate automatically nuzzled against Rio's hand.

"About two more hours and we'll take care of both of those problems. We'll kidnap Ryan away from the Sheriff's office if we have to."

Nate turned his head and kissed Rio's palm. "I think that sounds like a good plan." Ryan had left the small Texas town they'd been living in nearly two weeks earlier to take a job in Cattle Valley, Wyoming. Seemed the town needed a new Sheriff and they were looking for a bad ass with law enforcement training. Ryan fit their description to a T. Nate didn't think he'd ever seen a man who looked more like a rebel than Ryan.

With the shining, long black hair of his Native American ancestors, Ryan exuded confidence and sexuality. The town of Cattle Valley had been experiencing a few problems with protestors coming in and threatening its residents. The mayor wanted someone tough. Since Ryan looked more like a heavily tattooed biker than a Sheriff, he was perfect. Nate was just worried about what he would find. He and Rio hadn't yet seen Cattle Valley and Nate was born and raised in Chicago. It wasn't like he was snooty or anything, heck he'd loved Sommerville, the small Nebraska town where'd he'd met Rio and Ryan. Nate and Rio had been hired to investigate a scumbag in Sommerville who'd shot a good friend's partner. If you booted out the few assholes in that town, it would have been kick ass fun. But Cattle Valley...

At least from what he and Rio had been told, there were more gays that lived there than straight people. What would that be like? The town had been founded by a man whose son was murdered for being gay. Having no other heirs, the man had donated one of the biggest parcels of privately owned land in Wyoming. His entire financial portfolio had founded the town of Cattle Valley. Seemed the guy wanted a place where gay people could live without fear or prejudice. It was all fine and dandy with Nate as long as the town had a decent coffee shop and a good restaurant.

Rio started humming along to the radio, bringing Nate's attention back to that fine face. As he studied Rio's profile, he thought back to the night Rio and Ryan had saved him in a club in Lincoln. He'd gone with his friends Rawley and Jeb to the upscale gay club. Nate remembered trying his best to get over his attraction for Rio and Ryan that night. They were already a long standing couple, and it didn't appear they had a need for a third.

Since Nate had planned to make a weekend out of the trip to Lincoln, he'd rented a hotel room right down the street from the bar. When Rawley and Jeb said they wanted to take off, Nate happily waved them on their way. That was when the real fun began...

* * * *

Nate begged off the next dance and returned to his table. Finishing off his scotch and soda, he signalled the waiter for another. Deciding to brave the restroom, he headed to the rear of the club. You never know what you might find in a gay bar's restroom. Opening the door, he was pleasantly surprised to find it empty. "Excellent," he said unzipping his fly.

After a quick wash of his hands he went back out amongst the vultures. He had several men circling his table, trying to get him to dance but Nate's heart just wasn't in it. Drinking though, he thought as he spotted his fresh scotch and soda on his table, now that, he felt like doing.

Sitting down, he took several sips before one of the birds of prey landed in the seat next to him. "Care to dance?" The big oaf in leather pants said. *Who the hell wears leather pants in the summer?*

Nate shook his head and held up his drink. "No thanks, I'm taking a break."

The man smiled and nodded his head as he watched Nate closely. "I'll wait for you to finish." He ran his hand up Nate's thigh, and narrowed his eyes.

"If you want to keep that, I'd suggest you move on."

The guy rose and held up his hands. "Sorry," he said as he walked off.

Nate finished his drink. The booze seemed to be hitting him hard and fast. He went to signal for another but his arm felt too heavy to lift. Noticing his vision was starting to blur, he thought he'd had enough. "Time to get myself to bed," he slurred.

"I'll help you with that," the guy in the leather pants said, reaching for him.

Nate tried to get out of the man's arms, but his body wouldn't cooperate. What the hell was wrong with him? He felt his eyelids becoming heavier and realised he'd been drugged. "What de hell d'you pud in my dink?"

Bending over, the guy picked Nate up. "Just a little something to make you friendlier." Nate tried to squirm his way out of the guy's arms, but he couldn't keep his eyes open.

He heard a voice that sounded like Rio's, a split second before he was grabbed out of the man's arms. He managed to open his eyes enough to see Ryan holding him. "Drugged," he slurred slowly. "Need ta be sick."

Ryan looked at him for several seconds before looking back at Rio. "Take out the trash, while I see if we can get this thrown up."

Holding him close to his chest, Ryan carried him back to the restroom. Ryan sat down on the floor of one of the stalls and leaned him up toward the toilet. "Can you stick your finger down your throat?"

Nate felt his head fall back, helplessly. "Shit," Ryan said seconds before Nate felt a long finger work its way into his mouth. Ryan poked the back of his throat several times but Nate didn't gag enough to throw up. "Come on, baby, we have to get it up." Ryan tried again, using two fingers while applying pressure to his stomach.

Coughing, Nate finally was able to gag enough to throw up most of the several drinks he'd consumed. He felt another set of hands holding his head above the toilet and new Rio was with them in the tiny stall.

"Get a wet paper towel," Ryan told Rio. Seconds later, a cold towel was pressed to his forehead as another wiped his face and mouth.

"You think he got it all up?" Rio asked.

"Enough I think. He'll be dopey for a while, but I don't think it'll be enough to do any damage."

He was picked up again, only this time it was Rio who cradled him. Nate snuggled against Rio's chest. He turned his face enough to place a kiss on the skin visible above Rio's T-Shirt, feeling the vibration of Rio's groan as he made his way through the club.

The next thing Nate knew he was in Rio's arms in the backseat of Ryan's rental car. "Hotel," Nate said still slurring a bit, although he was feeling more alert.

"Think we should take him there, or back to the apartment?" Rio asked Ryan.

"Which hotel?" Ryan asked.

"Around the block, key card's in my billfold. Room two-forty-six." Nate was starting to feel a little better, but he didn't let on because he didn't want Rio to put him down. He felt the car start and pull away from the curb.

Within moments, Ryan pulled up to the front of the hotel. "You go ahead and take him in, and I'll find a place to park and be up in a minute."

"You think you can walk? They might look at us funny if I go carrying a grown man into a hotel lobby."

"Think so," Nate mumbled. He ended up having to rely heavily on Rio for support, but he made it to the elevator. "You'll have to get my wallet for me."

"Gladly," Rio said reaching his hand inside Nate's back pocket.

Nate moaned as Rio seemed to take his time. They were walking down the hall to their room and Rio was still fumbling around in Nate's jeans. When they stood in front of his room, Nate faced the wall and stuck his butt out toward Rio.

"Tease," Rio said in his ear as he finally pulled the wallet out.

"Not teasing," Nate said as he turned around to face Rio.

Picking him up, Rio lifted him until they were eye to eye, Nate's legs automatically wrapped around Rio's torso as he leaned in for a kiss. Snaking his tongue out, Rio licked at the seam of Nate's lips until he thrust inside. Fuck, Rio tasted good. Nate felt his cock throb in the close confines of his jeans. He ground his groin against Rio's as their kiss went even deeper. Rio started humping him right there in the hallway, and Nate couldn't have been more turned on.

"Goddamn that's hot," Ryan said, coming up beside them. "Where's the fucking key card, let's get into the room before we all get arrested."

Without stopping, Rio held up the billfold.

Digging for the key card, Ryan grunted. "I swear, if the two of you come without me, I'm gonna kick some ass." Ryan opened the door and pulled them both inside.

Rio carried him over to the big king-sized bed and fell down on top of him, never breaking their lip lock. "Shit," Nate heard Ryan say. He felt someone taking off his shoes and socks before hands felt their way up his cock to the snap of his jeans.

Ryan's hands tried to unfasten his pants, but with Rio grinding and humping against him, it didn't leave Ryan enough room. "Okay, stop, just fucking let me get the two of you naked."

Finally breaking apart, Rio fell to the side of Nate. He was breathing heavily as he tried to take off his clothes. Ryan, Nate noticed was already naked as he attacked the rest of Nate's clothes. By the time he was naked, Rio was too and the three of them moved as one to the centre of the bed.

"Wait, I need the condoms out of my front pocket."

Rio retrieved Nate's jeans and pulled out the strip of rubbers. He looked at them and then at Nate. "I don't even want to think about the reason these are in here." He tossed the condoms onto the bed and pulled Nate into his arms.

"You don't need those. From now on, it's just the three of us, no more cruising the clubs." He punctuated his statement with a bite mark to Nate's pierced nipple.

Nate looked at the two men. "You mean it? This isn't just a one off?"

Ryan shook his head, flicking the other nipple ring. "That's why we didn't approach you before. I knew Rio's feelings went deep, but until mine matched his, I wasn't willing to risk my relationship with him."

Swallowing, Nate arched his back as Rio continued to lick and suck his already sensitive nubs. "And do they? Go deep I mean?"

Leaning over, Ryan kissed him. His first taste of the heavily tattooed stud sent Nate's libido into overdrive. Reaching for the strip of condoms he held them up. "Please, someone make love to me."

"We're clean. We don't need those between us." Ryan tried to take the condoms out of Nate's hand but he shook his head.

"No, I've always worn protection, but I haven't been tested in almost a year, and until I can get to a clinic, we use these."

Ryan looked into his eyes and finally nodded his consent. Taking the strip, Nate tore off one of the rubbers and passed it to him. "Lube?" Ryan asked.

"Suitcase, side pocket," Nate replied, flipping over onto his stomach. Rio scrambled for the lube and Ryan ran his hands over Nate's ass.

"I don't want to make love to you this way the first time. I wanna look into your eyes when I make you come."

Nate froze. In all the years he'd been a businessman's bottom-boy, not once had anyone asked to make love to him face to face. Nate closed his eyes and said a quick prayer of thanks.

"Hey," Rio said, turning him over. "What's wrong?"

"I've never made love in this position. It just kinda threw me for a second." He could feel a blush creep up his face and turned his head away.

"Oh, baby," Ryan said, turning Nate's head. "Evidently, no ones ever made love to you. A fast fuck's fine when the time is right, but there's nothing like being made love to."

Ryan handed the lube to Rio, who slicked his fingers and touched Nate's rosette. He felt himself tense at the intimacy of the moment. He felt like a damn virgin which was funnier than hell, but he sure didn't feel like laughing.

Spreading his legs, he allowed Rio's fingers to work their magic on his body. Ryan took the opportunity to map every ridge and hollow of his lean frame. "So sexy," Ryan whispered against his throat. He moved down Nate's torso licking and kissing. Nate was going out of his mind with want, trying to reach enough of his men's skin to stroke and pet.

Rio shook his head, "Tonight's all about you, relax and enjoy."

By the time Rio had him stretched, Nate was insane, riding his hand and reaching for his cock. Rio pulled his fingers away and Nate opened his eyes. "Don't stop, so close."

"I know, but Ryan wants to make love to you, and I wanna watch." Rio stretched out beside him and rested his head on his hand. He nodded to Ryan and they both watched as Ryan rolled the condom on.

It was Nate's first real look at Ryan's cock. "Holy shit," he looked over at Rio.

"Why do you think I spent so much time preparing you?"

Nate looked back at the large, pierced cock. "Fuck that's beautiful."

After rolling on the condom, Ryan held his hand out for another one. At Nate's questioning look, he shrugged. "I've never tried a condom with the piercing, it's fairly new. I figure two would be better than one."

Nate grinned, "You do love me," he teased.

More books from
Carol Lynne

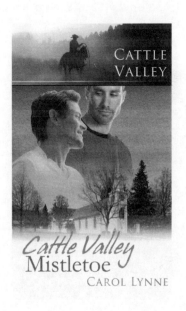

Book two in the bestselling Cattle Valley series

The Reverend Casey Sharp loves his church, his congregation and his community. He just wishes they loved him in return.

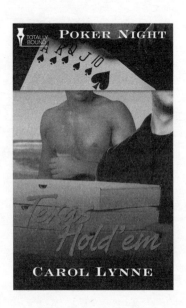

Book one in the Poker Night series

A pizza delivery never felt so good.

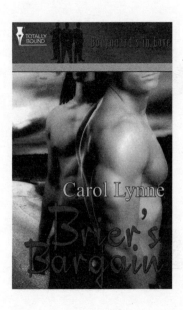

Carol Lynne

Brier's Bargain

Book one in the Bodyguards in Love series

Love is always special, but when you're a thirty-six year old man experiencing it for the first time, it's everything.

Book one in the Seasons of Love series

Seasons of Love follows forty years in the lives of two men, from the Spring of their relationship when love is new and to the Winter of their partnership of thirty years.

About the Author

An avid reader for years, one day Carol Lynne decided to write her own brand of erotic romance. While writing her first novel, Branded by Gold, Carol fell in love with the M/M genre. Carol juggles between being a full-time mother and a full-time writer. With well over one hundred releases, one thing is certain, Carol loves to keep busy writing sexy cowboys, shifters, bodyguards, vampires and everything in between. Although series books are her passion, Carol enjoys penning the occasional stand-alone title.

As founder and President of GRL Retreat, Inc., Carol helps organize the annual GayRomLit Retreat. Now in its sixth year, GayRomLit is an annual retreat that brings together the people who create and celebrate LGBT romance for a one-of-a-kind, must-attend gathering of dynamic, informal, and diverse fun.

Carol Lynne loves to hear from readers. You can find contact information, website details and an author profile page at https://www.pride-publishing.com/

PUBLISHING